G581: The Departure

Book 1 of the Gliese 581g series

By Christine D. Shuck

Also by Christine D. Shuck

Benton Security Services
Hired Gun
Smoke and Steel
Broken Code
Benton Security Services Omnibus #1 - Books 1-3

Benton Sicherheitsservice
Heiße Gefahr

Chronicles of Liv Rowan
Fate's Highway

Gliese 581g
G581: The Departure
G581: Mars
G581: Earth
G581: Plague Tales
G581: Zarmina's World
G581: Plague Tales II

War's End
War's End: The Storm
War's End: A Brave New World
Tales of the Collapse
War's End Omnibus - Books 1-3

Standalone
The War on Drugs: An Old Wives Tale
Get Organized, Stay Organized
Winter's Child
Short-Term Rental Success

Watch for more at christineshuck.com.

Table of Contents

Code Red

Date: 01.27.2104

Calypso Colony Ship

Somehow, he had to save them. Daniel's hair was matted on the left side of his forehead, still actively dripping blood from a gash near the top of his head. Each breath was a challenge. It felt as if he were underwater, sharp knives with each gasp in and thick bubbles on the way out. He tried to breathe in shallow; it hurt less when he did that. One of his ribs felt cracked, possibly broken and he tried to think clearly as dizziness and pain fought for his attention. Attention that was desperately needed elsewhere.

"I never should have left them." His fingers moved feverishly over the damaged keyboard and his vision blurred. The blood dripped into his eyes and a fresh wave of dizziness washed over him.

Oxygen levels must be low.

A dull red light flashed through the Cryo Deck, accompanied by the thick, oily smell of melted plastic from the handful of Cryo pods a few rows over. His mind, desperate to compartmentalize, to avoid the full panic he found rising inside, lingered on the memory of Janine's skin beneath his. The memory of Toby's small hand on his cheek, his brother Luke and his easy smile hung there beside him, real enough to touch. The years had passed easier for him – not knowing, barely realizing the truth until it was years gone. Were they all ash and bone now?

Each Cryo pod was equipped with a shrieking alarm. They were designed to emit a series of escalating warning sounds from a simple "Hey, something seems out of place" warning beep to a "The pod is failing and the subject will *die*," shriek that energized each nerve in a Cryo Tech's body to do something *now*.

But Daniel wasn't a Cryo Tech, Deeks, Daniel's poker buddy and best friend on Calypso was. And Deeks was dead, along with his assistant, Evers. Their lifeless bodies had been shoved into storage lockers at the far end of the Cryo Deck. And the doors leading to the rest of the ship, where there were others far more capable and knowledgeable than a Comm Tech could ever be were shut, the opening mechanism fried. Daniel was trapped and alone.

He could hear them, working at the doors, doing whatever they could to get through, the banging only adding to the cacophony provided by shrieking alarms.

All the doors on Calypso were thick, reinforced steel, with rods of titanium woven through for maximum security. Space travel was an uncertain thing, and all areas of the ship had double and triple protections to stop any hull breaches as well as prevent against the unlikely event of a ship-wide contagion. However, the blast doors were something new, yet another layer of protection that ensured that anyone remaining on the Cryo Deck had the best chance of survival.

It was ironic that this added security precaution might be their undoing.

The people in these pods were integral to the mission. Without them, those currently not in Cryo would have a hell of a time and that was just the realistic side of his brain talking. God damn it, *Sam* was in one of these things.

The screen on the console in front of him scrolled the same message...

OVERRIDE PASSWORD FAILURE

PERSONNEL RECOGNITION FAILURE

SYSTEM FAILURE - CODE RED

SYSTEM RESET ON ALL CRYO PODS IN 14:39 MINUTES

Daniel pounded the keyboard in frustration. The man on the floor to the right of his foot moved slightly and moaned. Like Daniel, he was bleeding heavily from several wounds – one on his head, where Daniel had slammed it against a pillar during the fight. Daniel gave the man a hard kick.

"You sonofabitch! What the hell were you thinking? Why would you do this? WHY?"

Daniel's left arm hung uselessly at his side. His left foot slipped sideways and he realized there was a sizable puddle of blood on the deck, accumulating over the long moment he had fought with the half-melted keyboard. The hole in his shoulder screamed red hot agony at him every time he moved, but the arm itself just hung there, whatever muscles it needed to move rendered useless by the knife still buried in it. It hurt, bad, and Daniel debated pulling it out.

"Not low oxygen levels, no. It's got to be from the blood loss, onset of shock."

He said it, mainly to himself, a part of him distanced from what was happening, the words sounding as if they were issuing from someone else.

"Yeah, blood loss. It affects higher brain function and reasoning skills."

His voice was barely registering over the endless shrieking of the alarms. Had his lips moved? Had he actually spoken out loud? Another wave of dizziness washed over him.

Behind him, the hammering at the doors had taken on a different tone. Sharper, higher grinding sounds, instead of the dull pounding. What was it? Some sort of saw? Daniel felt a flicker of hope. Perhaps they could break through in time, do something he couldn't.

But did he really have time to wait for the others to break through? Should he wait for the captain and the others to get here, so he didn't screw something up further? He wiped the fresh blood from his brow; droplets fell to the view screen below, almost obscuring the countdown.

The message continued to scroll...

OVERRIDE PASSWORD FAILURE

PERSONNEL RECOGNITION FAILURE

SYSTEM FAILURE - CODE RED

SYSTEM RESET ON ALL CRYO PODS IN 14:18 MINUTES

The door behind him looked untouched, despite the application of the saw or whatever they were using on the other side. It could be hours and from the looks of it, none of the people in the Cryo Pods had hours. How the hell had this madman done it? And why?

Daniel struggled to clear his mind, muddled and confused from the fight, filled with memories of the past. He had to stop this countdown before it was too late.

Beginnings

"Are we an exceptionally unlikely accident or is the universe brimming over with intelligence? (It's) a vital question for understanding ourselves and our history." - Carl Sagan

Date: 07.07.2092
Earth – Seattle, Washington

"For as long as man has understood the movements of the stars and planets –he has gazed at the meteors streaking across the sky and wondered what was out there, beyond in the great openness of space. Home of the gods and the unknown, our questions changed as we learned more about our world and the nature of space. Our curiosity drove us. Was there life out there, past our Earth, the cradle of our civilization? Were there other planets, ones we could travel to, that would support life, and even more importantly, *human* life? These questions have defined us, driven us to great heights, from bleak moonscapes to breathtaking wonders."

Daniel sighed and slumped in his seat as the presentation droned on. *Beautiful, great,* he knew all this. Every high school student had heard this speech, and the awe he had felt at the idea of space travel had dimmed slightly over the years. In past centuries and even recently after the Reformation, Americans had traveled to Europe as part of their coming of age. It was a year of decadent freedom and adventure before settling into the rigors of collegiate life, marriage, jobs, children, and responsibilities. Daniel had done all of this and more. Thanks to the smartly invested trust fund left to him and Luke, he had traveled far and wide. He had climbed parts of Mt. Kilimanjaro and he had traveled to the Moon. Untold thousands of others had done the same, visiting the moon or one of a handful of space stations now orbiting it and the Earth.

There weren't any rich kid flights to Mars yet, but given time, given another couple of centuries for the terraforming equipment to do its work seeding the atmosphere with just the right mixture of elements and Daniel was sure it would be the next new thing.

"Learn the Mysteries of Mars!" The vids already read, "Become a colonist on the newest frontier and become a part of history!"

The space stations provided links to the great beyond. *Wayfarer* orbited the Moon, serving as the training and launch point for Mars colonists who headed out on what was still a one-way trip for most to the red planet. Daniel wondered how they could stand it. The thought of living forever in domes sealed away from a frigid, airless, and dust-covered wasteland was unappealing to him. As for breathable air, well, that was a dream that was ten centuries or more in the future.

Still, humanity kept pushing the boundaries. The colonists who went there were a different breed than those who stayed behind. Their thirst was for knowledge, an understanding of a world alien from their own. And Daniel understood how they felt in many ways. Most were scientists and researchers - dedicated to creating a new world that would be home to humanity - a home away from home.

The presentation interrupted Daniel's wandering thoughts and brought him back to present, "For many years, scientists looked to the stars for answers to the questions of other planets. Over time, their ability to discern the movements of objects orbiting those distant stars grew. And then the world was rocked by the discovery of Planet G in the Gliese 581 system."

The speaker paused and smiled sadly, "And just as quickly, these discoveries were denounced."

Across the screen flashed images of old headlines that screamed:
Gliese 581g: A Black Eye for Believers in Habitable Earth-Like Exoplanets
And...

Earth-Like Planets Apparently Do Not Exist.

"This was an incredibly hard time for my grandfather, Steve Vogt. He would go to his grave convinced that Gliese 581g was there."

He paused and clicked to an image of a space telescope.

"The James Webb Space Telescope had an anticipated launch date of 2018, but it would not be launched until nearly 2033, due to The Collapse and Second Civil War. My grandfather would not live to see his research vindicated."

He gestured to the screen, "Shortly after its launch in 2033, my father Oliver Vogt turned the telescope once more towards the Gliese 581 solar system and found this …"

A tiny light, orbiting a red dwarf star was displayed on the screen.

The speaker smiled, "This discovery coincided neatly with the development of the first functioning Alcubierre-Mesner drive. This device, capable of warp speeds, was perfected a handful of years after Gliese 581g's re-discovery. The Alcubierre-Mesner drive was something previously described in science fiction tales. A dream made into reality."

Daniel sat up in his seat, leaning forward as the images of Gliese 581g with close-ups of rocky mountain ranges and deep blue-green waters began to flash across the screen. He could see others doing the same. The auditorium was packed, there were at least 12,000 seats, all of them filled, with others standing in the aisles and clustered at the back. Despite their numbers, everyone stayed silent, the silence punctuated by occasional gasps at the dazzling images on the screen.

The images looked familiar and yet…not. As if someone had taken a wrong turn with the paintbrush. The colors were somewhat different, the shapes of the plants, the rocks, the terrain - all slightly *off*. Daniel wondered if someday human children living on this tidally locked planet might look at pictures of Earth and think the same thing.

"World Geographic launched the D.O.V.E. probe on January 18, 2037." The speaker's voice rang out in the darkness. "D.O.V.E. stood for Discover, Observe, Verify, and Extrapolate - all of the steps that the most important probe mankind has ever invented would need. We needed to know if there was any hope of establishing a colony on this distant world."

"On board D.O.V.E. were hundreds of probes designed to collect and examine everything from the mineral deposits to the existence and makeup of surface liquids, along with untold numbers of environmental factors. These probes scoured the atmosphere, dug deep into the soil and plunged into the oceans and seas. Thousands of samples were taken and examined. The results were beamed back to the mother probe which in turn collated, summarized and transmitted the probe findings back to Earth."

The giant view screens zoomed back to the white-haired speaker, Dr. Anthony Vogt, and he paused, looking over the packed auditorium, smiled and said, "How I wish my grandfather, Dr. Steve Vogt could have seen the figurative olive branch that D.O.V.E. found on Planet G."

Daniel paid rapt attention now, this was the interesting part. He wondered if he would ever tire of seeing the details of this giant world. His eyes drank in the images that continued to flash over the giant view screen.

"On April 7, 2090, World Geographic received the first images of Gliese 581g, which we have now officially renamed Zarmina's World, in honor of Dr. Vogt's wife, and my grandmother, Zarmina."

Anthony Vogt gestured towards the screen and the audience gasped as footage of one of the sub-probes burst through clouds and a dizzying rush of sharp mountains and lush valleys stretched and moved. They sighed collectively as the probe skimmed an immense expanse of greenish-brown water, jerking to the left with the probe as its auto-navigation registered and avoided a large rocky mass protruding from the water.

"What we have learned in the fifteen months since the probes from D.O.V.E. have transmitted their data across the black void of space is absolutely staggering."

Again, the view screen cut back to a close-up of Dr. Vogt.

"My grandfather's dream of a world that humans could inhabit has come true. After years of study, after thousands of hours reviewing data and learning as much as we can about this amazing and promising world, I have the most important announcement of my life to make."

He paused for a moment, a glimmer of tears in his eyes and his voice rang across the auditorium.

"In honor of my grandfather who discovered Gliese 581g, and especially for the famous science fiction author who inspired my grandfather from childhood to study the stars, on this day, July 7, 2092, one hundred and eighty-five years after the birth of Robert Heinlein ... I am formally announcing the 2095 mission to establish a permanent colony on Zarmina's World. A brave group of human scientists, engineers, and forward-thinking individuals will carry our race and our future beyond our solar system, to a place unimaginably far away and alien to us."

The roar of the crowd was overwhelming. Many on their feet, applauding and cheering with excitement.

Dr. Vogt's grin stretched ear to ear, his teeth a brilliant white, and then the screen changed to close-ups of alien plants and sketches of the ship. He pointed to the ship, a giant version of the D.O.V.E. probe with additional modules added to the main ship stem.

"We have named the ship Calypso, in honor of the ship of the famed oceanographer Jacques Cousteau. Planning and construction, which began over five years ago, is now nearing completion. Calypso will depart in less than three years, on a trip that will take its crew to that distant star system, Gliese 581, and bring mankind to a new home and new frontier."

The crowd roared again in excitement, drowning out some of Dr. Vogt's words. The screen, however, now displayed a lengthy quote.

Dr. Vogt waited for a break in the cheers before continuing.

"Robert Heinlein once said 'A human being should be able to change a diaper, plan an invasion, butcher a hog, conn a ship, design a building, write a sonnet, balance accounts, build a wall, set a bone, comfort the dying, take orders, give orders, cooperate, act alone, solve equations, analyze a new problem, pitch manure, program a computer, cook a tasty meal, fight efficiently, die gallantly. Specialization is for insects.'"

There was laughter at the last sentence and a smattering of applause.

"We will fill Calypso with men and women who embody Heinlein's vision of humanity, people adept at numerous skills, brilliant in their specialties, autodidacts who drink up knowledge and increase their abilities each day that they live."

The crowd roared a third time as Dr. Vogt's voice rang across the auditorium.

"And we will send them to this untouched and brilliant place to learn what it has to teach us. To Zarmina's World!"

Daniel stood on his feet, feeling the energy of more than 12,000 people surrounding him, building into a frenzy. And at that moment, Daniel Medry wanted nothing more than to stand with them and fly to the stars.

World Geographic

"It pays to plan ahead. It wasn't raining when Noah built the ark." – Author Unknown

Date: 02.25.2097

Earth – Cape Canaveral, Florida

"Wow, that's...that's a lot of reporters." Anthony Vogt eyed the phalanx of reporters and cameras filling the amphitheater. For the moment he was out of view. Here in the sunny anteroom, wide, panoramic windows displayed the vast facility outside. He had taken a moment to peek out through the small window inset in the door.

Jenn Rivers, his newly appointed assistant, peeked as well and nodded, looking somewhat nervous. "It sure is."

Vogt, more at home in front of a telescope, alone on a mountain, kept his cool, but he could feel a rushing in his ears, the solid thump of his heartbeat accelerating. The last four and a half years had been filled with interviews, meetings with scientists and more, and now the countdown to departure was something tangible and real.

"I can't believe I'm here, at Cape Canaveral." Jenn said her voice full of wonder. Anthony had brought her up to date as quickly as he could in preparation for the news conference. Still, he thought, the girl hadn't had long, just a whirlwind two weeks to take in all of the details of her new job and that had included traveling halfway across the country in his wake.

Anthony smiled, "It's a lot to take in. The place has really grown and changed. It was far smaller than this fifty years ago." He pointed out the windows, anxious for a distraction, "Originally one hundred thirty-three acres, Cape Canaveral has nearly doubled its size since engineers supervised the filling in of the shallower northern section of the Banana River. You can see it there to the left."

Jenn craned her neck, following his finger as he traced the length of it. "It was really more of a salty, brackish lagoon rather than a true river, he said, smiling at her. "But filling it in helped enlarge the facilities here significantly."

"This is where all of the major discoveries on the Alcubierre-Mesner drives were made," Jenn said, enthusiastically. She had spent most of the weekend before studying the history of Cape Canaveral. "I read that the Cape also contributed significantly to helping build the *Gan De*, despite the station being managed by the Chinese."

"Yes, it handled the production of most of the main living modules." Anthony said, nodding in approval. "*Gan De* is under Chinese authority, but it still maintains an international crew."

"But the Cape hasn't been producing Calypso." Jenn asked, questioning.

"Well, yes and no. Calypso is massive, too massive to be launched from Earth's gravity. Most of it has had to be built in space, and in fact, the ship will never land on Zarmina's World. Once there it will be re-purposed into a space station and communications relay for the new planet." Anthony's eyes took on a dreamy quality, "I guess you could say that the *dream* of it has been collected here. The Cape is responsible for the main design, and they have done plenty of scale model testing here as well."

Originally chosen as a base for rocket launches to take advantage of the Earth's rotation, Cape Canaveral had fallen into disuse in the early part of the century, parts of its rich history lost to an occupying faction during the Second American Civil War.

Anthony didn't bother going into that history, from what he had seen in the past two weeks, Jenn had paid attention in school. She knew her history.

"The Ptolemy Colony is also responsible for some of the production since it is at a lower gravity. They assemble many of the pieces on the Moon, and then send the pieces up to the *Gan De* with boosters a fraction of the size it would take to push off from Earth."

"We've come so far," Jenn mused, "And now the Huygens Outpost on Mars are seeing their first generation born on the planet. It's amazing what has happened in the last fifty years."

Through the door they could both hear the growing murmur from the crowd of journalists.

"It's almost show time," Anthony said, checking his wristwatch.

The Seiko had been his grandfather's – passed down to him from his father. It seemed fitting to wear it today. He wished for the hundredth time that his grandfather could have seen this. His nervousness increased. There were so many people outside.

"Now the designs for the Mars colony Habs and atmosphere generators came from that building over there twenty years ago." He pointed to a low-slung building off to the right. "They were piped into space strapped to rockets and fed in pieces and parts to Mars over a period of about five years."

"The best is Calypso, though. The first manned ship to leave our solar system." Jenn said, her eyes on the cloudless sky above.

At night, with a small power telescope, the *Gan De* station could be spotted. With a more powerful telescope it was possible to see the Calypso, in orbit with the station, now 90% complete. Both orbited the Earth at 17,150 miles per hour.

Great things were happening here, but in Anthony's estimation, the impending departure of Calypso, was the greatest. For the first time in human history, man, and woman, would leave the solar system headed for a planet filled with boundless possibility.

"I can't help wondering if my grandfather imagined Calypso too when he first discovered the wobble and noticed the anomalies and shadows of something so incredibly far away." Anthony mused, "He must have dreamed of how it would look, what it would be like to stand on an alien world."

He glanced at the door, "With every step forward towards completion, it feels like vindication. I can't spare my grandfather those years of ridicule or questioning." He shook his head, "The media had a field day at his expense. But I can remind the world that it was Steve Vogt's work that brought them here to this place – the first extra-solar journey to another world."

In the amphitheater, he heard the noise die down and the introductions begin.

Anthony checked his watch again. It was an antique oddity, something that appeared in museums or on shelves behind glass. No one wore wristwatches anymore; most had stopped wearing or using them even in his grandfather's day. It kept perfect time, and the hands pointed to exactly ten a.m.

"Please welcome, Anthony Vogt." That was his cue.

He nodded to his assistant, took a deep breath, and stepped through the door, taking his place at the podium.

"Good morning, thank you for coming."

The cameras clicked quietly, bright pulses of light filling his sight with dancing spots.

"Four- and one-half years ago, I was given the honor of announcing the mission to Gliese 581G, also known as Zarmina's World. As you know, we had a few setbacks and the departure date was moved from 2095 to 2098. Last week World Geographic gave the world a firm date for departure, September 19th, 2098."

He smiled, "Today I am back with you to announce the official request for volunteers, brave new souls who will travel outside of our known solar system and far beyond..."

The speech went on for some time, the giant screens behind him flashed with images of the nearly finished spacecraft, the living quarters, and even more photos of Zarmina's World as Anthony outlined the parameters of the selection process the Selection Committee was looking for.

"And now, I have time for questions."

"Will you be on board the ship, Dr. Vogt?" Anthony laughed and shook his head, his hair a snowy white cloud.

"No."

He didn't explain further. They wouldn't understand anyway. Even if he did qualify under the stringent health guidelines, he was far too old to be considered as a colonist, and then there was the pesky problem of being terrified of actually being in space. He was quite happy exploring space through a telescope, his feet planted firmly on the ground.

"Dr. Vogt, can you tell us more about this seed bank we keep hearing about?"

Sue Davies, a petite, red-haired woman with a bony upturned nose asked. Anthony had sat down with her for a long interview more than a year earlier. Sue, who held a degree in Astrophysics, was more than just a journalist, she was a peer.

He brightened immediately. Genetics and astronomy were dual loves for him. He had made the case for collecting a wide variety of not just ova and sperm from the multitudes of Earth animals, but also those of humans.

Vogt, along with a host of others, had pushed for an extensive seed bank to be included on board Calypso. In fact, the collection was so extensive that it had taken a revamping of their storage techniques and a full re-design of the Cryo Deck, where the seed bank, along with over two-thirds of the colonists would be in stasis throughout the voyage.

The technology for growing embryos in artificial wombs was still being refined, but they had seen limited success. By the time Calypso arrived at Zarmina's World, the technology, if not with them, would be close behind. And they would need it in order to grow the domestic farm animals on planet; there was only so much space in the holds of the ship to store the creatures in Cryo pods.

Anthony nodded, "That is a wonderful question, thanks Sue."

He nodded to a technician off-stage and immediately schematics for the Cryo Deck appeared on the enormous screen behind him.

"The Cryo Deck was one of the sections on Calypso that underwent significant revisions. Once we realized that we had the opportunity to send out an A.R.C., we needed a few modifications in order to make everything work, and fit, within the space. So, we..."

Sue interrupted him, "I'm sorry, Dr. Vogt, but I hope you could explain what the A.R.C. is specifically?"

She smiled as she did it, to lessen the sting.

He nodded again, smiled ruefully, "Yes, thank you."

It was yet another reminder that his strengths were better utilized staring into a telescope.

"I need Sue to keep me in check; otherwise this talk might devolve into the fundamental differences between quarks and quasars."

The reporters laughed, and he continued.

"About fifty years ago, when the idea of deep space exploration became a reality, an ongoing theme was introduced, that of sending out A.R.C.s. An A.R.C. is an Advanced Reconstructive Colony, capable of re-creating, to some limited extent, a duplicate of Earth – through plants, fungi, sea life, animals and humans."

Behind him the vid screen raced with pictures, dizzying panoramic views of a vast herd of ruminants, shots of humans in every color and stage of life, and underwater photos of crab, coral, dolphins, sharks and more.

"Our colonies on the Moon and Mars both have their own A.R.C., which has typically focused on animal reproduction or, more specifically in the case of Mars, well-known breeds of farm animals in addition to 1,000 samples of human sperm and ova."

Anthony held up his hands.

"Now obviously, sending these specimens does not mean that we can reproduce all of them. That is, in some cases, years or even decades away. But A.R.C. is a treasure chest, a cornucopia sampling of who we are, as a species, and as a planet. In the case of Calypso and the long journey to Zarmina's World, we intend for A.R.C. to be our safety net. We are sending 250 brave souls, our best and brightest, to a place we can barely begin to fathom. They will need every advantage, including that of the rich, genetic diversity we can so proudly claim here on Earth."

"With over 50,000 ova and sperm, collected from each country and every culture on Earth, our 250 colonists will never have to face the possibility of inbreeding or extinction. And not just that, but they can have their faithful companions with them as well!"

The crowd laughed as images of dogs running and fetching balls resolved into a comical image of a cat, hanging onto the outside of a screen window.

"We have included over three hundred and fifty species of dogs and over fifty species of cats in A.R.C."

A new series of pictures flashed across the screen, showing different mushrooms and fungi in petri dishes.

"The Stamets Institute, founded in 2029, has graciously provided us with individual samples of their entire collection of fungi, over 140,000 varieties, which can be used for agricultural soil remediation and adaptation as well as their health benefits and continued research on Calypso."

The images changed, zooming in on a replica of the Cryo Deck.

"The Cryo Deck is absolutely essential to the future of a colony on an alien world. Because of this, we have included a secondary command center within the Cryo Deck itself, along with titanium rod reinforced steel blast doors, yet another level of protection for such precious cargo. In the case of a full systems failure aboard Calypso, the blast doors could be sealed and the most important cargo of all, A.R.C. and over two-thirds of the colonists would be protected and able to complete the mission to Zarmina's World."

Anthony paused, took a sip of water, and asked, "Next question?"

A keen-eyed young reporter raised his hand, "I've heard that there is an artificial intelligence that will be a new addition."

"Yes, you are correct. NARA, otherwise known as Network and Radio Administration, will be on board Calypso."

Vogt shook his head at the murmurs, "You would think we could come up with a sexier-sounding name than that, right?!"

Several folks laughed.

Anthony smiled in response, "Right, well, NARA is a sophisticated evolutionary step above the Siri and Cortana models. You may remember that they occupied smartphones shortly before The Collapse. Siri and Cortana, along with ALCON, created nearly six decades later, are all considered AI, but their collective mental capacity is that of a mere five-year-old."

The screen behind him flashed with a parade of images, depicting the benefits of NARA for the audience.

"NARA will be our on-ship and on-planet communications program and more. For instance, NARA will be able to detect heart rate, pulse, even give advance warning if a person is suffering a heart attack or needs medical attention."

The vid screen displayed a mannequin in a Calypso ship suit, a badge the size of a large button clipped to the left breast pocket.

"NARA is small, lightweight, and the unit is coded to the wearer, functioning as a communications unit, locating beacon accurate to within two feet, and as I mentioned earlier, also excellent for monitoring basic vital signs."

The vid screen scrolled dates, "There will be several specific seminars on NARA and its applications on the dates listed on the screen. So, any other questions regarding NARA can be asked then."

Anthony sipped more water, "Next question?"

An overweight, balding man shot his hand up, "What are the requirements or parameters for this mission? Is it true that families and children are being considered?"

Now was when the difficult questions would begin. He wasn't looking forward to explaining the age limitations, not at all, especially when it came to the gender disparity. But this is what he had signed on for. He nodded to the technician and began to answer the first part of the reporter's question.

Politically Correct

"Widespread intellectual and moral docility may be convenient for leaders in the short term, but it is suicidal for nations in the long term. One of the criteria for national leadership should therefore be a talent for understanding, encouraging, and making constructive use of vigorous criticism." – Carl Sagan

Date: 03.18.2097
Earth – Cape Canaveral, Florida

The conference table in the boardroom of World Geographic was cluttered with cups, papers, and, headed by one rather frustrated Anthony Vogt. His head was pounding. *Science should never be mixed with bureaucracy. In fact, bureaucracy seems to be the antithesis of rational thought.*

"All I'm saying is that we can't be elitists," one of the board members said, smiling gently and speaking as if Vogt were a small child.

He maintained a calm demeanor, but inside Vogt seethed with frustration. *Yes, they* could *be elitists. Moreover, they* should *be elitists. There was no need to send the weak or mundane when there were untold thousands of brilliant, overachieving 'tens of tens' out there, waiting for their chance to journey to the stars.*

"Mr. Elliott, with all due respect, we can and should be elitists in this matter. The odds against each of these individual's survival is staggering." Anthony pointed to the view screen. "They are not going on a picnic on some deserted island, we are sending them over one hundred twenty-one *trillion* miles away, alone, to an alien planet with 1.2 g's earth gravity that may, or may not, be capable of sustaining them. To simply send individuals who are not 'tens of tens', as the Selection Committee has chosen to refer to them, is idiocy."

Marshall Elliott bristled. Anthony realized that the man probably interpreted that last word as an attack on his own intelligence. And while the question of his intelligence was certainly an issue, it hadn't been his intention to insult the man.

Jenn Rivers, Vogt's assistant, sighed quietly, but Anthony, sitting next to her, heard. He realized that while she may have become used to his lack of tact, the board members had not. Her pursed lips sent him a definite "I told you so." She had tried to warn him before the meeting, even given him a note that gave a short summary of each board member, along with suggestions on how to handle them. It had been impossible to read it while fielding a flurry of calls that morning.

She slid it towards him, pointing to one line. It read; *Marshall Elliott will fight the 'tens of tens' approach. Avoid any references to intelligence and emphasize the versatility of multiple disciplines instead.* He nodded tersely, frustrated, wishing he had read it before engaging the blowhard.

He stared at Jenn's note for a moment, trying to figure out how to smooth over the effect his words had on Elliott. It was well known that Marshall Elliott, unlike most of the brilliant scientists and doctors that sat on World Geographic's board of directors, had secured his coveted position through obscene amounts of donations in addition to plenty of political maneuvering. That said, it wasn't in anyone's best interest to alienate the man. He was powerful, well-connected, and they had already had enough delays.

To Dr. Vogt's right, across the table and three chairs down, another board member spoke up, "I was under the impression that the D.O.V.E. probes had verified the ability for the planet to sustain life. That the topography and climate were Earth-like and that humans would be able to settle in the meridian with no problems."

Anthony frowned as he tried to remember the woman's name.

Jenn leaned over and whispered, "Trina Solbe, director of Art Acquisitions."

Anthony nodded, "The D.O.V.E. probe was detailed, but it couldn't tell us everything we needed to know. The D.O.V.E. probes taught us a great deal about the consistency of the atmosphere and its breathability, but we have no way of knowing if there are any allergens or airborne viral components. We also did exhaustive soil analysis, but until we are able to actually handle the soil directly, we have no idea if there are microscopic organisms that will find Terran crops too tasty to resist. That is why we have included enough fuel for

Calypso to make a return journey. It will be a close thing, but we must cover all our bases."

He pointed to the view screen, which flashed through facts and figures as he mentioned them, "We know that the gravity is 1.2 g's, so it is stronger than that of Earth by a significant degree. This is why we must test extensively for, and avoid, anyone with a family history of osteoporosis or other osteopathic difficulties or a family history of heart disease."

"We also know that there are plants on Zarmina's World, including what may be rather invasive and poisonous ones in the southern hemisphere, but we have no way of knowing until we arrive there whether or not plants from Earth will grow. Initial testing has indicated that Earth plants may need some genetic modification to be truly successful." He pointed to the list of specialties on the view screen, "That is why we need the multiple specialties in each of the colonists. We can't take our chances on having a few who specialize in only one area - each member of Calypso must have multiple specialties and be willing to learn and work as an understudy in others."

Solbe, a woman in her late sixties with soft white hair and lively hazel eyes, nodded, "And this other requirement? The listing on the I.Q.?"

Anthony nodded, "Yes, the Selection Team voted unanimously to set the requirement for an I.Q. level of one hundred thirty-five or more for all crew and colonists." A murmur ran through the conference room.

Solbe raised her eyebrows, "And how many have qualified under this particular requirement, Dr. Vogt?"

"Less than two for every one hundred applicants."

"And how many applicants are you currently processing through?"

"We have received nearly sixty thousand applications in the last week alone."

"So that would be..."

"One thousand one hundred and ninety-two applicants last week qualified as 135 or higher on the Strick-Bormann I.Q. test." Anthony allowed himself a small, almost smug smile. "All in all, to date we have over five thousand individuals who have passed the Level One testing."

"For a crew of 250?" Solbe smiled when he nodded, "Thank you, Dr. Vogt, it seems to me that the Intelligence Quotient is not a matter of elitism, but more of simply weeding through the vast number of applicants."

She turned to Marshall Elliott, who was still frowning, "It also establishes a baseline for those who will be given this amazing and challenging opportunity. "

Marshall Elliott was not deterred, "This other requirement, however, is ridiculous."

Anthony felt his temper flare again, "And that would be?"

"The age requirement. You have listed a maximum age, *maximum*, of forty-five years at the time of departure."

"Yes, this is due in great part to the higher gravity. Younger individuals, children even, will be able to adapt and survive better than those in their late 40's or 50's."

A pinch-faced woman in her late thirties seated next to Elliott chimed in, "And additionally, you have listed that at least," she paused and sifted through the packet that each board member had been given, "seventy-five percent of the female crew should be ages twenty through thirty. You aren't just elitist, you're *sexist*. I certainly don't see any qualification like that for the men."

Dr. Vogt's face flushed red with anger.

Jenn quickly spoke up, "Actually, Dr. Zahtjev, the Selection Team is made up of three women and five men. And it was one of the women who suggested we put in that qualification for the women. It was unanimously supported by everyone on the Team."

Jenn's interjection gave Anthony just a few seconds to cool off, and she had set the stage for what he would say next, "Again, we are not sending these people off on a picnic. We are sending them on a journey across trillions of miles, unbelievably far from home."

He paused and his voice softened, "We are asking those brave women to be the progenitors of mankind in a distant solar system. To be the first to carry new life on an alien world. To do so, they must be in perfect health and of optimum child-bearing potential. It is not sexist; it is a matter of being a realist. Most of these women will be in prime child-bearing age upon their arrival.

For the remaining twenty-five percent of women who are age thirty-one through forty-five at the time of departure, they are still young enough to possibly reproduce with IVF treatment if necessary, foster other children or even carry fertilized implanted embryos if their own ova are not viable. To not make these decisions now means that we send our best and brightest 121 trillion miles away to live their lives and die, without being able to pass on what they have learned to a new generation. We would be asking them to sacrifice not only their lives but the possibility of *producing* life. Would you deny them that?"

His explanations seemed to satisfy the more strident members of the board and the meeting turned to other areas of the upcoming mission. The Cryogenics tanks and the emergency procedures training were next on the agenda.

That evening, hours after the meetings had wrapped up for the night, Dr. Lana Zahtjev sat in front of her computer, staring at the screen. She knew she was far from beautiful. Men had never looked at her in *that way* and she had been unlucky in her few, limited relationships.

Yet something had moved deep within her as she remembered Anthony Vogt's words, paraphrasing them as she spoke them aloud in the empty room, "To live and die, without being able to pass on what I have learned to a new generation."

She bit her lip, a wave of longing washed over her. Most days it wasn't bad. Most days she could manage to ignore it, tamp it down, this complicated and disabling wish for something she did not have, had never really had. She had learned to accept her solitary existence as a thing she could not change. She knew she wasn't the easiest person to live with, her last serious relationship had never progressed past the occasional dinner and drinks.

The end had come when he had tried to kiss her passionately and to take the relationship, whatever it was, to the next level. When she had pulled away, he had called her an Ice Queen. That had hurt, in college, they had called her that too.

He had never contacted her again and when she thought of it, she did not even miss him much. The dinners had been nice, and the dialog had been intelligent and interesting, but as with the others, there had never been a spark.

Her hands moved over the keyboard, and the search results scrolled on the screen. Lana Zahtjev began to read, her lips moving silently as she read about the latest IVF treatments available.

Dr. Anthony Vogt, although he would never know it, had given her a gift. A name to the longing within her. It would take a full year for her to schedule it, but Dr. Lana Zahtjev stepped into the Happy Mothers Fertility Clinic on the day that Calypso left the solar system. Nine and one-half months later, she welcomed her daughter Eve into the world.

Tens of Tens

"It is not clear that intelligence has any long-term survival value." – Stephen Hawking

Date: 04.04.2097

Earth – Cape Canaveral, Florida

Dr. Anthony Vogt bowed his head and rubbed his temples. The conference room table was strewn with coffee cups and stacks of folders and the room was in an uproar. It was the third meeting for the Selection Team in charge of weeding through the list of applicants to crew Calypso. The first week had gone smoothly, but last week and this week had devolved into arguments over religion. More specifically, the question of whether there should be a minister or priest in the contingent.

The room had divided itself into three factions, those of faith, the atheists and agnostics, and those who felt that there was some kind of compromise to be made. Dr. Mendez was of the first variety, Dr. Lowenstein was quite clearly in the second camp, and Anthony found himself in the third. As for the other five members of the team, two had left in disgust moments ago, and the other three were positioning themselves on either Mendez or Lowenstein's side of the argument.

Sal Mendez and Oren Lowenstein stood toe to toe, red-faced and shouting.

Sal looked as if he were courting a coronary. His eyes bulged and his large beefy hands were curled into fists. He was tall, as well as wide, and looked as if he could stand to lose a good fifty pounds. His black hair bristled, and sweat flew from the tips as he shook with rage at the suggestion Oren Lowenstein had just made. From his neck up, he was bright red, except at the forehead which was actually starting to look purple.

"We are nothing without God!" he shouted at Oren.

Oren was slim, also dark-haired and despite the size difference, he did not look afraid of the larger man in the least.

"Oh yes, and whose God do we speak of? Hmm? The God whose Jews killed Christ? Or perhaps the Muslim's Allah, or Falun Gong?" His eyes snapped with anger, "Better yet, perhaps we should send the Mormons?"

Anthony tried to intervene, "If we could just..." Neither man paid any attention to him.

Mendez was a good man, but he was also a devout Catholic. And he had been known to argue, rather vociferously, for hours in support of the duality of faith and science. Lowenstein, whose father had been an Orthodox rabbi, was an atheist to the core and unafraid to call others, especially his fellow scientists, fools if they professed any sign of faith or belief in a higher power.

"God will judge the godless!"

"Do you believe in the tooth fairy and Easter bunny as well?"

"To send man out into the stars without faith to guide him is sacrilege!"

"Perhaps we should also bring hexes and make sure everyone knows how to ward off demons!"

"Blasphemer!"

"Idiot!"

"ENOUGH!" Anthony's bellow cut through both men's shouts and startled the rest of the room into silence. The abrupt silence allowed Anthony some respite from his pounding headache, but he knew he had very little time before it started up again. "We will show each other respect, and that includes all faiths, or lack thereof."

The folder that had started today's argument was that of Jacob Carter, age 44, a brilliant and respected psychotherapist who also held a doctorate in Ethnobotany. He was one of the handful of "over forty" age applicants, yes, but it was his recent conversion that had sparked controversy. Applicants were given extensive physical and psychological tests as well as essay-type questions designed to elicit as much personal information about the applicant as possible. Under the Personal Beliefs section, he had candidly written about his decision to attend seminary and become an ordained Methodist minister five years before.

"It is my dream that I may take the word of God to the stars, as a comfort to those of faith in the darkness of space."

A man who not only professed his faith, but was interested in proselytizing? This revelation had raised Lowenstein's fur, and he had said something disparaging about religion, setting off Mendez.

"Look," Anthony continued, ignoring Mendez's labored breathing, the man looked closer to a heart attack than he was comfortable with, "This is about choosing the tens out of the tens."

Oren responded, "Jacob Carter is a ten out of ten," he snapped, "despite being a..." He frowned slightly, "*Methodist*." He rolled his eyes.

Anthony jumped in quickly, "Yes, he is. He fits into our needed skillsets - his addition will make five total individuals with degrees in the various areas of botany. And Jacob is the only one with an *ethno*botany degree. His abilities as a psychotherapist are well known as well. He served as a crisis counselor during the Narine conflict and has passed all of the physical and psychological tests with flying colors."

His eyes ran down the summary page, then flipped to the back half, "Family history is negative for any mental illness, early death, or inherited diseases. His bone structure is optimal and his heart is good."

"Dr. Carter has also expressed an interest in studying Oceanology and assisting Fuller in exploring the anomalies reported in the Decca Strait and while he does not have any children, is fully functional and willing to either pair and reproduce with a suitable partner or adopt from an unrelated source carried by a surrogate."

He looked back at Mendez and Lowenstein. They had both slipped back into the plush armchairs that lined the long conference table and seemed to have settled down. Mendez was still pink and Lowenstein pretending indifference as Anthony read aloud to them.

Anthony continued, "Let's put him in the final 400 and move on, shall we? All in favor?"

The five men and women present each voted for Carter, even Lowenstein, who couldn't resist adding, "At least he's a Methodist," he stared dismissively at Mendez, "which means he is relatively reasonable."

Mendez' face flushed red all over again.

Anthony sighed. Next on the agenda were the couples and young families who had applied to join in the quest to Zarmina's World, including twenty gay and lesbian couples. After such a ridiculous fight over religion, Anthony was dreading the inevitable conflict over gay marriage.

He opened the first folder, "Jack Dunn and Kevin Edmonds, married ten years, one four-year-old adopted son. Jack is a videographer, historian, author, and experienced sailor. Kevin is well versed in communications and has studied extensively in Africa and South America on native building materials. It also notes under education that he has a minor in entomology and he has expressed an interest in cataloging new species once we are on-planet."

A murmur from the far corner of the room had begun immediately after hearing the names. It seemed that the homophobic contingent was about to rear their ugly heads. Anthony sighed in resignation and turned his attention to the elderly female board member. *Might as well get this over with now.*

The Final Cut

"Jealousy is a disease, love is a healthy condition. The immature mind often mistakes one for the other, or assumes that the greater the love, the greater the jealousy – in fact, they're almost incompatible; one emotion hardly leaves room for the other. Both at once can produce unbearable turmoil." – Robert A. Heinlein

Date: 11.20.2097
Earth – Seattle, Washington

Daniel Medry stood staring at the envelope. The news vid stream had been running coverage of the Selection Committee for weeks now, as the finalists had been selected.

"Uncle Dan, look at me!" Toby aimed his skateboard down the ramp, with only a small wobble. He was getting better, more confident.

Daniel smiled at him and waved, "Keep going, buddy!"

As applicants had been slowly weeded out, letters had been issued, carefully worded, kindly phrased, and he had dreaded each day's mail delivery, certain that he too would receive a polite "thanks but no thanks" printed on clean crisp white paper. The Selection Committee chose the National Mail Service for their notices, which now delivered via Autobot each afternoon.

"You gonna just stare at that envelope all day or are you going to open it?" Luke asked.

Daniel ignored him.

"Dad! Did you see that?" Toby yelled from the skate ramp.

Luke waved at the boy, "Yeah! You nailed it!"

He turned back to Daniel, "I've been showing him those old vids of Tony Hawk and his grandson. You remember the ones we saw? The ones dad gave us?"

Daniel smiled, his eyes still on the envelope, "Yeah, I remember."

They sent actual hard copies, not just emails or vidmails, which was the standard of the day. That choice, along with every other one the Selection Committee had made, was analyzed and vivisected ad nauseum by the news corps. Entire talk shows had centered on the leaked details of the selection process, including the decision to only send applicants whose IQs were demonstrably *above* the average.

Luke laughed, "We were obsessed. We spent every day of the summer out here on this ramp, practicing, determined to do bigger and bigger tricks. Until I fell and busted my arm up, that is."

Daniel nodded, "And I wouldn't practice without you."

"You said it wouldn't have been fair to practice without me. Instead, we spent the rest of the year learning coding."

"Nah, *you* spent the rest of the year learning coding, little brother. I spent the rest of it chasing Vicki Fields."

"Yeah, that sounds like you all right."

Just the other day on *The Informer*, a morning newsvid that tended toward inflammatory reporting, they had released a series of secret videos that showed two of the Committee members toe to toe, screaming about God. Daniel smirked, *The Informer* was filled with jackasses who would twist a woman's dying words into something deviant given the chance, but that vidcord had been especially damaging, resulting in calls for the Selection Committee to meet in a public setting.

It wouldn't happen. World Geographic, while political, still remained a private institution and the entire mission to the Gliese system was under its purview.

Daniel ran his finger under the flap, slowly easing the paper envelope open.

"I did it, I did it! Did you see? Uncle Dan, did you see?" Toby's excited voice distracted him for a moment.

"Yeah buddy, that was so cool!"

"He sure does worship you," Luke said, an almost envious tone in his voice.

"If he saw me all day instead of you, it would be all about you, little brother." Daniel reached out and punched his brother lightly on the shoulder.

There had been protests, heated debates, and even calls for the government to intervene in the face of "obvious favoritism and elitism." This had gone nowhere, and swayed no one on the Selection Committee by any great degree, who issued a statement declaring in no uncertain terms that if there were disagreements with the Selection Committee's choices, those individuals were free to build their own ship, and man it in whatever form they chose. This sparked yet another round of protests and calls for additional missions, further filling the newsvids with controversy.

Daniel felt the mass within the envelope, several layers of papers for certain. It wasn't thin, it was thick. *What did that mean*?

"Would you just open the damn thing?" Luke asked.

"Yeah, yeah, I'm getting to it."

His heart rate increased as he fumbled with the papers inside, slightly tearing the World Geographic embossed seal on the corner of the enclosed top page, his heart thumping a rhythm he could feel in his ears. The chance of a lifetime, an opportunity that would change his life forever, and one that would take him impossibly far from everything and everyone he had ever known – all of it lay inside of the envelope waiting to be unveiled.

"Well?" came Luke's voice.

"Holy shit. I...I got in to the last round."

Inside of the envelope was a letter and an airline voucher, dated for early January 2098. The letter was brief and to the point. He had been conditionally accepted into the Gliese program and would undergo two months of training and the last rounds of evaluation. Just five hundred applicants had made it this far, and his chances were now 50/50 that he would be accepted. Out of nearly 852,000 applications carried through from the last round, he was now in the final lap!

His brother clapped him on the shoulder, "Seriously? Damn, I would've thought that was like finding an iceberg in hell! What were the odds anyway?"

Daniel smiled, the letter in his hand a victory of sorts, a promise of the ultimate adventure.

"There were over thirty million applications submitted, with a total of two hundred and fifty actual crew member slots open, so my chances of being selected were one in one hundred and twenty thousand."

Luke whistled, "Damn, and they picked *you*?"

"Very funny little brother."

Daniel aimed a thumbs up at Toby again as his nephew swooped up and twirled confidently, the skateboard becoming a natural extension of his feet.

This park, named after the Swiss immigrant Ulrich Gabriel, who had owned an extensive farm and dairy herd, was home to so many memories. Here, in the days after his mother's death he had skateboarded for hours, not wanting to talk to anyone. That had been a dark time.

Years later, after the devastating loss of their dad, both he and Luke had slipped away from the house full of concerned neighbors and ended up here, wandering the wild part of the park, first in silence, and finally, near dark, with a plan. They wouldn't be split up. The next day Daniel had filed paperwork with the court requesting emancipation and also requesting guardianship of his younger brother. The house was paid for, and there was a healthy amount of money they could live on for years thanks to Dad's savvy investing.

"This place, it never changes. It looks the same as it did when we were kids."

Luke didn't respond for a long moment.

"Do you think you'll make the final cut?"

"I hope so."

"Why? Why would you want to go? You would leave this all behind? All of us, your home, your family?"

Daniel was silent for a moment, lost in the memory of that day. They had returned to the house, now filled with police and panicked neighbors. Daniel had credited the park with helping him remember what was truly important – his family.

And now, a dozen years later, he was considering leaving them. Daniel struggled with the thought of it. It had all seemed rather theoretical before, a distant dream, but this was reality. It was there in front of him, he had only to step on the plane and head for training.

"Daniel?" Luke's voice cut through.

"I...I guess so." *How could he explain this to Luke?* "I mean, damn, who knows what will happen at training, right? They'll probably take one look at me and say, 'Ah, hell no!'" He grinned at his brother, "I just want to be able to say someday when we are both old and gray that I *tried*. Y'know?"

Six weeks later Daniel found himself standing in line in Florida, staring at the enormous hangars where he and the rest of the future crew were to train. He stood near the entrance to Cape Canaveral, bag in hand, part of a line of applicants which slowly snaked down the sidewalk. He drank it all in, stunned at his luck.

"It still feels unreal to me. What about you?" A beautiful woman, dark curls pulled into a ponytail, stood behind him. Her eyes were a soft gray.

Daniel grinned at her, "Yeah, completely unreal. I'm Daniel, Daniel Medry." He put out his hand.

"I'm Sam." Her grip was firm and warm. She cocked her head to a guy with a friendly gap-toothed smile. His brown hair was cut short and his face sported a short beard. "This guy here is Mike Deekins."

Deekins shook Daniel's hand, "Everyone calls me Deeks."

"Nice to meet both of you."

Daniel, Sam, and Deeks talked, sharing information as the line inched forward. Sam and Deeks were both from the Alaskan Republic, separate now from the Reformed United States of America. The Republic maintained close ties with the RUSA as well as Canada. The Alaskan Republic was still sparsely settled, but they were fiercely independent.

In the weeks to come, Deeks and Medry formed a close friendship, joined at times by Sam, and the petite, attractive Kit Tanner, who Deeks was instantly attracted to.

Training and evaluations kept them busy, as did varying schedules and activities. As the weeks wore on, there was a steady stream of dropped applicants. Not everyone was cut out for space travel. There weren't just tests of athleticism or physical health, but also psychological tests, and even several tests that pushed the boundaries of many individual's deepest fears – claustrophobia, acrophobia, and more. Through it all, Medry and Deeks maintained, as did Sam, Kit, and a handful of others they grew to know well. Slowly, they were seeing their numbers reduced, edging ever closer to the final selection. There were, after all, only 250 spots to fill.

Cape Canaveral

"A human being is part of a whole, called by us the Universe, a part limited in time and space. He experiences himself, his thoughts and feelings, as something separated from the rest a kind of optical delusion of his consciousness. This delusion is a kind of prison for us, restricting us to our personal desires and to affection for a few persons nearest us. Our task must be to free ourselves from this prison by widening our circles of compassion to embrace all of living creatures and the whole of nature in its beauty." – Albert Einstein

Date: 11.23.2097
Earth – New York City, New York

"I don't care what the ads say," Jennifer Zradce tossed the strip of NearBacon down on the plate; "This tastes disgusting."

Nathan Zradce, who had been doing his best to hide his own look of revulsion at the taste of the faux pig meat, couldn't help but agree. He had managed to eat half of the strip before setting it down and digging into the eggs and toast.

The dream still tugged at the edges of his memory, although he was trying desperately to forget it. Cities filled with the dead, silent, except for clouds of crows feasting on the remains. He pushed the memory back down.

"Well, we tried it." He smiled at his wife, "And now we can feed it to the section supe's cat."

The section superintendent who managed the East Ground floor section was an older woman with three grown children. She had worked and lived in the same apartment for over 35 years. Each floor of the megaplex had four superintendents assigned to it, and the building clawed its way past low-hanging clouds, nearly one hundred stories tall. It occupied over three blocks of real estate in New York City, making its footprint one of the biggest of its kind in a city filled with enormous skyscrapers. With over four hundred units per level, the building was home to nearly eighty thousand people.

"Any news on the housing application?" Jennifer asked, pushing her egg around on her plate.

Nathan had dreaded this question and deflected it by fiddling with the remote, dimming the lights accidentally as he keyed in the sequence to activate the newsvid.

"Damn this thing," he complained, "I want to hear the news."

He ignored his wife's unhappy stare and clicked on the newsvid. Their apartment was so small that the screen didn't occupy a full wall, merely a swath of space no larger than a medium-sized mirror.

Jennifer hated the morning anchor, but she said nothing, watching as the screen swept over the images of thousands of dead pigs burning.

"The latest round of PCV-6 has left millions of swine dead or dying," the newscaster chirped, a smile permanently plastered to her face. "Scientists continue to work on this pressing issue while livestock prices soar in the Americas to over 65 Ameros per pound. And in response, shares in NearBacon have increased by 25 percent, despite a recent spate of complaints by consumers..."

As the news anchor continued her story, he could not help but remember more of the dream. There was a room filled with plants, all glistening silver with frost, and the greenery dead or dying.

"God, the news is always so damned depressing." He said, clicking to a different newsfeed.

"Nathan," Jennifer's voice was insistent, "we were denied again, weren't we?"

Nathan pressed the button and the newsvid winked off. He sighed; he had wanted to surprise her. Take her for a picnic at the lake in the evening, ask her if she was ready for a completely different sunset, and then show it to her. But Jennifer was persistent, if she thought he was holding out on her, she would worry at him until he spilled his guts.

"We were. I got the email last week and didn't want to tell you, and then this came in."

He pulled the letter out of his pocket. An honest-to-god printed on paper, letter that accepted both of them into the final phase of the selection process. He slapped it down on the table and leaned back to watch his wife's face.

Jennifer stared at the folded paper for a moment, puzzled, and then slowly reached out, unfolding it, her mouth set.

Nathan watched as her eyes scanned the page and her expression changed from one of dissatisfaction to one of shock.

"Oh my god," Jennifer's words had deserted her for once. "Oh my god, Nathan, we have been accepted!"

"The final phase, it isn't a for sure, but we go for training in six weeks."

He smiled at her. He knew she had been dreaming of something, anything, which would create an escape for them from this tiny apartment which was comprised of just 350 square feet. She had talked often of having children, which didn't move him as much as it did her. Children were often bewildering, and in the case of his childhood, disappointing to parents. He couldn't understand the underlying need she had to make more little creatures to fill up an already full world.

Despite their both holding a multitude of degrees between them, the newly instituted New York birth lottery simply hadn't come through for them. Not for the past three years' worth of applications. If they had a child, they would face such steep annual fines, as well as being cramped all together in this tiny apartment that they would barely be able to make ends meet. And forget being able to afford daycare or a good school.

Jennifer had insisted that they try for the Gliese program and sent in their application as soon as the invitation to apply had gone out. She had gushed about it, her eyes filled with visions of an empty world that had no limitations on the amount of space or children.

Jennifer jumped off of her stool then, enveloping Nathan with a crushing hug.

"Final phase! We can do it Nathan! We can make the final cut!" She pulled back, "Oh my god! Six weeks! I have to put in my notice, and figure out what to pack, and, and..."

She planted a kiss on his lips before reaching for her tablet to begin making a list of tasks. Nathan suppressed a laugh; his wife was a planner through and through.

Six weeks later they arrived at Cape Canaveral's front gates. The ride from New York had been bumpy, a storm was barreling in from the Midwestern states, and the skies had been dark and gray until they flew south far enough to escape the edges of the storm. Standing there, with their bags, the sky was clear and had just a slight nip to the air. It was early though, just past seven in the morning, and the temperature was slated to rise to 23° Celsius by noon.

They stood in a line of people slowly advancing through the gates of the Cape as they were processed through the Intake Center. There they provided the letter, scanned their National ID chips, and were issued a room number and a ticket for their uniforms.

An hour after arriving at the Cape, Nathan scanned his wrist over the chip reader at their room door. The room was literally half the size of their entire apartment and Jennifer giggled with excitement.

"Nathan, look, we even have our own bathroom, and I swear it is larger than the one back home!" She danced about the room before flopping down on the double bed. "I just can't believe we are here!"

The day was filled with orientation, a tour of the facility, and then a mock-up of Calypso, a full-size replica of the ship that was under construction in space, with the final touches and equipment testing currently underway. That evening, in the common rooms, they were encouraged to meet their fellow candidates.

Jennifer, who had haunted the forum boards for months, had used a password provided in the letter to join the Final Stage community board online and befriend several other of the attendees. They came from all points of the globe, but in particular, she had been talking with the finalists from the Reformed United States and the Alaskan Republic, and she pulled Nathan over to the group as soon as they stepped into one of the large rooms.

"Jennifer! Hey!" a dark-haired woman stood up and waved her over, "You look just like your photo, I'd recognize you anywhere!"

Nathan followed a few paces behind his wife. Social situations weren't really his thing. He would talk if someone spoke to him, but he never started a conversation, unlike his social butterfly of a wife.

"Sam! Oh, my goodness, it is so great to finally meet you!" Jennifer gushed, pulling the woman into a quick hug before turning back to her husband. "Nathan, this is Samantha Sydan, and," she turned back to the group, eyes narrowing in concentration as she took in the faces, "Let's see, you must be Daniel Medry, and you have got to be Mike Deekins, and you," she frowned in concentration, "You are Kit Tanner, right?"

The people identified laughed and nodded as everyone shook hands.

G581: THE DEPARTURE

Nathan remembered Jennifer talking about Samantha Sydan. Samantha's older brother was the captain of a supply ship that had just returned from a mission to the Mars colony, ferrying supplies and colonists to the Huygens Outpost. Jennifer had been carrying on endlessly about the folks she had met online, to the point that Nathan felt as if he knew them too. The evenings in their small apartment had been filled with monologues from Jennifer on the different people and their skill brackets as she learned as much as she could about what the Selection Committee was looking for in potential candidates.

Still, Nathan wished he was back in their room. This space was crowded, and he felt completely out of his element. But escape was not an option at the moment. Soon they were seated, with drinks in hand, and learning more about the people who they might soon be living and working with. As the drinks flowed and the sun set in the sky outside of the room, the question finally worked its way around the group.

"So why do you want to go to Zarmina's World?" Kit Tanner, a petite woman in her late 20s asked.

Daniel Medry, who had been making subtle overtures towards Sam Sydan, stopped and thought a moment before leaning forward, a smile on his lips.

"Let's see, a completely new world, with breathable air and actual atmosphere where I could spend the rest of my life exploring and never run out of places to go. What's not to like about that?"

Mike Deekins leered at Kit Tanner, "If you are going there, I'm on board, darlin.'" Kit rolled her eyes and turned to Jennifer.

"What about you, Jennifer?"

Nathan watched his wife's face turn dreamy, "Space to move and live. No limits on reproduction or those high annual fines that New York instituted last year."

Several of them groaned.

"I heard about that," Sam said, shaking her head, "That's just awful!"

Jennifer nodded, "And besides that, I'm a civil and mechanical engineer. The most frustrating thing about it is that I don't have space to plan a system that would work. I want to plot out the first colony, make it sustainable, expandable, and well-thought out. The thought of putting something together that doesn't include having to work around existing outdated systems is so appealing I can't even begin to express it!"

Sam grinned, "Don't I know it! I studied civil engineering as well, but I love botany and mycology. Just imagine the discoveries we will make on a new planet with different plant life! I worked for the Stamets Foundation during my sophomore year, and the possible applications of some of the fungal life that D.O.V.E. continues to report on are mind-blowing!"

Mike Deekins, who insisted everyone call him "Deeks" leaned forward, "Let's face it, we are all nerds and dreamers. I hope I end up in the final round due to my knowledge of the Cryo systems, but my true loves are sailing and marine biology. Just imagine what is going on in the Mediterre Sea."

Kit interrupted, "Did they settle on that name?"

Deeks shrugged, "When we get there, I figure it is all up for grabs, but the sea is in a similar shape, complete with a peninsula that looks a lot like Italy. Anyway, several of the D.O.V.E. probes caught movement on a large scale, possibly a whale? Once I get there, I'm heading south and establishing an outpost on the coast. We will have the tech for a fair-sized submersible as well as a survey ship." He grinned, "And like Jennifer said, all the room in the world. No bumping elbows or living in a tiny place, even though we have far less of that in the Alaskan Republic than you do down here in the R.U.S.A."

"What about you, Nathan?" Kit Tanner's voice turned the group's attention to him.

He had been happy sitting quietly, listening to the others, but now the spotlight was on him.

"Um, well..."

He had filled out the forms, submitted to the intrusive questioning, jumped through all of the hoops, and gotten to a finalist position without having to answer this question. And for a moment, he had no idea of what to say. The truth was he didn't particularly care either way. He had met Jennifer in college, they had gotten along well, and eventually that had led to an engagement and low-key wedding in a tiny garden in Manhattan with a small handful of friends and family. All her friends and her family, since his adoptive parents had died a few years earlier and he didn't really know how to make friends.

Marrying Jennifer, applying for the Gliese mission, eventually planning for kids and a life on a new world – these were all Jennifer's dreams. He was just along for the ride. He had no roots, no friends or family he called his own, and if Jennifer wanted to go, who was he to say no?

They were all staring at him, waiting for him to gush about exploring mountain ranges, deep seas, or cataloguing alien plant life. But for him, one place was pretty much the same as any other, alien life forms or no.

"I'm a closet artist," he lied glibly, "I can't wait to draw the skies of Zarmina's World, and the plant life too. It's going to be amazing!"

He ignored Jennifer's speculative stare. He couldn't avoid her questions later that night in bed.

"Nathan, why do you *really* want to go to Zarmina's World?" she asked in the darkness of their room hours later.

He lied again, thankful for the darkness so that he didn't have her staring at him and seeing through his lies.

"Why, children of course. We can have plenty of them, just like we have always wanted."

Jennifer said nothing. Later, after his breathing evened and dropped noticeably into sleep, Jennifer Zradce lay there thinking. She knew the closet artist line was bullshit and Nathan had never talked about having kids, or wanting much of anything. So why did he want to go to Zarmina's World? She had never really stopped to think about it, but now that she did, she realized that Nathan had never really seemed excited about it. Not that he had been against it, but as with most things, he wasn't enthusiastic about much of anything. He just sort of went with the flow. The apartment had been her choice, just like the wedding venue, the applications for new housing, and the race to a new world.

Eventually she accepted that there would never be a better answer than that. Nathan was rootless and without a great deal of direction. She had noticed it in college. It was always her that made the decisions, from what they ate to when they had decided to move in together.

It wasn't that she was a control freak, more that he simply didn't seem to care. He never objected, never argued.

Her mother, who had passed last year had said, "He's perfect, he would do anything for you. What more could you ask for?"

And she had listened to her mother, who had said the same thing about Jennifer's father, especially when he died the year after she graduated from college.

That was what a good husband was, right? Jennifer couldn't help wondering though; just what it was that moved Nathan. It was as if he hadn't discovered his passion yet and was settled on helping her find hers. In the end, without any evidence of him having other wishes or needs, she was happy that he was willing to follow her lead.

The four weeks of training and evaluation went well. At the end of it, Nathan and Jennifer Zradce were notified of their official acceptance to the Gliese mission. They were going to Zarmina's World.

One Last Hurdle

Date: 02.20.2098
Earth – Cape Canaveral, Florida

Nathan Zradce sat in the chair the psychotherapist had indicated on the first visit and relaxed. This was the third and hopefully final visit. They had run through the required questions the Selection Committee required answers for, then covered his basic history, touched on his three-year marriage to his wife Jennifer, delved into his professional career choices and discussed why he was willing to risk life and limb traveling farther than any human had ever traveled. The therapist was slim, attractive, and efficient.

Angela Di Marco had paused for a moment from reviewing his folder and history, her eyebrows raised and her mouth a moue of surprise, "You are adopted?"

Nathan nodded, "Yes, when I was eight."

"*Eight?*"

Nathan nodded, smiling slightly. This always seemed to catch people's attention, as if there was something that spoke volumes about a person in that age. Not an infant, free of damage, but eight years of living *before* being taken in by some sacrificing, saintly couple. His adoptive parents had been pretty close to saints, but they had often bragged that he was their easiest foster child turned adoptee.

Angela stared at him, then paged to the end of the folder.

"There is nothing here about your birth parents."

Nathan nodded again, "There wouldn't be. My records were sealed. My mother never told anyone who my father was, and she was committed to a mental institution when I was seven. I went into foster care then. I was one of

43

the lucky ones, my adoptive parents, Hal and Mary were absolutely amazing people. They adopted me just a year into being fostered."

He smiled, "I had a great childhood."

Angela shook her head, "So what was your mom like? Your birth mom that is."

A sudden flash of memory of Natalia Zradce singing to him, and to his brother Immanuel.

"*Sleep, sleep, sleep. Don't lie too close to the edge of the bed. Or little gray wolf will come and grab you by the flank. Drag you into the woods, underneath the willow root.*"

He managed to suppress a shudder at the memory of them, huddling in the middle of their beds afterward, legs and arms pulled away from the sides of their narrow twin mattresses, terrified that a wolf would come for them and drag them away to be devoured.

Nathan chose his words carefully, "I don't really remember much about her. A few snippets here and there, a lullaby maybe?"

Did they know? He didn't think they did. It was water under the bridge, but the scar on his abdomen gave a slight twinge in response.

During his physical, the doctor had noticed and commented on it.

"Huh, an old-school appendectomy scar. Got you just in time, huh?"

A typical appendectomy was now treated through laparoscopic surgery, but in cases of emergency, where an appendix has burst, a full incision had to be made so that the surgical team could be sure and clean out any contaminants from the abdominal cavity. Nathan hadn't corrected him. He watched the psychotherapist as she paged through the folder, her brow furrowed.

"You say that your mother was committed?" Angela said, suddenly looking up with a piercing gaze, "Do you remember the diagnosis? Or anything about what she was like in the time leading up to such a drastic measure?"

Nathan pasted a vaguely regretful look on his face, "Honestly, I really don't."

He shrugged and attempted a sad half-smile, "I believe she had a difficult time of it, perhaps a bad childhood? I really don't know. It wasn't talked about and it just seemed as if one day I was in one school and the next in a completely different one, and moved into Hal and Mary's house. They really took good care of me, but we never spoke of my mother."

Angela latched onto that last bit, leaned forward slightly, her interest peaked.

"Didn't you find that strange? Weren't you curious? "

Nathan shrugged, "I'm sure I had questions at the time, but the house was full of children, activities, and I just remember that Hal and Mary, well, Mary especially, were always encouraging my interests – primarily language and computers."

He smiled, "She worked from home. She was a software engineer, taught me basic coding my first winter with them and later paid for me to learn German."

His smile grew broader, "We used to tell jokes in German, for practice. They really fed my interests, y'know?"

Angela wouldn't let it go. She was persistent, that was for sure. "Surely when you grew older, in your teenage years or early twenties. You must have wondered, even looked her up."

I have to give her something, or she will never let it go. And besides, the visit had been public record.

He looked down, toyed with an unraveled edge of the fabric from the armrest of his chair. "I did look her up. A few years back. It was...it...it didn't end well."

He told her the truth of it, which was that his mother was as unhinged as they came, but that it was most likely due to a childhood and adolescence spent separated from her own parents, shuttling back and forth between foster parent situations, and worse, living through The Collapse.

"So how old was she when you were born?" Angela asked, scribbling furiously in her notebook.

"Mm, in her 40s, I think."

"And you were her only child?"

Immanuel falling to the floor, his tiny body arcing, his bones and tendons twisting in unnatural ways, head slamming against the concrete with a sickening crack, teeth clacking together hard. There had been blood, trickling from his mouth, a corner of his tongue caught between his teeth. Not enough blood to warrant the stillness that followed. That empty, dead stare as Nathaniel shook him, lifting him from the cool basement floor, their Legos spilled between them. Mother had buried him beneath a small willow tree in the back yard, humming the lullaby, tears running down her face. She had told no one, and no one had ever known. Only Nathaniel knew. He was so small then, without words, and lost without his twin brother.

"Yes, I'm an only child."

Angela nodded, staring at him pensively, and finally closed her notebook.

"Well, Nathan, thank you for coming in. I'll go ahead and pass your file on to the committee for review."

She smiled, "I do wish you the best of luck in all of this."

Nathan thanked her and left, wondering if he had just shot to hell his, and more importantly, *Jennifer's* chances of ever leaving Earth.

After he had left, Angela put a question mark down in the margins of her notes. The Selection Committee had been clear, mental illness and long space voyages did not go well together. This would need to be referred for further investigation with the committee. *The candidate appears stable despite the possibility of ~~traumatic~~ difficult childhood,* Angela wrote in the Notes section of her tablet.

Next up was Daniel Medry. Moments after Zradce had made his exit, Daniel Medry had checked in at the front desk. A small light went on in the corner of her office when a new patient arrived, and Angela reached a hand up to her hair, fluffing it slightly, and then freshened her lipstick before rising, walking to the door, and beckoning Medry to come in.

She couldn't help but want to return the attentions he had shown her the last two sessions. She knew it wasn't professional, but the man was sexy, smart, and funny – just the way she liked. He was irreverent, and surprisingly at ease around her, despite what was at stake. And those deep blue eyes, paired with that quirky smile. Angela was tempted to make something up on his records just to keep him on Earth.

But she couldn't bring herself to do that, it would be wrong, and some people were just lovely in theory, but not so much in practice. Medry gave hints of being the latter – he had the qualities of a rolling stone, a real "love them and leave them" type. He smiled at her with that quirky mouth, a flash of white teeth. Yep, Medry had her number and he knew it.

He took the seat that Zradce had barely vacated, leaned back, relaxed, and flashed her yet another grin that gave Angela a sharp thrill. She sat down across from him, wondering if she had made a mistake in her dress choice today. The skirt was shorter than she normally wore, and the blouse perhaps too flattering with its scoop neck and clingy fabric. She had known she would see him today, had it affected her clothing decisions? *Angela Di Marco, you are playing with fire.*

Off-kilter, she blurted it out, "Why do you want to leave Earth so bad, Daniel?"

God, why? She couldn't help the fantasy that flitted through her mind – him, her, twisted bedsheets. Damn *him and his sexy self.*

He blinked, "Well, good afternoon to you too."

That touch of normalcy broke the spell, at least for the moment, and Angela flushed in embarrassment. She had to take control of the situation. So instead of backing off, she pressed forward.

"Well?"

He considered her for a moment, probably assessing her elevated heart rate, noting her clothing, the touch of blush she had added to her cheeks this morning. He was the type of man who noticed such things. As he rolled her question through his head, his attitude changed and a look of pure joy stole over his face. The sexy look he had cultivated since laying eyes on her in their first session was gone, replaced by an almost child-like wonder.

"Can you imagine it? This other world? Breathable air, a rocky world like ours. The pictures the probe took don't do it justice, not really."

He sighed then, "I've walked on the moon, climbed parts of Mt. Kilimanjaro, walked where few humans have ever gone, but this.... what an adventure!"

He leaned forward, towards her, and the delight poured out of him as he continued to describe the photos and reports the D.O.V.E. probe had showed the world. As he did, a streak of intense attraction formed in the air between them. Angela couldn't help but share his excitement and a small part of her longed to see those alien landscapes, to walk on the surface of a distant planet and spend the rest of her life exploring the mysteries of an alien world. It wasn't her dream, it was his; yet he made it sound so amazing, the ultimate in adventure, the ultimate in being alive.

Medry didn't get any question marks or concerns written down in his file. Weeks later, along with a few twisted bedsheets, and Angela Di Marco signed off on Daniel's file. As far as the area of mental health, he was in great shape. She didn't mention that he was talented in other ways, and she knew better than to fall in love.

Medry had just passed the final hurdle.

Leave-Taking

"Human beings hardly ever learn from the experience of others. They learn; when they do, which isn't often, on their own, the hard way." – Robert A. Heinlein

Date: 03.26.2098
Earth – New York City, New York

Nathan Zradce had slipped away with the excuse of dropping off the bags of belongings to a local charity. That was true, at least mostly. Just one-half block down from the charity was Peak View Behavioral Health, a facility he had sworn he would never visit again.

The last time he had been here she had spit on him and then tried to claw his eyes out. She had managed to scratch him deeply on one cheek, tearing flesh with her ragged, half-chewed fingernails. The staff had been very apologetic, surprised at the level of vitriol the old woman had manifested.

"Normally she just sits here in the day room." The orderly had said.

"I've never seen her do that. She just stares out of the window and asks if anyone has seen Immanuel. Who did you say you were again?"

Nathan didn't answer. He had cleaned up his bloodied cheek with a paper towel from the bathroom and strode out. He hadn't bothered telling them that he hadn't really expected much.

That had been nearly five years ago. And here he was, walking through the front doors, his nose tingling with the smell of antiseptic and bleach. That *institutional* smell that reminded you forcibly, as if you were not already aware, that you were not in a welcoming place.

Nathan had struggled with the decision to come here. And he had struggled with it silently. His wife Jennifer knew that he was adopted and that his birth father had never been in the picture. The rest had been a fiction of sorts. He never told her about Immanuel. And as for his mother? When Jennifer had asked, he had told her she died.

When pressed for details, he simply said, "An accident. I don't remember much."

He wished that he could forget. The Selection Committee had known more of course. You don't send someone twenty-one light years away into space without knowing that a man's birth mother had lost her mind and was now locked up in an institution for the rest of her life, drooling from the anti-psychotics and staring mindlessly out of a window. He had said nothing about the attack and the physical exam had simply noted his abdominal scar as an appendectomy. He hadn't corrected them on that assumption. He had been accepted, so apparently, they had been satisfied with his answers.

Not much had changed in the building. Maybe some new paint. Nathan approached the intake desk, his steps slowing. *What am I doing here anyway? If she recognizes me, she might attack me again. If she doesn't, she will think I am Immanuel.* Either way, it wasn't going to be exactly therapeutic for either of them. But all Nathan could think of in answer was that he had to say goodbye one last time. He owed her that much. *No, I don't owe her anything. I owe it to myself.*

The woman at the intake desk was older and looked vaguely familiar. He gave his name, and her name and the woman eyed him for a moment. "I remember you. You came in years ago."

Nathan nodded but said nothing.

"You were her one and only visitor," the woman gave him a speculative look, "and I've seen you somewhere else too...recently."

When the mission finalists had been announced, their photos, along with their full names, had been shown on every newsvid world-wide. It was a big deal, just 250 of them, out of several hundred thousand applicants.

Nathan shrugged, "I guess I've just got that face."

Her lips pursed, "Perhaps so, but I am just *sure* I've seen you around somewhere, recently."

She waved one hand in dismissal at the thought, pushed over a clipboard, "Sign in here."

Nathan filled out the form and provided his ID card.

"It's policy, we need to dot all the i's and cross all the t's," she said, winking, as she handed him a visitor's badge.

He walked down a long hallway, through two sets of locked doors with intercoms and buzzers, and then an elevator to take him to the third floor. Another intake desk. This one didn't have any forms to fill out, and certainly no pens to write with. They weren't stupid, the patients on this floor had been known to make anything into a weapon. They counted every spoon and refused to issue anything resembling a weapon – patients learned to eat their Salisbury steak with spoons or their hands, their choice.

An orderly ushered him into a brightly lit room. The chairs were anchored in place and overhead the speakers played quiet, soothing music. At one corner an inane newsvid played cartoons, far out of reach of any prying hands, or spitting mouths, and several patients were staring slack-jawed at it, unmoving, one sagging slowly to one side. In all, there were about ten patients in the room, most of them in drugged, drooling stupors.

Natalia Zradce sat alone near a window, looking out with a wistful, somewhat lost expression. Nathan approached her slowly, shocked at how young she looked. He knew from the tiny box of documents he had received years ago that his mother was born October 30th, 2013. Which meant that he and his brother Immanuel were born on her 45th birthday – a fact he hadn't been aware of growing up. The picture of her holding two tiny babies in her hospital bed had been striking. In it, she hadn't looked a day over twenty.

There had even been a small sliver of a smile on her face. Nathan had always wondered who had taken the picture. Had it been a nurse? His father?

The birth certificate had not listed any father, and she had never told him who it was. Yet another mystery, he supposed.

The biggest mystery of all was sitting in front of him, swiftly approaching her 85th birthday although she didn't look a day over forty. Her hair didn't have a single gray streak in it. Her back was ramrod straight, and her eyes were clear. That was surprising when he considered her surroundings.

Perhaps she was doing better, perhaps they had a new wonder drug that took away the crazy and replaced it with sanity and kindness. A lovely fantasy, but highly unlikely.

She stared at him and he stared back.

"Natalia," bubbled the orderly, "look who has come to visit you! Your son Nathan."

The woman turned to Nathan smiling, "Natalia is one of my favorites, and she doesn't give us a lick of trouble, except a spate of nightmares in the early spring. Other than that, she is peaceful and quiet, just a joy to take care of!"

Early spring had been when Immanuel had died, his tiny body lifeless after a massive seizure. Natalia had prayed over his body for days, ceasing only when her son's corpse began to stink and draw flies. Nathan remembered it with such clarity. She hadn't taken his death well. Each night she had visited the tiny grave she had dug under the willow tree in the back yard. Nathan could remember peering out the window, desperate for her to return before the wolf from the lullaby came and got her. Then he would have been all alone.

Nathan didn't say anything in return, didn't even acknowledge the other woman's presence, and the orderly's smile slipped down at the edges.

"I'll just be right over there, Mr. Zradce, so you and your mother can have some privacy."

He managed a curt nod in her direction, his eyes never leaving his mother.

"Good afternoon, Mother," Nathan stumbled over the word.

Natalia Zradce's eyes flickered over him, "Nathaniel."

She said it so quietly, and her lips barely moved. He wondered for a moment if he had imagined it.

"I wanted to come to see you and tell you that I am leaving and going on a trip very far away," he said, the ground unsteady under his feet, almost as if he was floating.

His mother did not react. A fly landed on her hand and she didn't even blink, or move her hand to flick it off. It rubbed its front legs together, grooming itself or tasting the skin, he wasn't sure what, and she ignored it completely.

"Perhaps you have seen it on the news. The mission to Gliese 581g, Zarmina's World?"

Silence.

"It is very far away. It will take years to get there."

His throat was dry, standing there, trying to speak to this woman, this creature that haunted his dreams.

"I've decided that I won't be returning. I'll stay there on the planet and make a go of it. Start a family with my wife, Jennifer."

Silence.

She was staring right at him and not a single muscle moved, her eyes didn't even appear to blink. The seconds stretched, elongated, and were filled with silence. She seemed so perfect, so at peace, that what happened next terrified him.

She *smiled.*

It wasn't the kind of smile you ever want to see. Her teeth were gray, rotting from the cocktail of antipsychotics, sedatives, and poor oral hygiene after years of languishing within the walls of the psychiatric hospital.

Nathan felt his stomach flop in fear, watching as that crazy light he remembered so well gleamed in his mother's eyes.

"We are all going to die, Nathaniel. All of us."

He pulled away slowly, "Anyway, Mother, I wanted to come and say goodbye and to tell you..."

"The world doesn't know it yet, but it is all in motion, I've *seen* it, Nathaniel. Gluttony is one of the seven deadly sins."

"T-t-tell you that..."

After all of these years, the terror he felt in the face of her madness shook him to the core. He couldn't even manage to form his words right

She raised a bony finger and the fly, startled, flew away in a lazy arc. She pointed it at him.

"You won't die that way. You will live. But you will wish you hadn't. Oh yes."

He tried again, "T-t-tell you that..."

"Can you hear the screams of the dying, Nathaniel? Because I can. I can hear them screaming in agony and eating and eating and *eating.*"

She had risen from her seat now, a shambling horror of gray teeth and shiny mad eyes. Nathan took a step back. Behind him, he could hear the orderly rise up from the table she had been sitting at.

He couldn't manage to just say it, "I just wanted to tell you that I..."

She advanced as he backed up faster. She was a tiny woman, no more than five foot tall and he towered over her. This didn't make her any less terrifying.

The orderly had made her way to his side and was now advancing towards Natalia.

"Oh dear, well I think it is time for this visit to be up," she said, reaching for Natalia's arm, "Natalia my dear, why don't you..."

Natalia Zradce's hand flashed out, a blur, and the orderly let out a pained scream, a rivulet of blood dripping from the slash that appeared on her cheek.

And in that instant, there was chaos. The other patients, all of whom had been peaceful and zoned out moments before when he had entered the room, instantly moved into a state of high agitation.

He could not help but wonder if she had done it somehow.

Not just with her words or by bloodying the orderly, but with the madness that resided inside her. The energy of it was palpable, a taste of copper in your mouth and a feeling of twisting snakes in your stomach. He was sure she had done it, although he didn't know how. Nathan turned on his heel and ran for the door. He could hear the screams of the orderly and the patients behind him, but he didn't stop running until he heard the door to the room lock behind him. The intake desk personnel were already in motion, running towards the unit to shut it down and regain control of the patients.

Heart pounding, sick to his stomach and a headache beginning to form, Nathan made his way through the checkpoints until he reached the main intake desk.

The same woman was manning it and she chirped as he passed the visitor's badge toward her.

"I remember where I saw you! You are one of the colonists going on the Calypso, aren't you? My cousin's brother-in-law applied, but he was turned down. There was a lot of competition —— there had to be because he was a Rhoades scholar!"

Nathan muttered something, not even really knowing what. Then he bolted for the door. *What had possessed him to ever come here?*

Say Goodbye

Date: 05.27.2098

Earth – Seattle, Washington

The night was still cool, despite it being late May.

"Look there, Toby, next to Virgo, but before Scorpius, those faint stars there," the man crouched next to the little boy, as they both stared intently through the telescope at the sky.

"That's Libra."

"I don't see it," the boy whined, he shivered and huddled close to Daniel.

Daniel pulled off his jacket and wrapped it around Toby's tiny frame. Daniel sighed; he knew he should have bought the more expensive telescope.

"You can't go, Uncle Dan," Toby nuzzled Daniel, dwarfed by the jacket, "You can't go somewhere I'll never see you!"

Daniel's heart thudded painfully. He looked down at Toby's mop of blond curls, knowing every moment he spent with Toby and Janine risked exposing their secret. Toby had a father after all, and Luke adored the boy. Daniel, on the other hand, was a third wheel at best. He was great at weekend visits and taking Toby to the circus and carnivals, good for filling the kid up on sugar and greasy foods. He thrived at spoiling him rotten at every opportunity. That was his job, after all. Be the indulgent uncle, the fun guy who swooped in and gave Mommy and Daddy alone time and looked like Toby's very own personal superhero.

It wasn't really his style to be a dad. That was what Janine had said early on when she had broken the news to him that she was pregnant and pretty damn sure it was his and not Luke's.

"You aren't really dad material, Daniel." She had looked at the ground when she said it, "It just isn't your style."

"Luke doesn't have to know," she had said as Daniel struggled to think of something to say. "Besides, it was only once, and really, who would know for sure that Luke *wasn't* Toby's dad?"

Even though the brothers didn't look anything alike, Luke was dark-haired, while Daniel was blond. But their mom had sported curly blond hair. When Toby popped out seven months later with the same curly blond looks as his paternal grandmother and his uncle, who was to say it wasn't just a throwback to the past generation?

But Daniel knew. He knew it when he looked at Toby, when the boy sat with him for hours in the dark, peering at the sky. Beyond a doubt, Toby was his flesh and blood, his *son*.

The little boy leaned against him, "What's it like up there on Mars?"

"I've never been. They live in domes, though, there isn't any air, and won't be for hundreds of years. It's still pretty cold too."

"Will it be cold on the spaceship?" Toby asked.

"Nah, they'll keep it warm."

So how could he go? How could he leave his own child behind? Janine had asked him that too. The "just this once" had happened again, moments after he had broken the news to her two months ago.

Afterward, as they lay naked in bed next to each other, sweat beading on their skin, she had begun to cry, "How can you leave us, Daniel? How can you leave your own son? How can you go so far away, and never return? My God, Toby will grow up without you. Why would you go to such a desolate place?"

Daniel's tongue had felt thick and swollen. Telling her the truth was impossible. He loved her. But Luke loved her, had *married* her, damn it.

"And what about gravity Uncle Dan? Will you have gravity or just bounce around in the spaceship?" Toby was full of questions.

"There will be artificial gravity. The gravitational rings around the spaceship will make it so that, except for the far ends which are only used for storage, the entire ship will have the equivalent of Earth gravity."

Luke deserved better than to hear that his wife had cheated on him with his beloved big brother, the guy he had looked up to all his life. He didn't deserve to hear that Toby was Daniel's kid and that Janine had married Luke when she got tired of waiting for her true love to stop traveling the world and return to her. Luke didn't deserve the vision of Daniel and Janine in this bed, making the child he loved and believed was his own.

"Will Zarb...Zarb..." The little boy struggled to pronounce the word.

"Zarmina's World?"

"Yeah, Zarbeena's World, will it look like here, Uncle Dan? Like Earth?"

He ruffled the boy's hair, "It's different. The sky isn't blue, more of a white to red, and some of the plants are nearly black. We can breathe the air though. It is tidally locked, as well, because it so much closer to its sun."

"What does that mean?" Toby asked.

"Tidally locked? Well, the planet only shows one face to the sun, kind of like our Moon or Pluto and Charon."

Toby turned around and stared at Daniel in consternation, "But the Moon is either super-hot or super-cold!"

Daniel laughed, "That's true. But Zarmina's World is much bigger, and while there is a light side and a dark side, we won't be living in either, we will live in the meridian, the half-lit space between the two."

How could he explain that he had no other choice? That it would destroy all the trust and love and admiration his little brother had ever had for him?

I'm the screw-up here. Not Luke, not even Janine, and certainly not Toby. If I go, I can start again and leave them to their lives. They will be better off without me.

All of this swam through Daniel's brain as Janine had lay there sobbing next to him. "He's not my kid, Janine. He's Luke's and yours. We agreed on this eight years ago, remember?" His voice sounded remote and hollow. He sat up and gathered his clothes, slipping his jeans back on and searching for his other sock. He had to be gone before Toby and Luke returned from their fishing trip.

Janine's voice had sounded fragile and child-like, "And you can leave me too, Daniel? So easily?"

Better to make a clean break of it. "Yes," he said coldly and left her alone in the bed. He had closed the door behind him, wishing he could not hear her sobs so clearly. That had been in March.

"Are there animals, Uncle Dan?" Toby asked, nestling closer, his bony little butt digging into Daniel's inner thigh.

"Yes, the probes sent us back pictures of creatures that look a lot like deer, and a handful of other strange creatures. Most of them aren't much bigger than mice."

"Any dinosaurs?"

Daniel chuckled, "Sadly, no."

For two months, Luke struggled to come to terms with it. His big brother planned to get on a spaceship and head more than twenty light years away to find out if a planet *might* be habitable. He would never return, never grow old with Luke and Janine or have a family of his own.

"Mom and Dad are gone," Luke stared at his older brother in consternation, "and it's just been you and me since eighty-five. Daniel, you can't just leave."

Daniel couldn't look at his brother. He scuffed his shoe on the ground and looked up at the steady blink of the space station as it crossed the sky. It was the *Gan De*, the largest of the space stations and one of the oldest, named after a famous Chinese astronomer.

"I can't explain it, Bro, I can only tell you it has to be like this. You've got Janine and you've got Toby. You don't need me anymore. Not like you did then."

That awful night when they had lost Dad, somehow, they had stuck together, even in the face of well-meaning officials who told Daniel he would be better off letting them put Luke in foster care for a couple of years. Instead, he had applied for emancipation and then secured guardianship of Luke. He had refused to give up on his kid brother.

They had struggled, not so much financially, thanks to Dad's savvy investments, but certainly emotionally, for years. But they had made it, together

Toby sighed, "Will you try and tame the animals, Uncle Dan? And if you do, could you send one back to me?"

Daniel closed his eyes, imagining a life without this little boy, this piece of him. "Sure Toby, I'll do my best."

They were both silent then. He felt the boy slip into sleep a few minutes later, his breathing even and deep.

Luke had not understood how Daniel could leave.

"We could go with you, Daniel. Maybe it's not too late to apply. They would make an exception for family, right?"

Daniel smiled at his brother and shook his head, "As if Janine would go. Face it, bro, your place is here, with Janine and Toby. Mine is out there."

There would be more questions, arguments even, and eventually, Luke had shut up and grimly accepted that Daniel was leaving.

Departure

"The limits of the possible can only be defined by going beyond them into the impossible." – Arthur C. Clarke

Date: 09.19.2098
Calypso Colony Ship

Kit Tanner keyed a command on her comm link and activated NARA, utilizing the overhead speakers to clearly direct the attention of the large group of people jammed into the hallway.

"Hello! Welcome to Calypso! If everyone could please pay attention now. I will be showing you your living quarters for the duration of the voyage. I know you have all read the manuals," she paused and winked at them.

The manuals were a migraine-inducing monstrosity that some bureaucrat had insisted on creating. An inside joke among the crewmembers, the pages were crammed into a six terabyte program full of every possible response to an emergency scenario. One even included an unlikely situation in which the crew had to isolate themselves in their individual coffins in case of explosive decompression (as if that would work out in the long run).

It had been a constant form of amusement, "Just check the manual, I'm sure it's there." Or, "We've got explosive decompression and aliens boarding our ship via the waste ducts. Quick, consult the manual!"

They knew what they needed to know. Every one of them had been through hundreds of hours of training, drills and simulations, on land and in space. They knew about the living quarters, and a long laundry list of painstaking protocols and procedures, but the way Medry figured it if a pretty girl wanted to tell them again, he wasn't going to object. Not at all.

Kit pointed to the badge on her navy jumpsuit. Directly below the World Geographic symbol was her name.

She said it out loud anyway, "My name is Kit Tanner and I'm in charge of getting each of you settled in and oriented to the ship and the areas you will be working in. So please follow me."

Kit was good-looking and had straight brown hair and slate-blue eyes. Her slim hips and small frame were attracting a lot of attention, and not just because she was showing them where they would be living for the next five years. Deeks, Head of the Cryo section, exchanged glances with Medry and Aldridge, the latter quietly wolf-whistled under his breath. They all knew each other, but the guys couldn't resist teasing Kit, who was taking her first official duties on board Calypso rather seriously.

If Kit heard him, she gave no sign, and instead she briskly turned the corner and headed for a hatch marked Living Quarters. The hallway opened up, wider than usual, and on both walls, there were banks of capsules set into the bulkhead. The capsules were numbered and each had a door with a thumbprint reader. Each opening measured one meter by one meter and were 2.5 meters in length. The capsules were stacked three high, with footholds to the upper two levels. Inside each of them was a small area for personal items, and several cabinets for additional clothing storage.

Kit waited until the group had all filed in.

"We call these coffins because they are so small." She grinned, "Don't be put off by the nickname, these will become your private spaces where you can get away from everyone else. In as close of quarters as we will have, these spaces will really make the difference over the next five and a half years."

She pressed her thumb to the reader pad on coffin #018.

"This one happens to be mine. And as you will see it will open for no one else."

The door unlocked and Kit swung it open. The group shuffled about, each peering inside of the coffin.

"Now each of you received a number with your acceptance letter. This is your personal number while you are on board Calypso. It identifies you, your possessions, your personal coffin, your individual clothing sets and everything else. Forget the imbedded National I.D. chips or any other forms of identification, these three digits, and your thumbprint, will allow you access to your personal storage locker and just about anything else you can think of."

She looked down at the clipboard in her hand and then beckoned to James Aldridge, "Aldridge, your number is 121, correct?"

He nodded and grinned, pleased to be singled out.

"Right this way, then."

The rest of the group followed, "And here you are, Mr. Aldridge, in the 42nd stack, at the very end, bottom row. Now if you will just flip open the thumb reader, Mr. Aldridge."

He smiled at her, "You can call me James."

She smiled back, "Fine, James. Just put your thumb there."

He did as he was told, and the lock on the door cycled. "Now you can simply pull on the release and climb on in."

He pulled the release, opened the door and climbed inside.

Kit turned to the rest of the group, "Please take a few moments to locate your individual coffins now and go ahead and use the thumb reader to access them."

Medry moved to his coffin, #048, and opened it via the thumb reader. The opening made it appear smaller than it really was. Once inside he found it a little roomier. *Better than an* actual *coffin,* he imagined, *but not by much.* The coffin had a short tube to crawl through and then opened up into a small bubble of space. You could sit upright, even fit a second person in, but that was the limit.

The next twenty minutes were spent exploring the coffins. They had all been shown the prototypes during training, but these were the real deal. Each came equipped with individual climate control buttons. There were no sheets and the pillow had been built into the padded bed. When one of the others mentioned it, Kit explained that due to the limited amount of water on board, sheets and blankets were an unneeded option.

"By allowing each individual to control their environmental heating and cooling, there is no need for linens that would require regular washing."

She continued in a clear voice, "The coffins are equipped with a vacuum unit that is activated once a week, while you are on duty and not inside of the unit, removing hair and dead skin cells and any accumulated dust."

Daniel explored the functions built into the walls and listened to Kit, "You will each have access to a full database of music and televid entertainment as well as your own personal server access."

A keyboard popped out of the wall with a push of the button, flat and slim, fashioned out of what appeared to be titanium.

"All applicable systems are accessible through your thumbprint and crew member code, from anywhere on Calypso, including your individual coffin. Private files are encrypted and accessible only from a secure location, namely your coffin. You will also have full access to learning programs."

Kit paused before continuing, "As you are aware, we encourage everyone to learn additional skill sets that may be outside of your current profession. The general learning labs will be handling group learning opportunities, but there is a great deal you can learn from the stored information in the databases as well as any additional research that will be uploaded from Earth at turn-around."

Daniel was impressed with the entire setup. He could barely hear the others, despite having two of his group in nearby coffins, Deeks was below him in #047 and Jack Dunn was right next door in #051. He was pretty damn sure he wasn't the only one opening and closing doors and pushing buttons, yet he heard little from the other units.

Kit continued, "And as an added note, you will find that your coffin, with a bit of maneuvering, can hold two individuals for an, *ahem*, limited amount of time. After a few hours, it can become a bit claustrophobic."

Medry grinned and he could hear a couple of others laugh. He looked around him, yep, it would be tight, but getting someone, namely a slim, friendly woman like Sam Sydan into the coffin with him was possible.

"Also, you will find that the coffins are well insulated and you should not have any problems with sound transmitting through to your neighbors."

This earned no small amount of laughter. It seemed that Calypso's designers had thought of everything, including sex.

Kit began walking from one end of the hallway to the other, shutting the doors as she went, closing each of the coffin occupants inside. A few seconds later she linked into NARA again via the comm link on her ship suit.

Her voice came through a speaker set in the ceiling of Medry's coffin.

"I have set the comm link with NARA to Living Quarters and this affects all coffin inhabitants. The captain and other key crew members have the ability to send out global, ship-wide announcements to all crew. You each have the ability to call another crew member anywhere in the ship simply by dialing their individual code using the keypad next to the speaker."

She continued to point out features of the individual coffins, including a privacy feature that darkened the currently clear doors to an opaque black. As each member of the group played with the privacy feature, toeing the privacy on, soft lights appeared with dimmer pads set into the wall. Daniel was amazed at how comfortable the bed pad and built-in pillow was. It made sense. No one would be okay with a thin, hard mattress. Not with a trip of 121 trillion miles ahead of them. It enveloped and supported his body perfectly.

"We don't have time for a nap now. If everyone could please join me back in the hallway we will proceed to the communal living areas you will all be sharing."

The tour took them through the communal bathrooms, which were shared spaces with individual shower stalls, toilets and tiny lockers lining one wall. The lockers were again assigned to each individual according to thumbprint and number. As with the missing linens, there were no towels in the showers. Forced air blowers at the entrance and exit to each stall, rather similar in design to the blowers at the end of a car wash, forced the drops of water off and down a collection tube to be filtered and re-used. The same was true for the toilets, which utilized an effective filtration system, moving the solid waste through a processing unit that eventually ended up as nutrients for the 'Ponics Deck. The liquid wastes from the toilets and the showers were also processed through advanced systems that cleaned, clarified, and distilled it and eventually sent it back into the water supply.

The entries to the showers were locked and accessible only by the now-familiar thumbprint and keypad combination.

"Full immersion showers are only allowed every third day," Kit warned them, "And they are limited to four minutes. The auto-dispensers control the amount of cleansers used as these waters are returned, filtered and used in our hydroponics, then filtered again and put back through our own drinking water system. This will ensure proper balance in Calypso's closed system."

Others nodded, for extended space travel, for any long-term travel at all, one had to be mindful of the limited resources. And water certainly qualified as a limited resource in deep space.

There was a handful of rooms with tables, chairs, view screens and electronic whiteboards. Kit explained that these rooms had been set aside for multiple purposes, "Learning clubs, that focus on what we need to study to be ready for life on Zarmina's World," Kit gestured to a group already occupying one room, relaxing in the chairs as they watched vid clips of a popular comedian, "or something as simple as a social group with an interest in standup comedy."

She led them past other empty rooms, "The engineers who worked on Calypso realized that we will be on this ship far longer than any other mission. We need to be able to work together and live together, and with an average of twenty-five to fifty individuals awake and active during the five-year voyage, we have a vast array of talents and interests. The planners have tried to anticipate everything they possibly could."

At the end of the corridor was the Mess Hall which they had assembled in originally. It was the largest space any of them had seen to date. Although they had seen the schematics, as well as toured the Earth-side replicas, it was different seeing it in action.

Medry could see from the outlines on the floor that sections would rise up according to need, tables, chairs, and at the moment, a vast open palette to accommodate the groups being given the final tour and orientation before departure. According to what they had learned, the Mess Hall could fit every single citizen aboard Calypso. It might be a tight fit, but that meant the room was capable of holding the entire population, something they would only see in the last week of the voyage, if at all. The plan was to establish orbit, revive key personnel in stages, set up a base on the planet and then bring people down in groups, according to available resources and need. Some had already gone through the tour and been put into stasis in Cryo in anticipation for departure.

"The Mess Hall doubles as a gathering place where the Captain will hold weekly crew meetings. Monthly meetings will be held on the fourth Friday of every month and everyone is required to attend regardless of shift."

Kit smiled, "The only excuse for missing one is if you are in Cryo or sick as a dog in the Medical Bay."

Her lean form swished past Deeks, who appeared mesmerized, and Kit led the group out another door, "And speaking of Medical Bay, follow me, everyone!"

Two days later, most of the occupants of Calypso were safely tucked away in their Cryo pods while the crew stood in the Mess Hall and watched Earth recede from view, a rapidly shrinking planet that quickly became nothing more than a small bright light in a sea of stars.

It would take nearly three months to reach the outer edge of the solar system, a safe distance in which to engage the Alcubierre-Mesner warp drive that would take their ship far away from humanity's first home. They were finally on their way.

What We Need

"As our own species is in the process of proving, one cannot have superior science and inferior morals. The combination is unstable and self-destroying." – Arthur C. Clarke

Date: 12.23.2098

Earth – Kansas City, Missouri

"You want me to go *where*?" Edith Hainey set down her notes and stared at Scott Dorns, the head Virologist and her immediate superior, in shock.

He had the decency to look uncomfortable.

"It isn't until after Christmas," he replied, "Obviously with your family situation at present, you..."

Edith didn't need a reminder of her family situation. She lived it every day. Baby Jessica was a handful, after all, one of those children with two settings, blissfully asleep or awake and screaming. At forty-five years of age, Edith couldn't help but feel she was caught between two settings herself, the one that insisted she respond to a screaming child in the middle of the night and the other that demanded she leave the parenting to her unrealistic seventeen-year-old who had dreamily announced she was keeping the baby no matter what Edith said.

This same girl could sleep like the dead while her baby screamed in the very same room. This did nothing but wake up Edith at the far end of the hall. Edith was convinced she was the most unwilling and resentful grandparent who had ever existed.

"What about the conferences?" she asked.

She had been scheduled to attend two conferences in January already, one in London the second week of the month and one in New York at the end of the month, and now this?

Between the sleepless nights, Tom's lawyer calling her during the day with demands that she sign the paperwork or face being hauled into court again, and her son Tommy devolving into a petulant frat boy who was failing half his classes – Edith was well and truly beside herself.

"Oh, don't worry. You will be in and back out of there in no time." Scott said, smiling just a little too brightly, "Just four days in China, a few days back to report on the situation and then off to the conferences."

This wasn't how life was supposed to be, Edith reasoned. She had done everything right. As a child she had followed the rules, always received high grades, went to college and even worked part-time on campus to cover her living expenses. It was during her college years that she had met Tom. At first, it was perfect. They had met at a cattle ranch –– she was finishing her training in gene therapy and was working on her Master's thesis. He was the public relations rep for a nearby branch of EcoNu, a genetics and food production company that had recently expanded from Europe to the United States.

He later admitted that the job offer she received just a few months before graduating had more than a little to do with him. He had bent the ears of a few key people. Edith began working at EcoNu that fall, and they were married a year later.

Edith ignored Scott's foot tapping out a nervous rhythm on the floor. He could wait. Let the weasel sweat it for a moment or two. She knew how terrified he was of air travel, and his aversion to it was what had taken her away from her family and marriage at crucial junctures, helping to ensure its demise.

She had done everything right – even kept her career in the Hybrid Genetics division of EcoNu through the births of all three of her children. She had been faithful, even if Tom had not, and worked equally hard at her career, family and marriage.

But when the middle-aged spread had caught up with her, and Tom's extra-marital adventures came in the form of calls from random women in the middle of the night, even Edith had to admit that the marriage was dying rapidly. The killing blow had been their middle child, sixteen-year-old Liza's bombshell that she was pregnant and determined to keep the baby. It was all the excuse her husband needed to blame Edith, who was still reeling from her mother's death the year before, and exit their sham of a marriage stage right.

Scott looked increasingly nervous. "I can see about getting you an extra week of vacation and make sure everything is first class, the whole way there and back."

Edith stared at her computer, the lines on the page blurring. On top of everything else she needed new glasses; these old ones just weren't cutting it.

Scott shifted, nibbling at his lower lip. "Perhaps a mid-year bonus?"

Edith was sure he had a long line of excuses, including an intact family, the nerve damage in his back that limited his ability to travel long distances, and more to explain why she was the perfect person for the job.

While she was stuck going to China. *China.* And not the civilized section, oh no, some backwoods hell, one of the poorest parts of China, some place called Guizhou Province.

Scott had long thin fingers which were currently shuffling several documents around on the table next to him. Edith could see that there was an itinerary, travel documents, the works. This wasn't a question or even a polite request to think about it, this was a "we are shoving you on a plane whether you like it or not" kind of talk.

Edith sighed wearily, running her hand through her prematurely gray hair. It was feeling shaggy and irregular; she really needed to get it cut. She had missed the last appointment, just completely forgot it after a particularly sleepless night and then a fight with Liza over diapers or formula or God knows what. By the end of the fights, she really had no idea *what* had been the issue.

Liza was experienced at verbal repartee, having learned it well at Tom's knee. He had been such an excellent teacher, and Liza such a quick study. She could run circles around Edith, argue everything from how the sun and the moon orbited the earth to somehow twisting Edith's simple request to please throw the diapers into something other than the kitchen trash into a scorching attack on her own shortcomings as a mother and wife. She blamed Tom for this; he had been a spectacular role model at making Edith look like the unreasonable one.

Edith was worn out - from the divorce to the fighting at home and the endless crying of her tiny granddaughter. She was tired of arguing with Tommy over his grades and trying to convince him that studying was more important than girls and guitar solos. Perhaps a break from it all was just what she needed, even if it meant heading for some backwater hell. Just a few days for Edith to breathe and be able to forget that her life was a mess despite her best efforts.

She reached out and took the documents from Scott, sighing again, "Fine. Fine."

She ignored his rushed departure from her office, staring at the travel schedule. At least, she didn't have to worry about Joey. At twelve years of age, next to her, he was the most mature person living in the house. His grade card had arrived two days ago, straight A's and a note from one of his teachers extolling his virtues. She held onto that thought, one small warm light in the dark mess that was her life.

Guizhou Province

"The whole history of science has been the gradual realization that events do not happen in an arbitrary manner, but that they reflect a certain underlying order, which may or may not be divinely inspired." – Stephen Hawking

Date: 12.28.2098

Earth – Ghizhou Province, China

Edith had lost track of where she was, the time of day, and whether this made the fifth or sixth plane she had been on since leaving the Kansas City airport and heading for the Guizhou Province, deep in southwestern China. In the last airport, a young man who appeared to be in his early twenties had held up a placard with her name on it. He greeted her, an excited smile on his face, and introduced himself as Lin Huang, her assistant and guide.

His English was excellent, and Edith understood him well, which was a relief. As she had progressed deeper and deeper into China, she had noticed that the English translations on signs had rapidly reduced until there only sporadic, oddly written ones full of what her ex-husband would have referred to as "Engrish." Often, they made little sense at all.

Christmas day had devolved into bickering between Tom and the children, with Liza wielding her verbal weaponry, Tommy in a hazy hangover, and Joey, her only ally, preferring to eat Christmas dinner in his room rather than deal with the "family togetherness" that included his cheating father.

She had found herself looking forward to the flight away from all of them, except maybe Joey, although his retreat to his room had felt like abandonment, her only source of consolation and support, burrowing away in his safe zone. She had no safe zone, nowhere to retreat, and her husband and daughter had both sensed it, like sharks smelling a drop of blood in the ocean, and pulled out the heavy verbal weaponry. She had found herself smiling the next day as she left the house, listening to her granddaughter wailing and Liza completely clueless as she tried to soothe the tiny creature and quiet her siren screams.

Tom had volunteered to stay while she was out of town, but she had rebuffed him, sure his staying there would mean his girlfriend staying as well and she was damned if she would have the co-engineer of her failed marriage sleeping in *her* bed while she was gone!

Her musing on that particular subject must have shown on her face and been misinterpreted as pain or discomfort. Lin leaned across the aisle as the plane dipped and jolted, shuddering through the cloud-filled sky.

"Dr. Hainey, are you feeling ill?"

Edith replaced the bitter look on her face with a polite smile.

"I'm fine Lin, just fine. Please call me Edith."

The young man nodded and smiled, leaning back in his seat. Edith suddenly realized that, after 36 hours together, and, at least, four times of her reminding him, this young man was never going to call her by her Christian name. *It must be a cultural issue,* she thought to herself.

"We will land soon," the young man promised reassuringly.

Edith nodded wearily. She had slept a great deal on the different planes, but there was something about travel that just took it all out of her.

"I just can't seem to catch up with sleep, not since my granddaughter Jessica was born." She said to Lin. Edith refrained from mentioning that even before that, Tom had begun his legal attack while their eldest son, Tommy had filled the summer months with parties and endless debauchery. Young Tommy had lost his summer job the first week of June due to bad attendance and an even worse attitude. The new school year, which had begun in late August, had ended the fall semester with Tommy on academic suspension. His grades, like his attitude, were headed straight for the toilet.

The younger man smiled, "Oh, you are a grandmother? Congratulations! It is such a joy to have children, yes?" He looked so hopeful that Edith was sure he had never been kept up all night by a wailing child.

"Mm, a joy...yes." Edith was pretty sure that even Lin could read her lack of enthusiasm. His eyes slid away from her, to the tiny airplane window, which showed nothing but clouds.

Since the late spring, when Liza had announced she was pregnant and Tom had left, it just seemed that it had been one thing after another. Sleep was filled with dark dreams and waking up to reality was even more exhausting.

Edith turned her attention to the thick booklet that Scott had given her at EcoNu. The reports were exciting, showing phenomenal growth in the pigs as they responded to the EcoNu bio-engineered virus, growing at an unprecedented rate.

The virus, the latest in a decade of increasingly complicated versions, was truly elegant. EcoNu had the answer to world hunger in its hands if this strain proved out. And that, after all, was why she was here.

Before the Collapse, in the early years of the century, a series of increasingly virulent pig flu strains had swept through the United States and the rest of the world, ravaging the pig population, killing baby pigs by the millions. It had been so bad at one point, that just as the Collapse hit, along with the Second American Civil War, pork had spiked to over $23 per pound.

Edith's aunt Carrie, from her father's side, had been a young girl during that time and remembered eating her first bacon in years when her mother and sister moved to her paternal grandfather's farm in Tiptonville, Tennessee. There they had weathered the Collapse and Civil War with far less hardship than most. Edith still remembered her stories, though. Aunt Carrie had been quite a bit older than Edith's father Joseph, some fifteen years or so. Joseph had been born at the dawn of the Collapse and grown up in a world that was very different. The stories they had told had haunted Edith well into adolescence and adulthood, guiding her to a career in the bio-engineering field.

Just last month another news story had sent the prices skyrocketing yet again. The headline had screamed, *Bacon Prices Rise after Virus Kills Baby Pigs!*

EcoNu promised to change that history of shortages and uncertain supply with a virus that caused young pigs to grow exponentially in size, doubling the normal growth patterns, but not injuring them in the process such as now eradicated strains of chickens had suffered. The infamous Cornish Cross breed of chickens were no longer bred but instead held up as the worst possible example of breeding gone wrong. Bred to be slaughtered as young as six weeks, Cornish Cross fowl were prone to heart attacks and broken legs.

Broken legs! Edith mused as she paged through her reports. *And this had been an industry standard.*

A side effect of the Collapse and SACW, the Cornish Cross strain was too helpless to survive the chaos that occurred throughout the now Reformed United States of America. They were unable to forage and died in droves when electricity failed in the massive chicken factories.

Now granted, the pigs were showing shockingly low reproductive rates. That didn't sit well with Edith, nor did the smug speculation by some of the higher-ups that this could be considered a winning strategy. It smacked too much of Monsanto's death grip on the corn economy early in the century.

Edith had ideas about how to fix that, and had spoken to her manager Scott about it, but received a smothering, "Let's give it some time to resolve itself, shall we?" answer.

As if it would suddenly and magically resolve itself on its own.

It was the T2 enzyme, she was sure of it. She had worried about it, even as the team included it in the first cocktail of viral injections on the young pigs. Simple to fix, not so simple to eradicate once it was in a pig, but despite her emails to the team and her supervisors, warning of the possibility of such an outcome, the enzyme had stayed in the mix.

The reports in her hands showed that everything was going as scheduled, except for one small detail, a persistent low-grade fever in the young pigs. Where the average temperature for a pig usually fell between 38.6° and 39.5 ° Celsius, all of the pigs tested were hovering within the 41.2 ° and 41.6 ° Celsius range. Not high enough to be considered a high fever, but warm enough to be concerning.

Edith paged through the rest of the documents, checking other vital signs. The eyes were clear, appetite was elevated, and there were no signs of lethargy or illness other than the elevated temperature. Strange, and slightly concerning, but there was nothing to do but wait until the plane landed and she could see the animals herself.

The small plane bucked and swooped, and Edith slid the papers back inside of their folder and smiled briefly at Lin.

"I think I'll just have a little nap," she said, closing her eyes.

She hoped they would land soon; she was ready to have solid ground under her feet.

Just a Fever

"What standards will guide the genetic engineers?" – Leon Kass

Date: 12.28.2098

Earth – Guizhou Province, China

Guizhou Province was far more advanced than Edith had expected. The small plane descended through the thick layer of clouds, lurching and jumping so much that she regretted drinking the two cups of tea as they sloshed about ominously in her stomach. She could see an enormous city below them, tall skyscrapers mixed with massive apartment buildings, and even ancient-looking pagoda-style structures. For some reason, she had been expecting a more rural location. She had fully furnished the image in her mind, complete with dirt roads and a beaten down truck belching diesel.

Lin followed her gaze out of the window, "This is the city of Guiyang," he said, pronouncing it "Ghee-yang" and pointed to the large river they were flying over, "And that is the Nanming River, a branch of the Wu River. Guiyang has over seven million population. It used to be known as the Forest City," he smiled ruefully, "but those are all gone now."

There was a thick layer of smog hanging low in the air. It looked gray and oily.

"I had read that China had won the battle over decades of pollution," Edith said, her voice petering out as she viewed something obviously quite different.

Lin looked embarrassed, "Unfortunately Ghizhou Province is not as high a priority as some of the wealthier regions. There is, how do you say, corruption? It is a work in progress."

A moment of silence passed.

"Here is the runway now," he said, pointing out of the window.

She could now see the small air control tower. This was quite obviously not the main airport, but one specifically for smaller aircraft.

A few moments later the plane had landed and Edith breathed a sigh of relief. Her stomach was still unsettled and she hoped this would be the last plane ride for a while.

They disembarked from the plane and walked over to an ancient and battered Jeep. Lin bowed, his face flushing as he held the passenger door open for Edith.

"My apologies, Dr. Hainey, it looks quite rough, but I promise it is quite reliable."

Edith couldn't help but smile. Back home, Tom had jumped at the chance to trade up to a self-driving autocar the moment EcoNu offered it. She, on the other hand, had insisted on keeping her 2089 Simpatico. She loved the feel of the wheel in her hands, even though the kids had complained, and Tom had made fun of her.

"I might be stuck in my ways, but I like the feeling that I am in control." She had told anyone who asked, wondering if people who had eschewed e-readers for good old-fashioned books had felt the same way at the beginning of the century.

It took nearly an hour to reach the farm from the small airport, often on poorly maintained roads. No wonder they were in a driver-operated Jeep.

"Autocars operate using the Advanced Global Positioning System in combination with magnetic strips embedded in the roadbed itself," Lin explained, "This road has not been retrofitted with the magnetic strips yet."

The Jeep swerved to avoid a large hole in the road and bounced as it hit a smaller one. Edith braced herself for more as the road dwindled to nothing more than gravel and large swathes of muddy bog.

"Completely understandable," she said as they lurched and bounced over the rough road. Her teeth ached from clenching her jaw at each dip and jump of the Jeep. It was, after all, what she had expected when she had first heard of the assignment.

The low-slung buildings appeared in the distance before them.

"As you can see, the farm is a typical CAFO," Lin said proudly, wrenching the wheel to the right as the Jeep jumped through a large puddle. The mud spattering the sides of the Jeep reeked, as did the farm which could now be seen clearly.

"A mile to the west is a village of around 5,000."

"Ah, yes, a CAFO." Edith replied, trying to fake enthusiasm and failing utterly. Concentrated Animal Feeding Operations had been banned in the Reformed United States for nearly three-quarters of a century. Shut down by the Collapse, they were opened for a short time in the 2030s before being closed down again after a series of protests by animal rights activists as well as the Progressive party.

Edith had read the ample research that indicated that CAFOs were not only bad for the animals confined within them, they were also incredibly damaging to the environment and a breeding ground for disease.

"I'm surprised that EcoNu signed off on this." Edith commented coolly, and Lin stared at her in confusion.

"Dr. Hainey, they asked for it specifically. This is all, how do you say, to spec?"

The Quonset style huts were approximately four meters tall by five meters wide and stretched at least 25 meters in length. The smell, even when they were a quarter of a mile out, had been overwhelming. Edith would have asked more questions about EcoNu's orders if she hadn't been gasping for air, choking on the noxious fumes as the Jeep rattled to a stop.

The workers on site met the two at their car and quickly handed Edith and Lin rubber masks with gaskets and seals. Edith's eyes burned, streaming tears from the stench of methane as she fumbled with the straps. One of the workers helped tighten hers and once sealed, she was able to breathe again without difficulty. Without the masks they would not be able to withstand the putrid air. The outside of the facility was barren, and in the distance, she could see the waste lagoons brimming with liquid feces.

They weren't too terribly far from a village, at least, that is what Lin had indicated. Edith pursed her lips. How could the villagers stand it? One change in direction from the wind and the stench would hit the village head on.

This was why CAFOs had been banned in her country. The impact on the environment was devastating and the lawsuits had been going strong right before the Collapse.

Edith had read about it in her history books. After the Second American Civil War, all of the states except Hawaii and Alaska had reunited and many things had changed. The citizens' rights to a clean environment were high on that list. Corporations simply did not have the power in her country that they had earlier in the century. And from what Edith could tell, that was a good thing.

Edith stood there looking at the waste lagoons. Why would EcoNu okay a CAFO? What possible benefit could that have?

"Those waste ponds are nearly full."

Lin's expression was obscured by the mask.

"Yes, Dr. Hainey, they should be full soon, but there is a tanker coming to drain them tomorrow.

Edith watched Lin as he stood there, rigidly, his head bowed down. It was hard to tell, but she couldn't shake the suspicion he was lying at that moment. She just couldn't figure out *why*.

She felt as if she were missing something, and tried to remember the specifics about how waste lagoons were dealt with once they were full. She would have to look it up. It wasn't her area of expertise, nor under her control for that matter, but if the Chinese were messing up and violating any health codes, EcoNu would need to be informed.

Meanwhile, Lin kept his silence.

Edith's job was to test the pigs and ensure that all of the sampled swine were healthy. Or at least as healthy as swine could be in a CAFO. That was her job. Nevertheless, she made a mental note to speak with Scott Dorns about the waste lagoons. Perhaps the Chinese had misunderstood EcoNu's requests when creating the project.

"Oh my God." Edith stared at the massive numbers of pigs within the low-slung building.

It had almost certainly taken them around the clock effort to prepare for her visit. Despite this, Edith could not disguise her horror at seeing the reality of a CAFO up close and personal.

"We recently reduced their numbers. Any that were not growing as fast as the others were processed." Lin said.

"How many did you cull?"

"Fifty," Lin said, stiffening yet again.

She didn't call him on it, but now she was sure he was lying. If Lin claimed fifty, then the number of culled might have been closer to twice that. Edith tried to imagine another hundred head of swine crammed into the pens. She felt sick. This was beyond cruel. How could EcoNu have allowed this?

"These all received their last rounds of EcoNu growth inoculations yesterday." Lin said, sounding nervous.

"I'll need to sample at least ten percent. Blood, saliva, and feces if you don't mind," Edith replied.

She tamped down her reaction over the waste lagoon and the state of affairs inside of the building. Saying anything more would only make the man defensive, especially if he was doing what EcoNu had asked. She would wait and give a full report to Scott when she returned and submitted the blood sample work-ups.

Lin nodded and led the way to the small testing station, complete with vials for blood samples, lab coats and heavy-duty rubber boots.

Hours later, with racks of samples in coolers, Edith, and Lin entered a small, nondescript concrete building a short distance away. Here they rinsed off with water from a local aquifer, and drank some tea, before removing the lab coats and returning to the vehicle to make the drive back to Guiyang. Edith was pleased she wouldn't have to stay anywhere near the disgusting stench. Lin looked relieved that there had been no additional probing questions.

By evening, Edith was ensconced in a plush hotel overlooking the lights of Guiyang.

The next morning, she returned to the airport in a small autocar, well rested, slightly overwarm and sweating despite the cool morning air. Edith gave it little thought. She had been experiencing menopause symptoms for several years now and wrote it off as having to do with that. Especially since she had such a healthy appetite – she had eaten every scrap of the breakfast and then dug into the large bag of treats she had purchased for the kids yesterday evening. Her stomach rumbled again. She reached for the bag, wishing she had bought more.

While the autocar drove smoothly along, she composed a quick note to her supervisor.

TRANSMISSION PACKET
ECONU-HAINEYES TO ECONU-DORNSS
/BEGIN TRANSMISSION

COMPLETED REQUESTED SAMPLING OF 10% OF SWINE POP YESTERDAY. ALL SAMPLES INCLUDE WORKUP AS REQ'D. SLIGHTLY ELEVATED TEMP BUT NON-FEBRILE. GROWTH ON TRACK FOR OUR PREDICTIONS. WILL GIVE FULL REPORT UPON RETURN, BUT FARM IS SET UP AS CAFO WITH WASTE LAGOONS. WTH?
/END TRANSMISSION

In the weeks to follow, her schedule was filled with trips, conventions, and speaking engagements. She only had a few days of down time at home to see her family before flying to Europe, Latin America, and D.C. for various medical conferences.

Patient Zero

Date: 02.04.2099
Earth – Kansas City, Missouri

"What the hell? Oh man, Jace! Hey, *Jace*! I got a freak out here." Edith barely noticed the flustered pimple-faced teen that stared at her from the drive-thru window of Pop's Burgers.

He was soon joined by his manager, Jace Wyatt, who had just turned twenty-two the week before. Jace's eyes widened as he stared at the customer sitting outside the drive thru window. Edith was completely naked. Despite this, her forehead showed rivulets of sweat, which flowed easily from her face, and on down her chest, disappearing between a set of sagging, slightly wrinkled breasts.

It was an overcast day. In the sky above, the clouds looked like thick rolls of gray carpet. It was also unseasonably warm, at least 50 degrees, instead of the relentless chill of winter. Tomorrow another storm front would move in and they were all being told to prepare for a large snowfall, but for now, especially for this time of year, it was quite temperate, at least for Kansas City.

Edith felt hot, burning hot, and she was so *hungry*. It was all she could think of. The refrigerator had been cleaned out, she had literally sat on the cool tile floor of the kitchen that she and Tom had laid by hand some ten years before and drained every container of mustard, ketchup, and salad dressing. Some quiet part of her objected to this. There was this sense of wrongness, but it simply could not compete with the raging hunger she felt inside. It robbed her of thought, of anything more than the compulsive need to eat more in order to end the hunger.

"Uh...look lady, you have to uh," the young man's eyes trailed down the front of her, and he turned beet red, "you need to uh..."

"I need the food." She could barely speak, the heat was overwhelming, and her stomach was clenching and twisting. "Just, just give me the food." She had already paid for it, running the pay chip implanted in her wrist over the sensor. Behind the manager popped up another face, curious, wide-eyed, then another, and another, as word spread and more of the staff jammed into the small room. The bags appeared on the counter just inside the drive-thru window.

The manager handed her the bags full of combo meals, which Edith placed close by, her right hand shifting the car into park. She ripped into the paper wrappers, quickly stuffing a hamburger into her mouth, barely chewing and then gulping the bite down before taking another gargantuan bite. She repeated this, over and over.

Jace stared, as did the others crowding behind her in the drive-thru lane. Behind her car, a long line of cars snaked around the corner, the Comm was buzzing with folks ready to order, and several impatient customers began to honk or lean out their open windows and yell.

Edith ignored the honks of the cars behind her, still ripping through bags and wrappers, consuming the burgers and fries with a manic intensity. Pieces of wrapper slid down her throat along with the food. She seemed frenzied and her entire body glistened with sweat, beads of it rolling down her face, despite the cool temperatures.

"Ma'am, you can't park here. Ma'am?" The young man looked nervous. "Ma'am? You're blocking the way for the other customers."

She ignored him and continued to wolf down enough food to feed ten. A glance in the rearview mirror showed her a face she barely recognized. It was flushed, sweat trickled down her face, and considering it was February, that was plenty odd.

The manager, Jace, turned to one of the workers clustered behind him. "Call 9-1-1, tell 'em we've got an emergency here. This lady is *sick*."

"I'll say she's sick," Andy snickered, "She's naked as a jaybird! What a freak!"

Jace shook his head, "Nah, man, she's *sick,* not crazy. She's sweating, and all that food she's eating, there's something *wrong*."

He took a step back, wiping his hand on his clothes nervously, looking scared. "She's *sick*," He repeated and pushed his way through the crowd of workers. He would call it in himself.

Outside in her car, Edith continued to eat. It couldn't even be called eating really, she simply stuffed, swallowed, and stuffed some more. Occasionally she choked. The pieces were big, but she was so very hungry. She could barely see, barely register the growing crowd inside, and now outside, of the restaurant. No matter what she ate, or how much, her stomach seemed unaffected by the addition of food. It twisted, churned, and screamed in hunger.

Edith was desperate for the cravings to end. She shoved more food in, a bacon slice dragging along one edge, tracing a trail down through her until it came to rest, not quite at her stomach, bulging painfully above it. The small quiet voice of reason, one that entreated her to stop, that was warning her that something was terribly wrong...it was overwhelmed by the *need*, this *hunger*, which pushed beyond her natural boundaries into this dark abyss. The cool air from the open window, the honks from the vehicles behind her, and the curious stares of the growing crowd of onlookers...none of it mattered. The only thing that mattered was the need to end the gnawing emptiness, this terrible hunger that filled every fiber of her being and had grown in intensity each day for the past month. There was no room in her mind to question what was happening. The hunger pushed out everything else.

"Ma'am?" The handsome features of a paramedic appeared at her passenger side door. "My name is Mac Dolan ma'am, and I'm going to sit with you a minute." he said as he calmly opened the car door. His eyes were brown, with green flecks and they searched hers, his index finger moving from left to right, assessing her. He slid into her passenger seat, pushing the empty food bags and boxes out of the way so that he could take her pulse.

"Can you tell me your name, ma'am?" His hand was cool against her skin.

She could barely manage to speak, "Edith. Edith Hainey."

It sounded garbled coming out, her mouth was still full of food.

"Edith. Great." He smiled at her, a mouth full of bright white teeth, and stared at his wristwatch for a moment.

"Edith, do you know where you are? Do you know what day it is?"

The pain was coming in waves now, each larger than the last, and she was so tired. She had just finished everything in the bags, when suddenly everything changed. Edith groaned.

"Edith? Hey Edith?" Mac's penlight swept her eyes and he was close enough that Edith could smell his cologne.

There was a shifting within, and an intense lance of pain, a sense of something vital splitting open, and then, slowly, the tension left her. She stared into Mac's eyes. They reminded her of Larry, her high school sweetheart, such beautiful eyes.

Larry had been her first love, and they had made so many promises to each other. After graduation she had gone away to college and he had stayed, going to work for his dad's real estate business. Slowly the emails and phone calls had dwindled, until silence replaced the "I love you's" and plans for what they would do when she was home on summer break.

Her best friend Carla had said he was seeing another girl. The next year, Edith's second summer break back home had been harder than she thought possible. Larry was married, and the tiny girl who toddled in the front yard of his small house in Weston had had his eyes.

The pain was there and she felt it, but in a very detached way. The analytical part of her brain, what was left of it, realized what was happening. This is what it felt like; this was death. She had held her mother's hand near the end, felt the moment pass through her, and felt her mother's life drain from her body through her hands, and slip away.

Edith's eyes closed. As her head dropped, she heard Mac's voice calling to her from far away, asking her to stay with him, and in a dissociated way, felt her body being moved.

No more screaming grandchild, no more drunken collegiate son, no more hunger, just rest.

Guiyang Gone Bad

"This body is wasted, full of sickness, and frail; this heap of corruption breaks to pieces, life indeed ends in death." – Friedrich Max Muller

Date: 02.06.2099

Earth – Guiyang City, China

In the days after Edith Hainey's visit, Shen Luong, prematurely gray at thirty-five, was beside herself. Shen was in charge of facilities management at Dà Zhū Farms. A position she had been incredibly proud of until recently.

Her assistant, Xe, had called her the night before with troubling news. "The waste lagoon appears to be draining on its own!"

Shen had rushed to the site and discovered that they were indeed draining at a steady rate of one centimeter per hour.

This was not a good sign.

Dr. Hainey's visit to the CAFO pig operation outside of the city a mere five weeks prior had set the management scrambling in the days before her arrival. Shen had been instructed to accelerate the sewage lagoon venting schedule and lower the levels of the main lagoons to at least two feet below their current depth. The lagoons threatened to overflow on a daily basis, and regularly did during the rainy season.

"Seeing them at capacity may alarm the American doctor and threaten the farm's contract with EcoNu." Shen's manager had said. "Get the level down or we will all be looking for work."

That was the last thing Shen needed. Her husband had lost his job a few months earlier and they desperately needed her income.

The machines the farm manager had ordered used to dig deeper into the soil and enlarge the capacity of the pit, had caught and torn out an edge of the reinforcing base. Just a few inches of damage had quickly grown to a full foot, the foul sewage forcing its way from the lagoon through the fissure before dropping down, and then down yet again, following the line of gravity.

Shen surveyed the lagoon, thinking about the tragically short history of clean water in her country. Her assistant Xe chewed nervously on his already short, ragged fingernails.

"It's draining into the Nanming River." Shen said. It wasn't a question, but a statement. They were far too close to the river.

"Did you study your history, Xe?" Shen asked, almost conversationally. She was staring at a disaster of epic proportions and couldn't help but think of her environmental studies in college.

Her assistant just stared at her. Perhaps he was wondering if she was going to blame this mess on him.

Shen continued, not waiting for Xe to reply, "As late as 2015, shortly before The Collapse, our country was still struggling to provide their citizens with reliable clean water. By 2030, the wealthier provinces began implementing new, more stringent water controls. But here in one of the poorest provinces, it has always been a different story."

She thought of her family, a large extended one thanks to her parents' generation. Mama was one of five children and Baba was one of seven. Shen had cousins, along with countless nieces and nephews, scattered throughout the sprawling city of Guiyang. They all drank the water from the aged aquifers, all of them fed from the Nanming River.

"Did you know, Xe, that the Nanming River was once considered one of the most polluted urban rivers in all of southwestern China? It improved though; enough that people began to trust it again. And now this."

Shen felt sick. At this very moment, toxic waste from thousands of swine, which had been brewing and bubbling for weeks, was seeping into the aquifers that supplied all of the city's more than seven million inhabitants with water.

This was her fault. No matter that she had been ordered to do it by her superiors, she knew it was a gamble when she ordered it. Now thousands would pay the price. This wasn't a small leak; it wasn't a small amount of toxins. This would sicken children, adults, and the aged alike and Shen was to blame.

The virus, already shed and passed to the workers of Dà Zhū Farms, now found itself spreading through the open waters of the aquifer, waiting, replicating, and finally making its way en masse to the doomed city.

Shen had no idea what to do.

Far from Shen and Xe, in an impoverished neighborhood on the east side of Guiyang, Cheng's aunt Wang pursed her lips at the sight.

"You bury your mother in a *basket*?" She asked, staring at the coffin, a woven wicker affair which was guaranteed to be as green as possible and break down in the rich earth within just two years.

"You decided against the cypress or thuja wood?"

Cheng Liu had ordered the coffin three weeks earlier, when the progression of the cancer made it apparent that his mother would die soon. As the only child, all funeral duties fell to him.

Cheng stammered as he answered. His aunt had always made him nervous. "It, it, wa-was the most eco-friendly."

His mother's sister said nothing, just sniffed in disapproval at the sight of this simple, and unorthodox, coffin before her.

Cheng shoved down the hard roll of revulsion in his guts as his aunt removed the lid, exposing the yellow cloth which covered his mother's face and the light blue cloth that covered the rest of her body. His aunt had already burned the rest of his mother's clothes, just four outfits, in accordance with custom.

"What are you doing?" He asked, trying to sound authoritative and failing utterly.

"Making sure it is your mother. These *progressive* funerals, you can't trust them to get anything right." Wang said, staring inside.

"Mother don't be silly, of course it is Auntie." Jia said, coming to Cheng's rescue. "Here Cheng, help me cover the last mirror."

Cheng joined his pretty cousin, draping the fabric over the last of the mirrors while Wang returned to finish covering the statue of the Jade Emperor with red paper.

"And here is the gong, put it on the right side of the door." Wang ordered; her tone imperious.

Already the white cloth had been placed over the doorway.

Cheng glanced back at the woven wicker coffin. It sat on two low stools in the cramped front room, open, his mother resplendent in blue silk.

A part of him hated to do it, but he took the beautiful black wooden comb with inset mother-of-pearl his father had given to his mother early in their marriage and broke it in two, his aunt watching his every move.

"You must place one half in the coffin, and the other..."

"Yes Auntie, I know. The other half will go home with me. He tried to stand up to her, "I do know the customs."

"Humph, one look at that coffin and everyone will be certain you have forgotten all of our ways." She gave him a stern look, "As if anything you have ever done has not been in complete disregard for custom." She turned away, heading for the tiny kitchen.

Jia placed a hand on his shoulder and whispered, "Don't mind her, cousin, she rarely follows customs herself, she just likes to spout them to others. Sit down, sit down, I promise we will feed you terrible food and make you long to be back in Hong Kong again." She winked, patted his cheek, and then followed her mother into the kitchen.

Hours later, clothed in black from head to toe, Cheng sat at his mother's left shoulder as custom dictated, and listened to his aunt and cousin wail.

Aunt Wang's cooking, which had rendered the Buddha's Delight oily and overly salty, and the rice dry and tasteless, was more revolting than usual. He forced himself to swallow another bite when the time came to eat.

Jia leaned in, "I tried to stop her, but she insists on using far too much oil, and salt, at least you and I get to keep our girlish figures." Jia was irrepressible, and Cheng loved her for it. She was the one thing he missed, the only family member who had accepted him, and his choices, without any hesitation.

Despite the taste, Cheng's aunt, and many of the visitors were putting away massive amounts of the greasy food. Cheng forced another bite down, despite the grim visage of his mother's cancer-ridden remains beside him.

Just one day of mourning, it is unseemly," muttered Wang loud enough to be heard, "My father's funeral lasted for three days."

Cheng ignored yet another glare of disapproval from his aunt, saying nothing as a neighbor nailed the coffin closed and helped to adhere the yellow and white holy papers to the outside of it. It was custom, after all, and the family gazed away while the coffin was sealed. Cheng couldn't help but think that his aunt should have been born a century earlier, her entire life was steeped in superstition and the old ways.

After that, the coffin had been transported to the side of the road where additional prayers were offered, along with more slips of paper, before it slowly made its way to the cemetery, Cheng's head pressed firmly against the hearse for the entire journey.

As the joss stick burned, the coffin was lowered into the ground. Cheng, his aunt and cousin each tossed in a handful of dirt and then walked away from the grave on the steep hillside.

Cheng could see that his aunt was still furious with him. She muttered under her breath as they slowly walked home. It didn't seem to matter to her that the family's fortunes had dwindled sharply once his father had passed and his mother had slowly begun to fade. Cheng did his best to ignore her.

"What of the house, Cheng?" Jia had whispered as they walked away from the graveyard.

"I have made arrangements to offer it for sale. I hope it will be enough to cover the funeral costs." Cheng replied, quietly. Wang glared at them.

The simple structure held nothing for him. His life within it, a childhood and adolescence spent growing up within its walls, were framed in sadness and disillusionment. Always they had wanted from him something he was incapable of.

From the expectations they had of his future, "You must go into business or finance," his father had insisted in the face of his desire to cook with his mother in the kitchen.

Later, when his mother had noticed him staring for too long at a handsome neighbor boy, she too had let her displeasure be known. The house was a reminder of disappointment and repression. He had left the moment he was able, fleeing to the glitz-covered, forward-thinking metropolis of Hong Kong.

"Anything left inside is for you and Auntie."

Jia smiled at him and then looked sad, "You are leaving today?"

Aunt Wang had begun to complain loudly about the location of the grave, which apparently did not have the panoramic view she thought it should.

Cheng nodded, tilting his head towards his aunt and wrinkling up his mouth.

"I'm on a flight departing at eight tonight. I just can't take much more of this, you know? I don't know how you stand it."

The burial location Wang had suggested had cost twice what this one did. Cheng struggled to balance showing respect to his mother and wondering how important it really was to have a panoramic view of the smog-covered city while buried six feet under the earth.

Jia sighed. "It's bad of me, I know, but I'm counting the days until I can leave for college. Even if it is medical school."

Cheng slipped an arm around her. He knew that his pretty little cousin dreamed of being an actress, something her mother violently opposed. Aunt Wang was determined that Jia go to university and study medicine. The thought of Jia, who spent her days acting out scenes from her favorite movies or re-creating their costumes being sent to medical school, was such a deep disconnect that Cheng found himself filled with a profound sadness.

Jia was a dreamer, an artist. She didn't possess a mind for the sciences. No wonder she dreamed of escape to Hong Kong.

"I wish I could go with you," she whispered, "but Mama, she would forbid it."

Cheng gave his favorite cousin a quick hug, "Someday Jia, someday."

Once back at the house, Cheng changed into regular clothes and finished packing while the women burned the funeral clothes in the courtyard.

His aunt and Jia would take most of the furnishings, and he had no need for anything else within the house.

"Perhaps Jia could come for a visit when she is on break from school," he suggested, smiling at the excited look on his cousin's face.

"Perhaps," said Wang, her face shuttered and expressionless.

Cheng's heart thudded. *Poor Jia.*

"If you need anything, Auntie, Jia, just call me and let me know."

It felt awkward; the last string of their connection cut now that his mother was gone. His aunt nodded woodenly, saying nothing in return.

Jia hugged him tightly, "I will miss you, my cousin!"

The autotaxi was small, just a one-person affair, and he sat alone inside it, staring out of the windows. His chest ached not so much at the loss of his parents as at the loss of possibility. As infinitesimal as the chance might have been, he still had dreamed of a moment when his mother might accept him, not try to change him, and love him for who he was. And now, with both of them gone, he knew he would never have that moment. It was that loss that hurt more than becoming an orphan did.

The trip to the airport took far longer than expected, after several sharp stops and starts, the autotaxi informed him that there were delays due to an accident far in front of him.

He pressed a button on his Comm link and dialed Ang's number. His lover answered on the second ring. "Cheng?" His voice was still thick with sleep. They both worked late shifts and it was a few minutes before the alarm was scheduled to buzz them awake.

Cheng smiled for the first time in days at the sound of Ang's voice. "I'm delayed, some accident or something, I might miss the plane out, but there is one last one that I should be able to catch."

Ang sounded disappointed, "I was hoping you would get home early, Dayezhu, my big wild boar, and we could try out these new sheets I bought."

Cheng's grin grew wide. Ang always knew how to make him smile. Dayezhu, big wild boar, indeed. With his skinny bony body, he was anything but a big wild boar. Ang was a tease, exotic ice-blue eyes, a sensual mouth and a wicked sense of humor to go with it. Cheng couldn't wait to fall back into his arms.

His family, everyone except Jia, they didn't understand him, not at all. He wouldn't miss this city, and the loss of his mother and father in just the space of a few months hadn't really sunk in yet. It felt like an odd emptiness inside. He had lost them long ago, when his inclinations had first manifested. Their deaths hadn't affected him as much as the loss of their affections and approval had years ago.

"I'll call you when I'm at the airport. Love you."

"I love you. See you soon."

Accidents were rare these days, given that the automated vehicles had sensors which had a faster response time than any human. Cheng turned on the vidscreen, which immediately showed the cause of the accident far ahead, a vast number of people wandering in the road, and a line of cars slowed or stopped and unable to pass them.

What normally took thirty minutes would eventually take over two hours to drive from his parents' house to the airport south of the city. As the car inched forward, the wails of emergency vehicles echoed through the streets and Cheng stared out of the windows, watching scores of people lurching about, stepping into the roadway with little awareness of the danger.

On the Hequn Road, near the edge of town, things changed ominously. Hequn Road was one of several popular night food markets. There were scores of stalls selling prepared foods, clothing and more. This was a popular destination. Cheng had often walked this area, enjoying the night life and especially the Si Wa Wa, a pancake with shredded vegetables or fish in sour soup. There were dozens of stalls, and many delicacies to choose from.

Tonight however, as the sun dipped below the horizon and the yellow-tinged streetlights lit up the concrete, the crowds on Hequn Road were beyond anything Cheng had ever seen. There was an edge of violence and desperation in the air and the stalls were buried beneath the scores of hungry people. Some of the vendors were running, and not towards their stalls but away from them.

Cheng watched an enormous soup pot fly through the air, empty. He flinched as it bounced into the road, causing the autotaxi to jerk to a halt once more.

The city seemed to have gone mad. Beside the car, the crowd pressed close and to the left a man reached up on a scrawny tree and began tearing handfuls of leaves off of the branches and stuffing them into his mouth. A group of women were fighting over a roasted duck, eventually tearing it to pieces, steaming chunks of meat flying while the vendor yelled at them to stop. Everywhere he looked he saw chaos, violence, and voracious hunger.

He should have been disgusted, put off by the mindless eating and violence that surrounded him. Instead, he found himself craving hot pot and an egg cake his mother had made when he was little.

"Perhaps at the airport," he murmured to himself.

The car edged away from the crowd, finding an expressway and finally picking up speed. Behind him the city seemed to scream in agony and confusion. Something odd was happening, Cheng didn't understand it, but it terrified him. His flight was long gone by the time he arrived and he scheduled himself on a red eye departing five hours later, desperate to leave the city.

Whatever dark cloud had descended upon the city of his birth; Cheng wanted nothing to do with it.

What Have We Done?

"I've found out why people laugh. They laugh because it hurts...because it's the only thing that'll make it stop hurting."– Robert A. Heinlein

Date: 02.09.2099

Earth – Kansas City, Missouri

Tom Hainey stared at the briefing folder in his hands. It was nearly six in the evening. The sun had slipped beneath the horizon and dark clouds scudded menacingly in from the west, promising snow and more frigid temperatures. It was a Friday, and he should be at home with the children. Especially now, with Edith gone. His stomach rumbled and he felt a dark band of fear constrict his chest.

Tommy and Joseph, neither of them would even speak to him now. They were both still stunned at their mother's loss, as was he. Tom had moved back into the house temporarily after Edith's sudden and quite public death. His girlfriend had objected, loudly. He had stared at her and said nothing. She was loud and garish, her lipstick a blood red, her nails painted to match, and her hair was frozen in place with an overabundance of hairspray. Why had he not noticed this before? What had seemed bold and adventurous now struck him as uncouth and immature. Gina was young, just four years older than Tommy.

"I don't see why you have to move back into the house," she had said pouting, "They were fine when she was out of the country."

Tom felt a surge of anger. Edith was dead, the children all in shock and this stupid little girl could only think of herself.

"That was a *week*. And I checked in on them every day. She isn't coming back, Gina. My kids, look, I just have to go. You are welcome to stay here; I'll pay for everything."

He had been doing that already. The most she had contributed since moving in was to buy multiple bottles of wine, which she then drank herself.

She gave him a look.

"Well, I sure would hope so."

She batted her eyes at him, and Tom couldn't help but think she fit every stereotype that had ever been written about young girlfriends.

"Will you check in on me every day?"

How had he messed up so badly? What the hell had he been thinking? Edith had been with him, true to him, through everything. They had gone through the deaths of their parents together, seen tough times, and made three beautiful children.

Perhaps a little too beautiful. Liza knew she was pretty. A few snaps of her fingers and the boys had come running. But not the good ones, oh no, the crappy ones who were desperate to get into her pants and then run like hell when faced with a reality that they were unprepared for.

And of course, she had insisted on keeping the baby.

He had slept on the couch, unwilling to sleep in the bed he and Edith had shared for so many years, the one in which she had spent her final weeks before the virus kicked into full gear with such devastating consequences.

Within a week, Gina had moved out of the apartment and on to another middle-aged sugar daddy. A man who, like Tom, was desperately trying to ignore the creeping advance of middle-age by snaring a nubile young woman. He wished the guy luck and found that he was relieved.

Tom thought of his eldest son Tommy, who was currently making a career of glaring at him through a haze of alcohol and drugs, barely sober. His son hadn't waited long after the funeral before escaping the house to drink with his buddies and drown his sorrows over his mother's shocking end. As it was, Tom barely saw him, it seemed as if Tommy was doing his best to come and go when Tom was away from the house at work.

Joseph rarely left his room, especially when Tom was at home, and refused to even sit at the same table with him. The boy missed his mother. He also obviously blamed Tom for not being at home when he had been needed the most.

Liza, and his constantly screaming granddaughter were his only companions at the dinner table most nights – and Tom found that he almost preferred the screaming baby to Liza's sullen silence.

Most days Tom alternated between deep guilt, for he had been unfaithful to Edith for years, and a terrible dread over what was happening inside of him and the rest of his remaining family.

He knew it, he had even seen it coming. Edith hadn't, she couldn't even have dreamed of how deep the rabbit-hole went at EcoNu. He was sure of it. And now it was out, and he had it, and he knew it wasn't just him. A touch, a simple handshake would do it, had done it, to countless others. *Hug someone, let them breathe on each other,* he thought to himself, *that's all it takes.*

Tom's stomach rumbled ominously. He sipped more water and reached for the last of the sandwiches on the tray. He still had half of a bag of chips by his left hand. The meeting had barely started, and the tray, once heaped with small squares of delicately made sandwiches was now empty. Along the long conference room table, the same was true of every other tray, picked clean. He saw his colleague Anna Quinlan, Scott Dorns replacement, staring at the sandwich in his hand with an intense longing. His stomach rumbled again and he bit into it. At this point, the packets of sweeteners and powdered creamers were beginning to look good.

Tom couldn't help wondering how long he had. Was it a matter of days? Even weeks? Or would his life be measured in mere hours?

Edith had been gone seven days. The kids had all been exposed, especially the kids, along with hundreds if not thousands of others. The sheer possibilities of the spread of the virus were endless. Tom thought of the CDC and dismissed it, there was no point really, no way to detect it, and no way to stop it now.

"Dr. Haincy?"

A voice from the head of the table interrupted his mental wanderings. The sandwich was gone, down the hatch and his stomach screamed for more.

"*Dr. Hainey?*"

Kelly Armstrong, CEO of EcoNu, who would have been a stunningly attractive woman if she wasn't such a stone-cold bitch, was staring at him from the head of the table. For that matter, they were all staring. He swallowed dryly, not bothering to brush the crumbs from his mouth.

She spoke again, a patently false smile on her face.

"Dr. Hainey, are you with us? I was asking if you have had any progress on a kill switch for the virus."

Tom ignored the question.

"The virus is elegant, we made sure of that." His voice sounded rusty, unused. His stomach twisted with hunger, growling its discomfort. He grabbed three small packets, one sugar, and two powdered creamers.

"Yes, yes, I know. Your initial reports lauded it as the best feat of viral engineering ever seen." Her voice was sharp, grating.

"But what I am asking is..."

"You wanted it easy to implement, impossible to get rid of." He said, cutting her off. "How was it you worded it, ah yes, 'We must perfect a virus that creates total reliance on EcoNu, our pigs, feed, whatever was required.' After all, you wanted something that couldn't be copied, couldn't be stolen, and would stick in the genes of the product like some kind of proverbial glue." He ripped open the packet of sugar, tilted his head back and gulped it down. His guts screamed for more.

"Dr. Hainey, if you would please just..."

Tom practically snarled, "And what about the T2? The inclusion of that enzyme was completely deliberate and you should *know* there is no 'off switch.' How do you think the public will react when the second part of the virus makes itself known?"

In a strictly dollars and cents point of view, having a next-generation kill order within the growth virus had made sense. EcoNu was a for-profit company, no matter their carefully crafted public image. The T2 enzyme was EcoNu's ace in the hole. They would offer the viral therapy at a fraction of the cost that pig farmers were currently incurring (when the regular die-offs were factored in) and ensure that 98% of the baby pigs would survive infancy and grow to twice the size in half the time, ultimately saving on feed and upkeep.

"You called it 'a deal that had no downside'. By the time the farmers figured out that the treated pigs were sterile thanks to the virus, EcoNu could step in with our latest development, enormous factories that produce test-tube pigs - ensuring nearly complete control over the supply and production of pork here and around the world."

Kelly Armstrong tried to interrupt again, "Dr. Hainey, *please...*"

Tom railroaded over her, and from the look on her face, the CEO was quite unused to such treatment.

"I've seen the schematics. The factories are already being prepared. In less than a decade, EcoNu could have 80% of the worldwide market on pork secured and under its control. And when that happened, we would control the price of pork however we wished. But there won't be anyone left to eat the fucking bacon, will there?"

EcoNu had wanted world domination when it came to their products, and now they had it. He suppressed a giggle, his sanity teetering on the edge, it just wasn't what they had bargained for. And no one knew. Not yet anyway.

The giggle began to spill out, tears stood in his eyes. Tears of sadness? Perhaps. They began to roll down his cheeks, huge drops, and his entire body began to shake. He was laughing, this strange hybrid of hysteria – laughing with tears. He continued, despite the odd stares from his co-workers and the incensed look on the CEOs face. He couldn't help it.

If only he could go back and undo it all; be the husband his wife had deserved, that his kids needed him to be. But no, that wasn't going to happen, was it? He had screwed up royally. His kids hated him, the woman he promised to love for the rest of his life was gone, and he, he was a dead man. So were the people in this room.

When staring all of those realities head on, a little gallows humor made sense. It wouldn't take long for the world and the researchers at the CDC, to figure it out. EcoNu had customized, incubated, and released a virus that turned out to be capable of killing every last human on the planet – and all for the sake of a plate full of bacon with the EcoNu name on it. He choked out a giggle.

"Dr. Hainey?" Kelly Armstrong stared at Tom with narrowed eyes, "Are you ill?"

Tom's hysterical giggle bubbled up, "A kill switch? It's part of the herpes simplex family. There's no kill switch."

The CEO looked livid as Tom continued to laugh, chewed up bits of food and spittle flying through the air. Several of his nearby colleagues flinched away.

Kelly Armstrong's voice dripped acid, "And yet somehow you find this *funny.*"

Tom could barely breathe, the hysterical laughter bubbled over.

"We are the walking dead. Yet we sit here, on a *committee*, while outside the world..."

He jumped up from his seat, ran to the side of the room where the map showed outbreaks of the virus, starting with a huge red star in the middle of the United States, that star was Edith's. He stabbed at the stars, clusters of them in Europe, New York, California, the Midwest, sprinkled throughout Asia, a large cluster appearing in Guiyang, which he stabbed with his finger.

"Guiyang, home of over *seven million* people. At least it *was* full of people until China bombed it the hell off the map while trying to stop the virus. London, an international hub of travel, Paris, yet another hub, Rome and more. New York? L.A.! It is *everywhere*."

His co-workers were looking frightened.

"Edith," his voice hitched as he spoke his ex-wife's name, "Edith wasn't in all of these cities. It's broken past her; it is spreading to the entire world and it is far too late to try to stop it. *You* have it," he said pointing at the blond CEO. He turned his attention to Anna Quinlan who stared at his finger as if it were a gun.

"*She* has it, *I* have it. We all have it. There is no kill switch, there's only *death*."

His colleagues were wincing, drawing away from him, and one of the assistants had begun muttering urgently into a phone in the corner of the room. Tom bulldozed on through, ignoring the growing fear his co-workers were showing as they edged away from him.

"You wanted EcoNu to have a stranglehold on the production and sale of swine and damned if you didn't get it. Congratulations. Corporate bullshit, as if The Collapse didn't give us enough warning about what a corporation can do, will do, and *has* done just for an extra billion in profit."

As the security team entered, his voice gained momentum and he swept the room with his finger.

"You sealed our fates and we are all complicit. Now we get to pay the price. You are all going to *die*. Every. Last. One of you. We designed the virus to be highly communicable – 'infect other pigs,' you said, 'that way the farmers will have to come to us when the sterility kills all possibility of natural reproduction.' Just like the cornfields or the wheat in the early part of this century. Damned if we didn't repeat the exact same mistakes, do the same fucked up thing that blew up in our faces and meant changing the company name from Monsanto to EcoNu. As if a change in name would make everything all nice and clean again!"

The CEOs face narrowed with fury and surprise and Tom laughed again.

"Oh yeah, didn't think I knew that, did you?"

The security officers had reached him, "Sir, you are going to have to come with us."

Tom struggled in their grasp, his skin hot now to the touch, "One touch is all it takes," he screamed.

A split second later, he pulled loose from the grasping hands and his co-workers scattered, cowering away from him.

"We have all been infected, it's *too late* to find a kill switch even if there was one. We are all *going...to... die!*"

"Security, get him out *now*!" Kelly Armstrong's voice cut through the air.

Spittle and bits of food flew through the air as the security team grabbed him again and hustled Tom Hainey out of the conference room.

There was a terrible silence in the moments afterward. Anna Quinlan shook in her chair, and several others just sat in shocked silence.

Kelly Armstrong, patted her perfectly coiffed blond curls, straightened her tailored suit, and her hands went briefly to the pearl necklace at her throat before she sniffed and said, "Well, that was unfortunate. The man is obviously traumatized by his wife's untimely death. Truly, her death was shocking. It also must be pointed out that it has yet to be verified as having anything to do with EcoNu."

She took a moment and stared around the room, meeting each employee's eyes in turn.

"We cannot jump to conclusions as Dr. Hainey did, or collapse into a panic when there is not necessarily something to panic over."

She paused for a moment, waiting for everyone to recover from the ugliness of Tom's outburst.

"Ted," she said, turning her attention to the assistant who had called security, "ask the cafeteria to send up more sandwiches, and anything else they might have on hand. Also, please be sure to relay to Security that Dr. Hainey is to be taken directly to Two Rivers Hospital and that he is to receive the best psychiatric care possible, on EcoNu's dime of course. No charges will be filed, not for someone who is clearly grief-stricken over his recent loss."

The assistant nodded and scuttled out of the room.

"Now, let's get back to business. Dr. Quinlan, are we *sure* that the virus was from our pigs? Someone suggested that it was…" she consulted her notes, "similar in nature to a virus known as *pseudorabies*? Could I get a clear explanation, in layman's terms, to describe this situation better?"

Anna Quinlan, still shaking, managed a nod, and paged through the documentation.

"Yes, ma'am, I believe I can help with that."

Her fingers pulled the empty tray of sandwiches closer, swiping at the few stray crumbs, and trying desperately to ignore the yawning cavern that was her stomach long enough to get through the meeting.

"The Pseudorabies virus was the building block that we used to genetically engineer the virus. It's a delivery system if you will. The test subjects exhibit a small increase in overall core body temperature, accompanied by a sharp rise in appetite. The more they eat, the faster they grow and time to rendition is reduced from nine months to just under six months. This shortened time reduced the overall feed price and we are seeing a solid thirty-five percent savings. This means we can offer our meats for a more competitive price and increase the supply to more than double in the CAFO operations overseas."

The meeting continued, with Anna answering the CEOs questions, a semblance of normalcy returned to the rest of the group, and two more plates of sandwiches were delivered and immediately consumed by the occupants. Hours later, the memory of Tom Hainey being dragged out by security would stay fresh in everyone's mind. Although the halls had mostly emptied out at EcoNu long before the incident – accounts of it spread in bars, through emails and frightened whispers.

The next Monday only three-quarters of the workforce showed up and that quickly dropped off with each day that followed.

By the time a phalanx of CDC officials and military pushed their way through the tall glass doors of EcoNu's headquarters in Kansas City three weeks later, barely one in one hundred of the EcoNu workers remained. Many had already sickened and died, while others had fled in a desperate attempt to outrun a virus that was already deeply entrenched within them. The only thing they were successful at was in spreading it further.

The Hunger

"The whole history of science has been the gradual realization that events do not happen in an arbitrary manner, but that they reflect a certain underlying order, which may or may not be divinely inspired." – Stephen Hawking

Date: 03.10.2099

Earth – Kansas City, Missouri

A few wispy clouds scudded across the sky, but Mac Dolan barely noticed. Instead, his stomach gurgled with hunger as he crossed the short distance to the store, leaving his autocar parked in the loading lane in front, the door hanging open, engine still running, upon his exit.

He had cleared out the fridge, the pickles, the condiments, even the overly fancy bread his ex-girlfriend had raved about yet left behind when she moved out. She had managed to take two of the bath towels she had claimed to hate but left the bread. How many times had he heard her complain about how rough those towels were on her skin? That had been two months ago. And now that very same bread had developed a small fuzz of mold on one end. He ate it anyway. He had stared at it, sitting there alone in the empty fridge and actually felt his mouth begin to salivate as his stomach screamed for relief.

Seconds after consuming it, his stomach still gurgled, unfazed by the offerings, still aching with hunger. Some part of him was concerned, taken aback by this aberrant behavior. In the back of his mind was a nagging sense of wrongness, but it was overruled by the ravenous hunger he felt. Next, he had chugged the Tabasco sauce, hoping against hope that the need for more food would be abated somewhat, distracted possibly, by the burning sensation it made as it flowed from his lips to his tongue and on down his throat. It hadn't worked, still his stomach demanded more.

And now he was at Hy-Vee, the local supermarket, walking down the aisles, his temperature spiking and his stomach screaming for more food. He had reached the cookie aisle and his hand shook as he grabbed for bags of ginger snaps, knocking several of them onto the floor in his eagerness. He reached for one of them, unable to withstand the screaming, yawning *need* of his stomach any longer. His fingers tore at the packaging, bits of paper flying. He grabbed a fistful and shoved them into his mouth. Part of the packaging came with it. He swallowed it anyway, the thick paper scraping his throat as it slid past.

He didn't even notice the woman with her two small children stop and stare at him. He was hungry, so terribly hungry. Sweat rolled down his back, dampening his shirt. He choked on the bits of the dry cookie, the pieces catching in his throat, but did not stop. He filled his mouth with more, manically swallowing, feeling the tear of them as they were forced, some almost whole, down his throat.

"Mama, dat man is eating cookies," a tiny voice said.

The woman's oldest child, a little girl of three years with big brown eyes and immaculate pigtails was staring at Mac and pointing at his hand.

"Mama, I want some too!"

The child's mother stood rooted in place at the end of the aisle, mouth open in shock as she watched Mac finish shaking the crumbs from the first bag of cookies and rip open the second one. She stood there, staring, unable to turn away, even as her daughter began to cry.

He didn't seem to even hear the little girl, or notice that there was anyone else in the world there in the aisle, just him and the ginger snaps. He sat down, next to a shelf filled with Oreos, and began shoving the rough cookies down his throat, not bothering to chew at all now. Every once in a while, he would choke, even retch, as his body struggled to work with the unchewed food.

Mac's shirt was glued to his body, sweat-soaked and stinking. He hadn't bathed in two days, and since waking in a cold sweat he had ransacked the freezer of anything even remotely edible. He had barely waited for the food to defrost, gnawing impatiently on the frozen pizza as the peas defrosted in a pot on the stove. The peas had blackened and stuck to the bottom of the pot as he watched; he had forgotten to add water. It had taken an hour to clear the freezer and fridge completely. There hadn't been a lot, his appetite had been elevated for weeks now and he couldn't keep up with grocery shopping while working full time and going to school. When the last item had been cleared, even the crumbs wiped off of the shelves, he had walked away from the fridge. He had left his house, the front door wide open and walked out to his autocar.

Mac ignored the growing crowd, reached instead for a third bag. He tore it open, fingers shaking. In the distance, he could hear the manager of the store asking everyone to step out of the way as he and two police officers marched down the aisle.

Nothing really mattered to Mac, except the intense pain in his stomach. It seemed that the food he was cramming down barely touched that horrific need, but the food was what he desperately craved. It was hard to think, hard to get past the *hunger*. Just a few more bites, just a few, and surely, he would feel better.

A tightness had begun to build, starting in his stomach, moving up into his throat, a sense of fullness combined with the desperate hunger. Two conflicting messages in his body. The need to feel something, anything sliding down his esophagus was now at its apex.

He had lost all other focus, and the police officer speaking to him had no effect. He swallowed more Oreos, gagging and choking on the hard cookies.

"Sir, you need to come with us."

The officer was lean, fit and middle-aged, with a sprinkling of white peppering his dark, short-cropped hair. He pulled the bag of cookies from Mac's trembling hands and Mac felt a surge of panic. He reached for them and the officer's partner, a stout, middle-aged woman snapped one side of handcuffs onto his left wrist with a practiced, professional motion.

Mac attempted to speak, but the cookies in his mouth clogged all sound except a muffled gurgle, with pieces flying out in a small, soggy shower. He reached again for the bag of cookies, resisting the police now, his body thrashing as both officers tackled him and wrestled him to the ground. There was this terrible shift as if something was giving way inside him. He screamed then, and choked.

A wash of red glazed his vision, he couldn't breathe, and as the officers raised him to his feet, his hands secured in cuffs behind his back, Mac's knees gave way. One of the onlookers screamed at the blood trickling from his mouth, then the convulsions hit, his body flailing, attempting even as his esophagus detached from the bloated, and now perforated remains of the stomach, to empty the body of its excess. It was too late. It was all too late - inside of Mac's abdomen was a mass of food, stomach acid, and bile.

Mac retched, convulsed, and then lay still, a slow pool of blood and partially digested cookies spreading around him on aisle three.

Unhappy Meal

Date: 03.10.2099

Earth – Kansas City, Missouri

Dale Otterman was the County Medical Examiner by default. No one had hired him for this job and no one had said anything about a pay increase. His boss Jack West, who had run the morgue since Otterman was in preschool, had simply stopped coming into work last Tuesday morning.

Jack was the official County Medical Examiner, while Dale was the Assistant M.E.

Meanwhile, with no word from West or any answer at the door when the morgue director stopped by the house, Otterman had been tapped for his boss's load as well as his own.

The call had come in after he left the morgue for lunch. He was settled, the day unseasonably warm, and was in no hurry to return to work for at least an hour.

"We have an odd one," the dispatcher had said, and Dale instantly regretted answering his phone.

"I'm at lunch."

This was mostly true. He was nearly finished with the large sandwich he had bought from the food truck. He still had the chips to go, but he had a great view of the playground from the park bench which he hated to give up. He was partially shaded by a large oak and none of the rather vigilant mothers had noticed him sitting there, staring at a cute little girl in pigtails and a short jean skirt over a pair of polka dot tights. He wished he had brought his camera, but he had forgotten it next to his computer.

The last trip to a playground had been a disaster. He would need to avoid the west side of town for a while. A rather over-attentive grandmother had sized him up and pulled her twin granddaughters from the monkey bars before he could get more than a couple of shots of their thin legs and the edges of their frilled panties. Just downloading those illicit shots had given him a thrill. Right after he had snapped the photo, so sure no one had noticed, the old biddy had honed in on him and started cussing him out. He didn't speak Spanish, but the old bitch sure had been going to town. He had stood up from the bench and hurried away while she screamed invectives and gathered the little girls close to her.

He would never swear like that around little girls.

"The Chief of Police is here. He wants answers." The man was new but quite insistent.

Dale Otterman sighed, "I'll be there in thirty minutes."

He wanted to see this little girl take a ride on the seesaw one last time.

"Better make it fifteen, the Chief is waiting at your desk." The man replied before disconnecting.

Dale felt a flash of fear run through him. His camera was there. Had he wiped the drive?

Eighteen minutes later he was washing his hands in the sink. The Chief was tall, but portly, with a large sandwich and soda in his hand.

"Damn it, Phil. I told you I needed that report."

The Chief snarled into his cell phone.

In between noshing on his lunch, which happened to be his third full meal that day, he was apparently dressing down some poor sap named Phil. As soon as Otterman turned away from the sink, the chief hung up. From the sound of it, he disconnected the call while Phil was in mid-sentence.

"You're the new M.E., right?"

"It's not official yet, but, yes." Otterman would have said more but the Chief had moved on.

"Great. So, I need a rush on this. It's fucking weird. The guy walks into Hy-Vee this morning, started ransacking the cookie aisle and then collapses and dies. Thing is, he was a first responder on that Hainey case."

"I remember that case." Dale said, "Dr. West handled it."

After that, the old man had acted odd for two, maybe three weeks before he stopped showing up for work completely last week. No notice, no calls, nothing. Otterman didn't get it. The guy was nearly at retirement age, with a pension, why jeopardize all of that by abruptly quitting?

"What can you tell me about it since the good ole doc isn't here?" The Chief asked, leaning forward.

Crumbs spilled off of his shirt and onto Dale's tidy desk. Dale tamped down the irritation he felt.

"The Hainey case was perplexing. Jack took samples of the stomach contents, which apparently included most of the menu at Pop's Burgers, plus a large amount of condiments – whole-grain mustard for one. An adult human stomach can hold a maximum of 4,000 cc's, or four quarts of food and liquid."

"Ugh," the Chief interrupted, "*Four* quarts?"

"Yes. Anything past that and death would come a'knocking. Dr. Hainey's stomach contained 4,021 cc's, give or take 30 cc's for blood and other viscera. It was hard for Dr. West to get an exact amount due to the two tears that caused the stomach to spill into the abdominal cavity, causing the patient's demise."

He had never seen anything like it, nor had Jack. The last documented case of someone dying from stomach rupture due to overeating had occurred shortly after the liberation of concentration camps in World War II over 150 years ago. It was incredibly rare, in part because the human body has a series of protective reflexes that make such a thing nearly impossible. For instance, there were stretch receptors in the stomach that would cue the brain when the stomach is nearing capacity, and the brain, in turn, issues a statement that you are full and it is time to stop. If this message is not heeded, then pain, nausea, and typically regurgitation follow.

"You get the weirdest fuckin' cases, Doc. Makes me think that a good old-fashioned homicide has gotta be preferable to that."

Dale shook his head, "Actually, it is quite fascinating. Edith Hainey must have been in intense pain and discomfort by the end of her culinary misadventure, but there was *no regurgitation*. It was as if there had been some wires crossed in the brain and she had simply never gotten the message that it was time to stop eating."

The Chief eyed him, "Right. Well then, get on with your little freak show, Doc, 'cause I need answers."

Dale Otterman located his tape recorder, unzipped the body bag, and began with the standard external examination. He noted an appendectomy scar on the abdomen and a large pre-cancerous mole on the decedent's left arm. After the external examination was completed and he had carefully taken vitreous samples from both eyes, he proceeded to make the standard Y-cut on the corpse, efficiently peeling the patient's chest open like a book.

Immediately he saw the similarities. There was a large amount of undigested and partially digested food in the peritoneum. There appeared to be two significant tears in the stomach, which was stretched to an impossibly large size. He could feel the hard ridges of Oreo cookies, swallowed whole from the looks of it. Dale shook his head; *I know that could not have felt good going down.* Later examination of the esophageal tract showed abrasions along most of its length, all the way to the stomach.

He made his way down to the intestines, which were full and had been straining to eliminate previous meals at the time of death.

Jack had sent the samples from Edith Hainey to the CDC for evaluation, but they had quite a backlog thanks to some kind of emergency coming out of a backwater province in China. The Chinese CDC had been overwhelmed and demanded that the American CDC become involved thanks to an American-based company, EcoNu. The company was side-stepping charges from Chinese authorities who had shut down some big pig-farming facility there, after scores fell ill in a nearby city. The spin doctors had been hard at work, however. Apparently, it was the case of a faulty Chinese water treatment plant and had nothing to do with EcoNu. At least, that was what EcoNu lawyers were claiming as China continued to shout threats and point fingers at the American company.

The Chief was still waiting. As soon as he completed the autopsy and bagged the samples for Toxicology, he headed back to his desk. There sat the Chief, making himself at home at Dale's desk, feet up on the wood, and barking orders on his cell phone.

As soon as he saw him approaching, the Chief hung up and turned to him.

"Well?"

Dale said nothing, waiting for the man to move from his desk. The Chief didn't seem to be taking the hint. He stayed seated, leaned back, smirked, and repeated himself.

"Well?"

He felt a surge of anger. Dale feared cops, even working with them on a day-to-day basis had not taken that fear from him. He knew that his predilections were not within the acceptable range and most of his energies when not at work went into acquiring illicit videos that satisfied most of his desires. He had never used his work computer for any of it. He was careful, *very* careful, but still. Somehow seeing the Chief in his chair brought back all of those memories of bullies in the schoolyard. He bit the inside of his cheek and forced the words out.

"Undetermined. I'll need to wait for the tox screen to come back before I can say anything else."

Let the bastard chew on that. Otterman could have told him about the manner of death, which was narrowed down – Mac Dolan's death was not a homicide, suicide, or therapeutic complication. That left natural disease, highly unlikely, and thus the "undetermined" classification.

With a co-worker, a peer, he would have discussed it with interest, even pleasure. Dale Otterman was passionate about his work. That, pre-pubescent girls, and his love for eating out of a particular food truck every Monday through Friday was as well-rounded as the man got. But the Chief had already shown his colors. He was a bully, through and through, and Otterman saw no reason to pander to the fool, much less give him what he wanted, whatever that was.

The Chief looked *pissed.* Otterman had seen the same look in a quarterback's face in high school when he finally got it through his thick skull that Dale wasn't going to just give him the answers to a biology exam, and that he would actually have to work for it. The man stood up, towering over the medical examiner by at least seven inches, glowering at him.

Dale's mother, a petite woman who had suffered her husband's verbal attacks in silence, had often said to Dale, "Don't poke the bear, son."

But she had lived her life kowtowing to her domineering husband, someone not unlike the Chief here, who had thrown his weight around the house after spending his days in a dead-end corporate job, pushing paper and taking orders. Sometimes, it was fun to poke the bear, just to see a big man like the Chief make a fool of himself.

The Chief checked himself, looked as if he wanted to unleash on Otterman, but in the end, clamped it down and strode away, pausing only to say, over his shoulder, "Put a rush on those tox screens."

Dale Otterman had expected more. He watched the Chief walk out, slightly disappointed. As he watched the Chief swagger out of sight, his stomach rumbled slightly. He had photos to review and move over to a well-disguised thumb drive tucked away in his pen. But first, he would go ahead and grab a few snacks from the machines down the hall.

Hong Kong Outbreak

Hong Kong and southern China are in an area where everything comes together. It's like the perfect storm – animals, the virus, population density." – John Nichols

Date: 03.10.2099

Earth – Hong Kong, China

Ang was roused by Cheng's departure from their bed. He was a light sleeper, a problem in the congested city full of traffic no matter the time of day. He wore ear plugs and an eye mask and they used blackout curtains and sound dampeners that emitted white noise.

Cheng usually slept like a rock, barely moving once sleep stole over him, and this worked well for the sleep-challenged Ang. He would snuggle against Cheng, an arm draped over him. Lately, his lover felt warmer than normal, and Cheng had tossed and turned the entire night, making sleep impossible.

Ang groaned, pulled a single ear plug out, "Cheng? What are you doing?"

There was no clear answer, not much more than a series of complicated grunts. Ang tried to go back to sleep. He reached into the inky soup of sleep, tried to pull it back over him, back into a dream. He almost succeeded.

The sound of the refrigerator door dinging, warning that the door had been left open, pulled him back out again. He sat up, pulling the other ear plug out and sliding his sleep mask high up onto his forehead.

"Cheng?"

The apartment was mostly dark. Tiny strips of bright sunlight stole through the edges of the blackout curtains. The open-door warning on the refrigerator continued to chime.

"Cheng? Close the refrigerator, honey, our power bill is already too expensive."

Ang could hear Cheng rummaging through the shelves, opening what few containers remained. These past few weeks, Cheng's normally spare appetite had abruptly increased, and Ang had found the cabinets and fridge emptying at an alarming rate. It was nice, at first. Ang loved the feel of more than skin and bone when he pulled Cheng close. His lover was angular, even gaunt. At least he had been until recently.

Cheng still hadn't responded and Ang could hear him slurping something down.

Ang frowned, what would he eat if Cheng finished off the leftovers from his shift? "Cheng! Are you eating those noodles I brought home last night? Hey!"

The air was cool on his bare skin as he pushed aside the covers and padded over to the kitchenette. His lover was sitting there, bare assed on the cold cement floor, shoveling the noodles into his mouth.

"By all the gods, Cheng, you are going to choke! At least stop long enough to chew and swallow!

Cheng's voice was difficult to understand as he muttered around a large mouthful of cabbage, "Sorry. I'm just, I'm just so *hungry*. I eat and eat and nothing makes it better, I'm still as hungry as when I started."

Ang stared at him a moment, thinking of the rumors that had been hot and heavy about Guiyang and how travel to the city had been completely shut down a week after Cheng's return. And then there was that man who had been shoved out of the restaurant last evening after he began gulping down the soy sauce, fish sauce, and any other condiment in reach when his food hadn't come out soon enough.

"You have been this way since you came back from your mother's funeral." Ang reached out and felt Cheng's forehead, "You feel a little on the warm side, but not too bad. I'll go talk to Mama Han, maybe she will have some idea."

"I'm just so hungry Ang, I don't know what to do." Cheng ran his finger along the bottom of the paper container, desperate to get the last bits of sauce and vegetables.

He laughed sadly, "My mother would have loved this; she was always trying to feed me."

Ang felt a thick rope of fear coil inside of him. He had loved the new look at first. He had teased his lover, "I'll fatten you up like a pig," Cheng had smiled then, the first smile Ang had seen since Cheng had returned from Guiyang after the funeral.

"If you fatten me up like a pig, I'll never meet a nice girl like my mother wanted me to."

Ang had laughed and kissed him, "I'll send that nice girl packing, you are all mine my darling Dayezhu, and don't you forget it!"

Ang hadn't been worried then. A better appetite had smoothed out the hollows under Cheng's eyes, filled out his cheeks, and helped the ribs and hips look softer and less gaunt. But now? With the whispers of the city of Guiyang quarantined and under a communications blackout, the whispers of some mysterious virus had cropped up. Now he was very much afraid.

"I'm going to get dressed and go see Mama Han. Perhaps she will know what to do." Ang said, staring as Cheng began to pull out a jar of pickled fish, something he normally hated.

Cheng said nothing, just nodded, and dug into the jar with his fingers.

A few minutes later and Ang was out the door, exhausted and rather hungry himself as he headed for the dingy shop on the corner. Mama Han was the local herbalist, well-known for her traditional Chinese remedies. She was ancient, her tiny body hunched, the wrinkles cutting deep into her face, one eye clouded with cataracts, and the other beginning to film over. Despite this, she knew where everything in the store was.

The bell above the door dinged, rousting Mama Han from a half-doze in her easy chair near the window. Dressed in black pants and a black top with frog closures on the shoulder, she could have been at home in a 19th century tea shop. Her clothes were neat, but worn. She was taking in the weak morning sunlight, a ragged cat in her lap and another curled at her feet, keeping her aged toes warm. Her great-grandson, a boy of ten, sat in a corner reading from a worn tablet with a cracked screen. He looked up briefly when Ang entered before returning to his reading.

Ang bowed to the old woman. He and Cheng had seen her on a regular basis when Cheng's parents were still alive. Cheng had sent packages to his parents every week. Teas to strengthen his father's immune system, powders to ease the pain from his mother's spreading cancer, and other various compounds. Mama Han had made Cheng's parents suffering markedly less over the months, dispensing the wisdom she had accrued from more than five generations of Chinese herbalists, all here in this tiny shop.

"Ang," the old woman croaked at him, "this is early for you."

Ang nodded, "Yes, Mama Han. It is Cheng."

He proceeded to tell her about Cheng's slight fever and hunger, which had been growing steadily over the past few weeks. Mama Han listened to him, nodding occasionally.

"I hear bad things out of Guiyang. Some sickness, with scores dead." She said, shaking her head, "No one knows what this mystery illness is, or where it came from."

Ang felt the dark fear coil within him further. Here in this small, nondescript shop, which stank of the myriad of herbs and decoctions, even here he felt hungry, a place with more off-putting smells than the docks which constantly reeked of fish.

"Cheng was in Guiyang last month. He said that the last day he was there, something wasn't right, people acting crazy." His stomach gurgled, twisted in hunger. "Do you think he..." he couldn't even finish the thought.

His love, his world, possibly sick?

The old woman cleared her throat, a thick, bubbling sound. She reached into a greasy paper bag on her right. It sat on a black lacquer table, next to a half full teacup, which contained a greasy-green liquid inside of it. The bag was filled with spring rolls, two of which she held out to Ang and one which she took a bite from, slowly chewing. Ang ate one spring roll, it helped quiet the yawning growl of his stomach somewhat, and then the other, as he waited for Mama Han to speak.

"You bring him here. Let me examine him, maybe I find a better answer than just lotus leaf tea. This illness, whatever it is, is something I have not seen before. So, you bring him here."

Ang nodded and left the small shop, stopping only to purchase more spring rolls from a street vendor along the way. He bought two dozen, the two that he had eaten had barely dented his appetite. The apartment they shared was in a tall modern building, all concrete and glass. There were dizzying views from every apartment, which helped make up for the oversized shoebox feel of the place, just three hundred square feet in all. The scene which greeted him, however, caused him to drop the bag of spring rolls.

There were thirteen still remaining. They rolled about on the floor as Ang stared.

The tiny apartment was typically immaculate, both men obsessive about keeping the small space as neat as possible. It helped it to not feel quite as small. The pillows tastefully arranged on the small couch were the first thing Ang noticed. They were shredded, limp, their inside fiberfill missing, the cloth torn. But they weren't the only thing, someone had cut into their sofa, and there were huge holes of missing stuffing.

A small row of pots near the window that were usually filled with lemongrass, Thai basil and fennel were on the floor, the plants missing and dirt scattered in clods across the room.

Ang stared, taking in the scene before him, his brain struggling to understand what his eyes were showing him. Cheng was nowhere in sight, his shoes still neatly set on the mat by the door. His jacket as well. Who would break into their apartment and tear up the pillows and furniture? Hands shaking, he left the spring rolls on the floor where they lay and reached for a knife in the tiny kitchen. The refrigerator hung open, the empty container that had held the pickled cabbage was empty on the floor. He could hear thumps coming from the door to the bathroom.

"Cheng?" Ang's voice was barely above a whisper.

The Triads were still alive and well in parts of Hong Kong, but Ang had never crossed paths with them. Cheng had mentioned seeing several a few weeks ago at Feng, the popular nightclub he worked at, and there had been an altercation of sorts, one in which Cheng had needed to step in between a pretty girl and a member of the Hei Triad. Could this be some kind of payback? Ang inched slowly down the length of the kitchen, closer to the bathroom door which was partially closed. A crash of pill bottles came next, pills rolling on the floor, out of the bathroom and into the hall.

Ang's heart hammered in his chest, his palms slick with sweat and his stomach twisting, still hungry despite the spring rolls he had gulped down. He rounded the corner, peering into the bathroom, and let out a gasp of relief. The only occupant in the bathroom was Cheng. His skin was gray, shining with sweat. He choked on the handful of pills he had been attempting to dry swallow.

"Stop! Cheng, stop!"

Ang dropped the knife and reached for his lover, knocking the bottle of pills out of his hand. Bits of fiberfill were caught in Cheng's teeth, while broken bits of pills stuck to his tongue and mashed into his molars. Ang glanced at the pills, some were harmless, or nearly so, although one large bottle had been emptied in its entirety. His lover reached desperately for the pills that were now rolling around the floor like a set of demented dominoes.

"Oh God, Cheng! What have you done?" Ang tried dialing emergency services, his fingers shaking as he dialed 999 and was rewarded with a busy tone. "La shi!" He dialed again, only to hear a dial tone.

Cheng began pulling at the stuffing stuck in his teeth.

The third time Ang dialed, it rang once, "*All emergency services are under triage. Report to the nearest health center for treatment.*"

"Go tsao de!" He slammed a finger down on the disconnect button.

"Cheng! Please! Get up, get up, I'm taking you to Mama Han!"

It was a struggle, one that he barely was able to win. First Ang found himself wrestling with Cheng who, with extra meat on his bones, was a force to be reckoned with. By scooping up the pills, and insisting Cheng dress before he could have any more, he managed to lead his lover to the doorway, where the bag of spring rolls still stood. He doled them out, one at a time, leading Cheng down to the bank of elevators, then out of the apartment building into a heavy downpour. It soaked them, but it also gave them some level of anonymity as others hustled by, hunched under umbrellas and oblivious to the two as they lurched down the street. Mama Han's tiny store was less than a block away and Ang heard the bell clang in protest as the door swung open and he hauled Cheng, now out of food, into the store.

It was too late. In the quiet darkness of their empty apartment hours later, Ang huddled alone in their bed and cried. Seconds after crossing the store threshold, Cheng had begun to convulse, the sheer number of pills and whatever effects they were designed to elicit had been too much for Cheng's already ill body. As Ang and the old woman had tried to help him, one set of convulsions after another racked his body, and sent Cheng's head slamming down repeatedly on the cracked marble floor.

Much to Ang's dismay and despair, there was no autopsy. It was Hong Kong, after all. A city with over ten million people in it. One death was lost among many and by the time someone thought to read over what was initially labeled as a drug overdose, the city had already been consumed by the ESH virus.

Mr. President

"Far better to think historically, to remember the lessons of the past. Thus, far better to conceive of power as consisting in part of the knowledge of when not to use all the power you have. Far better to be the one who knows that if you reserve the power not to use all your power, you will lead others far more successfully and well." – A. Bartlett Giamatti

Date: 06.15.2099

Earth – Washington D.C.

Madeline straightened her husband's tie, kissed his cheek and followed him out of the dressing room. Her heels sunk into the thick carpet lining the living room of their suite. A small group of men and women waited quietly in chairs, their faces grim. They immediately stood as Gary Chen entered the room, a sign of respect to what might be the last president and First Lady of the Reformed United States.

The Oval Office was temporarily closed, thanks to the gruesome end of the Chief of Staff, Ian Warchowski. In the midst of giving a report the man had suddenly begun swallowing handfuls of foreign objects, including paper clips, a large jar of antique marbles, and far too many staples. Holding him down as he fought to ingest more had only led to the perforation of his stomach and esophagus. Madeline wondered if she would ever be able to walk into that room again and not see it replay a thousand times in her mind.

She could hear her husband's stomach gurgle. His appetite had been elevated, as had his temperature, for weeks now.

"I've got it Maddy. I know I do. I've felt hungry for days." He had said it in the darkness of their bedroom.

"Don't say that, Gary, please." She couldn't bear the thought. He had said nothing more, his hand reaching out to her in the darkness.

She wasn't blind. She knew, they all knew, what the symptoms were. She had watched him and others, seen their increased appetites, even as hers held steady, unchanging.

Why me? Why am I fine, but Gary isn't?

She could see him struggling with it, this need to eat more and more. He quickly ate a muffin. Madeline could see him eyeing the stack of them, obviously fighting his growing hunger in order to focus on the business at hand.

They had been up most of the night, all of them, and Alice, his personal secretary, was gray and shaking. The platter, heaped with muffins only moments before, was down to three.

Madeline's eyes tracked the room. Each of the occupants, except for her, appeared flushed. Each of them had eaten more than normal. She couldn't help wondering, *who will be left?*

She seemed to be the only exception, and she took a seat in the corner of the room. Her blue pantsuit was perfectly tailored, and her hair coiffed just so. No matter who sickened around her, she hadn't had a speck of fever and her appetite was its usual slight self.

How the rumor mill loved to talk about them, her and Gary, their marriage, their lack of children. Gary was particularly close-mouthed about it, keeping his personal life with her, and his public life as president, strictly separate. She knew that he worshiped her, even before they were married and, despite the efforts of many willing women attracted to his power and prestige, was completely devoted.

She smiled, remembering the first time they had met at a charity fundraiser. She had been stuck listening to her date complain about the very people the money was to benefit. From across the room, their eyes had met. She knew it sounded corny, but it had happened exactly like that, and he hadn't taken long to cross the wide room and stop in front of her, bowing slightly and extending his hand.

"Forgive me for intruding, but my name is Gary, Gary Chen. Your father asked me to speak with you about volunteering on the upcoming campaign." His olive complexion, liquid brown eyes, and intense stare had an immediate effect.

Within a week they were dating, two months later they were living together.

Their marriage did have political ramifications. Marrying Madeline gave Gary access to old money and prestige all in one fell swoop. When they had first spoke of it, she had warned him that their marriage would be open to endless speculation, especially due to his political aspirations.

"My family are one of California's original blue bloods. They had a fortune even before the 1849 gold rush, and afterwards, well." She had smiled at him, "People will say that you married me for my money and my family name."

He had smiled back at her, "And the Chinese-American contingent will denounce me for marrying outside of my ethnic heritage. So, we are both damned." He had winked at her, "Who cares what they think. Let them talk all they like. You and I will know the truth of it."

And it wasn't as if he were poor. Just the opposite. California had been inundated by the Chinese during and directly after the Collapse. Nearly two centuries of Chinese Americans lived there as well, but they were a far cry from the moneyed elite that descended on the west coast as the Reformed United States rebuilt itself from the ravages of civil war and financial disaster in the early part of the century. Chinese wealth was intrinsic to this rebuilding, and Gary's family soon controlled a large swath of the import-export business in Northern California. Gary had been groomed by his parents, a future planned for him before he ever entered the world, and politics had been the highway on which he had been set.

Madeline's family had large investments that had weathered the unrest. They had not been particularly excited about their only daughter being wooed by one of the invaders, "Nothing more than a modern wave of carpetbaggers," her father had exclaimed once, his lips pursed in disapproval as he stared at Gary.

There had been only one small hiccup. "I don't want children," he had said one night as they lay together in bed. His finger traced the sharp curves of her body. "Do you?"

At the time she hadn't. And now, faced with what felt like the end of the world, she was glad she didn't have one. It was yet another person who could be ripped from her by fate and murdered by a mere virus. In between those two moments had been ones filled with a general longing, one that didn't increase enough to be worthy of being admitted to aloud, but still.

"You are so beautiful," he had said that night, "I can't imagine your body ruined by childbirth."

Madeline thought of her cousin Elaina, who had three children and had a gorgeous body. What she had with Gary was profound, just short of worship, and she counted herself lucky to have found a man who loved her so deeply, passionately, even after fifteen years together.

"Mr. President, shall we go over the reports?"

Hollis Anders looked feverish and her usually quiet habit of occasionally gnawing her lips had apparently expanded to chewing her fingernails down to the nubs.

As Madeline watched silently from her corner of the room, Hollis pulled a small bit of hair out of her mouth, nervously tucking it behind her ear. Her lips were rough, cracked and bleeding in places.

"Yes, Ms. Anders, please go ahead." Gary said, sitting down on a Louis XIV era chair. Madeline could see that it would need to be reupholstered soon; there were a few pilled areas on the arms.

Hollis nodded, stared at the tablet in her hands and said, "The borders between Mexico and Canada have been shut for the past ten days. Most of the major cities and towns have been advised to enact quarantine procedures; however there has been a slower reaction than we had hoped for. Many of the city leaders have dismissed such measures as fear-mongering."

She continued, "The concept of a general quarantine is a standard, tried and true one, but given the instances of governmental overstep in the early part of this century, implementation is far more difficult in today's world."

Madeline knew exactly what Hollis meant. Although no one in the room had been born at that time, the history was clear and sharp in their cultural memory. Shortly before The Collapse, there had been strong militarization of police in and around major cities. This was done primarily under the guise of the War on Drugs, something that had been abandoned when the country collapsed into civil war, and later not taken up again due to its deeply unpopular legacy. The War on Drugs was now akin to human rights violations in American cultural memory.

Directly in the middle of that, was the legacy of the police, who had been subverted into a quasi-military ball bat that was used against the people for the slightest malfeasance.

Hollis added, "During the Reformation, massive changes were made that prevented such overreach from happening again. Unfortunately, those choices mean that the police and military are no longer what they were."

Hollis stopped for a moment, long enough to tear off her right index fingernail with her teeth and begin to nibble at the loose skin.

President Chen motioned for her to continue. Hollis stopped nibbling on her finger and resumed her report.

"There simply aren't enough troops to enforce quarantine, except in areas that already have a large troop presence. Mostly those cities with a nearby active military base. We are now getting reports from large sections of the country that are seeing the virus spread like wildfire. And it seems that the security procedures at the airports exacerbated the situation."

"How so, Ms. Anders?" Gary asked, nibbling on his own fingernails.

"People were placed in holding areas for testing. However, with the high contagion level of the virus, this resulted in even more people being exposed at airports."

She shook her head, "Held long enough to become infected, and then sent home, they have continued to spread the ESH virus. And outside our borders the numbers of infected are just as bad."

Hollis looked up from her reading as an aide came in with sandwiches and fruit, snatching a large sandwich and biting into it. It was a large bite, which stretched her already irritated skin, and her lip began to bleed.

"Thanks to the increased food intake, combined with a significant reduction in highway travel, most areas of the country are suffering severe food shortages. The food shortages themselves seem to be leading to extreme behaviors from the virus sufferers, who, responding to the compelling need to eat, eat anything they can. We have multiple reports of sufferers eating non-food objects – household cleaning products, wood, metal like Warchowski did, and um..."

Hollis faltered, choked back a sob, and bit down hard. The tattered lip split, blood welled up immediately.

Madeline felt sorry for the young woman. She had seen how Hollis and Ian looked at each other when they didn't think anyone else noticed. It seemed that in many ways, she was invisible, privy to secrets that Gary would never know.

Then, while waiting for the coffee to brew a week ago Hollis had taken Madeline into her confidence, "I know I shouldn't, but I really like Ian, Madeline. We just went on a few dates, but now he's moved back in with his wife." Tears had glistened in her eyes.

Until her sudden death the week before, Julie Warchowski had called her husband on an hourly basis, creating an impossible situation for him at work and forcing him to silence his phone, an act which he had obviously regretted after her spectacular death. Window blinds, that's what's for lunch. The metal variety, no less. Julie had eaten at least twenty of them before convulsing and dying. Ian had found her body that evening when he returned home.

Hollis' stomach rumbled audibly.

Chen nodded for her to go on.

"And there have been more reports of cannibalism."

The blood began to trickle slowly down her chin. Several others murmured, whether in response to the cannibalism or the fact that she was bleeding Madeline wasn't sure. Hollis licked at the blood, merely smearing it on her chin and a grimace of pain stole across her face.

"It says here that, um, most of the victims in that situation are either children or elderly."

She licked her chin again and looked about wildly. She stared at the empty plates, looking desperate.

"I need some food please," her pale blue eyes welled up with tears, "Anything will do."

Before anyone could send for more food, she rolled her tongue in her mouth, biting down hard.

Gary Chen stepped back and two of the remaining guards rushed in, grabbing Hollis and pulling her out of the room as blood began to pour from her mouth. The tablet fell from her hands, bouncing on the floor, flecks of blood coating it.

Susan Stryler, another aide, gave a horrified scream, "Oh God! She's eating her own tongue!" Even as she said this, Susan's face was a mix of terror and longing. Madeline had watched her quietly eat the remainder of the muffins along with ten sandwiches, snuck furtively while most eyes were on Hollis.

There was a quiet moment after Hollis' departure from the room. One of shock, of fear, and the growing realization that they all shared the same future fate. Madeline, forgotten for a moment, stood up, walked over on unsteady feet and reached for her husband's handkerchief to dry her eyes, laying a cold hand upon his feverish brow.

She had refused his request to leave the White House for safety weeks ago and reminded him that her place was by his side. She always knew just what to say. Just as Gary had been groomed for power, so had she. Even more so, since her family's legacy was deeply entrenched in California and America for generations of philanthropy on one side and politics on the other, with vast financial resources tying the two together. Gary, robbed of words, stood there, his eyes closed, focused on the cool, bony hand that caressed his brow.

Madeline spoke, her voice surprisingly calm, "These are terrible days, and we must focus on what we can do to hold this country together and care for those who need our influence and guidance."

She paused, took in the small group of staffers in front of her and consciously stepped into a role she had been born to.

"We know not the hour of our death, none of us, so let us take this time and focus on what we can do, together. It will help us stay strong through this."

She nodded to Susan Stryler, who was wiping tears from her eyes, "Susan, could you tell us about the rest of the report?"

"Yes, ma'am," Susan said, after clearing her throat and stuffing her damp handkerchief in a pocket, "We received a communiqué last night from the Interim Soviet Premier, Boris Naskilov, who has assumed temporary control of Russia after the death of..."

Susan went on to describe the state of Russia who had also attempted, albeit slightly more successfully, to close its borders and quarantine the ESH virus when it had broken out in their country in late February.

"It has been confirmed that the entire royal family in Britain are dead and there is rioting in key cities throughout Europe thanks to food shortages. There are also reports from our embassies in most of the northern and western nations in Africa reporting rioting and widespread fatalities."

Susan Stryler stopped, gulped from a water glass and shoved a sandwich down her throat. Her hunger had been growing for weeks now and she understood all too well what that meant.

She continued, "The fate of one Chinese city, Guiyang, are of particular concern. If Edith Sarah Hainey is considered Patient Zero, then the city of Guiyang may very well be known as Ground Zero."

"According to the reports, which were suppressed by the Chinese government until well after the news of Hong Kong broke, the water supply of Guiyang was corrupted by an American company, EcoNu. According to the initial findings of the CDC, this company is responsible for engineering a virus that they purposely infected pigs with, and which then somehow jumped to humans. EcoNu's goal was to bioengineer a pig which grew faster, was ready for market in just under half the average time, and there are other genetic markers in it that have not been identified yet. We have our top researchers working on it now."

"The contamination of the water supply was so widespread that within a relatively short time over 65% of the population had contracted the virus within as little as a five-day window. The activation of the virus had occurred exactly 35 days after infection. In less than a week, more than three and a half million people died, violently consuming everything in sight. The reports detailed that not a single plant, household pet, bird or even the entrenched rat population remained. Trees were cleared of leaves and bark, stores emptied of every last item, the shelves barren."

"And now the city of Guiyang is a smoking, radioactive hole in the ground," Gary Chen added, "Whatever the rest of the world might have hoped to learn from what seems to be the origin of the ESH virus, we are left with nothing. Damn it!"

He gulped down a handful of grapes that had just arrived, barely chewing them.

"So where do we stand?" Gary asked, as Susan stopped to wipe a spot of blood from the tablet. "How is this compared to other pandemics in the past?"

Susan looked up at him, "Mr. President, the world had seen some truly terrifying illnesses and disease. In recorded history we have seen the bubonic plague which decimated Europe's population by at least one-third. In World

War I, a strain of flu that primarily affected the young and healthy, led to more deaths than from actual combat. The AIDS epidemic killed over 52 million people over the course of nearly sixty years until its cure in 2039. And in the early 21st century, a series of diseases, including SARS, avian flu, Ebola and the Zika virus all had their turn."

She took a breath. "The ESH virus, however, has outperformed them all. In terms of mortality and communicability, it has eclipsed all the others that came before. We are looking at over one billion, that's billion, not million, dead in the past four months. Entire cities have had to be abandoned because the survivors are unable to bury or even burn the sheer numbers of the dead. And the ESH virus, it isn't done. From our calculations and from the results of the daily examinations we have all participated in, nearly every single individual in our government has already been exposed. We are dying sir, and there is no cure."

There was silence then. Those remaining in the room digested the facts that had been presented. Madeline watched it all and thought, *for years, man had looked out into space for an extinction-level event in the form of meteors or wayward asteroids, only to wake up and find it firmly in their midst.*

During the lengthy reports, two separate requests for food, and their corresponding deliveries had taken place. Not a single speck of food remained and Madeline noticed one of the staffers go from nibbling to fully chewing on a metal pen, denting the metal, desperate for more. There was no need to say anything, Madeline simply nodded to security and the staffer was ushered out the door. They had all had more than enough horror for one day.

"Issue the order for all domestic travel, air and ground, to be suspended and a full quarantine in place within our borders," Gary said, wiping away the crumbs from the small stack of sandwiches he had eaten.

"Also send a communiqué to Cape Canaveral and order a full quarantine of all space stations, along with the Ptolemy Colony on the Moon and Huygens Outpost on Mars."

He reached for Madeline's hand, and she smiled at him hoping to reassure him with her touch, "I want to meet again tonight with a full report from the CDC. We need to catch a break on this, folks, any kind of a break," he paused and smiled weakly, "After all, it's an election year coming up and I plan on being re-elected."

Two more staff succumbed before evening and President Gary Chen, the first Chinese-American president in the history of the United States, lasted three more days.

He died at four in the morning after desperately consuming the entire contents of their medicine cabinet, ingesting everything from cold medicine to three months' worth of anti-depressants in one go.

"You will list his cause of death as an accidental fall," Madeline insisted. This was close enough to the truth, after all. While convulsing on the overdose of medication, Gary Chen had repeatedly slammed his skull on the polished marble floor of the Presidential suite. Nearly his entire cabinet had preceded him in death.

At six a.m. on June 18th, 2099, Madeline Chen née Burnett took the Presidential Oath of Office. She would be the last American president.

The Center Cannot Hold

"Turning and turning in the widening gyre, the falcon cannot hear the falconer; things fall apart; the center cannot hold; mere anarchy is loosed upon the world." – W.B. Yeats

Date: 06.16.2099

Earth – Kansas City, Missouri

The line into the terminal at KCMI seemed to stretch into the distance without any discernible end. Eleanor Ridley-Briggs craned her neck, but could see nothing but a sea of backs and heads.

"Any idea what is going on up there, miss?" A short, elderly woman stood in line behind her.

Eleanor shook her head, "Sorry, I can't see a thing except more people."

The old woman sighed. "All of our technological advances, but we still end up in long lines. Well, I might as well get comfortable."

She perched on the side of her suitcase, which didn't look comfortable at all. She smiled up at Eleanor. "So where are you heading off to, my dear?"

Eleanor couldn't help but smile in return, "I'm actually heading back to Arizona now. I came for my grandparent's 50th wedding anniversary." She sighed, "I love it here. It has been a wonderful week; I hate to leave."

The old woman nodded, "This is home, isn't it?"

"Yes, I guess it is."

"Born and raised?"

"Yes, down in Belton."

The old woman perked up. "I *knew* you looked familiar. You are Mary Ridley's daughter, aren't you?"

"Yes, I am. And you are?"

"Becka Aaronson-Finley," she chirped, shaking Eleanor's hand with a surprisingly strong grip. "Your mother was one of my first students. Of course, she was Mary Jones at the time. I had just earned my teaching degree and she was in my fourth-grade class."

"Wow, and you remember her?"

"She was hard to forget." The cryptic response aroused Eleanor's curiosity. But before she could ask more, Becka began to pepper her with questions.

"So, you live in Arizona?"

"Yes, Flagstaff."

"Do you like it?" The old woman's eyes were a beautiful light blue, her hair still black in places where it hadn't turned gray.

"Not really." Eleanor heard the words come out of her mouth and was surprised. She hadn't really thought of it; the response had just been instant. "I guess I miss spring the most. And the landscape, it is just so barren and empty compared to here."

Becka nodded. "I feel the same way, I really do." She sighed, "I was blessed with three lovely children, and my husband and I moved to southern California for a few years, but I just couldn't enjoy it. It was so dry. I missed my plants and garden so much that we moved back and never left again."

"I promised my husband I would give it a try. We moved there two years ago and are both professors at Northern Arizona University."

"You are a professor as well!" The old woman laughed, "That I would not have expected from Mary Ridley's daughter."

Now Eleanor found herself very curious, but before she could ask for details, there was a wave of chatter moving down the line. In its wake was a team of airport personnel with a small machine on wheels. Eleanor couldn't quite see what they were doing, but the people in front of her were repeating what they had heard from the people ahead of them.

A blond, statuesque woman in front of Eleanor asked the man at her side, "But, *why* would they need to take our temperatures?"

"That weird virus, the one that the scientist, and several others, died from, they all had fevers. Almost undetectable, just slightly above normal. Jesus, I wonder if they will stop everyone with a body temp above 98.6 from getting on the plane."

He looked around concerned, leaned in and whispered to his wife, "Drink more of the ice water, babe, I don't want to miss visiting the new Disney-Pixar theme park!"

"If I drink any more water, Harold, I'll have to pee." The woman pointed to the restrooms in the distance, "And they are making anyone who leaves their place in line go to the *end* of the line."

The two began to bicker, voices rising.

"What's happening?" Becka asked, tugging on Eleanor's sleeve.

"It looks like they are taking everyone's temperatures."

Becka nodded and shrugged, "Well, I guess we will just visit a while longer while they get around to taking ours. So, your husband, tell me about him."

"Andy? Well, let's see. We met in college and married soon after we graduated. He spent most of his childhood moving from one city or town to another, all across the country. He really loves Flagstaff."

"And he hopes you will too?"

Eleanor nodded ruefully, "He hopes, but I guess I just miss home. Even walking the sidewalks reminds me of how different it is. In the winter they use a fine gravel to add traction through the snow. It remains year-round and walking on it reminds me of nails on a chalkboard. And none of my mother's bread or cake recipes work right due to the high elevation."

Becka shook her head, "It sounds dreadful."

"I shouldn't complain," Eleanor said, looking embarrassed, "It just isn't home. I'm never reminded of that more as when I come back for a visit."

"I will be visiting my youngest son, if they ever let us board the plane." The old woman smiled, "I have a new grandson to meet."

"Why congratulations!"

"Congratulate me after I survive the trip. I'm not terribly fond of this daughter-in-law, I'm afraid."

Eleanor managed a rueful expression, "I'm pretty darn sure that my husband's mother feels the same about me."

"It looks like we should have an answer soon," Becka said, gesturing towards the front of the line.

A small cart was drawing closer, a thermometer and digital readout prominently displayed. Behind it, the line split to the left and increased sharply, while those few who were directed to the right-hand side quickly disappeared into the distance.

Could all of the people on the left be sick? How widespread was this virus?

The blond, and her husband, were both shuttled to the left. And then it was Eleanor's turn.

The airline attendant placed the thermometer covered in a disposable sheath in Eleanor's mouth. A short three seconds passed and the machine beeped.

"Ninety-eight point four," the attendant read aloud. "Are there any more in your party?"

Eleanor shook her head, "No."

"Please move ahead to the right-hand lane and continue to your gate."

Eleanor paused long enough to call over her shoulder to Becka, "Best of luck!"

"Thank you dear, best of luck to you! And tell your mother hello, I'm sure she remembers me well!"

She may have passed the screening, but in the end, Eleanor never made it off the tarmac. She sat in a plane that was three-quarters empty for nearly two hours before the pilot updated her and the other passengers.

"Ladies and gentlemen, we apologize for the delays. We have received word from Air Control that all commercial travel has been suspended at this time. I am sure that this is a short-term measure, but for now we are being ordered to ground all domestic and international flights. This is a state of emergency issued by President Chen himself. Please retrieve your belongings and exit the plane in an orderly fashion after the plane has returned to the terminal."

Before the captain had even finished speaking, phones flashed, and a low drone of voices could be heard throughout the cabin. Eleanor sighed and called Andy first, leaving a message. He was probably finishing up his class right about now.

"Hi honey, they grounded all flights. I'll call you when I get back home with my parents."

Then she dialed her parents.

"Dad, they've grounded all flights. I'm sorry to make you drive all the way back, but..."

"Don't worry about it, honey, we are close. Your mother was starving, so we stopped for a bite to eat. I can be there in ten minutes. Just look for us outside the terminal entrance."

Her dad's voice was reassuring and Eleanor smiled at the thought of spending a few more days with them. After all, the state of emergency wouldn't last long and she was pretty sure she had detected a bit of relief in her dad's voice. He missed her more than he would admit.

A few minutes after she called, their car inched into sight, easily pulling into a parking spot as passengers from other flights streamed towards the light rail hub or filled the last of the autocar rentals, desperate to find room at local hotels.

During the car ride back, Dad said nothing and turned the radio to the local news while Mom, sat beside him, chewing her fingernails and systematically swallowing them, as they all listened in silence to the broadcast, which was simple, short, and terrifying.

"President Gary Chen of the Reformed United States of America, in conjunction with the CDC, has declared a state of emergency and instituted a travel ban effective immediately. The ESH virus is highly contagious. Return to your homes, all urban areas are now under quarantine. If you are traveling or away from home, you need to report to the nearest refugee camp for intake and health assessment."

The message repeated every thirty seconds on all channels.

Eleanor couldn't stop thinking about the hundreds of scared faces in the airport. *What was going to happen to all of them?*

Normally the trip from the airport to Belton took around 40 minutes. Instead of sliding through traffic at the posted 65 miles per hour, the Ridley's found themselves inching along, minutes turning into hours, and the highway slowly narrowing to one lane, as they moved into a phalanx of tanks and armed soldiers.

The Richards-Gebaur Air Reserve Station, closed at the turn of the past century, had been revamped in the past thirty years and turned into a visitor's center along with a small unit of active service members.

"Reminds me of Grandpa's stories of the Collapse," Dad remarked, as they crawled along. "Getting the military involved," he let out a troubled *whoof* of air. "This isn't good, not at all."

The car inched by one scene of mayhem, a motorist flailing and resisting several soldiers, yelling that his rights were being violated as he was dragged from a car, his wife and children screaming in panic.

Eleanor's fear mounted. Any moment now their car would be stopped and their identity chips scanned. Would they pull her screaming out of the car as well? Her home address was in Flagstaff, Arizona now, not Belton, Missouri. What if they decided she couldn't stay?

As if in answer to her fears, her dad spoke, "You aren't going to any camp, Sweetie, you are going home with us."

At the exit for Belton, another group of soldiers stopped her parents' car. Eleanor was certain that this was it, they would surely stop her and insist she be placed in one of the quarantine zones. Thankfully, one of the soldiers was a familiar face.

A boy she had gone to school with, she couldn't remember his name, but he smiled when he saw her, "Ellie Ridley! I haven't seen you in ages!"

Eleanor managed a weak smile back and tried desperately to remember his name, seeing his face so clearly in her memories, backlit against lockers and hallways. *Chemistry class, perhaps?* There was no time to figure it out.

The car behind them began to race its engine and honk, the driver clearly irate, and her classmate turned soldier waved their car on, intent on dealing with the troublemaker behind the Ridley's car. Eleanor and her parents were soon safely back home.

In the days and weeks to come, the entire area, including Belton, was full of violence and fear. The virus spread like wildfire, driving its victims to a state of unreasonable hunger, devoid of any calming influence. Food stores dwindled and tempers flared. By the fifth day, a full panic ensued as all of the nearby grocery stores ran out of provisions. By the end of the second week, it wasn't safe, inside or out.

Each day, she had checked in with Andy. The first week he was in fine spirits, but obviously missing her. The second week saw an ominous change, not just in Eleanor's immediate surroundings, but hundreds of miles away.

"I'm pretty sure I've got the virus, Ellie," Andy's voice sounded tense. "I'm so damned hungry I don't know what to do with myself and the stores are running low, real low."

All summer classes had been canceled, and he was home, alone and going stir crazy. "I swear to God; the gravel is starting to look tasty."

"Could you take an autocar, instead of the plane?" Eleanor said, desperate to get her husband out of there.

"Babe, they overrode the autocar controls, no one can leave town, not in an autocar at least. I'm stuck."

A week later the phone calls had stopped. There was no answer on his end, no matter what time of day she called.

Eleanor's mother was the first in the family to succumb to the virus. The radio and newsvids had all begun to describe it in careful detail - the elevated temperature, increased appetite, and in the end, an uncontrollable frenzy of eating. Eleanor's mother hadn't reached the final stage, some never did according to the newsvids, and it was possible she would be spared.

Eleanor and her father both saw the signs, but neither of them knew what to do, or even what to say, as Mary cooked bigger and bigger meals, eating more and more as each day passed. The pantry, usually packed overly full, brimming with usual staples of canned goods, snack foods, and all of the ingredients Mary used for her favorite baked items was slowly becoming more and more desolate.

And on June 23rd, at 1:05 a.m., Eleanor was jolted out of an uneasy sleep by the sound of her father screaming for her. Eleanor sprinted down the hall, blinded by the lights in the master bathroom, highlighting the gruesome scene.

Her father, dressed in his briefs, was desperately trying to peel a bottle of drain cleaner from Mary Ridley's spasming hands. Her body contorted, vomiting blood while still trying desperately to consume more. Blood, drain cleaner, spurted across the tiny room, splashing her father with caustic red froth, burning his bare legs as he screamed in horror. Eleanor rushed to help her father, to help him stop her mother from consuming the drain cleaner. She too felt the spray of the caustic liquid, across her face and forearms. It was far too late for Mary Ridley, however. Her death warrant had been signed the moment the virus entered her body.

Eleanor's father, a dapper man in his mid-sixties, would linger for just two weeks longer, severe burns on his arms and legs from the drain cleaner, bent and broken.

A mask of silence had descended after he watched his wife convulse to death on the floor of the home they had shared for over three decades. Eleanor, whose arms had also been splattered and burned by the drain cleaner, was one of the "lucky" few. She survived while her grandparents,

parents, and most of the family and friends she had known all of her life died within weeks.

It was there in her parents' house, stuck in quarantine, that she received the call.

"I'm so sorry, Ellie, so very sorry. It took me a while to find your phone number. I finally thought to check his phone for recent calls." Libby Johnson was their neighbor to the south.

Eleanor had said nothing, holding the phone, the unreality of it all made her feel as if the ground itself would begin to shift and crumble. Andy had been thirty-one years old and the picture of health. How had this happened? How was it even remotely possible?

"How?"

Libby stammered back, "H-h-how? It was the virus, Ellie. He, well, oh Ellie, you don't want to hear how. It was, it was the virus."

"How did he die, Libby?" Eleanor needed to know. "Was it food, or something else?"

She could hear Libby sniffle, "Oh Ellie, please don't..."

"Tell me, please."

"They think it was the pine needles that did it, Ellie. That's where they found him, there in the back and with the pine needles in his mouth. B-b-but they aren't doing autopsies anymore so it isn't for sure. There are just too many dead to be able to examine them all. They just..."

Libby's voice continued, her words blurring together. Eventually Eleanor just pushed End and cut off Libby's words.

Andy was dead. Mom was dead, and Dad was declining every day. In the past two days they had had to barricade the doors and windows. Well, she had. Dad just sat there, aging before her eyes. He hadn't moved, hadn't spoken, as Eleanor had hammered boards in place to hold off the hunger-maddened virus victims as they desperately searched for food.

Yesterday one had almost gotten in. He had been middle-aged, his hair receding, his face damp with sweat. He had tried to tear the boards off of a window before finally giving up, sitting down and beginning to eat grass. Hours later he had walked away erratically, obviously in pain, before finally collapsing at the end of the street.

Despite her close contact with her parents and friends and neighbors, Eleanor's temperature never rose above 98.6. She never felt the virus activate inside her. Instead, she would carry a spray of scars, an angry red for the first few months before they quieted to a silver-gray scar tissue, on her face and forearms, for the rest of her life - her mother's last moments painted indelibly on her skin.

Death by Monopoly

"We live at a moment when our relationships to each other and to all other beings with whom we share this planet, are up for grabs." – Carl Sagan

Date: 06.19.2099

Earth – Oak Grove, South Carolina

"When the world ends, what do you do?' Peter Satler wrote in his journal. It was an old-fashioned affair, made of paper, bound with leather, and a pocket on the inside held a slim pen. His wife, God rest her soul, had teased him endlessly about it, calling him a Luddite.

He missed Gina. Her absence was still a raw, gaping hole in his heart. He sat for a moment in silence, then continued to write, *"The newsvids are showing people in the cities wearing white surgical masks over their mouths. Just a touch, an errant breath on the wind, or a drop of sweat can spread the virus. It is cutting into our world, doubling down, sliding through families, communities and workplaces, leaving waves of death in its wake. Will it come for me and my children next?"*

"Dad? Have you seen my phone?" Peter's youngest daughter Taylor asked.

Peter closed his eyes, of course she would miss it - it had been a birthday present just a month earlier.

His stomach gurgled audibly, but he smiled brightly at his daughter, "Hi Sweetheart, are you ready for breakfast?"

"I'm starving, but..."

"Great let's fix some pancakes then."

Taylor eyes lit up, "With chocolate chips?"

"Sure thing."

Half an hour later, Bree had appeared from her room, her hair a tangled mess. "Dad, have you seen my tablet? It was on my desk the last time I saw it."

Peter sighed. Soon, Addison would wake as well. He was outnumbered and alone, but after listening to the newsvid last night, long after the girls had fallen asleep, he knew he had to do something. He had rounded up every electronic device in the house, dumped it all in a bucket and poured bleach and water over it. The wallvid was too large for that, so he had taken it out back and used a hammer. Not a single electronic device used for communication or entertainment remained in the Satler house.

"Come eat some pancakes, Bree honey, we made them with chocolate chips."

They ate in silence, ravenous, and Peter felt that the food barely touched their hunger, he could hear the girls' stomachs grumbling for more. As he mixed up a new batch, Peter emptied the last of the chocolate chips into the batter.

Outside, the world was warm and sunny with deceptively blue skies. It was perfect weather for the end of the world. The news of a mysterious virus had spread quickly in the past few months.

Addison arrived then, her spiked short hair unkempt, the smell of the pancakes having woken the teenager from her deep slumber.

"Pancakes? I'm starving!" She dug into a stack with gusto, focused entirely on shoveling the sweet treat in her mouth.

At first, news of the killer virus had been accompanied by skepticism, even morbid fascination - a virus that caused you to eat everything in sight until your stomach gave way? It sounded impossible, especially after several experts, all board-certified physicians, had explained that the body has several ways of preventing a person from overeating – discomfort for one and even if someone had managed to eat far more than their stomach could digest, they would simply toss their cookies and be done with it.

"Addy, have you seen my phone?" Taylor asked.

"No," Addison paused around a large mouthful of food, "Have you already lost it?"

Taylor bristled and Peter stepped in quickly, "Forget phones and tablets, girls, and give your dad a few hours of one-on-one time."

Bree rolled her eyes at Addison, "You know she lost it; she's like a little kid. Always setting things down and forgetting them."

"I didn't set it down," Taylor screeched, "I'm not some stupid baby!"

"Yes, you are, and now you're whining like some stupid baby."

"Girls!" Their argument momentarily silenced, Peter slapped more pancakes down on their plates. "We will play Monopoly and eat popcorn today."

His three daughters stared at him.

The thirty-five-day incubation rate had fallen to twenty-seven days, then twenty-three days and then the really crazy, scary stories started coming out. A coroner who had performed an autopsy on an EMT drank formaldehyde, instigating a particularly hideous death. This was the biggest piece of news until his stash of kiddie porn was revealed. That occupied the news for a day or two until it was replaced with a police chief who died after eating a large portion of his collection of antique coins.

Peter Satler had, after hearing that disturbing update, insisted that everyone remain inside away from possible contagions or dangers. The family could hear gunfire and sirens coming from the center of their small South Carolina town a few miles away. Peter had lived in New York for most of his childhood. There were always sirens or traffic or people yelling there. Cities, with their higher populations compacted into small spaces were rife with it - there was no escaping that fact.

But a town of 15,000? It was rare to hear a siren more than a handful of times each year. When the two grocery stores in town had closed their doors, unable to get deliveries due to the current travel ban, a formerly friendly, easygoing town had suddenly become a rather frightening place.

They had plenty of food at the house. Gina, Peter's wife, had been quite the do-it-yourself type. She had cajoled Peter into buying a house in the country, with acreage no less, and turned a dyed-in-the-wool city boy into a gentleman farmer cum cattle rancher. They had a small herd, just twenty-five head, and treated the creatures more like pets than food. Gina, who had grown up on a farm, had planted a large garden plot, raising all manner of crops and spent weeks canning each summer.

"We don't need to worry about anything except toilet paper, Sweetheart," she had told him, her round, tanned face smiling up at him.

And they hadn't, she had cooked better than any meal made in a restaurant and was the cornerstone of her family's existence.

That is, until the world had gone crazy. Soon after the stores closed, a virus-addled lunatic had smashed through the front gate on his all-terrain vehicle, running Gina Satler over and killing her instantly as she worked in her garden.

Addison, Taylor and Bree were still staring at him. "I'm not kidding girls, go get the Monopoly board."

It had been three days since the funeral. By now, he had grown accustomed to his daughters alternating between sobbing and screaming, or doing both at the same time. Take teenage hormones, add a dose of "Sorry kid, some asshole ran over your mother," and factor in the world going to shit with some crazy virus that will kill everyone. Take all of that, mix it around, and you have hysteria, mania and more.

He herded them all into the family room and pulled out the board, "We are going to play Monopoly."

"Now?" Bree looked rather shocked as if it had no place in this house of sadness.

"Yes, now." Peter's tone brooked no argument.

His stomach churned, "Addison, will you pop some popcorn for us?"

He began organizing the Monopoly board, placing the cards on Community Chest and Chance, before moving to the real estate section.

"And Taylor honey, you can be banker."

Taylor had recently delved into official teenage status with her 13th birthday nearly a month before, although Gina had remarked several times in the past year that Taylor had the teenage angst part down pat by the age of ten.

After the popcorn had been popped, the tokens chosen, and the game begun, the Satler family were happily distracted for hours. They were distracted enough not to realize that they had eaten all of the popcorn, along with two quarts of homemade salsa and the last two bags of tortilla chips. After that, another run to the refrigerator cleaned them out of hot dogs, an enormous jar of pickles, and two stacks of fresh tortillas.

They had been running low fevers and had elevated appetites for several weeks before the anchor of their family had perished in her beloved garden. The virus had slowly crept into them, and in the waning hours of the day with the sun long sunk past the horizon, the virus activated fully. The Satler family, already staggering from the loss of a beloved mother and wife were squarely in the eye of the hurricane.

Bree, the oldest, a few weeks shy of seventeen, screamed in frustration as her piece landed on Park Place, which had a bright red hotel sitting on it, a property owned by Addison. Bree and Addison were often in competition, and the game of Monopoly was only one example of how fierce the competition between the two girls, born just eleven months apart, could be. Her stomach was twisting in hunger, interfering with basic addition as she struggled to count out the $1,500, she owed to her sister.

Addison, who had scraped her bowl of popcorn clean of salt, seasonings and even the un-popped kernels of corn, eyed the money greedily. As her sister handed over the money, Addison's thoughts did not appear to be focused on the game. Maybe just a bite or two would help this awful hunger she felt.

As it slid down her throat, she gagged a little, the paper bunching against the back of her esophagus, sticking to the skin. She swallowed it down, reached over to her side, where the bank sat between her and Taylor and grabbed a fistful more. Taylor yelled for her to stop, but Addison ignored her, clearing out the $500 and the $100 slots before Taylor covered the rest with her hands.

Peter, in his own virus-induced fog, ignored them both as he tried to cram several sharp-edged houses and hotels down his throat. They hurt, a lot, but he was so *hungry*. It was a deep, grinding hunger. It wasn't something to be ignored, or dismissed. In fact, it never occurred to any of the virus victims to fight it, even if they could think past the immediacy of it, past the demands of the disease which promised to kill them.

As the two girls squabbled over the Monopoly money, eating their spoils, Bree eyed the squares of real estate, grabbing first one, then another, stuffing the hard, stiff paperboard into her mouth, the corners of it stabbing into her cheeks and gums, and then into her throat as she swallowed them down.

It wouldn't take long for the Satler family to down the remainder of the Monopoly game, slowed only by the board itself, which was too large to swallow whole and resistant to tearing teeth.

Major Tom

"This is the first age that's ever paid much attention to the future, which is a little ironic since we may not have one." – Arthur C. Clarke

Date: 06.21.2099

Juniper Supply Ship

"Can you hear me, Major Tom? Can you hear me, Major Tom? Can...you...hear...me?"

Amy's voice was clear over the Comm in his quarters. Captain Thomas Sydan rolled his eyes, how many times had he heard that joke? That damned old song always came up when he did a run with new crewmembers.

He couldn't help but smile at the thought of the voluptuous, and oh so attractive Amy Jenkins, even if she was spouting corny old worn-out jokes. She was Pacific Islander, with a voluptuous, impossibly tan body. Who could look at a woman like that and ever want some skinny chick again?

"Captain?" Amy's concerned voice came over the comm.

"Major Tom here, Amy, what can I do for you?"

He could almost hear her relief over the comm.

"Mathers is on Communications, Cap. He says he has a TP from the PLC, Captain's eyes only."

Amy's hair was jet black and she kept it long but braided. He had to resist the urge to tug on it when he passed her in the corridors. They had met two weeks ago, a good week before departure from the Ptolemy Lunar Colony, and hit it off instantly. This was Amy's first run to Mars on the Juniper and his second. The crews were constantly changing, especially now with all of the craziness going on down on good ole Terra Firma.

"You copy Captain?"

Less than a week ago, a state of emergency had been announced in the Reformed United States. By then, Tom had left the Chinese mainland heading for *Gan De*, the old international space station orbiting Earth, and then on to *Ptolemy Lunar Colony* a few days later.

He hit the comm link on his uniform.

"I'll be there in half a tic. Save me a seat in the galley, I'm starving."

The Juniper had left the colony yesterday, embarking on the long voyage to Mars.

The reports had been frightening, citing everything from isolated reports of cannibalism to a virulent form of pica. That one had been especially bad, although no one was knocking cannibalism, there had only been two reports of that, compared to the crazy pica on steroids that had killed at least 3,000 victims in the past three weeks.

"Will do, Cap!" Amy sounded chipper, back to her old self.

Tom's stomach rumbled. He had put on a few pounds and, despite the extra workouts he had been packing in, he wasn't losing them and he felt hungry all the time. *Keep this up, old boy, and they will retire you under the Roly Poly clause.*

There actually was a strict weight requirement, not that he was anywhere near being in danger of being in violation of it. Still, as the captain of the ship he needed to set a good example.

The first manned trip to Mars in 2066 had included bourbon shots at one-week intervals, beginning with the day of departure. That had set the tone for all missions that followed. Astronauts, much like sailors of old, were a superstitious lot. It wasn't discussed, and a blind eye was turned when a bottle was smuggled on board. Even now the bourbon shots served as a tip of the hat to spaghetti westerns and the "olden days" when men were men and women were scarce.

Last night, warmed by the bourbon, Amy had teased Tom into a lively debate over the necessity of knowing how to fly and land a spaceship so easily controlled by computer automation. At one point, she had put her hand on his. The sparks had been there, sizzling between them, distracted only by a particularly bad joke being told by one of the other crewmembers, something involving a battery and a bar.

Perhaps he could figure out a way to invite her to his cabin after shift. He slipped on his ship shoes and headed for the command center.

A few minutes later, and despite the growling of his cavernous maw of a stomach, Captain Tom Sydan read the transmission packet.

TRANSMISSION PACKET

PLC TO JSS

/BEGIN TRANSMISSION

QUARANTINE ON EARTH HAS FAILED. HUNDREDS OF THOUSANDS DEAD, MILLIONS INFECTED. QUARANTINE CAME TOO LATE – PLC AND GAN DE SPACE STATION ALSO SHOWING SIGNS OF ILLNESS.

SPECULATION THAT INCUBATION PERIOD OF THE VIRUS IS MUCH LONGER THAN INITIALLY THOUGHT AND THAT QUARANTINE HAS BEEN INEFFECTIVE. LOW-GRADE FEVER AND ELEVATED HUNGER ARE THE ONLY SYMPTOMS OF INFECTION. NO OTHER WARNING SIGNS UNTIL VIRUS ACTIVATES. DEATH AFTER ACTIVATION OCCURS WITHIN 24-48 HOURS. VIRUS 99% INFECTIOUS, 99% MORTALITY RATE. GOD BE WITH YOU.

/END TRANSMISSION

Death after activation occurs within 24-48 hours.

Those words continued to scroll through his brain, even after he closed his eyes.

Low-grade fever, hunger.

Now he understood the increased appetite.

The spot in the galley seat, with the voluptuous Amy Jenkins, was forgotten.

"Cap?" Mathers was looking at him with mounting concern.

He had known Adam Mathers for over a year now. The man had a family back on Earth, two young kids. He had told Tom about them, adding that he was going to request Earth-side assignments after this.

"A year is too damned long time to be away from your children, no matter how good the pay is, Cap." Adam had said as they watched the Moon rapidly dwindle in size in their viewports.

Tom had agreed. When and if he ever settled down, he would trade in his wings for tickle fights and a steady nine to five. Kids needed both parents.

"Get Sick Bay on the comm, Adam, tell them to suit up and prepare for full decontamination and isolation protocols. Stat."

He resisted the urge to touch his skin, or anywhere else.

Virus is 99% infectious. God, Amy had touched his hand last night!

"Tell them I'm infected, share the transmission with them. I'm transferring command of the ship to you until Max is on deck."

"Wait, Captain, wait!" Adam scanned the transmission, terror on his face. "We were all in that room with you together."

As Tom turned to leave, Adam reached out and grabbed his arm.

"*Tom!* If you are infected, so are we. We shared that shot glass. 99% infection rate? Shit. We all have it by now. Hell, maybe we already did."

There were eight crew members on the ship. And within minutes, it was confirmed. All of them were registering low-grade fevers ranging between 37.3 and 37.4 degrees Celsius. It wasn't high enough to even be considered a fever for most. Something one would barely think twice about. They all confirmed elevated levels of appetite, some for more than two weeks.

Hours later, Tom looked around at his crew filling the galley. Yesterday they had toasted to a safe flight through the darkness of space, and now, they were receiving reports from the Earth and the Moon filled with ever-increasing doom and gloom. The group was solemn, quiet, and they were all looking at him for guidance.

The follow-up transmissions, arriving within minutes after they had confirmed the presence of the ESH virus, were grim. This was a death sentence.

In the cargo holds below decks were 30 Mars colonists. Eight families, with children, in Cryo. They had been in Cryo since leaving Earth nearly six weeks ago. Before things had gone to hell, before anyone knew just how bad this virus was.

Tom stared at the people he would spend the last days of his life with. Amy, Adam, the others.

How long did they have, really? Days? Weeks? Or mere hours? His stomach clenched in hunger.

"I've been feeling hungry for days," remarked Matt, one of the lab techs, "Maybe more than a week now."

"Perhaps we should turn back?" Brett asked, he was barely out of his teens but a stellar navigator. This was his second mission to Mars.

Adam Mathers spoke up, his face haggard, "There's no going back. We have it, all of us, they would never risk us landing and possibly infecting people who have escaped the virus so far."

Amy put her face in her hands, "And we can't risk infecting Mars."

"Mars is dead if we don't bring them their supplies," added a short blonde.

Tom's brain felt full of sludge, but he finally remembered her name was Sarah. She took care of the ship's environmental systems.

"Mars is dead no matter what. Where are they gonna get any more supplies?"

The kid was speaking again. His eyes were swollen and his skin was blotchy. Then again, most everyone had had a crying jag by now, or it was imminent.

"We take this day by day," Tom said, "keep communicating with Earth and the Moon and learn as much as we can. Mathers, you'll collect the reports, give them to me, and we will have a meeting for all hands at 1800 hours each day."

He paused and made eye contact with each of them in turn.

"We need to stay the course of this. There might be some treatment, some alternatives we aren't aware of quite yet. Hang in there, everyone. Stay strong."

Later, alone in his cabin, Tom thought of the last message he had sent his sister Sam. The transmission packet was a year or more away from being delivered since the ship was currently in warp, shifting between the seams of space, pushing the barriers, there and not there.

He had been accepted for the Kepler mission, excited about the green light he had received to make a trip to another star system like his little sister was doing at this very moment. It wouldn't have been the same, it couldn't be, the Kepler system was over 1,400 light years away. The ship was being built in orbit around Earth now and was three times the size of Calypso.

The plan had been to fill it with nearly 1,000 colonists and crewmembers. Operating with a skeleton crew and self-automated, it would make the trip in just under 50 years although, for most, little or no time would pass at all.

He would never see it. None of them would. He knew it, deep within his soul, that there was no escape clause from this particular problem. Further transmissions from Earth had revealed that their greatest fears had been realized. The ESH virus was complicated, infectious, and viciously lethal.

Tom was a walking dead man, as was every other member of his crew. The only thing they could hope for was a relatively swift death.

If the poor souls in Cryo were very, very lucky they would not be infected with the virus. The ship would land, on auto-pilot, long after they were all dead. If they were able to keep themselves contained on the crew deck, the Mars colony could safely retrieve the colonists and the supplies from the floors below.

His wall comm beeped, indicating someone on the other side. He opened it, not at all surprised to see her. He didn't say a word, simply took her hand and pulled her gently inside.

"Cap?"

"Just Tom."

She managed a small smile, "Major Tom?

He smiled back, "No, just Tom." And then he kissed her.

And two weeks after that...

TRANSMISSION PACKET

JSS TO MHO

/BEGIN TRANSMISSION

CREW INFECTED WITH ESH VIRUS. INITIATED QUARANTINE ON DAY 9 OF MISSION AND RESTRICTING CREW TO CREW DECK. LOCKING DOWN REMAINING DECKS. FIVE DEAD, THREE WORSENING. MAY GOD HAVE MERCY ON OUR SOULS

/END TRANSMISSION

Six weeks and three days later, the Juniper supply ship landed without incident at Huygens Outpost. The transmissions from the crew had ceased entirely three weeks earlier.

Two fully suited colonists entered the lower levels of the ship, and over the next two weeks, working in stages with two other teams, unloaded the vessel of all the needed supplies and then revived the 30 Mars colonists, taking readings of each before bringing them inside of the colony.

Then they programmed the computers remotely to send the ship back into space on a short journey, one just long enough to turn around and send back to Mars. The thrusters set it on a collision course for the far side of the red planet, at full thrust, and the resulting explosion ensured that they had removed all danger of contagion.

G581: THE DEPARTURE

The transmission packet was deployed to Terran Planetary Command the following day.

TRANSMISSION PACKET

MHO TO TPC

/BEGIN TRANSMISSION

CONFIRM ARRIVAL OF JSS. ALL HANDS LOST. RETRIEVAL OF CRYO OCCUPANTS COMPLETE. ALL ADVISED QUARANTINE PROCEDURES FOLLOWED. NO EVIDENCE OF VIRUS FOUND IN MARS COLONISTS. JSS DESTROYED

/END TRANSMISSION

Time to Run

"There is just a thin veneer of civilization on our society. What is underneath is not pretty, and it does not take much to peel away the veneer." – James Wesley

Date: 07.12.2099

Earth – Boston, Massachusetts

The cracks and explosions outside were not fireworks. The children didn't understand this and whined in turns.

"Mom, you *promised*." Liam's whine was annoying, but it did little to stir Lila Mathers as she sat on the hard-plastic kitchen chair in Grace Whitley's kitchen. The transmission had come through last week, right before a solar storm interrupted all further communication.

TRANSMISSION PACKET

JSS TO EMC

/BEGIN TRANSMISSION

CONFIRMATION OF CONTAGION ON BOARD SHIP. ALL HANDS INFECTED WITH ESH VIRUS. INITIATING ISOLATION PROTOCOL TO PROTECT COLONISTS IN CRYO. PERSONAL MESSAGES FROM CREW TO FAMILY TO FOLLOW

/END TRANSMISSION

The personal messages had never arrived. The solar storm had seen to that. And now, as the Juniper Supply Ship moved farther from Earth, irrevocably far from efficient communications range, Lila's world was falling apart.

First travel restrictions, then quarantine, and now martial law had been declared. This in itself was terrifying and brought back the recounted stories of The Collapse, when the United States had crumbled into a civil war that had taken more than two decades to recover from.

"Mom..." Simon, just two years older than his brother knew better, but that didn't seem to stop him. He was pulling on Lila's arm. "You promised to take us to see the fireworks!"

Grace Whitley rescued Lila from her sons, recognizing the vacant look in the young mother's eyes.

"Boys! Listen to me. Those aren't the nice kind of fireworks. They are the bad kind, dangerous ones. They canceled the 4th of July this year because everyone has been getting sick. We can't go outside right now; we have to stay here."

She glanced nervously at her husband TJ, who was on his fourth glass of scotch and looking pissed. He glared at the boys, muttering under his breath. How much more could he drink? When would he blow his top? Grace worried that she had made a terrible mistake bringing Lila and the kids into the house, but what could she do? Lila was practically catatonic.

Yesterday Grace had called Lila for an update. The phone had rung until Simon's young voice had answered.

"Hello?"

"Simon? Grace asked, "Simon, this is Miss Grace. Are you okay? Is your mama there?"

"Yeah, but she won't talk to us. She just sits there and cries."

All of Grace's motherly alarms had sounded. "Simon, it will be okay. I'm coming over."

She had requested a car, biting her nails as the autocar slowly navigated the three short blocks to Lila's house. The street was filled with chaotic scenes, people running, a house on fire, and several bodies lying in the streets.

It had taken several minutes to convince the boys to open the door, but once inside Grace had just stared in shock.

"Oh my."

Simon and Liam were both dressed in pajamas and their hair was greasy and stiff.

"I tried to cook us something 'cause Mama just sits there, but I made a mess."

A mess was an understatement. The house had looked like a war zone. In their attempts to stay fed they had melted one plastic dish to the stove top, filled the sink full of filthy, stinking dishes, and eradicated the cereal and pasta supplies.

"What is that smell?" Grace asked as she caught a whiff from the hall.

"Liam clogged the toilet. I *told* him he was using too much toilet paper!"

Grace held her nose and headed for Lila's bedroom. The boys' mother looked like a ghost, hair dank and snarled, dressed in pajamas so filthy that they could probably stand up on their own.

"Oh honey."

Lila looked up at Grace and her mouth crumpled, "He's gone, Grace. He's gone and I don't...I can't..." Her voice trailed off as tears welled up in her eyes, tracing a pathway down her gaunt face.

Grace pulled the young woman into a hug, "Okay sweetie, it's going to be okay. Let's get you and the boys cleaned up, okay? And then you can come stay with us for a while."

Grace had guided her young friend into a shower, ordered the boys into a bathtub, packed a few changes of clothes and ushered them into the car an hour later.

TJ had been furious of course.

"We have our own problems, Grace."

Yes, she thought, *it starts with the fact that you don't give a damn for anyone except yourself.* It wouldn't have mattered if they were rich as kings, he would have used those very words. Having him home, restricted by the travel ban hadn't helped. She felt herself wondering *why* she had ever stayed with him after he had lost yet another job due to his surly, negative behavior. She should have sent him packing. He treated her worse than a dog, spoke to her like she was the hired help, and couldn't even be kind to their daughter.

"It's just until this blows over, TJ, they don't have anyone else and Lila is devastated," Grace tried to explain.

She was doing her best to stay calm, but the world had become a rather frightening place. This morning, she had tried to go out and buy some groceries, but there had been checkpoints, troops dressed in full riot gear with megaphones announcing that martial law was in place and that everyone was to return to their homes. No travel permitted. The stores had all been closed anyway. She had learned that after the fact upon returning home and listening to the newsvids.

That was also when she had heard the first gunshots. But they weren't the last. Through the morning and now in the late afternoon, the sounds of gunshots and other explosions had continued to pepper the air. They had drawn the curtains and forbidden the children from going outside, not even in the backyard after the newsvids had warned everyone to stay in their homes.

Lila Mathers just sat in the kitchen, unmoving, white-faced and in shock. Grace couldn't get her to eat and TJ just kept drinking and muttering whenever she walked by.

"They aren't family, Grace."

"We have to think of ourselves."

"This virus, we can't be taking in others, who knows if they are carriers or not."

He had been nose-deep in *The Examiner* for weeks, reading the quasi-journalistic, hate-mongering site with regularity, posting comments, and parroting every hateful thing the reporters wrote. *The Examiner* specialized in spreading fear and isolationism and Grace had been disgusted at the headlines, which blamed the victims, suggesting the mystery virus was merely an excuse for greed or some such nonsense. When the meager facts were not enough, the news agency often resorted to blatant lies.

Grace had spent months trying to be patient and kind with TJ, rationalizing his latest job loss away. Her own work as a researcher had been put on hold, just so that TJ wouldn't feel emasculated as he pursued his career and told her daily how important he was. And now, with the world crumbling around their ears, Grace had had more than enough.

"You should tell them to leave, Grace."

"Why don't *you* leave, TJ," Grace said, seething.

"What?" he looked at her in shock. She had always taken it, the snide remarks, even the cutting ones, and said nothing. This Grace was a new bird, someone unfamiliar.

"She is all alone TJ, and I won't hear another word on how we have our own problems or need to take care of our own."

She picked up the bottle of scotch, it still had two inches of amber liquid sloshing about in the bottom of it.

"What the hell?" TJ yelled as she marched into the kitchen and dumped the remaining scotch down the drain.

"What the hell is wrong with you?"

Grace whirled on him, "What is wrong with *me,* TJ? Well, let's see. You are here. That's one thing wrong. And then there is the world gone to shit around us. That's two. I should be working right now, trying to *help* figure this virus out, that's three. But instead, I'm here listening to your selfish bullshit."

She would have continued, but at that moment, her phone rang. Grace marched over to the table and picked it up.

The voice on the other end sounded rather gruff, "Dr. Wilkes?"

She had kept her maiden name, making sure it was on the certificate when she earned her doctorate, something that had raised the ire of TJ enough that she had considered having it amended and re-issued. Common sense had prevailed, however, and eventually, he had stopped sniping at her about it and how he had put her through medical school. He hadn't, but revisionist history was his forte.

"Yes, this is Dr. Wilkes."

Her voice was clear, strong and *loud.* TJ's face pinched in anger.

"Dr. Wilkes, Dr. Allen Lagunoff speaking. Dr. Brooks suggested I contact you."

Grace smiled for the first time in weeks. Janelle Brooks had been her mentor during her residency and was also the godmother of their daughter, Karen. She had made no bones of her opinion of TJ, calling him a pretentious ass on several occasions, once to his face. Grace shook her head, she had lost touch with Janelle a few years back after TJ had blown his top and smacked her, blackening her left eye. Janelle had offered to take Grace and Karen in if they needed a break. She should have taken her up on it. Instead, Grace had tried to save her marriage, convinced that Karen would be better off with her father in the picture rather than out of it.

"What can I do for you Dr. Lagunoff?"

The man did not beat around the bush, "We are putting together a group of researchers in a secure location to study the ESH virus, for both short-term response as well as examining its long-term effects. Since Dr. Brooks personally requested you, Dr. Wilkes, I hope you would be willing to join our team."

"Here in Massachusetts?" She asked.

There was a small pause, "No, the location is in Pennsylvania."

"I can't leave my family, and we have several people here with us, a young family that depends on us, that I can't just abandon."

"We are prepared to take everyone, Dr. Wilkes, as long as you all pass screening and are not positive for the virus, we can evac you with a military unit that is near you."

"How near?"

"They are approaching your front door now." Dr. Lagunoff said, and simultaneously there was a loud knock.

Grace jumped.

The next hour was a flurry of activity. First the lone man in an isolation suit at their door who took everyone's temperatures and collected and ran blood tests. TJ looked rebellious, muttered and grumbled, but submitted to their tests. Lila just stared listlessly at Grace when she tried to explain what was happening.

A few nerve-wracking moments followed while they waited for the results. Miraculously they were all clean. Between Karen being in school and TJ's business travel, their exposure had been normal to high, but none of them showed the markers for the ESH virus. Granted, the test was pretty new. It had been in use for all of two weeks now, but there hadn't been any progress of *stopping* the virus, only *detecting* it.

The kids and Lila had been taken out and put into a large autocar. A crowd was growing. There were plenty of scared people, and the soldiers represented help and security. But they couldn't help everyone, and the people that were stopped just a few houses away by the barricades would not stay still for long. The stores were empty, no travel meant no new food supplies, and the soldiers were eager to get moving before things turned ugly.

The one in charge turned to Grace, "We have to go. *Now*."

Grace went back inside with one to fetch TJ, who was still sulking in the family room, ensconced in his easy chair and growing more belligerent.

TJ flatly refused to be bundled into the autocar.

"They haven't even said where they are taking us," his words slurred, and Grace wondered where he kept the other bottle hidden, "This isn't some goddamn police state, Grace."

Grace didn't have any patience left. Why hadn't she left him years ago?

"Janelle is there, she wouldn't steer us wrong. It's a chance to stop this thing, and to keep Karen safe, along with Lila and the boys. We're going." She began to walk towards the front door, turned around and glared at him, "Stay if you want."

His look of disbelief, of shock, that she wasn't buckling under his will as she normally did, was evident on his face.

On the heels of the shock came anger, "You are not taking our daughter into some disease-ridden place!" He staggered up from his seat and lurched towards them.

The uniformed soldiers instantly reacted, one pulled Grace behind him, and the other aimed his gun straight at TJ. She had to do something, no matter how much of a shit her husband was, he didn't deserve to die here. And she certainly didn't want the soldier to shoot him, not here, not with his child just footsteps away.

"TJ, it's time to leave this place." She stared at him, willing him to see reason, "It's time to run. It isn't safe here anymore."

Now that he was standing, she could see that the other liquor bottle had been hidden in a pocket of the easy chair. More scotch, and, at least, five fingers down on a full bottle. He stared at her; bloodshot eyes full of something indescribable.

Perhaps it was his upbringing, full of at least two generations of angry, alcoholic, *mean* men. Perhaps it was an epiphany, standing there, realizing he wasn't ever going to be the man she deserved, or perhaps he was too drunk to even listen to reason.

TJ slowly turned his back on her, went back to the easy chair, sat down and pulled out the bottle. He swiveled in the chair, turned on the vidscreen with the remote, and ignored her.

"We have to go, ma'am."

"Right."

And they left then without a further word. Karen asked only once about her dad. And when Grace told her TJ had needed to stay at home for a while, the child actually looked relieved.

The autocar now loaded, turned and moved from the growing crowd into the gathering darkness.

How the World Ends

"All the evidence shows that God was actually quite a gambler, and the universe is a great casino, where dice are thrown, and roulette wheels spin on every occasion." – Stephen Hawking

Date: 08.17.2099

Earth – Seattle, Washington

He was all alone. And he was hungry, cold, and scared.

The line advanced slowly, sometimes it unraveled, jostled, and he often lost his place. He was small, one of the few remaining children that had been put on long yellow school buses and driven for what felt like days to the middle of nowhere.

Dad was dead. Mom was dead. *I guess that means the baby she had been growing inside of her was dead too.*

Toby scratched his head, it itched constantly and had for weeks now. He could feel the hard bumps of the lice on his hair. He dimly remembered a lice outbreak at his school when he was six, and they had immediately told all parents to treat their children, so it hadn't been bad. Some weird smelling stuff in his hair, a thorough combing and inspection and it was done. This, however, was far, far worse. His scalp crawled. His hair, now long and unkempt, was greasy and lank.

Another jostle in line. He caught an elbow in his chest and fell in the mud this time. The scab on his knee from an earlier scrap over bread opened up and the blood began to flow. He didn't cry, it didn't do any good to cry here. *Crying was for babies,* the older ones had taunted him, and he had enough to measure up to, his small size a mark against his survival in this harsh place.

He wasn't prepared for the soft, warm hand on his arm or the woman who had left her position leading a group of scientists to give him aid. He had seen them as they walked through the camp, a small group of clean white coats. They were the only clean thing here. Even the people running the camp wore stained and dirty clothes and looked worn out.

She helped lift Toby back on his feet and her bright green eyes stared at him, taking in his ragged appearance.

Years later, watching her across the table, he would wonder why he, of all those lost and frightened souls, had made her stop. Why him? Perhaps it had been fate that had drawn her to him on that day.

"Sweetie?" her hand gently raising him up out of the mud, taking in the bruises, the hollow circles under his eyes, and the knee now running with blood, "Are you okay?"

His eyes had flickered with surprise, some shock. No one had been kind, no one had really even noticed him since he was ushered onto a bus and taken away from the only home he had ever known. The weeks had passed, maybe longer, since anyone had held him, loved him, and told him it would be okay.

"I... I'm fine."

His voice betrayed him, cracking a little. He wasn't fine. Not at all.

"My name is Julie Aaronson, what's yours?"

"Toby Medry."

The camp director nudged her elbow, "Dr. Aaronson if we could just..."

"Yes, yes," Julie answered, looking distracted, "just as soon as we can patch this young man up."

"Of course, I'll have one of the staff take him to the First Aid tent," the director responded, signaling to a nearby staff member.

Her hand relaxed for a moment, almost letting go.

Later, years later, she said, "It would have been so easy to let you go. Certainly, that is what the staff there would have preferred. Besides, what did I really know about children? My brother Michael, he would have known. He had *five*, which seemed like an impossibly large number to me. I had simply never felt the urge to have kids. Until you came along, I was fairly certain I had been born an adult."

She hadn't let go. Instead, she reached down and took his hand, "No, I can take a moment to get this young man looked at."

Just a moment turned into an hour, the rest of the medical delegation left to be shown around by a flustered camp director while Julie saw to Toby's scrapes and bruises.

"Oh dear," Julie said, taking a close look at his hair. "That must itch terribly!"

Toby nodded.

"Well, I'm afraid we are going to have to cut it off, Toby. It's the quickest way to treat it, and I've been told they are out of the medicated shampoo. But don't worry, I'll find a handsome hat for you to wear if your head gets cold."

She pressed the stethoscope to his bare chest, listened to his heart, lungs, and checked his eyes, ears and throat.

"Well, Mr. Medry, I can see you haven't been eating enough and you look like you are dehydrated as well. Let's see if we can't get you fed and after that, you need a bath and some clean clothes. I'm going to make sure you get all the care you need."

Julie Aaronson stood up and beckoned to one of the camp workers.

Toby didn't want her to leave. It had been weeks since he had heard a kind word, felt a warm hand that wasn't pushing or shoving him around. The doctor was old, she had gray hair that was close-cropped and there were lines and wrinkles around her mouth and eyes, and in that moment, the thought of her leaving was overwhelming and terrifying.

He grabbed her coat sleeve, "Please..." he said, unable to put his emotions into words. It was all too much and he was so afraid, so lonely.

Julie turned back to him, her expression kind and concerned as she saw the desperation on Toby's face.

"Toby, do you want to stay with me? Is that what you need?"

He couldn't bring himself to speak. It was as if speaking it out loud would break open the dam and all of pain and loneliness he had held in since Mom and Dad had died would just burst out and never stop. Toby simply nodded, his eyes begging for her help.

Julie stared back, her green eyes glistening. She turned to the waiting worker, "I will be taking this one with me to my lab. We have room for him there."

Later that evening, when he had been fed, bathed, deloused, and Julie had found him the smallest set of scrubs she could and then rolled up the legs and arms, she had asked about his family.

"Dad died first, and then Mom. She was going to have a baby." Toby said, fighting back tears. "I'm not a baby, so I shouldn't cry."

"It's okay to cry, Toby. When your parents die, it isn't a weakness to grieve." Julie hugged the boy awkwardly. "Don't ever feel bad about that."

"I'm nine now, I think. My birthday is August 7th, so I shouldn't cry. Babies cry."

"Well, that's just silly. I'm sixty-nine, so I'm no spring chicken, and I still cry. Never be afraid to show who you are, it is what makes you special." She showed him a cot set up in the corner of an empty room. "I'll be right next door if you need anything."

A week passed and there was no word from the refugee camp, no one demanding the boy be returned. Toby found himself watching and learning from Julie, rarely wanting to leave her side.

Two weeks after she had found him in the camp, as they sat together eating breakfast, Julie looked thoughtful, "Toby? Do you want to stay here with me for a while? I mean, if you would rather be with children your own age, I would understand."

"I like it here." Toby said quietly. Over the past two weeks he had gained weight, the dark circles under his eyes had vanished, his ribs no longer jutted out sharply, and Julie had filled his room with books, a small desk and dresser, and new clothes and shoes. "I like staying here with you, Julie."

In the months that followed, Julie allowed him to sit in a corner of her lab and gave him any books he wanted. At first, all he wanted were books on the stars, and space.

"I'm going up to space, like my Uncle Dan," Toby said at first, dreaming of boarding a spaceship that would go faster than Calypso and beat his uncle to Zarmina's World. He would land there and be standing on the ground, waiting when Uncle Dan landed.

In time, however, as Julie peered at endless samples through slides, or ran scans, Toby found himself inching closer, peering at her work. Eventually, it became more, a mentor/mentee relationship. They lived and worked together, the rest of the year passing in a blur.

Neither of them could have seen this future when Toby had first felt her hand on his. But their choices on that day were life-changing.

Two years later, Toby now eleven, stared at the reports that littered her desk.

"Julie?"

The old woman was intently studying the latest cultures from a recently infected enclave of survivors from the hills of North Carolina. The incubation rate had escalated from a long 35-day cycle to just nine days from exposure to full-blown infection. The mortality rate remained in excess of 99%.

The connection to blood type had been verified enough times to be clear, only AB negative blood types had any hope of survival. It remained to be seen if the effects of the ESH virus would mutate enough that the survivors would be able to reproduce.

"Mm, yes, Toby?"

"The terato...terato..."

"Teratogenic?" Julie supplied.

"Yeah, teratogenic. That means no more babies, right?"

Julie looked up from the microscope. "Yes and no. Nature will out, Toby. All things defy extinction, and humans are more defiant than most."

She smiled, "We are a crafty, ingenious species which has survived some pretty heavy sh...," she amended what she was about to say, "Er, stuff."

"But what if there are no more babies?" he paused, "I mean if we all have the virus, and we are all sterile, then..."

Julie gave him a sad smile, "A poet, T.S. Eliot, once wrote, 'This is the way the world ends. Not with a bang, but a whimper.'"

Toby shivered, looked at the pages full of death and despair, looked down at his hands and thought of his mom and dad, and his uncle so many billions of miles away. Julie was good to him, kind, and patient. But he missed them. He couldn't help it. There was a hole in his heart, one that could never be filled.

Julie leaned over, took his hand and looked into his eyes.

"We survive, Toby, and dream and work for a better tomorrow. It's all that we can do. It is all any of us can do."

Toby met her eyes with a resolute stare, "I'll do my part, Julie."

"I know you will, Toby. I can see it in you."

She shifted off of the stool, rubbed her neck, and beckoned him closer to the microscope, "Would you like to take a look?"

He scrambled to sit on the stool and peer through the microscope at the virus slowly turning in the solution. Julie's hand rested on his shoulder, reassuring, kind.

Toby's eyes adjusted to the microscope and he stared at the thing that had taken his parents away.

Here was death, here was the threatened end of all that he knew.

He would study it.

He would defeat it.

Mars Needs Moms

"Mars ain't the kind of place to raise your kids. In fact, it's cold as hell." – Elton John

Date: 10.02.2099

Mars – Huygens Outpost

Outside of the Habs the atmospheric generators hummed constantly, working their slow, methodical process that meant that, in a handful of centuries, humans might actually be able to step outside with only a re-breather unit on. It was something for future generations to look forward to, but even then, the air would be far too thin for anyone to survive it without some kind of oxygen booster. The hum pervaded the Hab, a constant noise source that the inhabitants, such as they were, had long since ceased to notice.

Toya didn't think on this too long, she was simply incapable of it.

An accident in the Philadelphia Hab six months after she had arrived had seen to that. An accidental equipment failure had led to the deaths of two families as well as Toya's dad, who had been sleeping off-shift, and Toya who they had managed to revive.

The then six-year-old Toya survived, but not before sustaining significant damage due to oxygen deprivation which robbed her of her native brilliance. Before the accident, Toya had been a favorite in the Philadelphia Hab, capable of speaking three languages and showing a knack for computer programming. After she had recovered physically from the experience it was clear that she would be the mental age of a five-year-old for the rest of her life.

Toya's mother Selena had avoided being sent back to Earth due to Toya's condition by marrying John Snelling, a newly arrived meteorologist who was single and had already been sleeping with her since the voyage from Mars. A few months later, Lenny was born, and Toya had become a fixture in the Hab, racing about with the other children and, in later years, on her own as her companions had grown up without her and found their place in the colony's infrastructure.

But now John and Selena were dead, as were most of everyone else. Toya and Lenny were the only ones left in the Philadelphia Hab. Toya wasn't interested in the communications room, growing bored easily, she would rather play hide and seek or racing games with Lenny. Now that everyone was gone, there was no one to tell them to not run in the hallways. No one to punish or yell. Toya liked that. As the days went by, she found herself missing the other colonists less and less.

Toya waited for Lenny to get close, then stuck out her foot, tripping him as he raced down the hallway. Mom wasn't around to give her the sharp rap on the head she was used to receiving when she messed with her baby half-brother. He was a spoiled brat anyway and deserved a thumping or two. Toya, at nearly twenty years old, was built like a tank, whereas her eleven-year-old brother was a slip of a thing. Lenny weighed just over ten kilos, compared to Toya who was pushing thirty-eight. If they had been on Earth, with full gravity, she would have tipped the scales at over eighty-six, and Lenny at a mere twenty-seven, but Mars gravity kept them both light with a gravity of around 38% of normal.

Lenny, who had been running at full-speed, tripped on Toya's outstretched foot and left the ground for a full two seconds, twisting in space before slamming, with a scream into the far door. Blood jetted from his nose and he wailed in agony. Toya felt a twinge of fear, and found herself glancing about to make sure no one had seen. She kept forgetting they were all alone, and that the Hab was empty except for her and her now bloody and crying brother.

"Sorry Lenny," Toya said, picking him up roughly. "I didn't mean to."

"Yes, you did! You did mean it!" He held his nose, trying in vain to stop the gush of blood and failing brilliantly.

"Didn't."

"You *did*, Toya!" His tears mixed with the blood and snot. He was intelligent, Mom had mentioned that regularly, which had the nasty side effect of reminding Toya of how she used to be smart, but now was stupid, stupid, *stupid*. Toya couldn't help wondering if she could keep hitting him now, and make him stupid too. No one was there to tell her "no" except

Lenny, and he didn't count, because he was just a big, big baby covered in blood and snot. She dropped him down on the floor, eliciting another scream as his shin cracked against the concrete walkway.

This downward spiral may have continued, if not for the alarm that sounded at that moment, a single klaxon blast accompanied by NARAs calm voice.

PERIMETER ALARM
ATTEMPTED UNAUTHORIZED ACCESS OF AIRLOCK B

NARA served as the communications unit between the separate Habs throughout the colony. The Habs, five in all, had been designed to function independently and the residents of the separate units were only supplied with their own password. This gave them access to their Hab alone. Travel between the separate units was allowed, and encouraged, but it was like knocking on the door of a neighbor's house, a visitor couldn't just go barging in.

Lenny's eyes grew wide and the bloody mess and pain appeared temporarily forgotten.

"Toya! Someone else is alive!"

They ran to Airlock B, which was used for supply deliveries. Toya could see a suited figure standing outside of the grimy, dust-covered window of the outer airlock. Lenny hopped up and down, boosted by Mars gravity he managed short glimpses of what stood outside.

Standing outside, surrounded by corpses, stood a tall figure.

Toya frowned, "I dunno, he's a stranger."

Lenny sighed, "Toya, he's from one of the other Habs."

Shortly after the Juniper Supply Ship had landed, the auto-pilot settling the ship without incident, the colonists had gone on board, fully suited up. Lenny's dad had been one of them.

The crew were dead, this was expected, they had sent warning weeks before, but the colonists in the Cryo pods and the supplies on the floors below the crew deck were untouched.

Everything should have been fine. Lenny didn't understand what had gone wrong.

Dad had said that they were using the most stringent quarantine protocols possible. He had even described how they did it. First, they had opened the ship to the Mars atmosphere, then scrubbed the deck down, before activating the environmental controls and resuscitating each of the new arrivals.

"Maybe, or maybe he came on a spaceship and has the virus." Toya insisted.

Lenny rolled his eyes, "Our Hab has the landing pad for ships, and we would have seen his ship land. And besides, *we* have the virus already. We just didn't die."

It had taken a few days to completely clear the hold of all the supplies and equipment, but then, in accordance with directions from Home Base, the colonists had set the spaceship on its final journey, powering it back out of the atmosphere before programming it into an impact trajectory with the far side of Mars, hundreds of klicks from any Habs or atmosphere generators. The resulting explosion was designed to ensure that no one on Mars would catch the terrifying and deadly ESH virus.

"We don't have the virus." Toya insisted, petulant. She pushed Lenny away from the airlock and the buzzer sounded.

"Hey, kid! Let me in!" The figure outside had seen them.

"Yes, we *do*, Toya. Mom and Dad got it, *we* got it, *and everyone* got it." Lenny felt desperation creeping in. His sister was strong, and she wouldn't let him near the keypad to override the lockout.

Despite all of the colonists' precautions, the moment they woke up Ted Danziger, the last colonist to exit Cryo, the Huygens Colony had sealed their fate.

Dad had said that Danziger had the virus and just didn't know it. It hadn't spiked his temperature until he left the Philadelphia Hab for the Cairo one, stopping off at Hong Kong, London, and Sydney Habs first to inspect their atmosphere generators.

Toya had that look in her eyes, one that clearly told Lenny she was determined not to let him or anyone else have their way. Never mind the cluster of corpses outside, or the suited figure who was now banging on the outside of their Hab and sounding more irritated by the minute.

"Hey, look kids. It's safe to let me in. Open the airlock!"

Huygens Outpost, which boasted a population of 250 or more souls in five Habs scattered over several acres, was stripped down to a grand total of three survivors in just under four weeks. Lenny and Toya were two of them, and the third one was apparently knocking on their door now.

"NARA!" Lenny shouted at the artificial intelligence, "Let him in! Authorization B oh nine five!"

Toya looked furious.

NARA instantly complied, initiating the airlock protocols. The lights flashed a warning as the outside airlock opened, a rush of red, dusty air swirling in, the inside window frosting up from the cold Martian air. The figure strode inside, waving one hand at the children, and pressed the button to close the outside airlock. This initiated an entirely different set of flashing lights. The internal fans roared and the glass cleared of frost as the air was replaced with the oxygen-rich warm air from the Hab.

The second sets of lights stopped flashing after a long moment and the inner airlock door opened with the push of another button, the tall figure stepping through, his suit steaming a bit, the metal still ice-cold from the outside. It took several minutes for the man inside to emerge from the bright blue and white suit. Made for easy spotting on the Martian surface the garish bright blue was an affront to the eyes so close up. The material had an iridescent quality to it, and was guaranteed to glow for at least five hours in full darkness, also an added detection benefit. There were several layers, first the hard-outer shell, then the stretchy black insulating layer, followed by the third layer, a standard issue jumpsuit. Each of the Habs wore different colors. Toya's and Lenny's were green, and the strangers was red, indicating he had come from the Hong Kong Hab.

He was tall, with a shock of blond hair that had grown out of a standard crew cut, jumping into a mess of waves and disorganized sweat-plastered curls.

The man stared at the odd scene before him. Lenny and Toya stared back.

Lenny wiped his nose with the back of his hand, suddenly embarrassed of what he must look like – blood and snot smeared on his face, his tears not fully dried. And it had been a while since he had changed his clothes or washed his face. He looked down at his jumpsuit, it was stained and the blood from his nose had dripped down and spattered the grimy fabric with drops of dark red blood.

He was used to Toya, but he could tell by the stranger's reaction that her blank, slack-jawed stare and heavyset body had been noticed.

"Welcome to Philadelphia Hab, sir." Lenny said, "I'm Leonard, but everyone calls me Lenny, and this is my sister, Toya."

He held his right hand out.

The stranger stared at Lenny's hand, startled by the kid's civility, a direct contradiction to his ragged appearance. He reached out and grasped Lenny's hand firmly, a smile flickering over his face.

"I'll be damned. And here I was certain I was the only one. I was just about to try an override code when I saw you appear at the window."

He nodded to Toya, "Good to see both of you, by God, damn good to see you. I'm Michael Nix, from the Hong Kong Hab."

Toya rolled her eyes, "Duh, we know where you are from. Hong Kong wears red, everyone knows that, even dummies like me."

Michael's head cocked to one side and he regarded Toya, taking in her slack face.

"Right, well good to meet you both. Are you two the only ones left?"

"Yes sir," Lenny answered.

Nix shook his head, "No need to 'sir' me, Lenny. I'm fine with you calling me Nix, or even Mike. Just don't call me late for dinner!" He laughed alone at that.

Toya appeared to be growing bored with the discussion. She spun in circles and began to hum.

Nix stared at Toya for a moment before turning back to Lenny.

"You look like you have had a bad morning, kid, what say you get cleaned up and we scrounge up some lunch? You game?"

"Yes, sir, I mean, um, sure Mike." Lenny brushed at the already drying blood on his face, smearing it worse. "But we can't get into the Mess Hall food supply, so we don't have much food left."

Nix grinned, "Bet you're glad I showed up then. I've got codes to all the Mess Hall storage rooms. Before everything went to hell, I did the supply runs to each of the Habs in between growing the crops over in the Hong Kong Hab."

They stopped outside of the nearest bathroom so Lenny could clean up, and Toya twirled in place as they waited.

"Are you a nice guy or a mean guy?" Toya asked Nix.

"What do you mean?"

"Are you gonna let me run and dance or yell at me to stop?"

Nix laughed, "I don't much care either way to tell you the truth."

Toya spun away from them both, humming to herself.

He cocked his head at Lenny, "So, has she always been this way?"

"She nearly died when she was six," Lenny wiped the last of the blood from his nose with a wet towel, "Oxygen deprivation in one of the family Hab spokes."

The Habs were laid out in rings, with the central ring the common areas and the outermost rings the individual living sections, each family had its own spoke and section of a rim exclusively for their own use.

"Yeah," added Toya, "It made me stupid. I used to be smart." She said it with an edge of self-satisfied importance.

"I see."

Nix led the way down the corridor away from the airlock, turning right at an intersection of corridors and continuing down it before stopping at a locked door for Food Storage. He swiped his wrist over the code reader to the left of the door and the door lock disengaged.

"What did I tell you?" He said, winking at Toya. "Easy as pie. Now let's see where we stand."

He grabbed three bags of chips, tossed one to Lenny and another to Toya and lifted the supply tablet off of the wall. Each of the items on the shelves were tagged with RFID chips and the sensors recognized and removed the item from inventory when it was opened. The exception to this was anything grown on location.

The tablet screen sprang to life and Nix stared at the screen while Toya and Lenny ripped into their bags and devoured the chips with gleeful abandon.

"Lenny, help me run down this list, okay?"

They took the next half hour to review the lists of supplies still on hand in the Philadelphia Hab. Nix called off the tag numbers and Lenny counted them up and called the number back, darting through the labyrinth of tall shelving, climbing up into the racks like a monkey.

Nix nodded after a while, "Looks like we are in good shape here, far better than the Hong Kong Hab. I'm guessing that's got a lot to do with the bodies outside."

Lenny nodded solemnly. "They tossed out a bunch when the virus turned on. Others went out on purpose when they learned they had it."

Nix shook his head. "Wow. Effective I guess, but, wow."

There was an awkward silence and then the man clapped his hands together.

"Well, Lady and Gent, the good news is that we won't starve. The bad news is I've got no idea *when* we will get another supply run from Earth, if ever, so we are going to ration all of the good stuff."

He looked up to see Toya grabbing a handful of the small bags.

"Uh uh, Missie, we are going to ration that stuff."

She glared at him, "You *said* you were nice."

"Nope, I never said I was nice. I *said* I didn't care about you running and dancing, and I don't. But I'll be damned if you are going to eat all our snack foods."

"I don't like him," she said in a loud whisper to her brother, "He's mean."

Lenny just shrugged at his sister and kept eating the chips.

Later that evening, after dealing with several bodies that had been stinking up the individual family Hab units, Nix cooked dinner and they ate in the living room of Lenny and Toya's family Hab unit.

"So, let's talk long-term survival. We have extensive supply caches which, if we still had 250+ people would run out really quick." Nix began.

"However, with only three, we are in decent shape. We need to get the communications array back online, and..."

"The communications array was down?" Lenny interrupted.

"Yeah, the last big sand storm took it out. For all we know, they probably think everyone is dead. So, we need to get it fixed and let Earth know we are still here. That said," Nix looked at Lenny grimly, "You need to understand that they might not come for us."

"Why not?"

"It was bad here. You saw it for yourselves. But it's even worse on Earth. They might not have the resources to send out another spaceship to us. Not now, and maybe not for *years*. We need to prepare for that."

"And me and Toya and you, we are the only ones left?"

"Yep. And I'm gonna need both of your help making sure we can survive until Earth can come for us. That means pulling out the A.R.C. embryos, growing them in the artificial wombs they have been developing, and maybe turning one of the Habs into some kind of domestic animal garden of Eden."

The Mars colony had a limited version of A.R.C., mainly ova and sperm from domestic animals. There were humans as well, but those hadn't been tested. The colony had already been poised to begin its first batch of goat embryos in artificial wombs.

"My mom promised me a cat," Toya said, speaking for the first time in hours. "I want a cat. Lenny, grow me a cat, okay?"

"Sure Toya, right after you help me transform the center section of Cairo into a grassland for the goats."

"I want a cat, not goats."

"And you will get one, right after the wombs finish growing the goats."

Toya simply glared at him.

"Will Earth come rescue us?" Lenny asked, trying to wrap his mind around this new desolate future.

Nix shrugged, "I dunno, kid."

"We could build a spaceship then and take ourselves back home." Lenny persisted.

Michael Nix sighed, "Dude, I can grow plants like nobody's business. If it likes dirt or water, we're good. But building a spaceship? That's all you kid. Go for it. It's doable, but it just ain't in my wheelhouse."

He clapped Lenny on the shoulder. "Seriously, go for it. Meanwhile, I've got some goat embryos to start a'growing."

And with that, the discussion was over. They were stuck on Mars. At least until Lenny figured out how to build and pilot a spaceship. Outside the Hab, red dust swirled slowly.

Point of No Return

"Our lifetime may be the last that will be lived out in a technological society." – Arthur C. Clarke

Date: 10.04.2099

Earth – Yatesboro, Pennsylvania

Janelle Brooks smiled reassuringly at the small girl perched on the lab stool. Karen Whitley's blue eyes stared unwaveringly back at the older woman, showing no fear, despite the needle held in the research scientist's hand. On a table to Karen's right were several vials and rubber tubing.

"I promise it will only be a pinprick," Janelle said, "It will be over quick."

"I'm okay, Mama took my blood last week, before…" the girl paused, not finishing her sentence.

"Before she died." Janelle said gently.

Karen was only six years old, but she had taken everything in the past few months in stride, so matter of fact, just as her mother would have done. The girl was mature beyond her years, but she would have to be, Karen mused, *growing up with a father like that.* Janelle briefly wondered whether TJ was still alive.

Karen sat there, watching her expectantly, and Janelle set the needle beside the rest of the supplies, picked up the tubing and fastened it around the little girl's arm.

"Can you make a fist; show me how strong you are?" Karen clenched her hand closed, the veins in her tiny arm jumping out.

"Wow, you are doing a great job, Sweetheart!" She prepped her supplies, smiled at the girl, "Do you want to close your eyes?"

"No, I wanna watch." Karen replied.

Her dark blue eyes, edged with gray, held a look of intense concentration. Janelle hadn't worked with many children, but Karen was definitely not like other kids, her demeanor was one of someone far older than six years. Her

185

curiosity so obviously fed by her mother; Karen seemed at ease with Janelle. The remaining think tank occupants were men, and Karen barely spoke to them, preferring to stay by Janelle's side. She had taken to sleeping on a cot in a corner of the lab when Janelle worked late into the night. What a pair they were, both sleeping and eating in the same room, and rarely leaving, except in each other's company.

Karen watched as Janelle inserted the needle into her arm, her eyes never wavering as her blood surged into the first, second and, finally, the third ampule.

"We have the virus, right?"

Janelle answered, "Yes, honey, we have it."

Her thoughts flitted back to a sleepless night ten weeks ago, just two weeks after she had asked Allen Lagunoff to pull Karen's mother, Grace, back into the fray. She had meant to do good, she really had. Grace was one of the best, and not just as a researcher, but as a human being. Janelle had asked for her as soon as it was obvious how widespread the virus was - if there was a chance at all that her former student and friend was alive; Janelle was determined that she stay that way. Bringing her here, along with that sad little woman Lila Mathers and her two rambunctious boys, was an easy decision. And yet it had proved disastrous. They had no idea how the virus had spread to the people seemingly safely locked inside, and they hadn't realized it had until it was too late. Janelle felt as if she had doomed them all.

Knowing that the chances of avoiding infection outside of the bunker were slim to none had done nothing to alleviate her guilt. At the very least, she should have paid for the mistake with her own life. But Janelle, along with Karen and three others, an unusually high percentage compared with the rate of infection among the general population, had contracted the virus and survived.

"But our blood might be special?" Karen asked, pulling Janelle back into the present.

"Yep." Janelle smiled at Karen, "Yours especially, love, because overall you are an extra-special kiddo."

She finished with the draw, setting each vial into the waiting tray. *It all came down to blood really*, Janelle thought as she finished filling the vials, removed the needle and pressed on the small hole with a cotton ball.

"There. All done. You are such a brave girl!" Janelle leaned down after affixing the Band-Aid and kissed the girl's arm.

She tried at every opportunity to tell her god-daughter how special she was, desperate to fill the hole that Grace's absence had made in her young life.

"Miss Janelle?"

"Yes, sweetheart?"

"Why did you never have kids? Did you want them?" Karen asked.

Janelle sighed, "Oh yes, I always wanted to have a little boy or girl. It just," she struggled with the words. *How much do you say to kids at this age?* "I guess I never found the right person to have kids with."

In reality it was the *husband* part of it that had been the problem.

Finding the right female partner had proved especially challenging, thanks to her work schedule, its isolated location, and working in a field which was dominated by men.

Besides, Janelle thought, *when you set your heart on someone unattainable, it doesn't help those already astronomically low chances of finding a suitable mate.*

In many ways, Grace asking her to be Karen's godmother had been bittersweet. Grace had never asked, but Janelle wondered if she had sensed it, how much her interest in the younger woman had been personal as well as professional. Was there a dividing line? If so, Janelle had not ever really found it. She had been attracted to Grace in all ways - intellectually, emotionally, and physically. To her chagrin, Grace had appeared strictly heterosexual, although Janelle had held out hope that if she ever left TJ, things could have changed.

"I think you would have made a good mommy, Miss Janelle." Karen said, her earnest little face peering up at the older woman.

"Really, Sweetie?" her heart skipped a beat.

"Yeah, you have the mommy kiss."

Janelle's eyes filled with tears, "The mommy kiss?"

"Yep. All mommies have the mommy kiss. My mom said it is magic and makes things feel better quicker." She nodded, "And you've got it just like Mommy did."

She hugged the girl close, "Thank you sweetheart."

She closed her eyes, felt the tears coming fast and hard.

"You miss Mommy too, don't you?" Karen's voice was muffled, her face buried in Janelle's lab coat.

"Yes, yes I do Pumpkin, more than I can say."

Things certainly had changed, but not in the way that Janelle had hoped. Two weeks after being evacuated from the house she shared with her borderline abusive and alcoholic husband, Grace had shown signs of the illness, something a blood test that she had helped perfect verified. By that time, Grace had hugged Karen, and Karen had wrestled with Liam and Simon, and the boys had touched their mother, Lila, who was still mourning her husband.

Through it all, Lila Whitley had simply sat there, unable to do much of anything, barely eating, wasting away. The virus, when it activated in her, was akin to creating a mindless zombie. She had been desperate for food then, her stick-thin arms grasping, fighting against the restraints, feverish in her need to eat. They had tried to save the woman, tried to starve the virus out of her. The results had been bloody and horrifying. Lila Mathers had died after trying to consume her own tongue and cheeks, choking on the blood. The sight of Lila's last moments would occupy Janelle's nightmares for years to come.

"Miss Janelle?"

"Yes Karen?"

"Why is my blood special and not Mama's?"

"That's a great question, Sweetie."

Janelle began to describe human blood types, sketching a quick chart for Karen to see.

"From what I can tell, all of the people who contracted the virus yet managed to survive it have AB negative blood. This includes you, me and the others here in the facility who are left."

The girl stared at the chart.

"For you to have AB negative blood, one of your parents would have to be AB. Your mother was AB positive. Now for you to be AB negative instead of AB positive like your mom, your dad must have been either AB, B or A negative."

Karen was focused on the chart, "What is this O?"

"A different blood type, but one that you can't possibly have, because O blood types come from mixing A, B or O blood types, never the AB types."

"So, if my dad has AB negative blood, he might still be alive?"

Janelle's throat closed at the idea of losing the little girl. Grace had asked Janelle to find him when she realized she was infected.

"He loves Karen, Janelle. He might be the biggest and most self-centered asshole in the world, but he does love his daughter. Please promise me that you will find him after this. You will find him for Karen, won't you?"

Janelle had promised and watched the regular reports that came in from refugee camps, scanning the lists to see if the ill-mannered jackass ever showed up on them. He hadn't. Realistically he had probably drank himself to death, but there was no way for her to find out.

"I don't know, Sweetheart. He might be. God knows I've tried to find him. But he isn't at the refugee camps and he would have been evacuated like the rest of the survivors by now, so I'm just not sure what to think."

Tears began to form in Karen's sweet blue eyes and Janelle noticed that the girl's hair hadn't been brushed today. Did children this age know to brush their own hair? She wasn't sure. She wasn't sure of anything anymore. Who was she to try to care for this little girl?

Janelle hugged her close, "I'm so sorry, sweetheart. I know you must miss your daddy."

The little girl shook her head, "I want to stay with you, Doctor Jan,"

Karen's voice was muffled, her face buried in her godmother's lab coat. "Please don't make me go back to my dad."

Part of Janelle was surprised at this request, but mostly she was consumed with grief and guilt. She had brought Grace here, asked for her help, had hoped to save her from a loveless, abusive marriage. Instead, she had managed to sign not just her death warrant, but her friend's, and her friend's children. But in her arms was the future, whatever future the human race had - a little girl who needed her, wanted her. Perhaps there was a form of redemption here, or at the very least, forgiveness.

"I'm not letting you go, Pumpkin, not for the world."

Later that evening, when Karen was curled in a ball in the corner of the lab, one small hand straying from the mound of blankets, Janelle finished the workup on the blood samples and sent her findings to the tattered remnants of the CDC.

A response from a Dr. Julie Aaronson popped up within minutes.

TRANSMISSION PACKET

SEATTLE CDC OUTPOST TO RESEARCH AUTHOR BROOKS, DR JANELLE

/BEGIN TRANSMISSION

READ YOUR PAPER ON BLOOD TYPING CONNECTION AND CONCUR. PLEASE SEND ANY AND ALL DATA YOU USED FOR A VERIFIABLE CROSS-CHECK. WE NEED TO MEET AND COLLABORATE. CURRENTLY EXPLORING FURTHER TERATOGENIC ASPECTS OF ESH VIRUS. ARE YOU INTERESTED IN MEETUP?

/END TRANSMISSION

Janelle's heart leaped. Dr. Aaronson was well-known, a legend in her field of study. She had mapped the genome and cured leukemia five years before, creating a cure that was instant and effective, saving the lives of countless people in the process.

And she wants to collaborate with me!

Janelle wasted no time responding.

TRANSMISSION PACKET

RESEARCH AUTHOR BROOKS, DR JANELLE TO SEATTLE CDC OUTPOST

/BEGIN TRANSMISSION

IT WOULD BE A PLEASURE TO MEET YOU AND I AM HONORED. ATTACHED ARE FULL MOCK-UPS OF THE BLOOD TYPING AND VIRAL INDICATORS. LOOK FORWARD TO SPEAKING WITH YOU FURTHER.

/END TRANSMISSION

Janelle Brooks clicked Send and went to check on Karen. She was sleeping fitfully, her fist clenching, her eyes moving rapidly beneath her eyelids. She looked so much like her mother. Janelle contemplated picking her up and taking her to her cot down the hall and decided against it. Instead, she spread a blanket out and joined the girl on the floor. A few moments of listening to Karen's steady breathing was all it took to lull her into half-waking dreams of working with the famed Julie Lynn Aaronson.

Janelle's original message, along with consolidated reports from various agencies and governments around the world combined and eventually found its way to World Geographic's Terran Planetary Command. Miles away, in another facility with personnel locked far away from the dying populace outside, a message packet was broadcast deep into space.

TRANSMISSION PACKET

TPC TO CCS

/BEGIN TRANSMISSION

ESH PLAGUE NOW WORLDWIDE, ALL CONTAINMENT MEASURES HAVE FAILED. MISSION PARAMETERS HAVE CHANGED. ESTABLISH A PERMANENT COLONY ON ZARMINA'S WORLD AND ACCESS A.R.C. FOR ADDITIONAL GENETIC HERITAGE. UNDER NO CIRCUMSTANCES ARE YOU TO RETURN TO EARTH

/END TRANSMISSION

Sam I Am

"What a wonderful world it is that has girls in it!" – Robert A. Heinlein

Date: 11.02.2101

Calypso Colony Ship

"Buy you a drink, Sexy Sam?" Deeks asked, a sly smile on his face.

Daniel knew Deeks was full of it. The guy was so hung up on Kit Tanner that it was almost embarrassing. Apparently, he needed to overcompensate by messing with Daniel at every opportunity. Deeks leaned against a deck support and winked at Sam. Medry gave his poker buddy a half-hearted scowl.

Sam grinned back at Deeks and winked playfully at Medry. It gave him a jolt, and a touch of encouragement. They had interacted in a limited fashion since meeting at Cape Canaveral for training before departure, moving in different areas of the ship and performing different functions, but he found her fascinating and wanted to get to know her better.

Sam shook her head at Deeks, "Sorry Deeks, I've got a full hour left on shift, and I don't dare leave this guy unattended," she said, crooking a thumb at Daniel, "you never know what he'll get up to."

As the current head of the 'Ponics Deck, Sam was in charge of producing all of the fresh fruits and vegetables aboard the spaceship.

"I am surprised he hasn't burned the 'Ponics Deck to the ground." Deeks said, grinning at Daniel.

Sam laughed, "Well, I've hidden all of the incendiary devices on the Cryo Deck. It's up to you to keep them safe, Deeks."

The food that they produced on board Calypso not only fed the crew but was also being continually tested and experimented with. Any successful new strains increased their chances at productive crops once they had achieved planetfall. There were multiple experiments going at the same time, as they tested out new species of plants that would grow in the twilight conditions of the meridian.

Recently Sam and Daniel's schedules had lined up, which had resulted in multiple encounters in the hallways, outside of the Ready Rooms, and in the Mess Hall and Entertainment Deck. And of course, with Daniel's new study schedule, that meant seeing her here in 'Ponics as well. Daniel had volunteered for additional cross-training in medical and botany.

"Tell you what Deeks, why don't you shove this squash up your..." Daniel began.

"Now, now," her hand on his arm was all it took to take his breath away, "Don't fight over me, you two."

Daniel was about ninety percent sure that Deeks was just messing with him. He was also relatively sure that Sam preferred him over Deeks. His best friend on Calypso had really cranked up the flirting since Daniel had begun getting closer to Sam, which in turn had caused him to find more excuses to spend time with her.

The latest had been the shameless excuse to study under Sam, who was stunning physically in addition to being a brilliant scientist. If challenged, Medry would have admitted that what a woman *thought* was far more important than how she *looked*, one of the many reasons he felt so at home on Calypso. He was surrounded, after all, by autodidacts, "tens of tens" who tackled new ideas and learning like couch potatoes tackled salsa and chips, with gusto and enthusiasm.

Daniel grinned, sure now that Sam was flirting with him. She was beautiful and smart, the perfect combination.

"I just can't imagine *what* you are talking about, Dr. Sydan."

Sam laughed and handed him a tray of sprouts, "You need to get back to work on those back rows, Medry. And don't forget, we still have the squash to tackle."

For the past month, Daniel had been assisting Sam as they grew a unique strain of squash along the west wall of the 'Ponics Deck. The vines hung from straps attached to the walls. Any space that could be spared was taken up with vigorous vines. There were now flower buds forming, and since they were in a spaceship and didn't particular enjoy the thought of 40,000 honey bees sharing their living space, they would have to pollinate all of the female flowers by hand to ensure fruiting occurred.

Deeks, seeing the sparks between the two, and not as dedicated to standing in Daniel's way as it may have appeared, headed for the door.

"I'll see you later, Medry."

He stopped short of leaving, turned on his heel and asked, "Hey wait, Sam, do you play poker?"

Sam's eyes lit up, "I can't say that I have much lately, but I used to play poker with my uncle." She laughed, "He would rob me blind of my holiday candy. Valentine's, Easter, Halloween, Christmas - the old man was merciless."

"Well, that's perfect! We have a group that gets together every Friday, after Third Shift, beer, and poker, in the Mess Hall. Can I count on you being there?" Deeks asked.

Currently, everyone on board Calypso was assigned rotating seven-hour work shifts, while also adhering to the twenty-four hour "day" they had left behind on Earth. The general consensus was that when they arrived at Zarmina's World, they would continue this practice since time without regular sunrise and sunset had no real boundaries. Being used to a twenty-four-hour day, and with no real reason to change in the twilight world they would occupy, it made sense to continue the practice.

Sam nodded, "I usually work out on the Recreation Deck, get in my strength training and run some laps, but I guess I could put it off until Fourth Shift or go the next morning. Yeah, sure, count me in."

Deeks clapped her on the shoulder, "Excellent, I'll see you there!"

He saluted Daniel, "See you on Friday, Medry, prepare to lose all your money, you owe me."

Considering that Daniel had lost to him last week, he could only assume that Deeks was calling a debt in for making sure that he had a chance to connect with the Sam Sydan outside of a work capacity. In which case, Daniel certainly would owe his friend big time.

The next few days flew by quickly. He was learning some basic surgical techniques from Dr. Schrader and had assisted her with two small procedures. There were two other major experiments in potatoes and mustard greens going on using a reproduction of the red dwarf star's light spectrum. It was essential to understanding how much of a reduction in viability and production they could expect once they were on-planet. The hope was that, at least for some crops, they could be grown without UV lights, to conserve resources.

The next Friday evening, Deeks, Medry, and Sam sat down in the Mess Hall with Wes Perdue and Zach Jenkins for their regular game of poker. Sam fit in with the group quickly, beating them all soundly two Fridays in a row.

"After all," she pointed out, "my uncle taught me everything I know."

It would be two more weeks after that before she mentioned she had played poker competitively, managing to pay a huge chunk of her way through college on her winnings. By that time, she had cleared most of them out of their alcohol rations, entertainment allotment, and even collected IOUs that would keep her from having to deal with cleaning duties for the next two months.

On the fifth Friday, only Daniel showed up for the regular Friday poker round. By a quarter after the start of Fourth Shift, and the rest of the guys a no-show, Sam cashed in some of her alcohol rations and treated Daniel to several schooners of beer. She had helped grow the yeast on the 'Ponics Deck and was rather proud of the hoppy ale.

"Tell me about growing up in Alaska."

Sam's face lit up. "I grew up in the smallest, backwoods Podunk town you can imagine. More than two hundred miles from Juno, it had one pre-fab building that was a combination energy station, grocery store and post office. Other than that, and one hundred families scattered over nearly fifty miles, there wasn't much of what you would call civilization."

"I've told you about Luke, now you tell me about your family."

"My family? A pack of independent oddballs, I'm surprised any of us survived childhood, we were always getting into some mess. There was this time when we were grilling steaks in our backyard..."

As she spoke of her family her face turned first wistful and then mischievous as she described growing up with four other siblings.

"So, our dog had the steak in his mouth, and the bear was chasing after Benji, trying to get the steak. My brother Tom, who was in his idiot stage at the time, is chasing both of them because, as he explained later, that had been *his* steak and he wanted it back." Sam was waving her hands in the air as she re-enacted the moment, "And all I could think of was that Dad and Mom were going to kill us for not paying attention to the grill!"

After they stopped laughing, she said, "Your turn. Tell me more about growing up in Washington. I want to hear a funny one."

Daniel thought for a minute, "There was this fishing trip we all took a couple of months before we lost my mom to cancer..."

He shook his head, "Wow, that's a downer. The cancer I mean, I..."

Sam's hand covered his. "Go on." Her eyes held his gaze.

"Mom was feeling okay, even though she had just had chemo, so we went out on a three-day fishing trip on the lake. We fished all day and didn't catch a single damn thing. So, we were pulled up on shore that night, dinner was done, and I thought, 'I'll just throw in the line one last time.' I'd had such bad luck all day and that waterdog I'd been fishing with was long-dead, but I figured I'd give it one last go."

He paused, his eyes shining at the memory. "Mom was asleep there on the cushions at the back of the boat and I tossed in the line one last time. Only just as I'm waiting and wondering why I'm not hearing the line plunk into the water; my mom jumps up screaming."

He snickered, "See, I had hooked her blouse with my fishing line and that dead, cold waterdog had slid down into her shirt and against her skin."

Sam snorted and shuddered at the thought.

"She was screaming and jumping and my dad was trying to get it loose. Meanwhile Luke and I were laughing so hard we could barely breathe. That was something, I'll tell you!"

He laughed for a moment before sobering at the thought of his mother. They had never gone fishing as a family again, and Mom had died less than two months later.

"I miss my brothers." Sam said, as if reading his mood.

"Yeah, me too. Luke and I fought like hellions when we were young, but I miss him a lot."

They were quiet for a moment, and Daniel finished the beer, tipping the flask to get the last drops out.

"I've got my own bear story," he said, reaching over to run his hand along her arm.

"Yeah?" she didn't pull away.

"Yeah, it's true. It was a *stolen* bear."

"What? Okay, now you have to tell me!"

He shook his head. "Uh uh."

"What do you mean, uh uh? That's not fair at all."

"Gotta kiss me first." He winked at her.

"Well, that will cost you another beer." Sam fired back a smile on her lips.

They flirted and edged closer to each other as the night wore on. Eventually, they found themselves walking to the Living Quarters deck, their steps slowing as they reached the beginning of the rows, unwilling to part ways just yet. Daniel found his hand reaching for Sam's, a silent question hovering on his lips.

On the Living Quarters deck, between the long rows of individual crew coffins, were couples' billets. There were twenty of them in all, tiny spaces that included a bed and a tiny band of space with built-in storage above and below the bed. The built-in storage could also be converted into a small bunk. These would only be used at the end of the journey for the families with children. It wasn't that much more room than an individual coffin but the Couples Billets served their function well for chance encounters, budding relationships, or for actual couples to live and sleep together if they were on duty at the same time. As for the rest of the billets, during the voyage, they were assigned on a "first come, first serve" basis. There were only a handful of married couples on board and while one or the other was in Cryo, the individual coffins were used, leaving as many couple billets open as possible.

They were standing in front of one now and suddenly the liquid courage he had imbibed seemed to vanish from him. A silence cleaved the air between them, Daniel looked down at Sam's slender, long fingers intertwined with his.

"Shall we take this one?" Sam asked, her voice steady, saving Daniel from some fumbled come-on.

He hadn't slept with anyone since months before they left, a record for him, one which seemed to have robbed him of his normal lady-killer charm.

Daniel nodded and they each pressed their thumbs on the touch screen. The door opened. Shared rooms, during this long voyage, were strictly for couples. The Environmental section of the ship handled setting up the couples' billets for any long-term assignments. Otherwise, it was a one-use type basis - the thumbprints would be required simultaneously anytime anyone wished to enter the billet. It minimized misuse. The individual coffins weren't the most comfortable of sleeping situations, but using them meant more room for storage modules, which were of course filled with every possible item Calypso's crew would need to survive on Zarmina's World.

Daniel and Sam stepped inside and after a moment spent securing the door and kicking off their ship shoes, they fell into each other's arms. Hours later, sated and drowsy, they held each other, nestling close, skin still slick. Sam's hair, a mass of black curls, lay spread against the shared pillow ridge.

"I was wondering if you were ever going to make a move, Medry."

Daniel laughed, "I guess I'm a bit out of practice. It's been, well, it's been since before departure for me."

His thoughts flashed to a casual hook-up in a bar, shortly before departure. She had had flaming red hair, piercing green eyes, and been quite... *athletic.*

"Anyone special?" Sam asked, her fingers drifting lazily across his chest.

"No, I guess I tend to keep it casual."

Janine's words haunted him, *"After all Daniel, you aren't really dad material. It just isn't your style."* Who was he to be in a relationship? That was for guys like Luke, or Deeks, who, despite his incessant flirting with Sam and others, had given his heart to Kit Tanner and wasn't going to let go anytime soon.

Sam's fingers paused for a second, before resuming their meandering.

"So, you've never gotten serious? About anyone?"

Daniel realized then what she was asking. Of course, she would ask, it was normal, it was expected. They were all heading for a planet devoid of other humans. And it was natural to seek someone out who might be a good match for a mate, for someone to be a potential father of her children. That was what Sam was asking.

Billions of miles away, his son was growing up without him. Toby was better off, missing him as his uncle, not knowing he was something more. *It just isn't your style.* A good father doesn't leave his child, doesn't let him be raised by someone else. A good father, even a half-assed decent one, sticks by their kid, raises them and does dad things. Daniel had closed the door on that possibility the moment he let his brother think Toby was his. He didn't deserve to be called Dad, not by Toby, not by anyone. She deserved to know that, to not be misled or pin her hopes on him. He wasn't dad material; he wasn't even a good potential partner.

"I like you, Sam," he finally said, "You are sexy and beautiful and smart. You play a mean game of poker and I really liked tonight. But uh, I'm not really into kids and I suck at relationships. I just don't want you to get the wrong idea here about us, or where we might be going."

Her fingers stopped moving. Sam sat up, her hair cascading down her shoulder, brushing soft tendrils across his arm and chest. She was so damned beautiful and he liked her, a lot, he couldn't help but want to be with her. A part of him suddenly felt sick, he had said too much. In not wanting to disappoint her, he had pushed her away. Her gray eyes searched his, it felt as if she was reading the book of his soul, understanding the secrets within, places he didn't even understand or want to go.

Her voice was steady, but her eyes showed disappointment.

"I'm really sorry to hear you say that, Daniel. I think that,"

She paused for a moment, searching for the right words.

"I don't think you're the person you have just described. But for now, I'm going to go."

Crap. "Wait, Sam, I'm sorry, I..."

Daniel searched for words to fix what he had just said because he could see he had hurt her, this amazing woman who made him laugh, challenged him mentally, and who he had just had the most amazing sex with.

"Please don't go."

She reached for her clothes, slid them on, and then leaned over and kissed him.

"You are a good man, Daniel Medry, a far better one than you might care to admit. I think you are selling yourself short, thinking that way, and I don't think this is the real you talking. But I'm going to go now."

And with that, she was gone. Daniel watched her go, his protests dying on his lips. The next morning was his day off, the following morning was business as usual. Sam treated him as she had every other day he came in 'Ponics, although she now avoided any possibility of their touching, preferring to put distance between him and her. She told the guys that she had taken on a new study series on Friday nights and couldn't make the poker games anymore. Wes and Zach both heaved a sigh of relief, but Deeks gave Daniel a steady look of disapproval that first night. He had seen them laughing in the Mess Hall and knew that something had happened between them. But neither Daniel nor Sam talked about it, no matter how much Deeks dug.

He'd blown it. It would occur to him at odd moments, a flash of memory, Sam's body next to his, the feel of her skin, soft and silky, covering the hard muscles underneath, and the intimacy they had shared. As much as he tried to tell himself that it wouldn't have worked, he couldn't help feeling a deep ache of regret.

Dark News Indeed

"For the first time, we have the power to decide the fate of our planet and ourselves...This is a time of great danger, but our species is young, and curious, and brave. It shows much promise." – Carl Sagan

Date: 01.16.2102
Calypso Colony Ship

Daniel listened to the transmission twice, then a third time. He felt lightheaded and sick to his stomach. A rushing in his ears grew until he could hear nothing else – not the quiet movements of others on the deck, nor the steady hum of the ship. This simply could not be happening; it could not be true.

There were thousands of transmissions to go through. Now that Calypso had dropped out of warp and back into normal space, the ship could now retrieve the seemingly endless transmission packets that had been sent while Calypso's drives folded space and shot past decades of space travel in just a handful of years. Soon they would fire the engines in reverse, similar to how airplanes performed at the beginning of the century, using them to slow the massive ship and eventually slow them enough to place them in an orbit around their new home.

Daniel and his counterpart, Kevin Edmonds, who still looked as if he were suffering from the side effects of his long stasis in Cryo, were tasked with the handling of the high-priority messages. These were messages encrypted and sent from Mission Control, not just any run-of-the-mill "urgent" transmission from someone's grandmother.

Daniel pulled the headset off his head as it began to repeat a fourth time, twisting the thin wire in his hands. Beside him, Kevin was typing furiously. Daniel leaned over to read the words on the screen. It was the newest research on the subject of genetic alterations of beets. He remembered Sam mentioning it when he helped her out in 'Ponics. Several teams of scientists back on Earth had been working on the problem. They were trying to hybridize plants to grow in the limited spectrum of light a red dwarf star would provide.

Kevin was completely absorbed in the transmission he was transcribing. It ended a few minutes later and he looked up, took in Daniel's white, shocked expression, and immediately hit stop.

"You okay, son?"

Daniel just stared for a moment. The only thing he could feel was his stomach and it was threatening to hurl the contents of his breakfast, black coffee and toast, at any moment. He shook his head. He could not find the words.

Mystified, Kevin pulled the headset from Daniel's limp fingers, slid it over his head and hit the Replay button. Daniel watched as the older man's eyes widened and his face slowly drained of color. Kevin played it again, and then a third time, just as Daniel had. Finally, he slipped the headset off and handed it back.

He sat there for a minute, not saying anything, slowly digesting what he had heard.

"It can't be right," He said finally, "What's the date on that?"

Daniel found his voice, it sounded abnormally calm.

"October 24th, 2099."

Kevin shook his head, "That's what, thirteen months after departure, so that makes it, how long ago? Christ, Cryo fried my brain, what year is it now?"

"It's 2102, so just over two years ago."

"But that transmission, it said it had been, what, eight months or so since the initial outbreak? It couldn't possibly have spread that quickly."

He ran his hand through his hair. It was jet black with a heavy sprinkling of gray.

"We can't take this to the Captain without further details. We need to get all of the transmissions regarding this first."

Daniel nodded, his head spinning as the message replayed word for word in his memory.

"ESH plague now worldwide. All containment measures have failed. Mission parameters have changed. Establish a permanent colony on Zarmina's

World and access A.R.C. for additional genetic heritage. Under no circumstances is Calypso's crew to return to Earth."

Every man and woman on board had been fully briefed before shipping out. The chances of something going wrong, the possibility of never returning to Earth, had been discussed. Somehow, it had all seemed like such a remote possibility. The Moon and Mars outposts were going strong, and while Gliese 581 was considerably farther away, the technological advances had made even a 20.3 light year trip a reasonable, if involved, accomplishment. Every person on board knew they had a choice to stay and establish a colony, or return if the planet proved more than they could handle.

"Under no circumstances is Calypso's crew to return to Earth."

Reality, at least, a small piece of the many that would follow in the next few days, slammed into Daniel. They were on a one-way trip to an unknown, and possibly uninhabitable, planet.

A tiny, almost hysterical giggle rose in him then. Kevin looked over at him and arched one eyebrow.

"I was thinking about that joke about breakfast and sitting down to bacon and eggs. The hen was *involved* in supplying the eggs, but the pig was *dedicated*. I guess, I guess we're dedicated now too."

Daniel laughed again. It sounded hollow.

Kevin said nothing, pulled his own headset over his ears and entered a string of words into the search engine.

"Let's pull up all messages that match this search and divvy them up. When we have a clear picture of what happened, we will bring this to Captain Aaronson and the rest of the crew."

That had been 1015. The two men worked through lunch and well into the afternoon before stopping. Several times they had switched headsets so that the other could hear a particularly important set of details. Through it all, Kevin's mouth had tightened, lines appearing on his face, and both men's faces growing grimmer with each new development. It was now 1645, Daniel's ears pulsed, his stomach twisted in knots. His mouth was dry and his eyes red and bloodshot. Kevin looked just as bad. They both finished with their individual transmissions and slid the headphones off.

Kevin buried his face in his hands, his words muffled, "I need a drink, some food, and we need to talk to the Captain."

"We are only up to late 2099," Daniel objected, "perhaps things turned around."

Kevin snorted, "Turned around? Turned around? Christ on a stick, son, there's no turning around from *that*." He looked ill, his skin gray with exhaustion. "I have an ex-wife, a grown daughter, both back on Earth."

Daniel was quiet, thinking of Luke, Janine and Toby.

"Neither of them would talk to me after, well, after the marriage ended and I met Jack. I tried to say goodbye to my daughter before we, when we were..." He shook his head, "I'm sorry. You don't need to hear this. All of us left someone behind, and this is just, it's too much."

Daniel nodded, he felt the same way, "We uh, we need to take this to the Captain."

"Yeah, we do."

We Need to Talk

"To get anywhere, or even live a long time, a man has to guess, and guess right, over and over again, without enough data for a logical answer." –– Robert A. Heinlein

Date: 01.16.2102
Calypso Colony Ship

Daniel and Kevin emerged from Communications at 1645 hours and headed straight for the Command Deck. It wasn't far, just the other side of the same level. The captain maintained an open-door policy for all crew. There were only a handful on duty – a total of twenty-three currently on shift in total. The ship ran 24 hours a day, although Shift One from 0100 to 0800 and Shift Four from 1900 to 0200 were only minimally staffed.

Captain Aaronson was dictating the daily log, and looking over the digital reports from the half-dozen techs. Until Daniel and Kevin walked in, it had been a routine day, with only a slight mold issue reported on the 'Ponics Deck that was affecting the broccoli production. He nodded to the two Techs and motioned for them to sit as he finished the last part of his log. A moment later he was done. He toggled a button on the headset and turned towards them.

"Medry, Edmonds, what can I do for you?"

Kevin nodded to Daniel, "You found it..."

Daniel took a deep breath, "Sir, Edmonds and I have spent the past eight hours reviewing transmissions, and, I don't know how to say this any better sir, but there has been a Level Five extinction event on Earth."

The captain's face turned grim, "Level *Five?*"

"Yes, sir, a virus. They refer to it as ESH and it has spread world-wide and also affected the space stations, Moon, and Mars colonies. All space stations and both colonies appear to have completely ceased transmissions."

The Captain sat there for a moment, saying nothing.

"And Earth?"

"The virus was infectious through even limited contact. Initially there was an extremely long incubation period, thirty-five days or more, allowing for maximum transmission among the population. Over time the virus seems to have mutated and the incubation period has lessened to approximately eighteen days. The virus attacks the hypothalamus, in the lateral nucleus to be exact, and the affected literally eat themselves to death."

The captain rubbed his forehead, closed his eyes for a moment, and then asked, "The mortality rate?"

"The reports vary, but we are seeing averages of over ninety-nine percent."

"*Ninety-nine percent?*"

"Yes sir."

Captain Aaronson stared at Medry and Edmonds, both looked pale, sick.

"Due to the long incubation period, the virus was widespread before anyone knew what was happening." Medry added as he looked back down at his tablet, "Patient Zero is listed here as Dr. Edith Sarah Hainey. Also, there are reports of a large-scale simultaneous outbreak in the Ghizhou Province in China. As best as I can tell from the reports, the virus began there.

There were some earlier theories that it was possibly a variant of the VOS-MRSA mutation, a holdover from when we still used antibiotics. But those theories were apparently disproved. Also, there seems to be some kind of link as far as blood type. We are seeing reports stating that the only surviving population are the ones who carry AB negative blood."

The captain looked ill. The lines on his face deepened.

Daniel continued, "The incubation period also includes what they refer to as a 'whiteout period', where the infected is relatively asymptomatic yet infectious as hell. Originally it may have been as long as thirty-five days that a patient was infectious, yet asymptomatic. That led to widespread infection and by the time the CDC understood the situation, containment was impossible."

He stared at the captain, "Sir, they are ordering us to *not* return to Earth under any circumstances. I'll send you a synopsis of what we have learned."

Daniel tapped Send on his tablet and the captain's tablet pinged.

Captain Aaronson picked up the tablet and paged through the documents, silent. After a long moment, the captain said, "Say nothing, not to anyone. Collect all of the transmissions regarding this ESH virus and consolidate them for me in one main report. How long will this take?"

Kevin looked at Daniel, who shrugged, "We have a lot of data to go through. I'll create a search string, have the computer isolate all transmissions containing 'plague' or 'ESH,' and then we can follow the updates, consolidate them and give you at least a basic report by 1900 hours."

The captain nodded, "Do it. I want a full blackout on any communications packets until we fully understand what we are looking at. If anyone questions you on the communications blackout tell them that you are working on a project that I have requested. I'll handle any further questions from here."

He paused, "Let's hope things turned around."

Daniel nodded woodenly, "Yes sir, let's hope."

Kevin and Daniel got to work, and at 2100 hours, two hours past what Daniel had promised, they presented the full report to Captain Aaronson.

In all, the population of Earth had suffered such devastation that it would take decades if not centuries to recover from it. The ESH virus had infected over 99.95% of the population. The remaining fraction of the population had managed to successfully isolate themselves in remote enclaves, and violently resisted any contact with the infected. In cases where it had been thought safe and non-infected and infected had come into contact, the results were devastating. The uninfected contracted the virus and died within weeks. The virus had mutated, reducing the incubation rate from 45 days to less than two weeks. The mortality rate had not dropped, however, and remained a staggering 99%.

Another detail had revealed itself. Every single one of the survivors were of a specific, and rare, blood type, Type AB negative, which was present in only one percent of Caucasians, 0.3% of African Americans, 0.2% of Hispanics, and just 0.1% of all Asians. Overall, less than 0.4% of the world's population remained, just 14.5 million.

Daniel pointed to one report dated August 5th, 2100, noting the name of the researcher - Dr. Julie L. Aaronson.

He asked, "Do you know her, sir?"

Fenton nodded, "She's my aunt, my father's twin sister."

"Well, she's the author of a paper that is pointing toward early signs of possible complications with infection from the ESH virus." Daniel said, "As if the virus wasn't lethal enough, it has some early indications of teratogenic effects as well. It is causing high numbers of spontaneous abortions and miscarriages in humans.

He read further, "It also appears to be affecting the few remaining simian species who have also been hit hard by the virus. It indicated a possibility for high rates of infertility in the surviving population."

Captain Aaronson sat immobile, realizing the broad-reaching aspects of the disease that had ravaged Earth while he had sailed away into the darkest reaches of space. Their species faced extinction on its home world. At this very moment, lost in the darkness of space, Calypso held what might be the only population of plague-free humans left of a tiny blue planet known as Earth.

The next morning, the captain called a general assembly and solemnly reported the news from Earth for all of the crew currently on duty.

"We have been tasked to create a new colony on Zarmina's World, far from the dangers of this devastating virus," he told the stunned crew.

"We knew the possibility of returning home was small, but now we are certain. There will be no return to Earth. To do so would be to face certain infection and staggering loss of life. We are on our own, folks. And it seems that the fate of the human race rests in our hands."

The meeting devolved into a quiet panic, along with tears and anger. There were even calls for the ship to be turned around, an impossibility given their current trajectory. In time, the meeting ended, and the crew dispersed slowly through the ship.

Sam Sydan pulled at Daniel's sleeve. They had maintained a fully professional interaction since that one night together the year before. She had kept her distance, likely unwilling to get her heart entangled with someone who obviously was not ready to settle down.

"Daniel......"

He looked at her, his eyes burned with exhaustion, his head pounded.

"Could you keep an eye out? For a message from my brother Tom? He was captaining a supply ship on the Moon to Mars route when I left."

He nodded, "I'll keep an eye out. All of the crewmembers last names have been flagged, we will disburse the data on family as soon as we find it."

Her hand slipped up to his shoulder, reassuring and kind.

"Are you all right?"

Daniel considered her for a moment. He had only seen her in passing over the past few months. Their shifts had not coincided and she had distanced herself in a friendly yet professional way. She was looking for a future partner, not just a fun tumble in the sack. Daniel couldn't help but see her for what she was, an amazing, sexy, and smart woman. And at that moment he felt so vulnerable, in such raw pain at the thought of everyone left behind, lost in the chaos of the virus. Very possibly everyone he knew and loved, dead.

"No, I'm not." He said simply, pulling her close, "I don't think any of us are."

No News is Good News?

Date: 02.11.2102
Calypso Colony Ship

"My God, listen to this one. It is dated April 3rd, 2099." Kevin said, shaking his head. He had been tasked with presenting a coherent timeline of events to the Captain. He had slowly begun sifting through directed transmissions, those intended specifically for Calypso, and indirect transmissions, news, internet chatter and more that Earth beamed out into space in dizzying waves of information.

"It reads like some goddamn sci-fi novel but it is definitely related...

Medical Examiner's Gruesome Suicide Rocks Kansas City

This past Friday marked the most recent episode in a series of odd deaths in the Kansas City area. The body of a county Medical Examiner was found inside the morgue by a co-worker reporting for work at 9 AM. Dale Otterman, employed for over five years by the county, was found unresponsive and pronounced dead at the scene. While the cause of death has yet to be confirmed, investigators found a half-full drink bottle nearby that contained trace amounts of Formalin, a 10 % solution of Formaldehyde. The solution is readily available and used at the morgue for preserving tissue. "Otterman would have known that ingesting Formalin would be fatal", stated an investigator. The CDC has sealed off the area, and will continue the investigation.

"Jesus. The guy drank formaldehyde?" Daniel Medry rubbed his temples, trying to stave off yet another headache. His ship suit, normally form-fitting, hung loosely on his now-gaunt frame. It had been nearly a month and he was no closer to finding his family than he had been on the first day after learning Earth's fate.

"There have been reports of people dying from eating non-food items, rocks, paper clips. I've even found several cases of cannibalism." Kevin said, "This virus, it makes Ebola look like a walk in the park." He paused for a minute, and then asked, "How is the list coming?"

"It isn't complete. Not by a long shot."

For that matter, there wasn't really a real list, more of a collection of scattered documents, transmissions that had been thrown into space, some nuggets of hope, others full of despair. He had been working on creating a master list, one that cross-referenced the different continents. After all, some of the crew had family strewn across the globe, the three space stations and even the colonies on the Moon and Mars.

At least, for the space stations and off-world colonies, there was an answer – everyone was dead. All transmissions had ceased. That in itself was somewhat reassuring. It was an answer, one way or the other.

He had been combing through thousands of transmission packets. They were a nightmarish mishmash of information, some of it conflicting. Although World Geographic had planned for everything, well, perhaps not the end of the world, but just about everything else, down to coding the transmissions, it should have been easy. However, when the end of the world comes, and you are feverish, under the influence of a virus that makes you want to eat everything in sight, and dying, all of those coding strategies go straight out of the window.

The format changed, even before the news of the virus showed up.

Kevin had said, "This is probably due to the effects of the ESH virus spreading through World Geographic along with the rest of the world's population during the long incubation rate. Perhaps the virus also affected organization and other higher brain functions?"

The leader forms were missing half of the categorizations, and the details and wording were, *off,* as if the person composing the transmission was incapable of staying focused.

All he wanted to know was what had happened to his family – Luke, Janine, and his son Toby.

Daniel felt a twinge of guilt over this. How dare he call Toby his son? *Luke* had been Toby's father. He had been the first one to hold him in the hospital, to take him fishing and teach him how to ride a bike.

And what was I? Daniel thought, *I was no father. I was nothing more than a sperm donor.*

He couldn't run away from the reality of that.

Kevin shooed Daniel aside and took his place at the desk. "So, you have it by continent?"

"And then by country," Daniel replied, "I've been incorporating Europe first, as well as most of North America. I add the others in as I find them, but we will need others familiar with Russian, Mandarin, and several other languages to help me with the different alphabet systems."

He sighed, "My knowledge of Cyrillic and Asian orthography is, well, it's nonexistent."

Each of the occupants of Calypso knew at least two languages and could function relatively well reading, writing and speaking in both, and sometimes were passable in even more. At least one member of Calypso was adept, not just a working knowledge, but *adept*, at nine languages. However, finding someone who could read or write in Chinese would take a while and the Captain had put some projects on hold, thereby keeping several of the crew in Cryo for longer than planned, to conserve resources.

"And this name here?" Kevin asked. "What is this from?"

"A manifest. A list of kids being transported to a refugee center in August of 2099 in eastern Washington."

Kevin nodded, "So you have your answer."

Daniel shook his head, "No, I don't."

"Yes, you do."

"No, I *don't*!" Daniel felt panicked.

"Son..."

Daniel snapped, "Don't call me that."

Kevin's brows furrowed. A moment passed before he asked quietly, "What is it that you need?"

The loss, yawning within him, an abyss of darkness and despair, it clawed at Daniel.

"Some kind of an answer. What was Toby doing there? What happened to Luke and Janine?"

"You know what happened to them," Kevin spoke softly, "There are no more records of Luke and Janine past 2099, only Toby."

He ran a search string on Tobias Medry and found another document.

"It says here that a Julie L. Aaronson adopted him in February 2101. Huh, I wonder if she's any relation to the Captain. It lists Toby's birth date."

He stopped and looked at Daniel for a long moment. "You have more than most of us do, Daniel. Your nephew is alive."

"My *son*," Daniel whispered, his voice raw with emotion.

His brother Luke, Janine, both gone, and Toby, he was alone in the world and impossibly far from Daniel.

Kevin murmured, just as quietly, "Ah, I see."

He paused and then continued, "I have a daughter, Anna. I was married before, to a woman. My daughter, she...she didn't take my relationship with Jack well. We lost touch, were estranged, I left Earth without saying goodbye. And now," his voice hitched, "I can't find any record of her either."

Silence fell between the two men, both lost in their thoughts of loved ones impossibly far away.

"Jack comes from a large family, he had five other siblings. I've been doing my best to find out if any of them made it. I want to give him some hope to hold onto when he gets out of Cryo. And Simon, well, it was a closed adoption, so I don't even know who to contact."

Daniel's voice was raw, on the edge, "He was my son, Kevin. And I just left him there."

The older man stayed silent. There was nothing to say.

Mother Was Right

"But goodness alone is never enough. A cold hard wisdom is required, too, for goodness to accomplish good. Goodness without wisdom invariably accomplishes evil." – Robert A. Heinlein

Date: 03.18.2103
Calypso Colony Ship

"Mornin' Deeks." Evers nodded to his supervisor, logging into his computer on the Cryo Deck.

"Morning to you, Evers. You owe me by the way." Deeks grinned at his assistant, "I believe the total was five lagers worth of hooch for Friday's game."

Evers sighed, "Damned card shark. Well, I'll have to owe you. I'm out of my weekly allotment, Medry cleaned me out in the first round."

Deeks laughed, "Damn, and I owe *him* two lagers. I guess we both know who the real card shark is 'round here." His fingers danced over the keyboard at his terminal. "Looks like we just have one revival today."

"Yeah, I see him here. Zradce. He's swapping with Sean Platt." Evers paused and looked up, "He hasn't heard yet, has he?"

Deeks' smile slipped from his face, "No. I'll contact Dr. Carter, he will want to be here when Zradce is functional enough to hear the news. Go ahead and start the process, will ya? I'll tell Carter to be here at 1000. A couple of hours should be enough."

Evers nodded and walked away, toward the rows of Cryo pods in the main section. Here they stood, row upon row, over two hundred of their friends and shipmates, each in frost-lined double-reinforced Plasteel containers.

Evers keyed in the revival sequence.

BEGIN REVIVAL SEQUENCE ON ZRADCE, NATHAN
03:58 MINUTES UNTIL REVIVAL

Evers watched vapors begin to swirl, keeping a sharp eye on the readout on the unit. Reviving someone from Cryo was a cakewalk for the technician, but not so much for the revived. He remembered how it had felt waking up for the first time – he had felt high, confused, and none of his body parts had seemed to work right.

And then there was the whole, "Hey man, everybody is dead on Earth" news. That had taken some time to fully digest.

"I wish I could give you good news, Zradce, I really do." Evers said conversationally. The pod was still shut and locked, Nathan's eyes were closed.

BEGIN REVIVAL SEQUENCE ON ZRADCE, NATHAN
01:20 MINUTES UNTIL REVIVAL

"Here, you will need this." Deeks wheeled a cot over. "We don't want a repeat of last week."

Last week they had almost had the revived crew member crash and burn on the floor of the Cryo Deck. Her legs had buckled, and if it hadn't been for Evers quick reaction, they would have had to explain to the Captain how one of their best civil engineers had a concussion or worse.

BEGIN REVIVAL SEQUENCE ON ZRADCE, NATHAN
00:02 MINUTES UNTIL REVIVAL

"Here we go." Deeks said.

REVIVAL SEQUENCE ON ZRADCE, NATHAN COMPLETE
PLEASE RELOCATE REVIVEE TO OBSERVATION ROOM

The pod door had clicked open and Nathan's eyes were still closed, but his cheeks were pink now and his breaths shallow.

"Watching them come out of it never gets old. I mean, seriously, the technology of bringing someone to the brink of death and keeping them there for weeks, months, and years. It's amazing." Evers said, pushing the cart close and locking the wheels.

Deeks nodded, "The most efficient way to transport two hundred plus humans trillions of miles in space. But yes, it is amazing."

Deeks pressed a sensor to Nathan's chest, reading his pulse and more.

"Barely a blip of resources taken up, no food necessary, little wear on the ship or equipment, and the Cryo pods are designed to last for decades with minimal power usage." Evers mused, slipping into engineering mode.

"Yup, designed to ensure that no matter what happens on the ship, the sleepers within will survive, come what may. Impossible to break into as well." Deeks commented.

Nathan's eyes slowly opened. They rolled about, focusing on little.

Deeks commented on it, "The neurons are still trying to remember how to interpret the data. Hang in there Nathan."

He turned back to Evers, "Cryo affects the big switch, the true 'on off' button on a human being. And unlike a computer, our 'on off' switch isn't as easily recovered from when pushed."

Evers had recently been cross-training and assisting in Cryo. He had taken basic emergency response training on Earth and found that, despite having a degree in mechanical engineering, he had a knack for the entry-level medical studies as well.

"Hi Nathan, how are you feeling?" Deeks assessed their patient.

"I wha...uh...time to...can't..." Nathan Zradce struggled to speak.

"It's all right man. All the words will come back in a few minutes. You are in Cryo, by the way, it's your scheduled wake-up call and all that." Deeks smiled at him.

He motioned to Evers, "Give him some water, but not too much, just a few sips. I'll be back in half an hour. I've got some reports to upload to the Command Deck."

Evers nodded as Deeks walked away, and wheeled Nathan to the observation room. An hour later, Deeks returned.

"How is he doing?" Deeks asked, returning from his work station. He leaned over, a penlight in one hand and checked Zradce's pupils. They had stopped rolling about and the pupils responded appropriately to the stimuli.

Evers nodded, "Doing better, aren't you, Nathan?"

Nathan groaned, "I, uh, oh..."

Evers helped the man turn onto his side, hanging off the wheeled cart, before he lost what little was in his stomach. Evers wiped up a small amount of vomit.

"Sorry." Nathan croaked

"No worries, Zradce, it happens." Deeks reassured him. "It's a documented fact, nearly three-quarters of Cryo revivals toss their cookies within the first hour after waking up. It's a lot for a body to take, after all."

Evers handed Nathan his cup of water, "Just take small sips."

Jacob Carter arrived a few minutes later, passing through the titanium-reinforced blast doors that separated the Cryo Deck from the rest of the ship.

Deeks eyed Carter, "We will give you some time to talk with Dr. Carter here who has some news of Earth that we are sharing with all of the new revivals." He nodded at the doc, "Jacob, take all the time you need."

Evers moved as far from the Observation Room as he could, walking down the last aisle to check the readouts on A.R.C. Within the machine the size of a walk-in freezer was the entire repository of Earth's genetic history. Collected over the past two decades, it included everything from 3,000 species of fresh and saltwater fish, mollusks and crustaceans, to over 20,000 different animal species, along with human sperm and ovum from every ethnic region of the planet. There were also more than 50,000 species of plants and a staggering 140,000 different species of fungi. In other words, there was everything the colony needed to reproduce Earth's unique life on another planet. Somehow, in the light of the grim news from Earth, that seemed reassuring to Evers.

Here on the Cryo Deck the human species remained safe and untainted, possibly the only ones of their kind left.

Despite not wanting to hear the news of Earth, or Nathan's reaction to it, he couldn't help but wonder at how Nathan would react. Some people freaked, others wept, many were stoic. Often there was denial and panic. Having to see it, watching it repeated over and over, that was the difficult part.

He had met Nathan, they had all had time to meet each other, although some you knew in a distant sort of way. Zradce and his wife, Jennifer were nice enough. Nathan was quiet, and had kept to himself during training while Jennifer was a social butterfly. That was fine. Not everyone was going to be your best buddy. Both Nathan and Jennifer were more than competent. Jennifer held multiple masters in civil and mechanical engineering, and was scheduled to be awakened when they established orbit around Zarmina's World.

Evers wound his way back to the Recovery Room.

"We have a link for you to view in your quarters," Carter was saying, "It will give you suggestions on how to locate surviving family members as well as some appointments I have scheduled for you and I to meet. Remember Nathan, that I am always available to you if you are in need of immediate one-on-one counseling outside of those scheduled dates. We are here to help you deal with your loss."

One hour later, at 1100, Zradce walked out the door, still slightly unsteady on his feet. He had said little, responded just enough to fall within the guidelines of acceptable recovery behavior, and Deeks had signed his release.

Zradce finally made it to his coffin, his mind spinning around the dark truths he had just learned. The small amount of food he had managed to eat, sat in his stomach, churning, and his body still felt lethargic from the Cryo meds.

Mother.

He climbed in, slipped off his ship shoes, pulled up the links on his touchpad and tried to find the information on how to search through the survivor lists. There were no results when he searched, but he wasn't terribly surprised. He didn't look for his foster family, the ones who had taken him in after.

Those last moments with her haunted him still.

The madness in her eyes and her screams as they took her away.

If she had only known who he really was at that moment, he could have forgiven her. But she denied him, even then after so many years, erasing him, as if he wasn't important, as if he didn't exist.

Mother.

It had always been that way. Immanuel had been the one, her golden boy, her heart. The bond between mother and son had been far stronger than the bond between twins. He had never felt that connection to his twin brother that he had read so much about.

She had felt it, tried to make him be Immanuel in those months and years after his brother had died. Tried to remake the world into what she thought it should be. She had almost convinced him that he, Nathaniel, was really the one that had died. Not her Immanuel, oh no.

Mother.

And as before, as in all of the years since that terrible night and the loss of losing his twin, Nathaniel felt himself slip away. Maybe Mother had been right. Maybe he was Immanuel, the golden son, the one she really wanted, the one who should have lived. Had she died with his name on her lips? Had she died alone? Frightened? Or certain in her faith that these were the end of days, that this is what had been coming for a thousand years?

Nathaniel closed his eyes. He could see her better that way. Straining against the handcuffs, spittle flying from her mouth, screaming for them to let her go.

Schism

"A central lesson of science is that to understand complex issues (or even simple ones), we must try to free our minds of dogma and to guarantee the freedom to publish, to contradict, and to experiment." – Carl Sagan

Date: 04.14.2103
Calypso Colony Ship

At first, the meetings had been daily. Then thrice weekly. Then weekly. And now, Nathan thought for a moment, it had been ten days since his last meeting with Dr. Carter. *Jacob, call him Jacob.*

"How are things, Nathan?"

Jacob Carter appeared older than his forty plus years. The last few months had aged him. Perhaps it was the challenge of keeping the crew in a good head space, not an easy job with everything that had happened.

"Fine."

"Define *fine.*"

Today would be a challenge. But Nathan was up to it, just this one more session and, if things went well, he could be free of the mandatory meetings.

Nothing to see here. Nothing at all. The world ends, everybody dies, and really Doc, it's all fine around here. Nathan Zradce had never held much stock with psychotherapy.

Nathan smiled, a small one, because otherwise he would have some dumb shit-eating grin on his face that would scream *liar!* And then he would be here for another twelve weeks shooting the shit with a guy who wanted to peer inside his brain.

"Really, I'm doing okay. No nightmares, nothing."

"That's right. You had a dream about your birth mother. You mentioned it at the end of our session so we didn't get a chance to get into detail about that."

Jacob glanced down at his notes, missing a myriad of conflicting expressions that flickered across Nathan's face before disappearing once again behind a mask of casual indifference. *Why the hell did I have to go and mention a nightmare? Now Carter will never let it go!*

Jacob continued, "So, you mentioned that you were adopted at a young age? My records don't even show it. How young were you?"

Nathaniel pretended to think a moment, "Huh, let me see. I dunno, maybe eight or so?"

"Eight *years*?"

"Uh…yeah, I guess, somewhere around there."

Jacob scribbled a note on his computer tablet. It was rare to see someone actually use one of the handwriting programs on a tablet. Most found it easier to either transcribe notes using sub-vocal intonation or through a basic keyboard program that recorded the strokes you made directly on the interface. Jacob Carter was using an actual program that would read his loopy, unique handwriting and translate it into recorded notes. Few even knew the art of cursive writing it was that rare.

"That's not particularly young, Nathan. What are your memories of her?"

"I don't have any."

Spittle flying from her twisted deranged mouth. Hands clawing in the air as the officers wrestled her to the ground. "Immanuel! Immanuel! Give me my SON!"

"None?"

Nathan shrugged.

"No. None at all. My foster parents are the first people I really remember. Hal, my foster dad and his wife, Mary. They adopted me, but I wanted to keep my last name, so we just added theirs as a middle name. They were great folks."

Jacob scribbled with his stylus a little more, then stopped and frowned at Nathan.

"I guess I'm still stuck on you not having any memories of your mother at the age of eight years. Memories are typically formed beginning at around age three. We don't tend to remember much before that time, but we certainly do remember important figures, like parents, and by age eight, well."

His voice trailed off and he stared speculatively at Nathan. "How did she pass?"

Bundled into a straitjacket, fighting, clawing, even after they injected her with the strong anti-psychotics. Screaming his brother's name from inside of the ambulance.

"Was it sudden? Or after a long illness?" Jacob persisted.

Nathan felt the pressure building in his head. Right at the temples, those gateways to the psyche, the pain was setting in.

"Immanuel! You let me GO!"

"She had a mental breakdown, at least, that's what they told me."

"And you have no memories of her? And no siblings? What about your father?"

The pain continued to build, spikes of agony in time with his heartbeat.

"I have to protect him!"

It took effort to shrug now that a headache was settling in to stay.

"I'll cut you." Maniacal gleam in her eye. Standing in the filthy kitchen, a large, sharp knife in her hand. "You tell me where Immanuel is. TELL ME!"

He had been so frightened of her when she was like this. She was unpredictable, dangerous.

Nathan could see Jacob was still waiting. He was waiting for Nathan to answer.

"No, no siblings, sorry to say."

"Where is Immanuel, you little snake. What have you done with him?" He remembered it all too clearly. It had been on a cold winter's day, the wind howling, shaking the small house, and he hadn't been able to escape outside as he did in the warmer months.

"My dad was never in the picture. I guess he wasn't too excited about having a kid. My mom never talked about him. I was lucky enough to get plenty of siblings when my foster parents took me in. We were a full melting pot, kids of all colors, all ages. Hal and Mary, they were great."

Her standing there, blocking his escape into his room, into his closet where the darkness was his friend and his mother left him be. "I need to find Immanuel. The end of times is nearly here. All of this," she waved the knife around her in a vague circle, "ALL of this will blow away at the end of days. We will be reborn, comforted by the fires of the righteous. God will clothe us in soft raiments and we will eat manna. We will ascend and sit at the right hand of the Almighty. It has been written."

Jacob didn't seem to know where to go with all of this information.

"I guess I'm just a little surprised you didn't mention this sooner."

"You, YOU are the devil's spawn. I see the mark upon you, shining from your head like a curse. Where is Immanuel?" He had stepped back from her, desperate to hide and wait out the wave of crazy, but he could see there was nowhere to go, except maybe outside in the storm.

Nathan shrugged again. His head screamed in protest.

"I guess it just didn't occur to me. I had a good life with Hal and Mary, they were great."

"Yes, you've mentioned that."

"I guess I don't know what else to say. I had a great childhood. The typical bumps and scrapes, I shoplifted once as a teenager and they both really took it seriously, made me pay for the stolen merchandise and volunteer with some youth groups. They were just..."

"Great." Jacob supplied.

"Uh, yeah."

"And have you checked on their status since your revival from Cryo?"

She was bleeding. Her hand clenched around the knife so hard that the metal sliced into her skin. "Tell me where he is, you disgusting little snake." Why did she always blame him? She had always loved Immanuel best. For every step he took backward, she took one forward. The blood dripped onto the floor, making fat red blooms on the faded and stained carpet.

Nathan stared down at his hands, slumped forward in his seat.

"Hal died five years ago from cancer. And shortly after, Mary passed away too. It wasn't even a year."

He twisted his lips into something he hoped resembled a sad look.

"It was as if she died of a broken heart. There was a huge funeral. They had fostered more than seventy kids over the years."

"You are a lying little snake. Tell the truth. WHERE is Immanuel?"

"I'm sorry to hear that, Nathan. Any word on your foster siblings?"

"Don't say another word. I know you, and I know him, you are nothing, Immanuel is clean and good."

"Those kind of records are rather hard to look up. A lot of them are sealed – especially those who were in the foster care system. And as for the others, well, honestly, we just didn't keep in contact after Hal and Mary died."

"You never called them Mom or Dad?"

Immanuel is everything you are not, Nathaniel. I'm going to find him, even if I have to come through you to do it.

"No," Nathan managed to laugh, although the pain in his skull was debilitating, he had to get out of there, "They were pretty laid-back in that sense. Mary especially was a big proponent of not making kids call their new parents Mom and Dad. Something about that being a 'special title, not to be pushed or misused.'"

He shrugged, "Even in my case, where I was adopted and not just fostered, they left it up to me. I had been calling them by their first names for a full year, so changing would have felt...odd."

This seemed to satisfy Jacob. He scribbled away with his stylus for a moment more, and then looked up.

"So... overall, how do you think you have handled the news from Earth?"

The knife flashed towards him. Pain, like an electric shock, jolting into his body. Red, bubbling from the wound in his stomach. Screams. Who was screaming? Him? Her? He stumbled away from her, the room spinning, opened the door and stepped out in his bare feet. The cold wind slapping him in the face and blowing through his clothes as if he were naked. Walking to the next house, his steps slowing, erratic, ringing the doorbell. The woman who had answered had screamed, backing away from the open door.

"It's been tough. Really tough. I, uh, I wish my wife was here right now. But I'll see her when we obtain orbit around the planet, so, yeah."

Police. Paramedics. Holding her, holding him. "It will be okay, son. We've got you."

Jacob Carter stared at him and Nathan struggled to keep a small smile on his face. One that hovered somewhere between "really sad" and "we will survive."

Mother. Struggling. Screaming. Fighting to get free. The knife was out of her hands, on the ground, covered in red.

"I'm going to go ahead and inform the Captain that you are cleared from the mandatory counseling sessions. As I am sure you are aware, if you ever need me, I am happy to fit you into the schedule or talk to you, day or night."

A tall blond woman, turning away and speaking into her radio.

"We've got an eight-year-old male, abdominal wound lower right quadrant, heavy bleeding. Blood pressure is ninety-two over thirty-eight and dropping, oh two sat, eighty percent on five liters of oh two with non-rebreather mask. I'm increasing the oh two to seven liters. Alert the PICU we are in route. ETA three minutes."

The gurney rising, moving, the dull gray clouds and icy wind abruptly cut off by the sterile ceiling of the ambulance. Sirens.

"Stay with us, Nate. Do they call you Nate or Nathan?"

"Thank you, Jacob. I will definitely reach out to you if I need to talk to someone."

He pasted a vaguely grateful, relieved look onto his face.

Siren wailing. The vehicle shaking over a rough pothole. The tall blond woman holding his wrist.

"Nate? Can you hear me? Hang in there, kiddo, we are close, just another minute."

Nathaniel made it through the rest of the pleasantries and nodded goodbye to Jacob. He walked steadily through the door of Jacob Carter's office, into an empty hallway, and sagged against a wall as soon as the door closed behind him. His head, it didn't seem possible that it could hurt this much and not simply explode.

He stood there a moment, allowing the ship wall to prop him up, then gathered his wits and moved on down the corridor. It wouldn't do for Carter to come out and see him like this. Nor anyone else. Too many questions and Nathaniel had had enough questions to last a lifetime.

Blue scrubs leaning over him, along with bright, bright lights. His eyes hurt from staring into them. "The bleeding is heavy, but I think the abdominal aorta is intact. We'll need to check it out. Prep him for surgery."

Nathaniel counted himself lucky. Everyone was either on shift or at lunch. He climbed into his coffin and cradled his head in his hands.

A petite woman in slacks and a yellow blouse stood at the end of his hospital bed.

"Hi Nathan, I'm Laura, your social worker. I'm here to check on you. Are you doing better?"

His head nodded.

"I'm going to be arranging for you to stay with a nice couple when the doctors tell me you are ready to leave. They have taken care of lots of children, I am sure you will fit in well there."

He managed another nod.

"You won't be going back home, Nathan, your mom is in a hospital too, but she has to stay, probably for good, so she doesn't ever try to hurt anyone else."

She had paused, taken his hand in hers and said softly, "Your mother is sick, Nathan. I looked up her records, we had her in our system from years and years ago. She was an orphan; did you know that?"

He had shaken his head. Mother had never talked about the past. Except...

"She sometimes talked about 'Other Mother.'" His voice was barely a whisper.

Laura had nodded, "Maybe that was the foster family that adopted her. We learned about the abuse after she ran away at seventeen."

She squeezed his hand, "You aren't a bad child, Nathan, and your mother, she's sick. I'm so sorry this happened to you but I promise things are going to get better now. I know you will like your new family; they are so looking forward to meeting you."

Nathan's face was wet with tears, the pain pulsed through him, and he said it out loud, his voice hollow and overly loud within the small space.

"She didn't ever love me. She wanted Immanuel. I was the one who should have died, not him."

He spoke the words in his coffin, they hung there in the air, but they were 35 years too late. He hadn't said it to the case worker, he hadn't even told his wife. No one had known about Immanuel. No one, except for Mother and him. As it was, he barely remembered his brother. Just a handful of cloudy memories. He struggled to remember those last days.

Why had Mother loved Immanuel more? Even with those few wispy memories, there was a disparity. The look in her eyes when she gazed upon his brother. The twist in her mouth when she turned and noticed Nathaniel. There had been a difference, despite them looking and acting alike.

"The difference between you is day and night. He was the sun, but you," her mad eyes burned into him, across millions of miles of space, "you are nothing but darkness."

Perhaps, in some unknown way, he had caused this to happen. He mused on that while lying in a hospital room, waiting to be discharged. The nurses were kind. They tousled his hair, brought him treats, spoke to him kindly. And Laura had visited every day, telling him about the new family he would go and live with.

Inside of his coffin on Calypso, Nathan wept. His head felt as if it would burst. He hadn't remembered, hadn't thought of those terrible days for so very long. He had buried it. But in the end, he knew the reality of it, the truth about who he was.

"I heard your mama tried to kill you."

A pinch-faced girl, thin and twitchy, she had been waiting outside of the foster family home, waiting to get him alone.

"Heard you were evil deep inside and your mama tried to make you clean, Nate. Is that true?"

Nate, everyone called him Nate, and they had never asked, just called him that. He compromised by thinking of himself as Nathan, which felt as if it fell somewhere between the two.

Nathaniel shook his head, "No, I'm not bad."

"I think you are. I think you are filled with the devil and you will kill us all."

She poked at him with a stick, sneering.

She hadn't been smiling later. Not when he tripped her with that same stick, causing her to fall down and break her wrist. She had screamed then, but Nathaniel had sworn up and down it had been an accident. No one disbelieved him. Apparently, Angelica was anything but angelic. She had avoided him after that and been taken away soon after.

Mother had said that the world would end in fire. But there was more, much more. The more he thought about it, the more he remembered that final visit with her. She had spoken of the end times, Nathan remembered. Devastating plagues, war, and famine. The virus, now there was a plague for you. Mother had said that they all deserved to die. And from what he could see that was exactly what was happening.

What he didn't understand was why the plague hadn't affected anyone on board Calypso.

In her saner moments, if they could even be called that, Mother had lectured him. She sometimes forgot her own assertion that Nathaniel had been the cause of his brother's death. As if Nathaniel had reached into Immanuel's heart and stopped it in its tracks.

"You have to be a soldier of God, Nathaniel. Sometimes God needs help. He needs you to bring his will forward and apply it to everyone, even if they lack the true faith."

Her eyes had burned into him, "You must be a soldier of God. Wield your faith like a sword!"

Nathan's headache suddenly dimmed. As if the light had been turned from the brightest setting down to a mere soft glow. Was he really a soldier of God?

Nathan felt a great piece of his insides giving way. He slipped away, a construct of the loss of his mother and brother. He wasn't Nathan. He never really had been.

Nathaniel. Immanuel. Soldier of God. He was all of them in one. The others didn't realize the truth, but he did. They were doomed. They had escaped their fates by happenstance, by some kind of perversion of science over the will of God. It was time he changed that and became the soldier of God Mother wanted him to be.

Nathaniel fell into a deep, dreamless sleep.

End of Days

"After this I looked, and there before me was a door standing open in heaven. And the voice I had first heard speaking to me like a trumpet said, 'Come up here, and I will show you what must take place after this.'" – Revelation 4:1

Date: 04.15.2103

Calypso Colony Ship

"Morning, Nathan."

Nathaniel forced himself to nod and mutter "Morning" in return as he passed Wes Perdue outside of the Mess Hall. He had slept late, the dark dreams had held him until he had awoken, later than usual. He was running late, but he desperately needed to eat before his shift began. Everyone else had already been and gone and the Mess Hall was empty.

He filled the tray with fruit and a round of freeze-dried oatmeal and watched as the hot water from the tap slowly dispensed covering the small disk in liquid.

The dreams still lingered in his mind.

The 'Ponics Deck, glistening bright with frost, the plants hanging limp, dark slicks of green, bordering on black. Ice glistening from the vents, his breath clouding in the air. It had felt so real.

He sat down at a table, picked up a strawberry and froze, the berry halfway to his mouth.

The hand slapped down, stinging, as it knocked the piece of bread from his hand.

"You didn't say grace, Nathaniel," his mother's voice sharp and authoritative at his ear, "Other Mother always made sure I said grace before eating. How many times must I tell you this?"

"I'm sorry Mother," his voice said, "Please, I'll say it now."

"It's too late, Nathaniel, Other Mother said that it is too late to say grace after you try to take a bite. You have sinned and must be punished. Now go to school," she pushed him from the chair, "and remember to always say grace."

He set the fruit down, his stomach now rumbling ominously. He had to be punished.

He cleared his tray, placing the uneaten food into the compost bin, the silverware, dishes, and tray into the compact dishwasher in the wall of the Mess Hall. The washer blasted the food away with a mixture of water and air under high pressure. Any solids were collected and dumped into the compost bin.

Three hours later, the small amount of work he needed to do was done, his mind was clear, and his focus razor sharp. It was the strawberry that had done it. That cursed fruit, impossibly grown aboard this ship so far from Earth.

Mother clicking off the newsvid, "A new fruit, created in laboratories, what would Other Mother say about that?"

Mother turned on Nathaniel, who was working on his schoolwork on his student tablet.

"Nathaniel! Listen!"

He jerked his head up, meeting her gaze. Today was not a good day. He could see the madness in her eyes.

"Other Mother said, 'You must not eat fruit from the tree that is in the middle of the garden, and you must not touch it, or you will die.' The fruit they have made is wrong and evil, Nathaniel, Other Mother was right!"

He was alone in his small cubicle in the Programming Section, one of several others working away at various coding jobs needed on board as well as for the colony that would be established upon arriving at the new planet. The interface blinked, waiting for his next command.

His stomach, empty and growling in class. "Nathaniel?" Miss Rose, his teacher was standing next to his desk, "Did you have breakfast?"

"No, Miss Rose. Mother said the food coupons weren't right. So, we ran out yesterday. Mother says she can get more today. But not any of the bio...bio...bio jen..."

"Bioengineered foods?"

Nathan nodded.

"I see."

Mother had a list of foods that they couldn't eat. It made shopping a challenge, and with the latest round of releases of bio-engineered foods replacing what couldn't be produced on a massive scale, the list grew longer and longer, and their bags of food became smaller and smaller.

Nathaniel's teacher must have said something. The next day there were two Child Protective Services workers there, examining Natalia Zradce's kitchen. As both workers backs were turned, she shot him a look that promised he would pay for his mistake.

His mind kept returning to the dream. Ice on the inside of the viewports in the lounges. His breath steaming in frozen air. He could feel the bitter cold as he walked the empty halls of Calypso.

Despite the dreams haunting him all these hours, Nathaniel's stomach rumbled. It had been long enough, three hours now, he could stop and get food. He left his cubicle, walked to the lift and rode down to the Mess Hall. He filled his tray with the offered protein cube, fresh greens from the 'Ponics Deck, and filled a water cup from the wall dispenser. Perhaps if he asked forgiveness for eating this evil food at the same time as he said grace, it would be acceptable. The room was full and he felt out-of-place as he sat down at an empty seat and bent his head.

"How long has it been since you prayed, Nathaniel?" His mother, turning on him the moment the CPS workers left. "Look what your sinful ways have done now! Remember, blessed are all who fear the Lord and walk in obedience to him."

Her hands on him, hard and bony, her fingernails claws in his skin, she had pushed him into the small closet at the end of the hall. Shutting the door, she had whispered through it as the lock slid into place.

"Son though he was, he learned obedience from what he suffered."

The door had not opened again for two days.

That had also been the last day he ever attended school.

"I didn't know you were a devout man, Nathan."

Nathaniel was jolted out of his whispered prayer as Jacob Carter sat down in an empty seat across from him.

Nathan nodded, and dug into his meal.

Carter smiled cheerfully, despite a somewhat awkward silence.

"In case you didn't know, I head a group that meets weekly. If you are ever interested, do let me know. We send up prayers, discuss theological questions and more. Seeking solace in the Lord with other like-minded people around you can be a comfort in itself. You are more than welcome to join us."

Mother, in a froth of fury over unwelcome visitors at their door, "They pretend to be prayerful, while asking for money. Ha! They don't pay attention to the word of God; they ignore it and do as they please. Other Mother often said, 'If anyone turns a deaf ear to my instruction, even their prayers are detestable.' The fools!"

Nathaniel realized that Carter was expecting some kind of response.

"Uh, yes, right, I'll keep that in mind."

He finished eating his meal and left in silence.

His mind returned to the last dream as he walked down the hall. It had centered on the Cryo Deck. He had walked in through the enormous reinforced doors, hoping to see his wife. Instead, once there he could see the machines showed no lights, no readouts, and as he looked closer, he realized the pods were filled with skeletons, mouths frozen open. Each pod was filled with the same image, grinning in a macabre rictus of death.

Back at work, alone in his cubicle, he could still hear his mother speaking, as real as if she were standing behind him.

"It is the end of days, Nathaniel. You are the great prince, foretold to arise and protect your people. Other Mother said that there will be a time of distress as has not happened from the beginning of nations until then. But at that time your people – everyone whose name is found written in the book – will be delivered. You must step forward now. God demands it.

He stared at his workstation screen; hands immobile. Mother had been right about so much. She had said the world would die and so it had, billions rotting in cities, the survivors fleeing, hiding from the corruption death had wrought upon the streets, waterways, and the land itself. And then there were the people left in the world. Just a few in the face of so many dead, barren, unable to bear children.

Truly they were cursed by God. All of Mother's visions, they had all come true. Now he was left wishing he had died, just as Mother had predicted, because he didn't know what to do. How was he supposed to usher in the end of days here, in this spaceship so far from Earth?

What if the dreams last night had been a message? What if he was supposed to make it all happen? The thought stunned him. He sat there at his workstation, unmoving, immobile, until shift end, his thoughts resolving into a plan. As he left work, Nathaniel's steps veered away from the Mess Hall and headed instead for his coffin, where he climbed in and immediately dimmed the lights and keyed his window to the opaque privacy setting.

The dreams, they were a message. He was sure of it.

First, I dreamed of 'Ponics, filled with frost and dead plants. Then the second dream, on the heels of the first, of the ship empty, lifeless and cold. He thought. *The Cryo Deck, filled with the dead. That is my destiny. The dreams were a message. End of days. Mother was right.*

After all, he was the one, Mother had said he would live and he had, when all of Earth was dying. Now he just had to finish what had been started. It was the end of days, and he had a duty to help the poor lost souls on Calypso, to help do God's work.

He pressed a button and a keyboard slid out, his personal work station ready. He typed in a search string and watched as the screen filled with code.

Nathaniel realized for the first time what he truly wanted in life. After so many years of blank nothingness, no guide to follow, and no mission to fulfill – his way was finally clear. He would find a way to end this unholy existence. On Earth, dying was simple. Here, God needed his help. He would make them all proud –Mother, the Other Mother, God... *everyone.*

Success would not be judged in moments or days. It would be judged by the dead.

All that was left was bringing his shipmates through to the other side.

This Empty World

Date: 04.15.2103
Earth – New Athens, Central North America

"Good morning, Madame Chairman."

Janelle Brooks stood with Julie Aaronson in the brightly lit atrium of the new capital and shook Madeline Chen's hand. Outside the world was beginning to wake up from its winter slumber. The mornings were still chilly and the nights definitely required a warm coat.

Inside the atrium, however, it was warm and moist. The room was filled with lush green plants, a stream of water ran through it on the eastern side, and the fresh scent of earth mitigated the lingering chemical odor of the extruded plasticrete that was being shaped in the massive 3D printers. The city was nearly 75% complete; occupying what had once been vast ranchlands in the plains of the Reformed United States of America.

Madeline smiled and motioned to a couch and several chairs, "Please, sit."

Janelle sat next to Julie on the couch and Madeline chose a chair across from them.

"I understand you have been working together since the outbreak began."

Julie nodded, "Nearly, we began collaborating about three years ago. She smiled at Janelle and took her hand, "We formalized our partnership last year.

"And you have two children, is that correct?" Madeline asked.

Janelle nodded, "Yes, we both took in orphans during the crisis. We finalized Toby and Karen's adoptions last year in the same ceremony. They get along well, despite the age difference."

Julie was staring at the walls of the atrium, which twisted in curves, first widening, and then slowly closing towards the top. Fifty feet above them was an enormous skylight and the morning sun glinted off of the white surfaces.

"This is magnificent," she said, intrigued by the formations embedded within the structure, "even better than the pre-construction sketches had indicated."

Madeline Chen nodded, "I am glad that you like it. The architect Shigoro Hitagashi designed this building and most of the others under construction now. I'm particularly impressed with the way the light moves through each of the buildings through the course of the day."

"And this entire city, it is being constructed almost entirely out of plasticrete, isn't it?"

"Yes, indeed it is."

Julie nodded in approval. "I've heard great things about the polymer. It's non-toxic, durable, and extremely versatile."

Madeline smiled, "I can see you have been doing your homework. Were you also apprised of the health benefits of the new construction?"

Janelle nodded, "We have been following that closely as well Madame Chairman. The HEPA E-20 is being used in all of the buildings, correct?"

"Yes. We will have the HEPA filters in every public and private building in this city. That, along with clean energy generated through the solar fields, wind farm and the geothermal applications, and this city will be completely 'green' without any of the half-measures we had to take with already established cities."

"It will give people the highest quality of life that Earth has ever seen." Julie added.

"Yes, indeed it will." Madeline paused, "But you didn't come here to discuss architecture, did you?"

"No, Madame Chairman, I'm afraid we did not." Janelle answered.

"Well, I have to admit, before we get started, that I'm a fan of your work, Dr. Brooks, as well as yours, Dr. Aaronson."

"*Our* work?" Janelle asked, startled.

"Yes, I minored in Bioscience in college," Madeline replied. "But my parents were insistent that I make Political Science a priority, so," she sighed, "here I am. The widow of a politician and the Interim Chairman of the Terran United Planetary Government. Just saying it out loud makes me miss the hard sciences even more."

Janelle shook her head, "I had no idea. Well, that certainly will make my report easier to relay."

Madeline laughed, "Go easy on me, I hate to admit how long it has been since college!"

"Of course," Janelle said, and queued up the information on her tablet. "I've sent you all of these documents, but here is where we stand. Thanks to the iDent chips here in the Reformed United States, as well as the ten variants employed in most of the countries around the world prior to the virus outbreak, we know that our current world population stands at just over fourteen and one-half million, with another half to three-quarters million UPs, four hundred thousand of those are within Chamaral Falls in Mauritius and the rest..."

Madeline blinked, "Did you say...*ups*?"

"Sorry," Janelle looked embarrassed, "Uninfected Persons, UPs for short. We started using the term last year and it just sort of stuck."

"Right, that makes sense. The UPs are all of those who remain in the enclaves and haven't been infected with the ESH virus." Madeline said.

"Exactly. In any case, our total world population is hovering at right around fifteen million, one hundred seventy thousand."

Madeline nodded, "That's about in line with what I had been apprised of."

Janelle gestured to Julie, "Dr. Aaronson has been studying the teratogenic qualities of the ESH virus and she has sent you a summary of her findings."

Julie keyed up her figures.

"As you may know, prior to the ESH virus, anywhere from ten to twenty-five percent of clinically recognized pregnancies naturally end in miscarriage. This number was possibly closer to fifty percent, the majority of those ending in the first days, long before a woman even knows she is pregnant. Additionally, it should also be noted that 80% of all miscarriages occur in the first trimester."

Madeline Chen nodded and motioned for Julie to continue.

"In the first few months of the ESH outbreak, I noticed a sharp spike in miscarriages and stillbirths, even among women who had entered their second and third trimesters. Now I wasn't sure if this was a side effect of the virus entering the system during the pregnancy and perhaps killing only the fetuses that were *not* AB negative, so we did extensive testing once we saw the trend in some of the refugee camps. There was no correlation, many of the fetuses we tested were AB negative blood types, so they should have survived the ESH virus."

Julie stopped, sipped from the glass of water sitting in front of her and continued. "My next theory was that the shock of the ESH virus invading the maternal host was detrimental to the fetus. This took some time to disprove, a full year in fact. The ESH positive women who attempted to get pregnant were continuing to miscarry in record numbers."

"The percentage?" Madeline asked, straight to the point.

"Over ninety seven percent, Madame Chairman, in the..."

"*Ninety seven percent* of pregnancies in ESH positive survivors end in miscarriage?"

"No ma'am, ninety seven percent of pregnancies miscarry in the *first trimester*. Overall, we are looking at closer to ninety-nine-point-six-five percent of all pregnancies ending in miscarriage. Worse, this might not end with the first generation, or even the second."

"*What?*" Madeline Chen stared at Julie, her face turning pale.

"There's more. From what Dr. Brooks and I can tell, and this is in the process of being verified by a team outside of Munich, the embedded herpes virus markers indicate that there will be a far higher infant mortality rate as well. Possibly as many as seventy-five percent of those babies who survive until birth may die before their second year."

As if it weren't enough that the survivors were hanging on by threads in refugee camps all over the world. All of them waiting as the massive machines printed new homes which promised to clean the air still reeking of death, and protect them from the illness which had ravaged every corner of the globe.

The cities, filled with unending scores of the dead, were unlivable. The stench had faded, but the environmental hazards remained as millions of decomposing bodies filled the buildings, streets and tunnels of the cities. Many of them had been razed by incendiary devices, starting with the cities of Guiyang and Hong Kong. Lagos and Kinshasa on the African continent had also seen fit to cleanse by fire, as had Moscow and St. Petersburg in Russia.

"I...I don't know what to say," Madeline said softly.

"We have to take action, Madame Chairman, *now*." Janelle said, "As it stands, Earth's population is smaller than it has been in over three thousand years. And if we don't do something about it, that number will be halved within three decades."

"What do you suggest?"

"Put simply? We need an organized breeding program." Julie added, bulldozing through the shocked look on the Chairman's face.

"If we don't institute it now, and promote genetic diversity and a benefit-based breeding platform, we will lose the opportunity completely."

There was a moment of silence as Madeline Chen scrolled through the reports, her lips moving slightly as she read the proposal.

"You are suggesting a massive change to how human families exist," Madeline exclaimed, paging through her tablet. "This is reminiscent of a caste system in concept." Her eyes widened at a particular passage. "A system which *rewards* women for having more babies than they can take care of?"

Janelle nodded, "I know, it seems like a lot to take in. Especially since we were all raised with the threats of population control and large families faced *more* taxes rather than less. But please understand, Madame Chairman, I first obtained my master's in social science before going into the biosciences. We have spoken with others extensively as well for this report. If we don't change how we think about reproduction *immediately* our species is likely doomed to extinction."

"There are artificial wombs," Madeline began.

"Yes, and those are failing at a spectacular rate. We have hopes that, given time and advances in technology, we will be able to ferret out the failure points, but right now, the artificial wombs can successfully produce lower life forms, but not humans. We don't know *why* yet, but the children come out developmentally and psychologically stunted. Imagine a generation of children like that." Janelle warned.

Julie chimed in, "By focusing on and rewarding those who are able to have children, we maximize their breeding potential. No human is exactly alike; some may have better success than others at carrying a fetus to term. Please keep in mind that those miscarriage numbers are *averages* and do not represent the individual so much as the whole of the breeding population tested at this time."

Madeline's face still carried a look of horror, "And this next bit," she said, stabbing at the words on her tablet, "You want to lower the age of reproductive consent to *sixteen*?"

"For at least twenty years, yes. We need to maximize reproduction potential." Janelle said, adding forcefully, "Look around you, Madame Chairman, look around at this empty world and tell me you think that everything is going to right itself on its own. That this beautiful new city will actually have children. We are at a tipping point and we must act, now."

An hour later, Janelle and Julie were escorted back to the waiting shuttle. It would take them back to Genesis, Mississippi, the first of the new cities to be built and one of three new survivor cities in the North American continent. Madeline Chen, while Chairman of the Terran United Planetary Government, counted the three cities in her territory.

"She thinks we are nuts." Janelle said, grim-faced.

"That she might, but the reality is there, in black and white. It might stomp all over our American sensibilities or the message of 'one child is enough' that we have all been hearing these past twenty or more years, but damn it, we don't have time for that," Julie fired back.

"The entire UPs population aside, we have just under four point five million women of breeding age left, and in twenty more years, that number will drop to less than one point five million women if we don't do something about it. We are facing an extinction level event."

Madeline Chen sat for a long time in silence after the two scientists' departure. Her Comm link had flashed, indicating she had messages, but she had set it to "Do Not Disturb." The other people would wait, just until she could digest these grim details.

There were hours of meetings left in the day, and reports from the salvage missions going on in New York, Washington, and San Francisco. There were hundreds of people working their way through the cities, recovering what art they could. The loss of the Greater Los Angeles basin to El Nino-fueled wildfires had spurred recovery efforts. The art and historical artifacts that had been lost in southern California was mind-numbing, but there were other far older areas of the world in which there were even more historical and literary treasures.

Madeline had been told that there were frantic efforts going on in Rome, Cairo, and other ancient bastions of humanity. They couldn't save everything, not even a fraction of it, but the salvage teams were doing their best.

She paged through the messages on her tablet. The packs of dogs, wild now that their owners were gone, roamed the cities. It had become such a problem, especially for the recovery teams, that the remainder of the military were dispatched to cull their numbers down. The situation was nearly as bad for the formerly domestic cat populations, but cats were far better at caring for themselves than the dogs. And they didn't hunt in packs like their canine counterparts. The only good news from that quarter was that the rat population in New York City had finally been eradicated.

She reviewed the documents Janelle and Julie had prepared for her, scrolling through them on her tablet, words and phrases jumping out at her. What they were suggesting was nothing short of fascism. An enforced registry and breeding program? Women spending their lives as living hosts for babies? It was shocking and she struggled to wrap her mind around it.

And then there was the space expedition side of it. Dr. Aaronson, whose nephew was captain aboard Calypso, had actually suggested that they send the rest of the UPs to the Gliese 581 system. As if they could just whip up a spaceship! Not a single piece of the ship could be built by ESH survivors, not without risking contamination and death of any UPs who climbed aboard the vessel. It was insanity.

They had learned the hard way, over and over, that to approach an Uninfected Person and make contact, regardless of stringent safety procedures, was to introduce death into their midst. They had lost hundreds last November when a settlement in the Appalachians was exposed, and again in northwest Washington a month later.

There had been no discussion of possible cures or retroviral therapy in the proposal. No ideas on how to eliminate the ESH virus and re-integrate the UPs population in with the surviving population here on Earth. And worst of all, no hope for eliminating the teratogenic effects of the virus on fetuses.

Madeline felt ill.

She had been so strong since Gary's death. He had treated her like a fragile, glass doll for the entire course of their courtship and marriage, but Madeline had survived when her husband and billions had not. She had flown over the wreckage of the Reformed United States, as well as much of the rest of the world, and seen the devastation. Empty cities, heaps of the dead whose putrid smell was carried on the wind even now, four years later. The highways filled with cars, and more bodies, whose decaying effluence had poisoned waterways and soil, filling even the green cities with contamination. The world was now overrun with every kind of animal *except* for man.

She had survived it all. She was stronger than she looked.

Her tablet beeped, a message scrolling into view.

TRANSMISSION PACKET
TUPG TO ACTING CHAIRMAN
/BEGIN TRANSMISSION
FAINT SIGNALS DETECTED FROM MARS. THREE SURVIVORS REMAIN. ALL ESH POSITIVE. MORE UPDATES TO FOLLOW WHEN SIGNAL BOOSTER IS IN PLACE.
/END TRANSMISSION

A glimmer of hope. The Mars colony had been declared a full loss, but apparently, they had been wrong. It was something to hold onto, a tiny victory in a sea of loss.

The spring sun poured through the windows, warm, reassuring, but Madeline rubbed her temples slowly as she felt the beginnings of a migraine forming.

She had been set with an impossible task. Somehow, she had to convince the rest of the world to listen, and follow, this daring plan. She would probably be vilified. But if she did not take action, the future of the human race was doomed.

Madeline's hands strayed to her flat belly. No child had ever grown inside of her. Gary had always treated her like a delicate doll, capable of breaking if handled wrong. In many ways, she had been just that to him, a doll to be displayed, almost worshiped. He had loved her, and she him, but never had the subject of children ever been more than a thing that other couples did.

Perhaps it would help if she announced that she would do her part as well. At the age of thirty-nine she was on the outside edge of fertility and the chances of carrying a child to term were riddled with more than the average number of problems. Despite this, her willingness to commit to the breeding program would go far in helping others accept the radical changes on the horizon.

Madeline imagined an embryo taking root inside of her, turning her flat stomach into a round bubble of life. It certainly couldn't hurt to try. For the first time, the idea of having a child brought a smile to her lips.

Outside of the enormous white building whose twisting spires were reminiscent of a double-helix strand of DNA, a city continued to rise from the plains. Set between Missouri and Oklahoma, in what was once endless prairie, the latest in technology dictated every street, sidewalk, and building. Soon the ESH survivors would come here, to this new city, and settle into life again.

But for how long? The city plans included schools, daycare centers, and playgrounds. Madeline thought of these, sitting in her atrium in the city center. For the first time she wondered, would they ever see children fill them again?

Cabbage and Beets

"There are no conflicts which cannot be resolved unless the true promoters of them remain hidden." – L. Ron Hubbard

Date: 04.22.2103
Calypso Colony Ship

Sam's hair was tousled, the short haircut she had given herself last week was curly and generally unkempt. Staying over at Daniel Medry's coffin was close and uncomfortable, but recently, it had been almost necessary. It helped her not give in to the despair she had felt since learning of Earth. She knew too that she was falling, hard, for Daniel. Plenty of others were seeking comfort, and the Couples Billets had been claimed several nights in a row. Daniel and Sam had found something reassuring about the closeness of Medry's coffin and Sam staying overnight had become a regular thing. Legs and arms entwined, sometimes making love, but more than anything just being close to one another, a reassurance that they were not alone.

She slipped into an open Ready Room and rinsed her face, smoothed the bigger spikes of hair down, and keyed in her personal code for a clean jumpsuit from the clothing dispensary. Damn it, she was late. Not that it mattered that much. As the current head of 'Ponics, she had some flexibility on arrival time, but she was hyper-aware of how important it was to maintain a routine, especially now.

Although the ship had learned of Earth's fate over a year ago, the information packets and responses from Earth were scattered and infrequent. Mix in a few solar storms with bureaucratic ineptness and you got an endless series of missives that seemed to contain nothing but heartbreaking news.

Sam was struck by the lack of foresight from Earth. Yes, they were going through the biggest crisis the world had ever seen, but you would think that someone would recognize the need for coherent, organized information.

There were 250 souls on this ship, all with families, friends and lives back on Earth.

And with every single one of those people, the first question upon their lips when they heard of the ESH virus was, "My family, are they alive?"

Sam's heart ached still, thinking of Tom. He had been almost five years older than her, and it was his interest in space, in becoming a captain of a spaceship that had first infected her with the yearning for traveling to new worlds. Growing up, they had been close, closer than most siblings she knew. He had never kicked her out of his room, not even when his friends were over, not even during the teenage years when a ten-year-old kid sister was usually the opposite of welcome. Even after they had grown up and headed their separate ways they had kept in touch.

He had been so excited, and a tiny bit jealous when she had been approved for the mission to Zarmina's World.

"You got me licked, Sis," he had said, "But not for long. I've applied for the Kepler mission."

The Kepler mission had been slated to leave in 2105.

There had been a spate of extrasolar inhabitable planets found shortly after Gliese 581 was discovered (and temporarily discredited) right before The Collapse. When the James Webb Space telescope had been launched, those planets were quickly identified and D.O.V.E. vessels sent to Kepler and other systems. Kepler's mission had been announced in 2095, just three years after Gliese 581. The D.O.V.E probe to Kepler was equipped with the prototype Alcubierre-Mesner warp drive that Calypso had. The probe hadn't had to deal with human crew, so the warp hops were quicker. It had returned from Kepler with fantastic views of a planet very Earth-like in appearance. For that colony mission the entire crew would be in Cryo for nearly 50 years, emerging from stasis only after the ship had achieved orbit around the planet.

One of the packets that had been given to her shortly after the news of Earth broke had been from him. He had been accepted for the Kepler mission. That had been the plan at least. Until the world had died. A mission which would never happen now, couldn't, she imagined.

When the word had come that he and his crew died somewhere in space she had been wild with grief. Why hadn't they picked him for Calypso's crew? Why her? Why did *he* have to die?

Perhaps that is when she had begun to fall for Daniel. He had listened, not offered any senseless platitudes.

Tom was gone, and she wasn't.

Daniel had said, "The key to actually *living* our lives is understanding and accepting that."

Sam slipped into the clean jumpsuit and pulled on her ship shoes. They were a soft, stretchy fabric with a thin layer of memory foam insole that molded to her feet perfectly. Time to stop wallowing in her sadness and get on with her day.

She was just leaving the Ready Room, nodding to another crew member who was waiting for his turn, and was heading for the cafeteria for something she could take with her to the 'Ponics Deck to eat when her suit com crackled. It was Laney Deeds, her newest assistant, one of the youngest of the crew members at twenty-two years.

Upon hearing the news of Earth after being taken out of Cryo three months ago, she had spent the first two weeks crying before finally snapping out of it, focusing on her work with a quiet intensity.

"Sam? Sam? We have a huge problem in 'Ponics, something happened to the temp controls!"

"Be there in a half a tic, Laney."

Sam sprinted for the tube. The tubes were small, two-person affairs, elevators of sorts that ran between the decks. They were constantly in motion. One only had to step onto the ledge and step in quickly, and the tube would take the single occupant to the next floor, or the next, only reversing when it had come to either end. There were eight floors in all, but only four of them were in use right now.

The rider could jump off the tube into a pocket double airlock, and if already in a spacesuit, progress through the airlock doors into those decks. There was no need to do so for anyone but those tasked with performing routine monthly inspections or supply retrieval.

The decks were not currently pressurized or heated since they were intended for storage. That would change once they arrived and established orbit. Everything that a new outpost would possibly need was down in the lower levels, including the machines that would make the building and manufacture of their new society possible.

Sam jumped off of the tube and took the remaining three meters to the 'Ponics Deck door at a fast jog. The corridor was clear, and she felt a burst of cold air as she slipped through the doorway onto the 'Ponics Deck. *Cold air. Frigid.* Her breath puffed out in clouds as she took in the disastrous scene in front of her.

Plants glistened with frost. They were limp, bunched up and dark green, some already black. She looked at the long rows of potatoes, lettuce, and her eyes locked on the delicate carrot seedlings that had been emerging in Row 5, along with the strawberries in Row 6 beyond that. All of them indisputably dead.

"Pull the reports, Laney, I want to know when the temps dropped and why." Sam barked.

She closed her eyes. This was a disaster.

The ship depended on this food. It made the MREs more palatable, raised morale, and meant that their food stores would last longer. They needed every possible morsel of food to stretch. Who knew for sure if crops would grow in the alien soil? They could conduct all of the experiments they wanted to, but the reality was until they were actually working the soil on Zarmina's World, it was all a crapshoot.

Shit. It had gone wrong on *her* watch. No matter what the outcome, Sam felt responsible. And this just two months before her shift ended and Nagel Lowry took over. He was an exacting man, and she knew he would find a way to blame her. Despite all of the screening processes of the Selection Committee, in the end, they had filled the ship with highly intelligent, no-nonsense, innovative types who tended not to play well with others. The Committee had discussed it at length and decided that it was worth it. No matter how hard one tried, not everyone was going to get along. Overall, the crew of the Calypso were hard-working, exacting, and meticulously detailed. It was better than having the opposite inclinations.

Laney was shivering as she began scrolling through records.

Sam tapped NARA to life on her comm mike, "NARA, crewmember one-nine-oh, please connect me to Environmental."

The computer program handled the communications network on Calypso, tracked all personnel and handled information retrieval for over ten different databases that contained the combined knowledge of 50 different countries.

NARA's voice responded in a cheerful monotone, "Connecting to Environmental Engineering, one moment please."

"Environmental...Jenkins here." Zach was a close friend.

"Zach, Sam here. I've got *frost* in the 'Ponics Deck."

"Come again?"

"The temps are currently reading one degree Celsius in here," Sam replied.

Zach paused, "Negative on that, I've got all systems showing 18 degrees Celsius. Sam, is this some esoteric April Fool's joke?"

Sam allowed herself a small smile, "Sorry Zach, I'm not kidding. I can see my breath down here and we've got massive damage to all the crops. It must have been this way most of the night."

"Sonuva...I'm coming down now. Jenkins out."

Moments later, Zach arrived. He was clean cut, his short black hair spiked. The usual smile was gone from his features, replaced by a grim expression.

"Holy hell, it's *cold*. What did you do to it, Sam?"

She gave him a pained look, "Right, blame me."

Zach headed for the control panel and opened the door, digging into the pack he had slung over his shoulder for a mini-laptop and jack. Plugging into the system, he began running a diagnostic.

After a few moments of staring at the screen, watching the code scroll, he hit a key, pausing the readout.

"Well, that's not right. What the..."

Sam, who had moved down the rows, checking the individual plants, looked up.

"What have you found?"

"A piece of code that, well, it doesn't make sense."

His brow furrowed. It occurred to Sam that Laney was watching him with an intensity that seemed a little *more* than just professional. Sam couldn't help but grin, and hid the motion by turning away.

The girl had been so sad, and Zach was single and quite attractive. One of his sisters was also on board. Zach had come from an interesting background, a family filled with seven siblings, all adopted, from all corners of the world. Zach had been adopted from Taiwan. His adoptive mother had been white, and his father was from Nigeria. He had made Sam laugh over tales of growing up in a predominantly white town in Tennessee.

"It looks like perhaps a programming glitch. I can't explain *how* but it looks as if there was a command embedded that reduced the temperature down to one degree Celsius at 0100 hours this morning." Zach shook his head, "What it doesn't explain is why the alarms didn't go off. We have redundancies on top of redundancies to protect from this kind of thing happening."

He looked up and met Laney's eyes and smiled a wide, white-toothed smile. The girl looked embarrassed and turned back to her work. Zach glanced over at Sam and quirked his eyebrows in confusion.

Sam gave him a significant look, tilting her head towards Laney, who was arms deep in plants, and nodded. Guys needed help sometimes, it seemed, and after a moment, an "oh" of surprise had formed on his face and Zach smiled even wider.

Sam figured she would be seeing Zach around 'Ponics more, and not just because of the malfunction. He had moped when she hooked up with Daniel, and she hadn't realized until then that he had wanted anything more than friendship. It wouldn't have mattered, whatever Zach's fantasies were, he was firmly a colleague in Sam's eyes.

"I need to report this to the Captain," Zach said and headed for the door.

"Let him know I will be there as soon as I've got an accurate count of our losses." Sam answered in return, "And please get the heat back on in here. Otherwise, all we will be eating is cabbage and beets...and maybe not even that."

Zach nodded and slipped out the door.

Sam and Laney got to work.

Let Her Go

Date: 06.26.2103
Calypso Colony Ship

Seeing the apprehensive look on Sam's face brought it home to Daniel. He was standing there on the Cryo Deck, just a few steps away from Deeks' desk. For the first time he felt completely out of his element.

Sam was on the prep table, dressed in boy shorts and a tank top and looking sexy as hell. She also looked vulnerable and sad. He had caught her in time. She was scheduled to spend the next eighteen months in Cryo and be revived right before planetfall.

Medry, you are a complete dick.

He knew it. He had pushed Sam away for a week now. And for what? Because of how he felt about her? Even he knew that was stupid. Cryo wouldn't last forever, and he knew she wanted some future with him, she'd as much as said so.

Kids.

He had read once some sappy sentiment that Janine had posted on her and Luke's fridge. It had read, "Making the decision to have a child – it is momentous. It is to decide forever to have your heart go walking around outside your body."

Sappy...but true.

And Sam had said it. After months of blissed out moments together, her thoughts had finally turned to the future, to what their lives would be like after planetfall. She wasn't the only one. Knowing the fate of Earth had reminded everyone of how fragile human existence truly was. There had been some who wanted to start having babies immediately, before planetfall. At the other extreme were those who were voicing their fears over becoming the equivalent of brood mares, and asking if the artificial wombs could be adapted to support human embryos.

Whenever it even looked like the conversation was going to head in the direction of babies, he'd cut in, changed the subject, and shut her down.

She wanted kids. And all he could think of was Toby.

His...son. And he had left him there. Left him to die, alone, abandoned first by his biological father, and then through death, by the only parents he had ever known.

Plenty of kids had been left orphans. A world *full* of people had died horribly. Toby wasn't alone in this, and Daniel knew it, but it didn't change anything. Daniel had left his *son*, his *brother*, the mother of his child, and thoughtlessly abandoned them to an unspeakable fate.

They had all had to report to Jacob Carter for evaluation after the news of Earth's fate had gone ship-wide. And just because Daniel and Kevin and the captain had had some more time to accept it, that didn't count for much. Everyone ended up talking to Carter, he was the Psych on duty, and the man everyone had to spill their guts to. Captain's orders, you go until Carter tells the Captain you don't have to anymore.

He had done his mandatory hours with Carter, cried, howled, and then put his heart and memories in a nice little pocket. He's passed and gotten out of the required sessions in record time. Until now. Until the conversations started going to babies, kids, families, and planetfall.

He just...*couldn't*. He couldn't talk about it. He couldn't imagine Sam's belly growing full and round with his child.

It's just not you, Daniel. You aren't exactly dad material, are you? Across the distance of billions of miles, a dead woman's voice still haunted him.

"Daniel, I..." Sam was directly in front of him now.

He put a finger up to her mouth, then leaned in and kissed her. "I've been a dick, Sam. And you don't deserve that." He took a deep breath, tried to get past the logjam in his throat at the thought of telling her about Toby.

Sam's expressive gray eyes filled. She played the tough chick well, but once you got past that rock-hard exterior, well, he had seen an entirely different side of her since they had become lovers. Sam was the best of both worlds, smart and sharp-tongued to keep him on his toes, intuitive and sensitive.

In some ways, she reminded him of Janine, and in others, reminded him of someone Janine could never have been.

"I've got something to tell you. Something about my family I haven't told you about."

Her eyes widened a little.

She knew of his family, who hadn't talked of their families? She had talked of hers, of a brother who had captained ships to the Moon and Mars. He had held her close when they had received word of his death. They had grieved together.

Evers, who had been prepping Sam, had quietly moved to the opposite end of the Cryo Deck. Deeks wasn't on shift yet. There was just the two of them.

Daniel took a deep breath and told her the truth about his affair with Janine, his brother's wife, and Toby. She listened quietly.

"I left him there, Sam. I left him to face a world full of death and loneliness." Daniel caught his breath, his chest hurt just thinking about it, "How can I even think of bringing another child into the world after doing something like that? And could you even look at me and want a child with me knowing that?"

Sam said nothing, simply pulled him close.

They stood there for a moment and then he said quietly, "I'm in love with you Sam."

"I love you too, Daniel."

Moments later, Mike Deeks ambled in, now on shift.

"Time for a nap, Sexy Sam?" he asked.

Despite his flirtatious words, he barely looked at her, intent on his job. Medry wondered if Deeks was still pining for one slim and attractive Kit Tanner.

After handling the transition of all personnel from Earth to Calypso, Kit had gone directly into Cryo. Like a majority of the folks in Cryo, she would not be revived until just before planetfall.

Sam hugged Daniel one last time and nodded to Deeks, extending her arm.

"Can I stay until you go in?" Daniel asked.

She nodded and he squeezed her hand, and then moved out of Deeks' way.

Daniel watched as Deeks fitted Sam with an IV, inserted the cannula in her nose and filled a syringe with a bright green fluid that swirled inside. He wasn't much for needles, especially if they were going into him, so he hadn't really watched when being prepped for his stint in Cryo.

The drug, combined with a gas similar to nitrous oxide would bring Sam's body into an altered state of consciousness, allowing Deeks to administer another drug which would reduce all body functions to a crawl. Combine this with just the right timing in cooling and Sam's body would enter a state of what was essentially hibernation.

They had first experimented with it during the long in-system trips to the Mars colony. Six months in each direction, since they couldn't use the first-run warp drives in-system, and it had been an excellent alternative to feeding two dozen people for half a year before getting to an inhospitable planet with limited resources.

It had also worked well for a couple of cases of cancer that couldn't be treated at the Mars colony. They had discovered that the hibernating state that Cryo provided slowed down the spread of the disease significantly. It had saved the lives of a handful of people over the years. The in-system drives developed in the past ten years had negated the need for hibernation within their solar system, but it had been the perfect solution for a trip such as this one.

Daniel watched as Sam's eyes fluttered and slipped closed, her slim, long fingers flexing slightly as if she were grasping for something just out of reach. Daniel ran a hand through her hair, smoothing down a few stray hairs, while Deeks waited a moment and then slid the next injection into her before pushing a button on the bottom of the table.

The entire assembly shifted, the sides of the Cryo case extruding from a section of the floor and enveloping the table with Sam on it. The sides slid up, straps tightening into position and the clear viewing window was temporarily clouded with cooling vapors. Daniel had never watched the process before, and he sucked in his breath.

It was one thing to be in Cryo, or even to come out of it, and quite another to see it done to another human being. It was more than disconcerting. It was terrifying.

Deeks continued to watch the various readouts displayed on the front screen of the Cryo pod, absorbed in blips and lines, which were incomprehensible to Daniel, but apparently made perfect sense to Deeks.

Deeks nodded, murmuring to himself as the blips and lines slowly lessened into barely discernible bumps and valleys.

He looked up at Daniel as if noticing him for the first time and clapped a hand on Medry's shoulder, "She'll be fine buddy. It all looks good."

Daniel helped Deeks shift the Cryo pod upright, guide it via the built-in rails to an open position in the eighth row, and heard the machine click into position in the floor. The portals for the Cryo chems were built into the floor, along with the oxygen supply and more. Each pod plugged into its own set of pipes which were controlled by the Cryo Deck's main computer.

The mist had cleared slightly, and Daniel could see Sam's face. She looked dead. It was unnerving, to say the least. As he stared at her face, he thought about what a future with her would be like planetside. Who knew? Perhaps she would wake up from Cryo and decide to find someone else, someone who gave a damn about family and kids, someone reliable, who wouldn't just abandon a child to a world full of death.

Medry sucked in his breath. *Damn it.* He wasn't okay and he knew it. He needed to talk to Carter again, maybe the psychologist could help him be the man Sam deserved. Maybe.

Daniel slipped out of the Cryo Deck and headed for his workstation. He was fifteen minutes late.

This Doesn't Make Sense

Date: 07.01.2103

Calypso Colony Ship

The Mess Hall was empty, quiet between waves of personnel coming through for food. In one corner, Zach Jenkins' food cooled as he reviewed the piece of code again, reading through it, checking the syntax – it just didn't add up. If Wyatt were here, she would be able to make sense of it. Whoever had written this was covering their tracks well.

Jacey would be able to ferret it out too, she had a nose for rogue code. Zach was brilliant, but when it came to comparing what he could do with Jacey Wyatt, he might as well be in remedial English class.

He rubbed his eyes. He'd been at this for days. Everyone else was moving on, convinced it had been some weird glitch, but that was not what he was getting. Someone had *done* this to the 'Ponics Deck. And whoever had done it had known exactly when to strike.

In most cases, the decks ran on four seven-hour shifts which overlapped each other. But for something like the 'Ponics Deck, there was no need. Or at least, there hadn't been until now.

The Captain and Nagel Lowry, the head of 'Ponics now that Sam Sydan had gone off shift and back into Cryo, might not have been willing to call it sabotage, but they had both agreed to immediately bump up the shifts, waking up another Tech from Cryo to handle the 1st Shift instead of leaving 'Ponics unattended for six hours. So, the schedule was now full, with overlaps at either end.

And yet they won't entertain the thought that this might be sabotage, Zach thought to himself.

He missed his sister Mali, who was on board, but in Cryo along with Jacey. She would have known exactly what to say to convince them, but it seemed impossible for Zach.

"I have to find the other half of the code," Zach mused, "and then they will believe me."

"I believe you, Zach." Laney's voice broke through the fog of commands and code.

He blinked and looked up, surprised to see her standing in front of him. He had been so absorbed in his work he hadn't even heard her approach. The soft ship shoes that everyone wore were quiet, but still, the girl had snuck up on him.

On her tray were two muffins, she handed one of them to Zach, "Here, you should eat something."

"I have some cabbage and beet soup here," He said, reaching for the bowl.

It was cold and a thin skin had formed on top. Zach gave it a half-hearted stir and wrinkled his nose. It smelled bad too.

"It doesn't taste good. Try the muffin." Her eyes were a startling shade of green, bright, not pale. He found himself wondering if she wore contacts.

Laney smiled back at him.

Christ, he was staring at her like an idiot.

Zach brushed her fingers with his as he reached for the muffin, took a bite, "Thanks."

"No problem."

"How's Sam's replacement, Nagel, doing?"

Laney gave a pained look, "He's, ugh."

She looked around, making sure no one was within earshot and lowered her voice, "Sam was fun, but I swear Nagel Lowry carries around his own personal storm cloud. Apparently, we have been doing everything wrong and it is a shock we haven't managed to kill off more plants while Sam was in charge. The man is impossible!"

Zach grinned.

"Side effects of having a bunch of brainiacs, some of us are impossible to work with."

"I'll bet you aren't impossible to work with."

It spilled out, and when she blushed, he couldn't help but smile in return.

Laney took the plunge and sat down across from him. Zach was exotic and down-to-earth at the same time – his Asian features juxtaposed with a slight Southern backwoods twang.

It was a small ship and word spread worse inside the metal walls than inside of a small town. Zach had looked Laney up. She had come from a big family, the same as he had. He had seen how hard she had taken the news of Earth. Her eyes had been bloodshot and swollen from crying for weeks after they woke her up from Cryo. Even after that, she had been quiet, withdrawn, and he often noticed her coming or going from Jacob Carter's office, which was just down the hall from Environmental Systems. Zach had watched Laney in the Mess Hall and the other common areas, wishing he knew what to say. The truth of it was that seeing her grieving had been almost reassuring. He knew they were all hurting, but she wasn't afraid to show it.

"How have you been?" he asked, thinking that, for the first time in a long time, her face wasn't blotchy from crying.

"I'm doing okay, I guess. It still hits at weird times." Laney answered, her brilliant green eyes meeting his gaze.

"Yeah, me too."

There was a long moment of silence.

Zach broke it first, "So, no one else thinks this was sabotage. I feel like Cassandra, doomed to tell the future and not be believed."

Laney nodded, "So let's figure out how to convince them. We need proof."

"It's hidden in billions of lines of code," Zach said morosely.

"What search strings are you running?"

"You know code?"

"Just enough to be dangerous." She took a nibble from her muffin and grinned again.

Zach looked at the girl and realized that, code expert or not, at least she was willing to help, and she believed in him.

He returned her grin, "All right, yeah, so let me show you what I've been running so far."

Their heads bent together and Laney eventually moved around the table and slid into the seat next to him to see the screen better. For the next few hours, they were absorbed deeply in their work, shoulder to shoulder, only stopping when a new wave of crew members came in, looking for food.

They were not successful that day or the next, but they kept searching. Zach couldn't explain *why* he believed that there was a saboteur among them, but he did. It didn't hurt that he had a great excuse to spend hours with a good-looking girl.

Zach's skin was a smooth olive, his hair jet black, and his brown eyes with their slightly angled corners were warm and welcoming. Laney was pale, with brown hair and forest green eyes. Where his fingers were warm, hers were ice cold.

"Poor circulation," she said in response to his surprised look. "My hands are always cold."

"Well, we can't have that." Her heart jumped when he smiled and enclosed her hands within his, warming them.

Working on a project together, even something as endlessly monotonous as sifting through millions of lines of code, was, *fun,* and Zach found himself not wanting to find the proof if only so they could keep looking.

They met after their shifts. Weeks turned into months as they sifted through the 'Ponics Deck programs, finding sub-routines and dead ends. It became routine, meet in the galley, work on two tablets, stop and discuss any odd bits, and move on. They would work for a few hours, then say good night to each other and head to their individual coffins.

By early December, their easy friendship edged into something more.

"We keep talking about those old action movies but we never get around to watching them." Zach mentioned one evening as they sat down to look at a new section of code. "Why don't we knock off early and watch one?"

Laney grinned, "If you can finagle some popcorn out of the supplies, you've got a deal!"

He laughed, "Aren't you going to ask what movie?"

"Nope, surprise me."

They knocked off early, neither of them focused on the code. Instead, Zach found that he was nervous. Could he be reading Laney wrong? He had only limited dating experience.

Later that evening, after they had said good night and returned to their own personal coffins, Zach could still feel the cool tingle of her lips on his.

He had selected the original Terminator movie, the director's cut with the 100th year anniversary edition commentary.

Laney had never seen it. He had enjoyed watching her jump at all of the right moments, practically crawling into his lap during one of the final scenes in the factory. Later, as they left the small theater room, her hand had fit into his so naturally.

"Did you like the movie?"

"I really did! But..."

"But what?" he asked.

"I guess I just figured it would be some high lit movie from the way you described it." Her face assumed a serious expression, "I believe you called it, 'A seminal storyline that illuminated a string of dystopian worldviews in the years prior to The Collapse.'" She giggled and he pulled her close to him, finally having found the nerve to kiss her.

It was more than a physical attraction, Zach had realized just how much he liked how Laney thought, what she said, and how she worked on problems. She had a fierce independence, based on the stories they had swapped, and he felt this easy, comfortable attraction to her. Something in the way that she sat, leaned in, twirling her hair around one finger as she stared at the endless lines of code. And her easy smile, which had been showing more and more with each week that passed.

The next day, in between their searches for evidence of sabotage and long, lingering kisses, they reminisced about their childhood.

"I grew up in the Everglades," she said, "There were still plenty of alligators out in the wild, so my parents made sure my brothers and sister kept a close eye on me."

Zach laughed, "We didn't have any 'gators in Tennessee, but we had plenty of snakes, including the timber rattlesnake."

Laney sighed, "I'm so used to the outdoors that is been hard here on the ship. I think I'd even take running into a 'gator or even a rattlesnake if it meant having dirt beneath my feet again!"

"I know exactly how you feel. The closer we get to planetfall, the longer it seems to take."

Laney had told him how her parents had chosen to homeschool her and her siblings. It had allowed her hours of freedom and encouraged her love of exploration. Her father had worked for World Geographic, one of the countless engineers who had designed spaceships, including the Calypso. She had spent endless hours at the now-defunct NASA Space Center seeing and touching the actual capsules, rudimentary as they were, that had brought Americans to space, and to the moon for the first time. This, bookended with her fascination with plants and their processes had led to dual degrees of Mechanical Engineering and Environmental Science. This had been an apparently irresistible combination for the Selection Committee.

In the two years before the final selections, the World Geographic Selection Committee had flagged all applications that listed multiple disciplines for special consideration. They wanted folks who were more than just one-trick ponies and Laney had been on the short list. She had sent in her application form two weeks before her seventeenth birthday.

Stolen kisses and small intimate gestures were where it all stopped, however. Laney had laid it out quite firmly, after all.

"This ship, it is an artificial construct. I like you Zach, I really, really do. But I want out of these confines, away from feeling stuffed shoulder to shoulder with everyone else before we take this any further. I don't want your feelings to change, or my feelings for you to change, once we are out of these ship walls." She had said it earnestly, pulling away once his kisses became more passionate.

Zach had to admit that it was a little disappointing, but he understood how she felt. It was too close of quarters. Everyone was in each other's faces right now. There was no real privacy at all. And despite the time that had passed, they were all still working through the loss of friends and family back home. After he had been revived from Cryo nine months ago, learning the news had hit him hard. Like everyone else he had searched for his family. His parents were gone, of that, he was sure.

Later updates had included the knowledge that only a certain rare blood type was being spared. Somehow, it provided just enough resistance to the ESH virus to give some kind of immunity. He didn't know the blood types of any of his siblings, however, and records were incomplete. His sister Amy had been aboard the Jupiter Supply Ship and she and the rest of the crew had been reported as deceased just a few weeks before Huygens Outpost had ceased all communication and went dark. As for the rest of his siblings, he had no answers, but as he and the rest of the Calypso crew were learning, that was an answer in itself.

He still had Mika, although she was oblivious, unaware of her loss, waiting for final orbit before she would be pulled from Cryo, and told the news. At least she would have him to lean on.

Spending hours with Laney reminded him that, despite all of the terrible things that had happened on Earth, and the crippling loss of his adoptive family, he was very lucky to be surrounded by good people. Perhaps that is why it was so important to him to find the person who was responsible for the 'Ponics freeze.

One day Zach stopped in mid-scroll.

"Oh my God, I…" He stared at the line of code. "Oh my God."

Laney leaned over, resting her chin on his shoulder, "What? Where?"

Zach pointed and she stared at it, her lips moving silently as she read the lines of code.

"Oh wow, that's, that's…"

"Elegant?" Zach supplied.

"Yeah." She stared at him, and grinned, "You found it."

"Yeah, I did." Zach stared at the code.

"Time and date? Can we trace it back to its origin?" Laney asked.

Zach nodded and they bent to their work, shoulder to shoulder, uncovering the last piece of the puzzle.

Moments later, there was a shift change and some other crew members filed in. As they did, Laney tensed and pointed to a string of commands that identified the workstation of origin.

"That's it! Oh my God, Zach, what do we do?"

"It's a public workstation," Zach said, "It could be anyone."

"So, what do we do now?"

Zach stood up, closing the notebook, and gathering his belongings.

"We go to the Captain *now*, before something else happens."

They made their way to the Command Deck. There were two people in line in front of them. Zach stood, shifting from foot to foot, unsure of what to do next.

Laney stared at him, at the others in line, and grabbed the notebook from Zach, "Come on, we can't wait on this."

She strode into the Captain's office, leaving the two other crew members standing in her wake.

"Sir? You need to see this, it's important."

She set the notebook down on his desk and ignored Nagel Lowry, who looked rather outraged, having been interrupted in the middle of a lengthy, and rather boring, oral dissertation on the status of the 'Ponics Deck.

A few minutes later, the Captain had several other crew members in for the second round of explanations. The questions were still flying fast and furious as a klaxon alert began to sound.

NARAs voice sounded over all speakers.

WARNING CRYOGENICS SYSTEM SHUT DOWN

SYSTEM FAILURE - CODE RED

SYSTEM RESET ON ALL CRYO PODS IN FIFTEEN MINUTES

The room dissolved into chaos.

Forever Sleep

"I have noticed that even people who claim everything is predestined, and that we can do nothing to change it, look before they cross the road." –– Stephen Hawking

Date: 01.27.2104

Calypso Colony Ship

The Cryo Deck was preternaturally quiet. Daniel Medry was running a little early and the shift change wasn't for another fifteen minutes, but it had been a quiet day. The transmission packets were mainly medical in nature and included updates on the ESH virus and the now clear teratogenic nature of the organism. Even as the death rate leveled off, the birth rate had plummeted. Women were miscarrying at a phenomenal rate – and not just in the first trimester, but the second and third as well. That was pretty much all he had gotten out of the report before he forwarded it on to Carrie Schrader who headed the Medical Bay. She held more medical degrees than he could list and was studying the ESH virus in detail during this relatively quiet time before they achieved orbit and planetfall. Once there, everyone would find themselves occupied by the daily challenge of creating a civilization in their new world.

Reading about the ESH virus often made Daniel's stomach clench and roil uncomfortably. Perhaps it was the insanity of it all. *How a company could design a virus and unleash it - without any concern for what would happen if it made the jump from swine to human. Who does that? And all in the name of profit.*

And look what it had done. Highly transmissible, nearly 100% fatal in humans, and now those who were still alive were facing the possibility of extinction. They were all carriers. They had seen their family and friends die horribly, and the survivors were now struggling with infertility and astronomical rates of fetal and infant death.

He thought of Sam in Cryo. She wanted kids, and after the past six months without her, he had certainly had plenty of time to think. He had finally acknowledged that he wanted the same. He could never make it right, what had happened to Luke and Janine and Toby. He could never go back to Earth and hold his son in his arms. But he could have those children that Sam wanted so much. And now, after months of contemplation and introspection, along with what he considered an unhealthy length of abstinence, he was looking forward to their future life on Zarmina's World. His dreams had been filled with children as of late – all black-haired children with deep blue eyes.

Damn it, Sam, I miss you.

He walked into the Cryo Deck. He needed a good poker game and maybe a nip or two of scotch, the diversion would help get those gloomy statistics from the transmission packet out of his head. He didn't need to know that the human race might be doomed, might actually die off due to its own stupidity and capitalistic greed. Deeks would get him out of his rut and make him laugh – Deeks was good at that.

It was quiet on the Cryo Deck. Too quiet.

The space was large. It had to be. Over 200 of the occupants of Calypso were in the pods at any one time. Feeding 250 mouths while traveling 1.2 quadrillion miles for nearly five and a half years would have taken more space for food on the ship than was possible, hence the alternative. Most of the inhabitants of Calypso had gone into the pods before the ship even left Earth's solar system and they would not be revived until after planetfall. For them, no time at all would have passed. Daniel himself was supposed to be there now. He would have been if Earth and its denizens hadn't decided to die off in the hundreds of millions. All of the updates, the transmissions from Earth, they had multiplied exponentially. As a result, this had kept Daniel and Kevin far busier than anyone had ever planned.

The deck held pods arrayed in multiple rows of twenty, stretching back on tracks built into the floor. On either side of Cryo were rooms designed to hold four padded tables each. These rooms were used to prep Calypso's inhabitants and also serve as recovery rooms. There were four of them, two on each wall. At the far end of the deck were several offices and rooms.

Here was the main control deck for the pods, workstations for the crew who worked the Cryo Deck, and storage of equipment and supplies.

Usually, he could see Deeks or Evers in one of the front rooms once he passed through the blast doors. Evers was young, not even thirty years old, but he was already balding. The lights on the deck managed to light up his head like it was a lightbulb, but today, there was no telltale sign of the Tech.

"Hey, Deeks! Evers! Where are you two troublemakers?" Daniel called.

There was no answer.

He headed toward the back of the deck. Maybe Deeks had his headphones on and couldn't hear.

In front of Medry were two rooms along the back wall of Cryo. The one on the right, the control room, was dark. The lights were off and only a few of the control lights flickered through the half wall of tinted glass. Daniel turned to the room on the left and walked towards it. Reaching the doorway, he felt for the switch and flipped it on. Light flooded the room.

Lockers lined two of the walls of the room. The room also contained two workstations where Deeks and Evers typically sat. A work tablet lay on the floor, its screen cracked. But Daniel barely noticed. Instead, his eyes were riveted on the trail of blood leading to the lockers...a *lot* of blood.

Like something out of a horror movie.

"Deeks...Evers...if this is some kind of a prank," Medry said slowly, "It isn't funny."

He walked forward, stepping over the bloody drag marks. It certainly *looked* like blood.

Any minute, one of those bastards is going to jump out and scare the living shit out of me, I just know it.

But instead, his hand pulled on the lock and the door to the nearest locker swung open. And in true horror movie fashion, a body slumped out of it, eyes staring, a garish red slash forming a ghoulish death smile on the throat below.

Daniel's heart stuttered, Deeks, Daniel's friend and poker buddy, was staring up at him. Worse, stuffed behind him and now also sagging out, was Evers, also sporting a horrifying scarlet slash across his throat. His windpipe was torn and hanging half out.

A scream of horror rose in Daniel's throat as he spun on his heel, straight into Nathan Zradce's outraised arm, which was slashing down towards him with a bloody knife. His assailant's knife sliced along Daniel's scalp as he feinted to the left and shoved the man hard. This only resulted in Daniel slipping in the blood on the floor and falling, his head cracking twice against the deck, knocking him out with the second blow.

It was the wail of the alarms that roused him moments later. That and the smell of burning electrical wires. Daniel forced his eyes open, wiped the blood from them. His head was bleeding profusely. He couldn't see Nathan, *where the hell had he gone*? Maybe he had seen all the blood and thought Medry was dead. Maybe. Daniel struggled to sit up; his head was pounding.

It didn't make sense. None of it made sense. He turned, wincing in pain, to look at the lockers. Deeks and Evers were still there, still dead, and now the Cryo Deck was screaming that something was wrong. He couldn't see to the hallway outside –– were the blast doors closed?

His mind reeled. How had this happened? Why?

Zradce, the man had attacked him. And, Daniel's head ached as he tried to catch up with this lightning quick turn of events. Nathan must have killed Deeks and Evers too. But why?

And what was the man doing now? Had he been the one to close the blast doors? To set off the alarms in Cryo? Why would he do that? His own wife was in Cryo!

None of it made sense. But as Daniel grasped the situation in front of him, he knew he had to do something. He looked for a weapon, any weapon, but found nothing except the broken tablet on the floor. It wasn't much of a weapon, but he had to try. He eased out of the room, doubled over and nearly passed out when he bent low to move past the tinted glass half wall of the control room.

Doing so was painful, but he had the element of surprise as he entered the room. Nathan Zradce's back was towards him. He was slamming a heat wand from Engineering down on the controls, the smell of sizzling plastic and electrical conduit filled the air. Daniel gathered up all of his strength and slammed the broken tablet into the back of Zradce's head.

Nathan screamed in pain, dropping the heat wand and stabbing with his other hand as he turned towards his attacker. The knife missed with the first slash and came down with such ferocity the second time that his left shoulder shuddered in response, the knife digging into meat and muscle, burying itself to the hilt. Blood sprang around the knife, soaking Daniel's shirt and Nathan's hands until his fingers slipped from the blade.

Daniel, fighting for his life, kicked Nathan's legs out from under him and slammed him hard in the face with the tablet. He heard Nathan's jaw crack as he hit the floor and was knocked unconscious.

He ran to the half-melted control panel as NARAs voice issued over the speakers:

EMERGENCY SHUTDOWN OF ALL CRYO PODS INITIATED

SYSTEM RESET ON ALL CRYO PODS IN 14:47 MINUTES

If Daniel didn't do something soon, everyone in Cryo was going to die.

Our Father

Date: 01.27.2104
Calypso Colony Ship

Daniel's ears ached from the constant wail of the alarms. His head swam. A cut ran across the top of his head, leaking blood. He had felt an unnerving softness in a section of his skull the one time he had reached up a hand to explore the damage. His forehead was a mass of red and drying blood. If he could have seen his own reflection, he would have discovered that his handsome face looked like something out of a horror movie.

The alarms continued to wail, their red lights flashing, and Daniel's stomach twisted with nausea. He tried in vain to remember what to do when a person goes into shock.

"Stop the blood loss, that's one."

He looked at the handle of the knife protruding from his shoulder, should he pull it out?

"Yeah, maybe not. Think Daniel, think. There has to be a way to stop this countdown."

He tried the Comm link on his suit. If he could connect with NARA, he would be able to talk to the crewmembers outside who were working on getting in. Perhaps they would know what to do.

"NARA, crewmember oh-four-eight, connect me to Captain Aaronson please."

No response.

"NARA, crewmember oh-four-eight, connect me to Environmental."

Still no response.

"NARA?"

The Comm link remained silent. Whatever this madman had done, he had managed to block the link between NARA, the rest of the ship, and him. Daniel was on his own.

At his feet, the moaning had turned to a hysterical giggle and recital of scripture. The screen on the console continued to scroll, the minutes counting down.

OVERRIDE PASSWORD FAILURE

PERSONNEL RECOGNITION FAILURE

SYSTEM FAILURE - CODE RED

SYSTEM RESET ON ALL CRYO PODS IN 13:49 MINUTES

"Our Father who art in Heaven, hallowed be thy name..." The man at Daniel's feet said.

Daniel kicked him, hard.

"Shut up, you crazy sonofabitch and tell me how to stop this countdown before every one of them dies!"

The man giggled, his mouth a mass of blood and broken teeth. Daniel's right hand ached from the beating he had given the lunatic.

"Thy kingdom come, thy will be done, on Earth as it is in Heaven." He giggled again, "And in the stars, where all of God's love is possible."

He might have continued, but Daniel kicked him in the head and he fell silent and lay unmoving on the floor of the Cryo Deck.

The view screen now read...

OVERRIDE PASSWORD FAILURE

PERSONNEL RECOGNITION FAILURE

SYSTEM FAILURE - CODE RED

SYSTEM RESET ON ALL CRYO PODS IN 13:13 MINUTES

The whine of the saw or drill was beginning to have an effect on the door behind him. He thought he could see a white-hot glow in the upper left corner. He looked back at the screen.

OVERRIDE PASSWORD FAILURE

PERSONNEL RECOGNITION FAILURE

SYSTEM FAILURE - CODE RED

SYSTEM RESET ON ALL CRYO PODS IN 12:55 MINUTES

No, he couldn't wait for them. He had to do something. He wiped the blood out of his eyes and looked around the room. Two hundred fifty pods, with at least two hundred of them filled with a human being vital to their mission. He couldn't get to all of them in time, and how could he choose which ones to save? His eyes stared at them, arrayed in rows, the occupants peaceful in their suspended animation, unaware of the terrible danger they were all in.

He had screwed up so damned bad, leaving Luke and Janine and Toby behind. Everyone he had loved. He had run from them, into the blackness of space and an uncertain future, so sure that they would be fine without him.

But they hadn't been. He didn't even know if his son was still alive. The plague knew no boundaries, gave no quarter, and spared no family. They were lost in the waves of the dead and dying, lost to him forever through time and space. He couldn't help them. In truth, he had abandoned them.

Daniel felt a sudden surge of understanding for *why* the man at his feet had done what he had. The sense of loss, of overwhelming futility and horror at the thought of every loved one gone and dead had haunted each of them for over two years now. There had been times when Daniel had wished he was back there, that he too could be counted among the dead. It seemed fitting. Existing without them, knowing he was helpless to ever return, or change the past, had filled him with a blackness that did not fade or shrink with time.

He headed for the nearest row and began with the first pod. He typed the code each member of Calypso had been taught as part of their safety training into the tiny keypad on the individual Cryo pod.

Words appeared on the pod's view screen as vapors swirled and the frost lining the inside began to clear.

MANUAL OVERRIDE INITIATED
BEGIN EMERGENCY REVIVAL SEQUENCE ON AXLER, JASON
03:58 MINUTES UNTIL REVIVAL
SYSTEM RESET ON ALL CRYO PODS IN 12:12 MINUTES

Each Cryo pod listed the occupant's name. Daniel didn't know everyone – he had trained with many of them, but there had been so little time, so many hoops to jump through. He stared at Jason. He looked familiar, but he didn't know him well. The frost vanished and Daniel could see a slight frown on the man's sleeping face.

Daniel began working down the line. The individual pod sequences had to be initiated, cycle through, and complete before the system purge. It took four minutes for an emergency revival sequence. This meant he had to get to every occupied pod, type in the sequence and be done with all of them before the purge countdown hit the four-minute mark.

His sluggish brain tried to figure out the numbers. How long did it take him to input the codes? He wasn't sure, maybe five, maybe ten seconds? His brain, running low on blood, struggled for what seemed like forever to try to average how much time it would take to initiate the revival sequence on all of the pods.

At the fourth one, his fingers slipped and the screen flashed.

MANUAL OVERRIDE ATTEMPT NOT VALID
EMERGENCY REVIVAL SEQUENCE NOT INITIATED
RE-ENTER PASSWORD
SYSTEM RESET ON ALL CRYO PODS IN 11:14 MINUTES

"Can't do both, Medry."

Daniel's voice was a hoarse croak, barely penetrating the wail of the alarms.

"Focus on entering the code. Keep going."

He re-entered the password, his fingers numb and clumsy, and he was rewarded with the standard message.

MANUAL OVERRIDE INITIATED
BEGIN EMERGENCY REVIVAL SEQUENCE ON JENKINS, MIKA
03:58 MINUTES UNTIL REVIVAL
SYSTEM RESET ON ALL CRYO PODS IN 11:07 MINUTES

Was this Zach Jenkins sister? Daniel thought it had to be. Zach had mentioned her recently, wished she was awake to help him track down a mystery he had been working on. Zach was from a large family of siblings adopted from across the globe. Mika's skin was coal black, her dreadlocks glistened with frost.

Daniel willed his feet and hands to move faster. He ignored the dizziness he felt. Now was not the time. He moved on down the line. Sam needed him, they all needed him. When he moved too suddenly, his vision would narrow, darkening around the edges like an antique photograph, tunneling his thoughts. Even breathing felt difficult, as if the air had turned to sludge in his lungs.

MANUAL OVERRIDE INITIATED
BEGIN EMERGENCY REVIVAL SEQUENCE
03:58 MINUTES UNTIL REVIVAL ON FARNSWORTH, DAVID
SYSTEM RESET ON ALL CRYO PODS IN 10:56 MINUTES

Farnsworth, he was the alternate First Officer, Martin Phoenix's contemporary. He remembered David had served the first half of the journey. He had been awake when the news of Earth broke, on duty for only a few more weeks afterwards. Daniel frowned, trying to concentrate, wasn't he related to the Captain somehow?

Daniel's thoughts kept sliding sideways, disappearing into inky memories of his family. He moved slowly, deliberately, and felt Luke and Janine's presence, close enough that he imagined he could smell the floral notes of Janine's favorite shampoo, the one he had bought for her, kept buying for her because he loved how it smelled. It was as if Luke was standing next to him, his hand on Daniel's shoulder.

"Keep going brother, don't stop."

Daniel wanted to tell Luke he was sorry, kept trying to form the words as he stood in front of the next Cryo pod, trying to remember what it was he wanted to say, something he needed to do, both of them seemed the same, tangled memory mixed with hallucination, and Luke's hand on him.

"You gotta keep going, brother. You have to save them."

Daniel nodded to Luke, reaching out to key in the code.

MANUAL OVERRIDE INITIATED

BEGIN EMERGENCY REVIVAL SEQUENCE ON TANNER, KIT

03:58 MINUTES UNTIL REVIVAL

SYSTEM RESET ON ALL CRYO PODS IN 10:52 MINUTES

Daniel stared as the frost cleared and he could see Kit's face, her lips slightly parted. He thought of Deeks, dead in the back room, and her, waking up now. At least he had managed to save her. He kept going, moving slow.

Vision in Red

"We have also arranged things so that almost no one understands science and technology. This is a prescription for disaster. We might get away with it for a while, but sooner or later this combustible mixture of ignorance and power is going to blow up in our faces." – Carl Sagan

Date: 01.27.2104
Calypso Colony Ship

He wasn't going to make it. The access door glowed white hot, but the crew still hadn't broken through. The alarms continued to shriek. The intensity of them hammered his already battered skull, and he could feel his pulse jumping in time. The heavy, coppery taste of blood filled his mouth. His tongue had been lacerated at some point, perhaps during the fight, or when he hit the floor of the Cryo Deck, his teeth digging deep into the sensitive organ. It was swelling, and still bleeding, He tried to spit out the mouthful of blood, but it just dribbled down his chin. He had no strength left to spit, it seemed, and the world tilted, his vision blurring.

Daniel kept moving, his feet clumsy, stuck on legs that felt heavy and unyielding. He keyed in the sequence, it beeped, and he tried again. On the third try, the words scrolled.

MANUAL OVERRIDE INITIATED
BEGIN EMERGENCY REVIVAL SEQUENCE ON YOUNG, NISKA
03:58 MINUTES UNTIL REVIVAL
SYSTEM RESET ON ALL CRYO PODS IN 10:29 MINUTES

Four rows to go, with nearly eighty innocent people still in their pods, completely unaware of the grim fate that awaited them. His friends, people whose talents the entire colony depended upon. But despite this, Daniel was moving slow, struggling with every ounce of his being.

It had taken him three tries on the last pod to enter the correct sequence and initiate the emergency revival. He was barely able to stand; his hands were cold and they shook. The blood from the blow he had taken to his head still ran freely, and he squinted out of one clear eye, too tired to bother wiping his face.

His mind was wandering too. Perhaps it was blood loss, perhaps Luke and Janine weren't really there, but damned if they didn't seem so real. Luke looked exactly as he had the day Daniel had last saw him, Janine as well, wearing that sad, disapproving look she could get. His vision blurred again, and he wondered if he would see Toby.

"No," came his own voice, slow and slurred, as if he had been drinking, "Toby isn't dead. At least someone you love is still alive."

Luke's specter nodded at him. Janine's just looked pissed.

"I have to save them," Medry muttered, cold and clumsy hands reaching for the next Cryo pod.

He pressed the keys, blacking out momentarily at a critical juncture, repeating it once, then twice, before it came out right.

MANUAL OVERRIDE INITIATED
BEGIN EMERGENCY REVIVAL SEQUENCE ON LYONS, THEO
03:58 MINUTES UNTIL REVIVAL
SYSTEM RESET ON ALL CRYO PODS IN 10:22 MINUTES

The crazy bastard who had done this, who had murdered his friends Deeks and Evers, lay unmoving on the Cryo Deck floor behind him, a pool of his own blood spreading from his nose and mouth. Medry couldn't help but hope that the man was dead. His mind simply could not conceive of a world in which his actions made sense.

MANUAL OVERRIDE INITIATED
BEGIN EMERGENCY REVIVAL SEQUENCE ON DRENKOWSKI, SARRA
03:58 MINUTES UNTIL REVIVAL
SYSTEM RESET ON ALL CRYO PODS IN 10:18 MINUTES

Sarra, she and Kit had both come from Chicago, and had been friends for years. He remembered that from training. That and her practical jokes. She was also a veterinarian and well-versed in the artificial wombs they had on board, having helped develop them.

He leaned for a moment on the pod he had just initiated. His eyelids felt heavy and his legs and arms were like lead weights. He closed his eyes, just for one sweet blessed moment. He was so tired.

Falling against the pod was what jerked Daniel back to consciousness. The knife slammed into the meat of his shoulder, then ripped loose and fell to the floor with a dull clang. The shock of the impact was enough to pull him back to present, more awake than ever, and lucid, for the moment. He entered the code on the pod in front of him and then stared dumbfounded at the screen.

MANUAL OVERRIDE INITIATED
BEGIN EMERGENCY REVIVAL SEQUENCE ON RUBINOWITZ, LITA
03:58 MINUTES UNTIL REVIVAL
SYSTEM RESET ON ALL CRYO PODS IN 10:05 MINUTES

How could over thirteen seconds have elapsed since the last pod? He had only closed his eyes for a second! He had just over ten minutes to go, and countless pods left. He continued to move down the line of pods, inputting the emergency revival sequence and moving on as soon as he saw the familiar words begin to scroll on the screen.

He was so cold. The world swam around him, dimming to gray splotches when he moved his head too quickly.

He still needed to reach Sam. He had to keep going. All of these people, they needed him to save them. He peered at the display and slowly entered the code.

MANUAL OVERRIDE INITIATED
BEGIN EMERGENCY REVIVAL SEQUENCE ON DUNN-EDMONDS, SIMON
03:58 MINUTES UNTIL REVIVAL
SYSTEM RESET ON ALL CRYO PODS IN 10:01 MINUTES

This one was a little boy. The name that flashed across the screen, Dunn-Edmonds—that was Kevin's kid. *Thank God.* Daniel's mind flashed to a memory of Toby's face smiling, framed in tow-headed curls. His heart thumped harder; the loss of his son knifed deeper into him. How could he have left him? If he had only known what was to come, what the fates of those who had been left behind would be. If only he had known. But, how could he? How could any of them have known?

The 'would haves' and 'should haves' had been driving him nuts for over a year now. He had no right to miss him, no right to call Toby his son. What kind of man leaves it to another to raise his son? What kind of man has an affair with his brother's wife?

"You are a piece of shit, Medry." Daniel muttered out loud.

Janine's specter nodded, smirking as if she had been waiting for him to figure this out all along. Who was he to think he could save these people? He was a fuck-up of the worst degree. He shook his head, earning himself another wave of dizziness.

"Piece of shit or not, you are all they have right now, so suck it up."

He moved to the next pod and keyed in the sequence.

MANUAL OVERRIDE INITIATED

BEGIN EMERGENCY REVIVAL SEQUENCE ON LOWRY, ELLEN

03:58 MINUTES UNTIL REVIVAL

SYSTEM RESET ON ALL CRYO PODS IN 9:56 MINUTES

Was this Lowry's wife? She looked young, far younger than Nagel. He thought of Nagel, uptight, by the rules, the 'Ponics deck a far different place under his supervision. Especially for those used to Sam's management style.

The wound in his shoulder was worse with the knife out. Six more pods on this row to go, they all seemed to blur together. His foot slipped and he fell hard. He was running out of time. Worse yet, his body was running out of blood.

Fade to Black

"Never frighten a little man. He'll kill you." -- Robert A. Heinlein
Date: 01.27.2104
Calypso Colony Ship

Somehow, Daniel got back up. Fighting dizziness, nausea, and an overwhelming feeling of weakness, he had stumbled to the next pod and the next until the row was nearly complete. Behind him, he could hear sounds of pods opening, of people emerging from them.

Recovering from Cryo wasn't an instantaneous thing. It held a revived sleeper in a grip of disorientation for minutes, even hours. Each person reacted differently, but it was not unlike waking from a very deep sleep. Behind Daniel, as he struggled with maintaining consciousness, men and women, even a handful of children, suddenly found themselves tumbling from restraints, arms and legs flailing, their sluggish brains bewildered by the cacophony of sound and light that surrounded them. Some fell in heaps on the floor, while others moved towards the blast doors like moths drawn to a flame. The doors glowed white hot as the rescuers continued to break their way through.

Daniel didn't stop. He couldn't. He made his way to the next pod and keyed in the sequence.

MANUAL OVERRIDE INITIATED
BEGIN EMERGENCY REVIVAL SEQUENCE ON LOWRY, NANCY
03:58 MINUTES UNTIL REVIVAL
SYSTEM RESET ON ALL CRYO PODS IN 9:07 MINUTES

Nancy was young. It was hard to tell, but she didn't look like she was more than five years old. He was almost to the end of the row. He moved onto the next unit and began to input the emergency override code.

Just one last row after this, Daniel reminded himself. *Just twenty more pods to go.* The little girl in the last pod had reminded him of how Toby had looked when he was asleep. Toby couldn't be older than her by a year or two. *Wait no, Toby was a teenager now.* Luke's specter stood near him, mouth moving soundlessly. What was he saying? Daniel wanted to stop and ask his brother so many questions - Could Luke forgive him? Was Toby all right? Had Luke and Janine's deaths been quick? As the last question hit Daniel's brain, the hallucination that was his brother tilted his head and shook it sadly.

Daniel's heart lurched painfully. He didn't want to think of how it must have been for Luke, or for Janine, worse to know that Toby had probably seen them both die.

The Cryo pod beeped at him.

MANUAL OVERRIDE ATTEMPT NOT VALID
EMERGENCY REVIVAL SEQUENCE NOT INITIATED
RE-ENTER PASSWORD
SYSTEM RESET ON ALL CRYO PODS IN 09:02 MINUTES

Daniel cursed and typed in the code again. This time, it worked. His fingers trembled and they felt thick and clumsy. He moved to the next machine.

A fresh wave of dizziness washed over him and his vision blackened around the edges. He held still and it cleared, his gaze focused on the man behind the glass, dark-haired, with a thick mustache. It was Saul Cramer. He headed the engineering staff.

Daniel's mind flashed back to training at the Cape, Saul's strong, broad hand eclipsing his, "Name is Saul. I'm an engineer, or so they tell me. Between you and me, I prefer the term grease monkey. If it can be fixed, I'm your man."

When Environmental had the glitch months back, they had revived Saul long enough to ensure that it wasn't something mechanical before putting him under again.

MANUAL OVERRIDE INITIATED
BEGIN EMERGENCY REVIVAL SEQUENCE ON CRAMER, SAUL
03:58 MINUTES UNTIL REVIVAL
SYSTEM RESET ON ALL CRYO PODS IN 08:55 MINUTES

Daniel moved on to the next pod, his vision blurring. He sucked in a breath. He had found her, *finally.*

MANUAL OVERRIDE INITIATED
BEGIN EMERGENCY REVIVAL SEQUENCE ON SYDAN, SAMANTHA
03:58 MINUTES UNTIL REVIVAL
SYSTEM RESET ON ALL CRYO PODS IN 08:50 MINUTES

The frost began to clear and Sam's lovely eyes were still closed. He wanted to stay, wait for her to wake up, but there were more pods and very little time. He knew this intellectually, but his body was uncooperative and alien. He felt trapped inside of a bag of blood and bone that seemed bound and determined to fail him.

Luke's specter swam back into focus. His brother looked sad now, said something that Daniel could not hear and pointed to the next pod, beckoning for him to hurry. Daniel nodded to his brother, which was a big mistake. The drum in his forehead kept time with his heartbeat, which seemed unnaturally fast. The room spun and his foot slipped to the side, coordination failing him again. Daniel struggled to stay conscious, but he was losing the battle. He keyed in the manual override for the next pod, then the next in the row. There were still eight occupied pods left. He keyed in the sequence.

MANUAL OVERRIDE INITIATED
BEGIN EMERGENCY REVIVAL SEQUENCE ON STRYDER, ERIC
03:58 MINUTES UNTIL REVIVAL
SYSTEM RESET ON ALL CRYO PODS IN 08:44 MINUTES

Daniel headed for the next pod and distantly wondered how the floor had managed to tilt up to meet him. Darkness claimed him.

On the cold metal floor, Daniel's eyes slowly opened. The ceiling was groaning and clanking. It was one of many noises that did not make sense. Another was the vision of Sam, somehow leaning over him, clad in the standard fare for Cryo, a tank top, and boy shorts. Her hair and skin were still damp, and her hands felt ice cold on his skin.

"Daniel?" she asked, her voice still thick from the drugs.

In addition to her voice, there were scrabbling sounds coming from the ceiling, which now sounded like the biggest rat in history coming through the venting. Daniel could also hear several of the revived. They were coughing, calling out, several were crying. Cryo was complicated, coming out of it with no one to monitor you, or help explain things, was disorienting.

The wail of the alarms added to the cacophony, and if that were not enough, it appeared that the crew had begun to break through the door. Daniel could hear Captain Aaronson and the others calling to the newly revived crew sitting in heaps on the floor near their open Cryo Pods.

Daniel tried to stand, tried to simply sit up, but his limbs seemed disconnected from his brain. Nothing was moving, no matter how much he willed it. Consciousness can be such an elusive thing. The wailing alarms seemed to fade away in a roar of nothingness and he could see his field of vision closing down as if he were staring into a long black tunnel where only a little bit of light remained.

"Daniel!"

He was so tired now, even his tongue felt thick and heavy as he struggled to push out the words, "Got to...open...the pods, use the emergency revi...seq...sequen..."

He could feel Samantha shaking him, screaming his name, but the blackness claimed him then, and he knew nothing more.

Last Row

"When one's expectations are reduced to zero, one really appreciates everything one does have."
– Stephen Hawking

Date: 01.27.2104
Calypso Colony Ship

The alarms were shrieking. Not just in the Cryo Deck, but everywhere else. Once the purge sequence had been enabled, the Control Deck had been alerted. All major functions were routed through there, and Jenkins and Perdue had been on the Command Deck speaking with Captain Aaronson when the alert sounded. There was an instant concern, especially once the men on duty realized they had been locked out, physically and electronically. Captain Aaronson issued a general alert. People were streaming out of their coffins, pulling on clothes, and running to their emergency stations.

The reinforced titanium doors were closed and locked.

"None of the overrides are working, sir." Martin Phoenix said, his fingers jabbing at the control panel.

Captain Aaronson slapped the Comm link on his suit, "NARA, crewmember oh-oh-six, connect me to the Cryo Deck!"

UNABLE TO CONNECT

CRYO COMM INOPERABLE

"NARA, disengage locks on Cryo Deck doors."

UNABLE TO COMPLY

MANUAL OVERRIDE INITIATED

EMERGENCY REVIVAL SEQUENCE INITIATED

ATMOSPHERE BREACH CONTAINMENT PROTOCOLS
INITIATED

SYSTEM RESET ON ALL CRYO PODS IN 14:25 MINUTES

Zach Jenkins shook his head, "You can't have both at the same time. Someone inside locked it all down, initiated a Level Five event *and* ordered the system reset." He ran his hand through his hair, "I don't know how that is even possible."

He tried his Comm link, "NARA, crewmember two-one-two, connect to Cryo Deck please."

UNABLE TO CONNECT

CRYO COMM INOPERABLE

"Captain, someone inside those blast doors has done this. This is no accident." Zach said.

"Can you fix it?"

"No sir, this, whatever they have done is not only beyond my capabilities, but even if I could, it would have to be from the other side of these doors. Cryo was equipped with an entirely separate control system, one that could be operated and maintained autonomously from the deck in case of breach or environmental failure."

The captain cursed, "We need to get through those doors. *Now.*"

Within a handful of minutes, the plasma torch arrived and was put to work. As the metal began to melt, the fumes quickly affected everyone nearby.

"Environmental, we need the ventilation increased on this deck." Fenton barked. Zach Jenkins felt the strong pull of the vent, clearing the hallway of fumes, and smacked his forehead...*why didn't I think of it earlier?*

"We can access Cryo through the vents, sir! It will be a tight fit, but I think I can make it." He had to yell it twice before the Captain heard him over the blast of the torch.

Captain Aaronson nodded immediately, looked around and focused on Wes Perdue, "Take Perdue with you. Go!"

Jenkins and Wes Perdue set off at a dead run towards the maintenance tubes. They were young and slim, smaller-boned than most of the rest of the team currently hovering outside of the Cryo Deck. It would be a tight fit, but Zach was sure he could do it. He knew just where the nearest access point was. He had studied the schematics of Calypso over and over while waiting for his application to be approved, and right now, five years later, it just might pay off. Five yards down and left at the corridor, in the corner, was an access panel.

"Shit, we need a hex driver," Zach looked towards Equipment and Supply, but before he could decide on whether to head there or run back to his coffin for one, Wes Perdue was on his knees with a small pocketknife clutched in his hand.

Damned if the kid didn't have a Swiss Army knife, complete with screwdrivers and the rare hex driver. It was small and difficult to work with, and it took what seemed like an agonizing amount of time to remove the hex nuts from the access panel, but they were finally successful.

Wes snapped it back closed, pocketed the knife and grinned, "A genuine Victorinox Cybertool Lite," he said as they pulled off the access hatch, "A family heirloom and my dad's gift to me before we left Earth. They gave me hell at boarding, I was three ounces over my weight limit."

It was pitch black inside, and Zach gulped back his fear of dark, enclosed spaces. There was no time to feel claustrophobic now.

Wes looked at him and then into the dark tube, "I'll go first if you want."

Zach shook his head, "You don't know the way and I do. I studied the hell out of every inch of Calypso while we were in training."

He closed his eyes for a moment and reviewed the air supply system in his mind. Straight up, sharp right eight meters, then up again and across. They should be able to drop right into the middle of the Cryo Deck, in between the second and third rows of Cryo Pods.

"C'mon Jenkins, we gotta move." Wes was itching to dive in.

"Yeah, yeah, I got it. Follow me."

A few seconds later and Zach was inside. Damned if it wasn't close, worse than getting used to the coffins. Arms in front, clawing and clutching, and legs and knees pushing him along. Zach's legs had slightly better mobility. His shoulders bumped against the sides of the vents and he quickly learned to wiggle them from side to side to help his forward momentum. Behind him, he felt his foot connect with something and Wes yelped.

"You all right, man?" Wes' muffled reply came back in the affirmative, but the kid hung back a little more after that. There was nothing like getting kicked in the face to curb your enthusiasm.

The 'up' sections were easier than Zach thought they would be. There were tiny foot and handhold indents in the vents. Between those and the fact that he barely fit as it was, it was simply a matter of wriggling up the first few feet and using the foot and handholds to pull and push the rest of the way. Inside of the vents, the alarms were significantly muted. Zach could hear Wes grunt and gasp as he wriggled along behind him.

After what seemed like an interminable amount of time, Zach heard Wes gasp, "Christ on a stick, man, you better know where you are going, because sure as shit I don't want to get stuck in this damn tube."

"Trust me, we're almost there." Zach laughed, then he stopped, realizing that just getting there was not enough, they still needed to get *out* of the vents and *he* didn't have the right tools.

A few moments later, he could see flashes of red lighting the vent. There was the hatch. He moved past it, calling back to Wes as he did, "It's all you man, you got the tool." The alarms wailed as Wes wrestled with the vent and cursed behind him. There was nothing Zach could do, no way to turn around or give the kid a hand.

"The hex nuts are on the *outside*," Wes yelped in pain. He had used the knife to separate the slats in the vent wide enough to feed his hand through and attack the hex nuts from the outside. As he struggled blindly with the tool, Wes sliced his hand open, cursed and nearly dropped the Victorinox in the process.

Agonizing seconds passed and the alarms continued to shriek. Below them, Zach could hear others calling out from inside the Cryo Deck, confused and disoriented. The access hatch finally gave way with a clatter and Wes half climbed, half fell out of it, clearing the way for Zach to back up and slide out. Wes had rolled out of the way before Zach dropped with a thud to the deck below.

They looked around, the shrieking cacophony of the alarms was intense and the red emergency lights lit up streaks of some dark substance on the Cryo Deck floor. Wes reached down, touched a thick drop. It was blood from the feel of it, sticky and mostly congealed. There were streaks and drops of blood everywhere, mostly on or around the damaged control panel.

One man lay motionless at the foot of it and streaks and drops of blood led away, towards the long lines of Cryo Pods, ten rows of twenty-five pods each. Most of the Cryo pod doors hung open and the newly revived were sitting in stunned heaps on the deck floor or stumbling to their feet, some heading for the main door which now had a large glowing hole in it. The

Captain and most of the crew on the other side were still trying to cut their way through.

Zach ran towards a group of newly revived, he hoped to head them off before they got too close to the white-hot door. Cryo left a person a bit addled for the first few hours. It was similar to waking up from anesthesia, there was no telling what they would do. In most cases, a person was revived from Cryo over a period of nearly a day, watched carefully, and when fully oriented, sent on his or her way with a buddy to keep an eye on them.

The alarms and lights were disorienting and Zach figured there were at least two-thirds of the people from Cryo in various states of ambulation, confused as hell, which he had to watch over. Two women and one kid were about ten feet from the white-hot door, lurching towards it like zombies.

He turned and called out to Wes over his shoulder, "The purge is still counting down, get the rest of the Cryo pods open!" He grabbed the nearest woman by the shoulder, spun her around and sat her down, jumped toward the second and slid an arm around her waist as he grabbed for the little girl next to her and picked her up bodily. The heat from the door was hot on his face as he stopped both from burning themselves on the white-hot metal.

Wes turned and ran for the last row of pods, nearly tripping over Daniel Medry and Sam Sydan. She looked confused and was kneeling on the floor next to Medry. The shrieks of the alarms changed in tone. It didn't seem possible that they could take on a more urgent tone, but they did and Wes knew they had very little time left. He ran to an occupied pod and keyed in the emergency revival sequence.

MANUAL OVERRIDE INITIATED
BEGIN EMERGENCY REVIVAL SEQUENCE ON MOSS, SEAN
03:58 MINUTES UNTIL REVIVAL
SYSTEM RESET ON ALL CRYO PODS IN 04:06 MINUTES

"Shit!" Wes screamed in panic, he ran to the next pod and input the sequence. They had just six seconds to get the rest of the pods started on the emergency revival sequence.

MANUAL OVERRIDE INITIATED
BEGIN EMERGENCY REVIVAL SEQUENCE ON ZRADCE, JENNIFER
03:58 MINUTES UNTIL REVIVAL
SYSTEM RESET ON ALL CRYO PODS IN 04:01 MINUTES

Just five more to go. Somehow, he had to get to them

MANUAL OVERRIDE INITIATED
BEGIN EMERGENCY REVIVAL SEQUENCE ON GONZALEZ, ESTEBAN
03:58 MINUTES UNTIL REVIVAL
SYSTEM RESET ON ALL CRYO PODS IN 03:56 MINUTES

"Oh, God, no!" He ran to the next pod, his fingers flying over the flat glass screen.

MANUAL OVERRIDE INITIATED
BEGIN EMERGENCY REVIVAL SEQUENCE ON DUNN, JACK
03:58 MINUTES UNTIL REVIVAL
SYSTEM RESET ON ALL CRYO PODS IN 03:52 MINUTES

He could see the mist beginning to clear. But he knew it was futile. He had gotten there too late. His heart skipped a beat. Jack Dunn was Kevin Edmond's partner. They had a kid together.

MANUAL OVERRIDE INITIATED
BEGIN EMERGENCY REVIVAL SEQUENCE ON COOK, ELIZABETH
03:58 MINUTES UNTIL REVIVAL
SYSTEM RESET ON ALL CRYO PODS IN 03:47 MINUTES

It was too late; it was all too late.

Wes stared for a moment. Elizabeth's face was peaceful, her dark hair in two long braids. They had met at the Cape during training. She had been instantly recognizable to so many of them. A talented journalist, she had written extensively on the Narine conflict and exposed two political vote-buying scandals in the years before departure. During introductions, she had talked about writing the history of the first extra-solar colony – it was mostly likely one of the reasons the Selection Committee had picked her.

The alarms shrieked and Wes left her pod to initiate the revival sequence on the last two, even though he knew it was useless.

MANUAL OVERRIDE INITIATED
BEGIN EMERGENCY REVIVAL SEQUENCE ON MICHALKO, HEATHER
03:58 MINUTES UNTIL REVIVAL
SYSTEM RESET ON ALL CRYO PODS IN 03:43 MINUTES

The locks would not release until the emergency revival was completed and an entire reboot on the system would crash it in the middle of their revival sequence. It was a built-in flaw the creators of the Cryo pods had never envisioned and it was going to kill five innocent people.

MANUAL OVERRIDE INITIATED
BEGIN EMERGENCY REVIVAL SEQUENCE ON BRUEHL, LLOYD
03:58 MINUTES UNTIL REVIVAL

G581: THE DEPARTURE

SYSTEM RESET ON ALL CRYO PODS IN 03:38 MINUTES

Wes stood helplessly as the countdown inexorably wound down. Lloyd's cheeks sported a heavy five o'clock shadow. He had been a pompous jerk during training, determined to outperform everyone until his first experience in zero-gravity had made him lose his cookies. Afterward he had been less of an ass. Wes wouldn't have considered him a friend, or even someone he wanted to hang out with, but he didn't deserve this fate.

Wes barely noticed that his face was wet with tears. He grabbed a wrench from the deck floor, sticky with blood, and began to try to break through the thick armor of one of the pods.

Overhead, through the speakers, NARAs calm voice declared,
EMERGENCY REVIVAL SEQUENCE COMPLETE
SYSTEM RESET ON ALL CRYO PODS IN 00:03 MINUTES

Wrench in hand, Wes ran back to the sixth to last pod, the display now read:
EMERGENCY REVIVAL SEQUENCE ON ZRADCE, JENNIFER
COMPLETE
SYSTEM RESET ON ALL CRYO PODS IN 00:01 MINUTES

The lock cycled and the door to the pod opened. Jennifer Zradce slumped into his arms; her eyes still closed.

The entire deck went black.

The Door to Hell

"Think of how many religions attempt to validate themselves with prophecy. Think of how many people rely on these prophecies, however vague, however unfulfilled, to support or prop up their beliefs. Yet has there ever been a religion with the prophetic accuracy and reliability of science?"
– Carl Sagan

Date: 01.27.2104
Calypso Colony Ship

Fenton Aaronson always began his day the same way. His wife Joanna had been amused by it. She had teased him about his "intransigent ways." This woman who had captured his diehard bachelor's heart was full of large and complicated words.

And while some would use words like that to show off, Joanna did it with the ease and thought of someone who knows more than most and doesn't see the point in hiding intelligence or flaunting it – simply using it for the strength that it is.

Each morning (although morning on a spaceship was rather subjective), he would begin by stretching each finger, each toe, before moving on to his legs, his arms, back, and neck. He would breathe slowly, intentionally, and although his mind was full of thoughts for the day, plans he had or ideas he wanted to consider implementing, especially now that they were so close to their destination – he would intentionally push all of them aside and focus on his body.

This had served him well. Seven years before departure he had been going through his morning routine and felt something slightly off in his abdomen. This had continued for three days before he decided to go and have it looked at. It had been a small benign tumor, easily removed, and easily dealt with. The doctor had been rather skeptical at first when Fenton had suggested they do a scan. But she had decided to humor the tall, handsome man in her care. The tumor had been small, they had caught it early on.

After he had finished this stretching, meditative few minutes, Fenton typed a short note on his tablet:

INTRA-SHIP COMMUNIQUE
CAP TO MESS
/BEGIN TRANSMISSION
EARL GREY W/HONEY AND MILK, PROTEIN AND FRUIT OF DAY
TY, CAP
/END TRANSMISSION

Fenton dressed in his blue shipsuit and headed for the Mess Hall.

"Mornin' Cap," the cook nodded to him and handed him a tray.

"Thanks Les. How's the finger?" Fenton asked, nodding to Lester's left hand. He had cut his finger badly a week ago.

"Nearly healed, thanks to the Doc." Lester held up his finger which sported an angry red healing line. "She used that new skin graft tech on it."

Fenton smiled and carried the tray to the nearest occupied table. He made a point of sitting with crewmembers at each meal. It helped keep him connected to what was going on with them, especially since the news of Earth.

He nodded to several others in the room and approached Nathan Zradce.

"Mind if I sit?"

Nathan stared at him silently, blinking for a moment before nodding.

Fenton sat, surveying the contents of his tray. One cup of Earl Grey tea, with a spoonful of honey and a splash of Almost Milk, a protein cube and a small handful of strawberries. It had taken some time, but they finally had recovered from the 'Ponics Deck failure that had killed off most of their fresh fruits and vegetables.

The only plants to survive had been cabbage and beets, which were hardier than the rest of the plants. Everyone had gotten very, very tired of eating the two, no matter how creatively they were prepared. He smiled at Zradce and sipped his tea.

"How are things in your department, Nathan?"

Again, there was silence, a couple of seconds where Zradce remained utterly silent and unmoving, the fork paused halfway to his mouth. "Um, fine, sir."

"Looking forward to planetfall?"

"Um... yes."

Fenton, having run out of things to say, finished his meal in silence, and bid Zradce goodbye. Nathan nodded his head, avoiding eye contact.

In his ready room a few minutes later Fenton typed a message.
INTRA-SHIP COMMUNIQUE
CAP TO CARTER, JACOB CM#121
/BEGIN TRANSMISSION
UPDATE REQUESTED ON CREW RESPONSE TO ESH PLAGUE. ANY CM'S THAT WE NEED TO BE CONCERNED ABOUT?
TY, CAP
/END TRANSMISSION

A short time later the reply flashed on his tablet.
INTRA-SHIP COMMUNIQUE
CARTER, JACOB CM#121 TO AARONSON, FEN CM#001
/BEGIN TRANSMISSION
CURRENTLY HAVE ONE CREWMEMBER ON SUICIDE WATCH. JUST OUT OF CRYO, LOST ENTIRE FAMILY. OTHER THAN THAT, FOUR OTHERS CURRENTLY IN TWICE WEEKLY THERAPY SESSIONS. REST OF CREW SEEN ON AS NEEDED BASIS WITH NO POTENTIAL ISSUES OR CONCERNS.
LET ME KNOW IF YOU NEED ANY MORE INFO, CAP.
JC
/END TRANSMISSION

Fenton nodded. Zradce had never been the most outgoing crewmember. When it came to intellectuals, it was a crapshoot. Some were relatively functional introverts, others struggled in their attempts to interact with others.

Carter had explained it once, "Extroverts outnumber introverts almost three to one. However, introverts form nearly seventy-five percent of those people with IQs over 160. This is why we have built in as many extra spaces in Calypso as possible. Our crew is predominated by them."

Zradce was probably just fine. But still, there had been something about his reactions that seemed... off... somehow.

There was no time to dwell on it further. It was time for the Landing Committee meeting, a go-ahead now that the last of the staff heading it had been revived and given time to recover from the side effects of Cryo. The Committee members filled his ready room and Anton Webster took the floor.

"We need to make a decision on which of the three possible landing points will be Sagan Base." He began, "I know they each have their particular merits and concerns. Go too near a river and we risk flooding, too near the mountains and there will be the challenges of higher elevations and temperature fluctuations."

"The truth be told, we aren't able to know everything there is to know about Zarmina's World," Martin Phoenix, Calypso's First Officer pointed out. "There are plenty of questions that a probe, no matter how complex it was, simply cannot answer."

Settling a new world was rife with challenges and danger. The future of the human race, especially the ones here on this ship, depended on making the right choices.

"Well, the reports I've read indicate that we will have one hell of a volcanic eruption on the western edge," Kevin Edmonds added. "The last thing we want to do is settle the plateau. Unless you like breathing in choking ash and ducking as volcanic rocks the size of autocars fall from above."

Fenton turned to him, "So, you're sure?"

"As sure as I can be of these things. I'm a seismologist, not a volcanologist, but all the signs point to an eruption within the next eighteen months, and we've seen the debris field from previous eruptions, the plateau is definitely within range."

"I think that brings us down to two options then. Any objections to removing the plateau from the potential list of sites?" Fenton turned to each of the Committee members in turn, and everyone stayed silent.

"Very good then. For the record, we now have the Mediterre coastal option or the as yet unnamed plains. I would like a full list of pros and cons from both before we narrow it down. Edmonds? I'll need a seismological workup for both locations please."

The meeting wrapped up and it was on to the next one, a final consensus of who would need to remain in Cryo until past planetfall and who needed to be revived.

Things were definitely revving up now that they were within weeks of their destination. In a few days a score of twelve more crew members would be revived, putting their numbers at over fifty-four crew active on deck, the largest number they had seen since departing Earth over five years ago.

Right before lunch was the Systems Status meeting.

"Nothing much to report Captain," James Aldridge, the acting head of Environmental Systems reported. "The 'Ponics Deck was a doozy, but it's been quiet for months. There was that weird Environmental Systems glitch a month before which we caught before disaster struck. Other than that, there are no major concerns, everything is looking good."

The end goal was in sight after all, and none of them wanted a delay in their arrival. After five years of monotony, they were all itching to leave Calypso behind and start their new lives on the surface.

Fenton joined his First Officer, Martin Phoenix, for lunch in the Mess Hall. There were two recent Cryo revivals sitting at one table. They hadn't been out of Cryo for a full day yet and were lurching about, limbs and brain still not connected fully. He recognized both of the women and was thankful that they already knew the news from Earth. Over the past few months, as sleepers were pulled out of Cryo for one reason or another, usually a change in shift personnel, the terrible details of the ESH plague were relayed to them. It was often crippling news. There was no one on board who wasn't affected in some manner or another. No one who hadn't lost a friend, a family member, or even their entire community to the virus.

Still, it was like reliving the pain all over again each time someone new was pulled out of Cryo.

Ellie Satler had described it well, "It is like having your heart broken all over again. You would think it would get easier, but it doesn't."

As Captain, he couldn't avoid those grieving souls any more than Carter could. It made him wish for planetfall even more, so the last of those in Cryo could be revived and they could all move on from these recirculating cycles of shock and mourning.

Fenton paused in his ready room after lunch to review the latest environmental reports on the southern continent. Deposits showed it rich in ore, which would be where they would set up the autonomous mining operations and provide the colony with much-needed iron ore for steel and other building materials. He noted that there was a disagreement between two of the authors, one questioned whether the deposits were as extensive in the south and pointed to an eastern deposit that was possibly closer to the surface and larger. It was, however, positioned near another active volcano with significant seismic activity.

He stopped to rub his eyes. Fenton hadn't been sleeping well since Joanna returned to Cryo. If Joanna had been awake right now, she would have told him he worked too hard. It would be six more weeks until she would be revived. Her role was essential to planetfall and like most of the others, she would not be revived until they had achieved their final orbit. He sighed, counting the days until she could be back in his bed and in his arms.

"We have to meet with the 'Ponics Deck supervisor, Nagel Lowry at 1300 Cap,"

Martin interrupted Fenton's thoughts of Joanna.

"Just a quick meeting to review all the fail-safe procedures they have implemented and discuss the potential failure ratios. By the way, Zach Jenkins is still concerned about exactly *how* the failure in 'Ponics occurred and has been tracing through the computer code to determine its origin."

"Is he still crying sabotage?" Fenton asked, somewhat bemused.

Martin shook his head, "No, he's backed off from saying *that*, but he still seems pretty suspicious of the whole thing. Lowry says it isn't anything to worry about, but I've been checking in with Zach on a regular basis, just in case." He smiled then, "And Laney Deeds has been assisting him lately. It seems that those two are growing close."

Since the news of Earth, Captain Aaronson had asked Martin to add an additional report to his list, that of tracking relationships and even possibly steering work relationships towards personal relationships. When his First Officer had looked surprised, Aaronson had explained, "My job is to the mission, and the mission parameters have changed. We get to play matchmaker now."

An odd stance for the captain to take, but one that Martin appeared to enjoy as time went on.

Fenton nodded approvingly, and then added a note to meet with the iron ore project coordinators. Moments later, Nagel Lowry arrived to give his weekly report on the status of the 'Ponics Deck and Fenton beckoned Nagel and Martin to sit down. Already there was a queue forming outside of his Ready Room, the afternoon rush had begun.

Moments later, as Lowry droned on about some kind of atmospheric regulator design that would increase crop yields, Zach Jenkins and Laney Deeds barged in, tense and excited.

"We have proof of sabotage on the 'Ponics Deck, sir." Zach said, as Laney nudged him.

Nagel Lowry looked furious, "You can't just..."

Fenton interceded, "Proof of sabotage, Jenkins? Well, I'm sure Lowry here will want to know all about it. Let's see what you have found."

And just as the two began to explain the code they had found, a ship-wide alarm sounded, NARAs voice issuing over all speakers:

WARNING CRYOGENICS SYSTEM SHUT DOWN
SYSTEM FAILURE - CODE RED
SYSTEM RESET ON ALL CRYO PODS IN FIFTEEN MINUTES

Fenton froze, trying to understand the ramifications. System reset? If the Cryo pods reset with an individual still inside, the occupant would die from lack of oxygen.

With forty-four crew members awake, that leaves two hundred and six in Cryo. Two hundred and six of their fellow crewmembers who could die during a system reset.

"Maintain an open link on the Command Deck and shut that down," Fenton barked at the crew members that had appeared at his door, "Jenkins, Perdue, you are with me. We need to get to the Cryo Deck and see what the hell is going on. Everyone, we need to *stop* that system reset!"

WARNING CRYOGENICS SYSTEM SHUT DOWN
SYSTEM FAILURE - CODE RED
SYSTEM RESET ON ALL CRYO PODS IN THIRTEEN MINUTES

The minutes became a blur of desperation, frustration and terror. Martin had radioed through Fenton's comm informing him that they had been locked out of Cryo via the Command Deck interface, the bridge's computer access to the individual Cryo pods blocked. NARA's access to the Cryo Deck had been disabled, and Fenton was staring at the blast doors locking them out physically.

As the moments had ticked by, the overhead speakers calmly issuing a countdown that would result in the deaths of most of their crew, Fenton's thoughts had strayed from the bigger picture to the image of Joanna's face. Had he really spent his entire life without her? And could he now bear the thought of losing her and living the rest of his life regretting not having met her sooner?

WARNING CRYOGENICS SYSTEM SHUT DOWN
SYSTEM FAILURE - CODE RED
SYSTEM RESET ON ALL CRYO PODS IN ELEVEN MINUTES

Her son, Alex, recently revived and part of the Landing Committee, had arrived with scores of others. There was a deep fear in his eyes, and Fenton, caught in a quiet moment between issuing orders, beckoned him over.

"Mom is in there."

It was a question and statement. Alex was a great kid. Joanna had given birth to Alex when she was just eighteen. His dad had stayed in the picture until after the young man's 12th birthday, before disappearing into Europe and never resurfacing. Joanna had raised the boy alone after that and done a fine job of it. Fenton had been pleasantly surprised by Alex's mature attitude and quiet confidence. At the moment, his stepson looked anything but confident, but he was staying calm, and that was important.

"We're gonna get in there, Alex. I'm doing everything I can to get your mom out of there."

The young man nodded and stepped back. The corridor was too crowded.

Fenton turned to the gathering crowd, "Those with experience in using plasma torches, stay. I need Medical Bay prepped and a team here stat. And if you are neither of those things than get the hell out of this hallway. NOW!" he barked. The crew members scattered.

WARNING CRYOGENICS SYSTEM SHUT DOWN
SYSTEM FAILURE - CODE RED
SYSTEM RESET ON ALL CRYO PODS IN EIGHT MINUTES

The men cutting with plasma torches were coughing, the skin on their faces turning red from the intense heat. They didn't falter.

"Get Environmental to double the air flow through here!" Fenton bellowed, coughing, his eyes watering from the fumes.

The order had been relayed and the increased air flow helped a little. The crew continued to cut into the door.

"Get some breathing masks in here, everyone else, fall back to the next hallway," Fenton ordered, still coughing.

Zach Jenkins pulled at his arm, "We can access Cryo through the vents, sir! It will be a tight fit, but I think I can make it."

Captain Aaronson nodded immediately, looked around and focused on Wes Perdue, "Take Perdue with you. Go!"

WARNING CRYOGENICS SYSTEM SHUT DOWN

SYSTEM FAILURE - CODE RED

SYSTEM RESET ON ALL CRYO PODS IN TWO MINUTES

The hole grew, molten metal dripping onto the floor, and they were able to catch glimpses of people moving within. Had Jenkins and Perdue been successful? A large piece clunked, opening a hole large enough and several of the crew members, along with Fenton, surged forward, quickly jumping through the large red-hot opening and into the Cryo Deck.

"Get to the pods and initiate emergency revival on all..."

It was too late.

WARNING CRYOGENICS SYSTEM SHUT DOWN

SYSTEM FAILURE - CODE RED

SYSTEM RESET ON ALL CRYO PODS IN ZERO MINUTES

The system reset clock had reached zero and the entire Cryo Deck was plunged into darkness. This elicited several screams of panic from those of the revived who were relatively cognizant of their surroundings. The only light showed through the molten-edged hole in the door from the hallway beyond, casting the Cryo Deck into a nightmare of shadows and movement.

As crewmembers surged into the darkness, the Cryo Deck lights blinked back on, revealing a chaotic scene.

There were Cryo revivals in every state of recovery, some ambulatory, some not. Near the main control panels for the Cryo Deck was Nathan Zradce, unconscious and barely breathing. Down one length of Cryo pods lay Daniel Medry, also unconscious, and bleeding heavily.

"Breathe, damn it, breathe!" Wes Perdue had a young woman half out of a pod, tears tracking down his face as he struggled to perform CPR.

Zach Jenkins had found a wrench and was using it to smash his way through a closed Cryo pod, desperate to reach the person inside now that the pods had powered down.

At least five Cryo pods had not finished with their revival sequence when the system reset itself.

Blood was spattered at intervals, long gory streaks of it. Two bodies were dark lumps lying on the floor in the farthest room.

"We need a medic here!" shouted one of the crew members and Dr. Schrader stepped through the smoking doors, two assistants behind her carrying gurneys.

Somewhere in this mass of people was his wife, Joanna. His eyes cut over the black-clad figures, all Cryo revivals, and focused his gaze on the last Cryo pods near the end of the line.

Zach Jenkins continued to smash against one of them, sobbing now, desperately trying to reach the partially revived occupant inside. Jenkins had to know it was useless, they all did. A shutdown in the middle of a revival sequence caused irreparable harm to the subject.

Humans, cryogenically suspended, their circulatory and respiratory systems slowed to a crawl, were not easily revived. The mix of Cryo drugs had to be just right, and even after the initial sequence had been completed by the Cryo pod, the effects of Cryo were difficult, and some suffered side effects for hours, even days afterward. But to have a pod shut down in the middle of the cycle - that was a death sentence.

Oh God, where was she?

Then he saw her, hair slicked back, her eyes unfocused, grasping the side of one of the Cryo pods, trying to keep her balance. He made his way past others, ignoring the shouts of his crew, his eyes on her alone.

Forget the noble captain who put everyone before his own personal life, Fenton Aaronson wove his way through the mass of Cryo revivals, crew members, and bloody mess to lock his arms around his wife.

"Jo, oh god, Jo. It's okay, I've got you." His words were muffled in her hair, the feel of her against him such an unimaginable relief.

Those agonizing moments outside of the Cryo Deck, unable to get through and unsure of *what* had caused the anomaly, Fenton had felt as if the air had been removed from his lungs.

He was too old to be in love like this, Fenton had reminded himself countless times. A confirmed bachelor of nearly fifty years, meeting Joanna in the last days before they left Earth, thrown together by circumstance, he had found that love, unlike this ship, didn't have a warning system of any kind.

He had locked eyes on Joanna, and felt something in him turn, like a key in a lock, and been instantly and hopelessly smitten. Never had a woman made him feel vulnerable, powerful, and giddy, *never*. But Joanna did. He held her in his arms, trying to find a way to breathe again, as other far more level-headed members of his crew tended to the newly revived and injured.

Behind him, the edges of hole they had cut into the Cryo Deck smoked and glowed. It felt as if he had stepped through the door to hell. Joanna trembled in his arms, still suffering from the after-effects of Cryo. He could see her son, Alex, making his way through the mass of people, his eyes frantic.

"Alex! Here!" he called to his stepson, beckoning the young man over.

A group hovered around Zach Jenkins, one of the men pulling him away from the prone form on the floor. The woman was dead and Zach was shouting and sobbing, fighting with others trying to pull him back, desperate to continue CPR. But the shock of the system reset, coupled with the incomplete revival sequence had been too much. Captain Aaronson's eyes took in the other four Cryo pods, all shattered, populated with lifeless bodies.

Five dead. His mind worked, stared at the two bloodied men on the floor who were now being attended to by the medical staff.

With his wife safe in his arms, he came back to himself, remembered his duties, his responsibilities to the ship and all of the occupants.

"Stabilize those two men and make sure they are restrained, both of them, until we can sort this all out," he said, his voice steady and loud, garnering attention and response from the crew.

"Anyone with medical experience please report to Dr. Schrader and assist in assessing all revivals and escort them to either their individual coffins or the Mess Hall until their recovery is complete. There will be a ship-wide meeting tomorrow morning at 0800."

He held Joanna close, put his lips to her temple and breathed her in. *God, he had almost lost her.* Fenton reached out to Alex and pulled the young man into their embrace.

Under Suspicion

Date: 01.31.2104

Calypso Colony Ship

Fragments of speech, movement, hands on his arms and head, checking him, assessing.

A voice, "Stay with us." Whispers, competent fingers holding his wrist.

"He's bleeding out, and I'm barely registering a pulse. We need him in Medical, *stat.*"

Daniel tried to speak, to ask about the Cryo pods, to ask if they had gotten everyone out in time. He managed a hoarse croak.

The hand moved to his undamaged shoulder, gave it a brief squeeze.

"Shh, hang in there Medry, you are going to be fine, buddy, just hang in there."

He slipped away again.

Darkness in the Medical Bay, only runner lights, and Daniel ached all over. He couldn't move his arms, his head throbbed and his mouth felt stuffed full of cotton. He could see an IV bag hanging from the bunk. A distance away, on the other side of the cabin, was another still form. Daniel couldn't tell who it was, and he was in too much pain to care.

He tried to bend his arm up to his battered face and couldn't seem to do it.

A familiar face appeared before him. Dr. Carrie Schrader, the Medical Bay director. Her green eyes searched his, and she smiled a small, tight smile.

"You need to rest, Medry." She inserted a syringe into the drip line, reached out and adjusted one of his bandages, "You lost quite a bit of blood."

Before he could open his mouth and ask about the Cryo pods, a warm rush entered his arm, and his words and thoughts turned to mush. The darkness rushed in again, his last sight before oblivion claimed him was the doctor's sharp gaze.

Life existed in a drug-filled haze, with only brief lucid moments. Light. Dark. He had a sense of time passing, but how long? Hours? Days? He slept, barely able to think when he did manage to claw his way to consciousness.

Daniel heard voices arguing.

"I don't care what you or the captain or anyone else thinks, Daniel did *not* sabotage those Cryo tanks, he saved us! You are fools and I'll be damned if you are keeping me away."

Sam.

He struggled to open his eyes.

"Ms. Sydan..."

The voice sounded like James Aldridge, who was one of the youngest active crew members. He had been eighteen when he signed on for the voyage.

"That would be *Doctor* Sydan to you."

Sam was in the corridor outside of Medical Bay by the sound of it. Daniel managed a weak smile at her outraged tone. She only pulled the doctor card when she was truly pissed. And considering that a disproportionate amount of crew held a doctorate in one field or another, and sometimes multiple fields, she had to be pretty pissed to bring it up.

Steps sounded in the corridor, and Carrie's voice sounded perturbed, "You both need to keep your voices down. These men need their rest."

"My apologies, Dr. Schrader," James said, "I was just explaining to Ms... I mean, *Dr.* Sydan, that she could not visit Medry alone."

"And why not?" Carrie asked.

"Well, he, I mean, the captain, that is, Medry, he is still under, umm, suspicion," the young man stammered.

Carrie sighed in annoyance, "James, I hold the codes to unlock those restraints, not Dr. Sydan. Medry isn't going anywhere, neither is the *real* saboteur, especially since he will most likely never wake up from his coma."

Sam slipped through the door, a grin on her face. Daniel could hear Carrie as she pulled Aldridge away, her voice fading as they moved down the corridor.

"Come on, give them a few minutes and walk with me. I need a cup of coffee and maybe some of those amazing bagels that Lester promised he would make us."

Sam locked her eyes on Daniel, her face anxious.

"Oh, Daniel!" He managed a crooked smile, although every piece of him throbbed in pain. "I'm so sorry I couldn't get back to you sooner!"

She stroked his battered face, and then pulled her hand back when he flinched in pain.

"How long..." Daniel was surprised at how difficult it was to speak, "has it been?"

"Four days. Until now they have had at least two men outside Medical Bay at all times. The captain has been here himself most days."

"God Daniel, purple is not your color." Her eyes traveled over him. "Neither is black, yellow or mottled red."

Her tone was cavalier, but the tears trickling down her face were anything but.

Daniel tried to reach up and wipe away the tears, but his hands couldn't seem to move. He wiggled his fingers, felt a hard ridge of metal against his wrist.

"They have you restrained." Sam said, "Captain's orders. I'm so sorry, Daniel, I tried to tell them. It's complete bullshit. I know you were the one who got me out, got the other Cryo pods open before the system reset, but they said that they had to follow procedure. I've been trying to see you ever since!"

"It's okay, Sam. I'll explain and it will be okay."

"I know it will, Daniel. I'm just... it's just that... you saved so many lives. You are a hero. You know that, right?"

Daniel shifted and felt a fresh stab of pain from his shoulder. "I didn't, make it, to the end of, the last row of pods, did they get to them in time?"

Sam looked away, ran her fingers over the uninjured parts of him, "I should see if they can give you something for the pain, now that you are awake."

"Sam, did they, did everyone make it?"

She avoided his gaze, "You need water. I'll see if I can get you some."

"Sam," Daniel croaked, "please."

Sam closed her eyes for a moment and then turned back to him.

"Without you, we would have *all* died. You saved so many people, please don't forget that."

Her eyes brimmed with tears. "Wes Perdue and Zach Jenkins were the first in. They came through the damned ceiling a couple of minutes before the rest of the crew cut through the blast doors."

She paused; a tear trickled down her face. "I couldn't remember the codes, Daniel. Later, hours later, they came to me. I should have helped; I should have done something."

His fingers gripped hers, holding tightly, she sniffed and took a deep breath.

"Zach ran to stop a handful of the revivals, they were headed straight for the white-hot blast doors, still out of it from Cryo. Wes headed for the remaining pods and began keying in the sequence. He got two of them in time."

"How many didn't make it Sam?"

Another tear escaped, and then another. She met his eyes, but her lip trembled. "Five people. A girl, Heather Michalko, and the journalist Elizabeth Cook. Also, Esteban Gonzalez, Lloyd Bruehl, and... and Jack Dunn."

Daniel closed his eyes. "This is all my fault."

Sam looked shocked, then furious, "No, it is *not* your fault. You didn't do this, *he* did it!" She stabbed a finger across the room at the other bunk.

"You saved over two hundred lives. You saved *me*, Daniel. You saved Kevin and Jack's son, Simon. You almost died from your injuries in the process. None of us can forget that."

She held his gaze, bent down and kissed him gently on the lips, "You saved us all."

Tribunal

"Human judges can show mercy. But against the laws of nature, there is no appeal." – Arthur C. Clarke

Date: 02.09.2104
Calypso Colony Ship

Daniel made his way slowly into the captain's ready room, a man on each side of him. He almost laughed at the absurdity. He could barely walk, what did they expect him to do? Fight to get free? Grab a wrench and start swinging?

He didn't object. He knew that the tribunal was just that, a chance to explain the facts as he knew them. The others hadn't been there, hadn't seen Zradce hammering at the main control panel, damaging it so that stopping the system reset was impossible. It had nearly ensured the deaths of 206 people in the process. They hadn't seen the two men fight after Daniel tried to stop the destruction of the control panel, or his attempts to revive those in the Cryo pods before the system reset. All they had seen was the blood and chaos, two men on the floor, and the damage already done.

"They need to hear your side, Daniel," Sam had said, "once they do, the charges will be dropped and they will know the truth."

She had stayed by his side, sleeping in the Medical Bay, refusing to leave except to perform her duties. Her hair was tousled and he reached out to smooth down a duck tail that had formed near the back. "How are things on the ship right now?"

Sam sighed, "I have been busy on the 'Ponics Deck trying not to trip over a handful of botany techs, all fresh out of Cryo and eager to do something, anything with their days. There are plenty of experiments left to run as we ready the small plants for transplanting to the surface." She rolled her eyes, "But it is so damned crowded we do more shimmying about than anything else. We have four full shifts, and it is a hive of activity, just like the rest of Calypso."

With all of the extra bodies on board awake and moving about, the Medical Bay was a quiet haven, only the beeps of the machines and low voices punctuated the silence.

"In the common areas, it is absolute chaos throughout the day, and barely quiets during the Fourth and First Shifts." She grinned, "I get better sleep here on the floor of the Medical Bay than I would in my own coffin."

"What have they done with everyone?" Daniel asked.

"Well, the newly revived have been separated into two groups and set on a working, leisure, and sleep schedule that balances their numbers as much as possible. However, it is such a sharp departure from the skeleton crew we had operating since departure, it has really put a strain on everyone. I swear, I can feel my heart rate increase and anxiety build up each time I'm out in the halls. I haven't seen more than twenty people at one time and in one place for *years*. They can't even have a ship wide meeting all at the same time, there's no room for everyone to attend."

Daniel glanced over at the opposite side of the room. Nathaniel Zradce lay there, still in a coma, and Dr. Schrader had said that the chances of him ever recovering from it were very small.

There had been swelling, followed later by minimal brain activity, and Carrie had put it bluntly, "If he ever does wake up, which he mostly likely won't, in all probability he will be unable to walk, talk or even feed himself. We need to consider the Zero Protocol."

Zero Protocol was the last resort, a decision that required a majority vote from a tribunal. It meant consigning a human being to the blackness of space, jettisoning their body, living or dead, into the void. It was not a decision that any of them would take lightly.

They had all agreed to it, as part and parcel of joining this mission to Gliese 581. If you violated the rules, if you endangered others, or if you sustained injuries that could not be reasonably remedied without using up a set amount of resources, then Zero Protocol would be voted on and enforced.

The harsh realities of traveling 22 light years from your home planet through the void, meant risk. And everyone depended on everyone else – there could be no exceptions.

Without it being said, Daniel knew that he also faced that possibility. If they believed him guilty of sabotaging the Cryo pods and murdering five innocent people, he would pay for it with his life.

There were voices at the entrance and Daniel felt his heart rate increase. It was time for the hearing. It took one of the men and Sam to help him out of his cot and onto his feet. Slowly they made it out of Medical Bay, down the hall, and past scores of staring faces. Did they think he was guilty? Or did they consider him a hero? He couldn't tell, especially since he was focusing on simply standing upright and walking, a monumental task considering how battered and broken his body was.

Daniel felt like he had run a marathon by the time they made it to the Command Deck. Sam had slipped away as they approached the 'Ponics Deck, telling him she would see him after her shift. Carrie Schrader followed Daniel into the tribunal.

He stood in the captain's ready room in front of four people, three were members of the tribunal, and Captain Aaronson, who was presiding over the hearing.

He sat down slowly in the chair they had for him, shaking from the effort it had taken to walk the short distance from Medical Bay.

"Daniel Medry," the captain looked up from his tablet for a moment, "Thank you for coming." Captain Aaronson studied him intently, "Mr. Medry, are you sure you wish to testify? I understand that Dr. Schrader has advised that we delay any questioning until your injuries have healed more."

"Yes sir," Daniel said, focusing on taking shallow breaths and timing his words to avoid the most intense spikes of pain, "I just want to get this over with. I'm able to testify."

The captain regarded Daniel steadily, "All right then. Before we begin with the questions, I would like to introduce the members of this tribunal. Before you are Ellie Satler, Director of Facilities Management aboard Calypso, Jackson Sebring, Pro Tem Commander planet-side, and Martin Phoenix, First Officer. Mr. Medry, do you have any objections to the members of the tribunal as it stands?"

"No sir."

"And do you wish to name a member of the crew as counsel during this tribunal?"

"No sir."

"All right then." The captain looked down at his tablet, "We have received several first-hand reports and testimonies already. They have given us an overview of the events by personnel who entered through the ventilation shortly before the system reset. We have received numerous testimonies by those revived from Cryo, but their memories are fallible due to their drugged state. We have also had several accounts from the crewmembers who were first through the blast door hole. We have a pretty good understanding of that end of things, and I'm hoping you can clarify some of the events prior to all of that."

"Yes sir. I'll do my best."

"Excellent. Please begin with an explanation of why you were in Cryo to begin with."

"My friend Deeks, er, Mike Deekins, and his assistant Stuart Evers were on duty. Deeks and I play poker every Friday night in one of the lounges. It was right at the end of shift for Deeks, and I had come by to see if he wanted to grab a meal with me at the Mess Hall before the game began."

"And what happened next, Mr. Medry?" Ellie Satler asked.

"I noticed that the control room and offices were dark. It was also very quiet. Not that Cryo is loud, but usually I hear Deeks and Evers talking. There was nothing until I got to the back rooms where they usually sit."

Ellie Satler nodded, "Go on."

"I turned on a light and saw one of their tablets on the floor, its screen cracked. Then I saw blood, a large amount of it. I saw that the blood was leading in a trail away from their desks and towards the locker area, where the Cryo gear is stored. That's where I found the bodies." Medry's voice hitched and his broken rib blazed hot pain.

"So, you and Deeks were friends?" Martin Phoenix asked next.

"Yes sir. Deeks was a good friend. We met in training at the Cape."

"Tell us what happened next, Medry." Captain Aaronson pressed.

"I was attacked, sir. I turned and Zradce was coming at me with a knife. If I hadn't have turned around at that moment and blocked his attack, he probably would have killed me."

Jackson Sebring's steel gray eyes bored into him, "I see from the initial interview two days ago in Medical Bay that you stated there were two separate attacks. How did you survive this attack? Why do you think he stopped the first time?"

"I don't know. I know I must have gotten knocked out. Maybe Zradce thought I was dead." Daniel shrugged, an agonizing mistake as his injured ribs screamed their objections. "I just know that I woke up on the floor, blood in my eyes and the alarms screaming."

"So, you are saying that Zradce closed the blast doors and programmed in the countdown?" Ellie Satler asked.

"Yes ma'am. It certainly wasn't me. I tried to stop it, but he attacked me again and I was stabbed in the shoulder at that time."

"Did he say anything? Anything to indicate *why* he would have done this?" Ellie pressed, her eyes intent.

"No ma'am, just scripture."

"What?"

"Bible scripture, he recited the Lord's Prayer."

Martin Phoenix leaned towards the captain, "Carter mentioned he had seen Zradce praying at meals, but the personnel records clearly state that he was an agnostic."

Fenton quirked an eyebrow, "Apparently that changed. Not that it is unusual given the circumstances, we have seen the numbers grow exponentially with Carter's prayer group." He motioned for Daniel to continue.

"We fought briefly and I managed to subdue him. I tried to open the blast doors and stop the countdown, but he had damaged the master controls significantly. I knew the crew were trying to get through and thought that there might be time for that, but then I remembered the emergency revival procedure we were taught in training."

"Go on."

"I began entering the manual override on each of the Cryo Pods, but I was injured and it slowed me down."

Jackson keyed something into his tablet, muttered under his breath, and showed it to Ellie and Martin in turn.

"Go on," Ellie prompted.

"Each row held twenty people in Cryogenic suspension, and there were eleven rows in use." Daniel looked down at his hands, the memory of his panic foremost in his thoughts. "I kept falling and I passed out a couple of times."

Martin Phoenix took the lead through the next set of questions. "Medry, are you aware of Jennifer Zradce's testimony earlier today?"

"No sir."

Martin nodded, "She is understandably concerned that her husband is being blamed for something that someone else might have done, specifically *you*."

Daniel felt a surge of overwhelming sadness for the woman. He had met her a few times, but Sam and Kit had known her better, even been friends, during the last phase of training.

"I can understand that."

"How is that, Medry?"

"How hard would it be to wake up and hear the kind of news she had?"

"Mm," Martin Phoenix stared at him before asking, "Were you and Zradce well acquainted?"

"No sir. I knew him, but we weren't friends. We might nod hello in the halls, but that was about it."

The questions continued, revisiting every step Daniel had taken, every moment he could remember.

Toward the end, Carrie Schrader had stepped in, concerned at the pallor of Daniel's complexion as he struggled to breathe while answering the rapid crossfire of questions from the three officers.

"I want to make it clear that I object to any continued questioning of my patient. Daniel sustained significant injuries and has not sufficiently recovered from them."

Her lips were set in a tight line and she glared at them in turn, especially Martin who had asked several detailed questions, leaving Daniel gray-faced and gasping in pain as he tried to answer them.

By the end of the testimony, they had hashed out every possible second of the day in question. Medry's testimony implicating Zradce as the saboteur was unnerving and disturbing. They were still digging, trying to determine motive. And Zradce was in a coma, showing minimal brain function. Who knew if he would ever wake up, much less be able to defend himself?

His wife had testified. She had been the lone voice of support of her husband, confused beyond measure and in denial.

Daniel staggered back to Medical Bay, exhausted, held up on each side by the men who had escorted him to the tribunal. He was relieved to return, too weak to do anything more than sleep.

Captain Aaronson had entered the final piece of evidence after Medry was led away. Just three words, at the end of a straightforward report on some electronics maintenance. Zradce had apparently stuck it in the document almost as an afterthought...

Mother was right.

Ellie Satler looked at the report, "What did he mean, 'Mother was right?'"

Aaronson shook his head, "It was a standard report from five months ago. No one even noticed it until we were reviewing every report Zradce had filed." He gave a short, bitter laugh, "I doubt anyone had ever read it all the way through. I sure as hell hadn't."

The captain closed his eyes and when he opened them, they looked haunted, even guilt-ridden, "What if the crop failures, and the Environmental glitch weren't random? Could Zradce have been behind all of this?"

"It would mean that he had meant to kill his own wife, sir, along with the rest of the crew." Martin Phoenix said quietly, his eyes brooding over the concept.

"We need to know why he would do that. Has there been any luck in decrypting his personal logs?"

The captain shook his head, "Not yet. Zradce specialized in security, which could be how he managed to stop the Command Deck override protocols and initiate the system reset in Cryo. Medry certainly doesn't have the background for that. We have techs working on breaking through the encryption. And there was also a request sent to Earth for any additional family records."

"Other than that, there is nothing in his personnel records beyond the information you have in front of you. Earth won't be able to respond for a long time and we have heard from Zach Jenkins and Wes Perdue on what they saw upon entering the Cryo Deck. As for the computer terminal used to enter that particular string of code that overrode the environmental controls, well, it was a station he used, along with one other crew member."

"And the other crew member?" Ellie pressed.

"The other crew member, Lloyd Bruehl, is one of the dead." Fenton looked at the others, "I think we all know who was responsible, even if we can't understand *why*."

Martin Phoenix shook his head, "I wonder if it even *can* be understood."

Captain Aaronson returned to his tablet, looking up at the three members of the tribunal, "Is the tribunal ready to render a verdict then?"

All three nodded. He double-checked the viewscreen in front of him, it was still recording, as it had been the entire day through each of the testimonies.

"Well, let's do this formally then. Martin Phoenix, First Officer aboard Calypso and member of the tribunal, what is your final judgment?"

Martin answered, "I find Nathan Zradce guilty of sabotage and murder."

The captain nodded and moved on to Ellie Satler and finally Jackson Sebring. Their answers were unanimous.

Nathan Zradce had been found guilty of sabotage and the murder of five innocent crew members.

Aftermath

"Happiness and strength endure only in the absence of hate. To hate alone is the road to disaster. To love is the road to strength. To love in spite of all is the secret of greatness. And may very well be the greatest secret in this universe." – L. Ron Hubbard

Date: 02.12.2104
Calypso Colony Ship

Calypso had never seen as many people on its decks as it did in the weeks that followed. The coffins were full, the couples' billets were at capacity, and voices could be heard throughout the decks no matter the time of day. It seemed that even the soundproofing on the coffins and billets was sorely tested, and tensions began to run high. What had once been a rather quiet ship was now a noisy, bustling place. The quiet out of the way places had been invaded by the newly revived and the first few days of joy at having been saved from dying, dimmed to feeling cramped and edgy.

"Just eleven days to go." Daniel said, running a hand along Sam's body. They were both inside of his coffin, and despite the sound dampeners could hear a loud argument going on outside of one of the ready rooms.

"It can't come soon enough," Sam groaned, "I had forgotten how much I dislike crowds. I feel like I can barely breathe."

Outside the women continued to yell, one insisting that the other had taken a full immersion shower just two days ago. With the entire crew of the Calypso straining all resources, full immersion showers had now been limited to one per week. This hadn't been a popular decision, partly due to the smell that quickly filled every corridor and public space.

"Wow, listen to those two go." Daniel laughed. It sounded as if several others had gotten involved, raising the volume in the hall significantly.

"The number of arguments has risen in tandem with the stench." Sam sighed.

There had been two fights, one broken nose, and Medical Bay was filled with an endless stream of supplicants in search of everything from condoms to sleeping pills.

"Carrie is ready to throw in the towel and tell them all she's going to become a hermit," Daniel snorted. "You should have seen the line of people outside of Medical Bay this morning. I think Carrie gave me a clean bill of health just so she has one less person in her face. Not that I can blame her."

He shifted; a small grunt of pain escaped his lips.

"Did you hear about Zach and Laney getting together?" Sam's fingers traced his injuries; her touch was gentle. "They were the ones who tracked down the piece of code that Zradce wrote which altered the temperatures in the 'Ponics Deck."

"Yeah, I remember Zach." Daniel said, pulling Sam on top of him, his mouth on her neck, "He thinks he is close to cracking Zradce's encryptions. That will make the tribunal and the captain happy. Zach said there was another possible issue with the Environmental systems. They ran diagnostics everywhere after the sabotage on Cryo and some weird codes came up that didn't make any sense."

"I *saw* her taking a shower two days ago!"

The voice was strident and the speaker had apparently moved, now standing directly outside of Daniel's coffin. Other voices joined hers, but not in agreement.

"Would you damned well shut up? I'm trying to sleep in here," came the muffled voice of another crew member.

Sam and Daniel began to laugh, their potentially intimate mood broken. "Like I said..."

"Eleven days can't come soon enough." Daniel finished for her. "I am right there with you, love."

The ship-wide meeting of all crew members was held the day after the Cryo sabotage. Daniel had missed it, but Sam had filled him in later.

"No one wanted to return to Cryo, not after the sabotage." She had told him, holding his hand as he recovered in Medical Bay. "Lowry made it clear that the impact on the food stores would be significant. They have enacted measures to reduce the caloric consumption for all adult crewmembers to fifteen hundred calories per day. Anyone younger than eighteen will be allowed their full caloric allotment."

The deaths had been difficult. Of the seven pods that Wes had initiated the emergency sequence on, only two of the occupants had made it. Simon Dunn-Edmonds, aged four years, had been pulled out just in time along with Jennifer Zradce. The last five, trapped inside of the pods and only half revived, had run out of oxygen and suffocated by the time the system reset completed and the locks had released. It was a design flaw that the engineers of Calypso had overlooked, a weakness that Zradce had discovered and exploited.

The five dead, one woman, one fifteen-year-old girl, and three men were mourned. Each of them had been talented and gifted, and their absences were a giant wound that had no time or space to heal. For those who had been in Cryo for the full voyage, the news of Earth came as an additional shattering blow.

Outside of Daniel's coffin, additional voices could be heard. They had recently deputized eight of the crew members to serve additional peacekeeping duties on Calypso to help ease tensions and quickly subdue arguments. Two of them seemed to have arrived and the voices quieted.

"How's Kit doing?" Daniel asked. Sam and Kit were spending time together, more so now than ever, as Kit worked through the loss of Deeks.

"She went to Carrie the other day and put in a formal request from A.R.C." Sam said quietly. "She asked for Deeks' sample."

Nearly everyone on board had submitted to egg or semen sampling before departure. Duplicate samples were stored on Earth as well as in A.R.C. on board Calypso. In a way, it was a taste of immortality. If something happened, and their lives ended, some part of them would still remain. The "just in case" was suddenly very much a reality.

"Wow." Daniel turned it around in his head, thinking of his friend, wishing for the hundredth time that he had arrived just a few minutes earlier.

"What did Carrie say?"

"She said it wasn't up to her. So, Kit went to the captain."

"And?"

"Cap thought about it for a day, talked to Carrie and Carter and gave her the green light." She sighed, "They were really into each other, so who knows, it probably would have happened if he had made it."

Daniel nodded, mostly to himself. It would have. He'd known Deeks had it bad, and from the way Kit had responded to him at training and before departure, he was sure the two would have hooked up.

"It just seems like a lot for her to take on. Being a mom all on her own, with the colony just getting started and all."

Sam shook her head, "She's tough. It's devastating to her, losing Deeks like she did, but I'm telling you, the minute she got word from the captain, she was down in Medical like a shot. She said she'll be implanted next week and I swear, Daniel, it's the first time I've seen her smile since waking up in Cryo."

She added, "Did you know he named her in his will? All of his personal effects, he willed them to her just two weeks after she had gone into Cryo. It included a personal log full of notes written to her counting the days until they were back together." She sighed, "So damned romantic."

She groaned, "Oh, and did I tell you about the rumors that are being spread? Some are trying to say that the ESH virus and reports of the widespread deaths on Earth are lies."

"What?"

"Oh, and that these false reports are being used to push a misogynist agenda and force women to abandon their work in order to bear large numbers of children."

"That's ridiculous!"

"Kit and I are working together to try and touch base with each of the women. We are asking them to consider having children just until the kinks in the artificial wombs had been worked out."

"How long will that be?"

"Well, Martin Phoenix seems to think it should be soon, but I don't know. They have a team working on it now."

"I'm not romantic enough, am I?" Daniel asked Sam, hoping to try again now that the commotion outside had dissipated.

"You have your moments." She smiled, "Would it be terribly un-romantic to tell you I have an appointment next week to get knocked up?"

"What?"

"I want kids. You know that."

"Yeah, but."

"Not all of them have to be yours." She said cheerfully.

Daniel's hand fell away, "Okay."

Sam laughed then, "From A.R.C., silly. What, did you think I meant someone on board?!"

"Um, okay, yeah, for a minute there I did."

"And?" she asked.

"And what?"

"Is it a problem?"

Daniel paused and thought for a moment. He thought of his son, Toby. He imagined the Earth, empty, the cities filled with the dead. He could see Deeks' face, along with Kit's, Luke's, Janine's and so many countless others. Life was so tenuous, so fragile.

This life that they were heading towards. It was full of unknowns. The probes continued to stream data about Zarmina's World and they had learned so much in the past few months as the ship slowly decelerated and the planet steadily grew in size, filling the view screens with their future.

Sam's voice interrupted his thoughts, "You aren't okay with it, are you?"

Daniel pulled her close. "On the contrary. I find it kind of sexy. New life on a new world. It is your body, Sam, and just know that I will be honored to be called Dad by any and all of your children if you are willing to have me. I know it took me a long time to figure it out, but I'm glad I did. I'm in love with you."

The next day, Daniel was honored in front of the entire assembly for his heroic efforts. He still moved slowly, his wounds had not completely healed, but he was recuperating quickly.

After the ceremony a petition had been circulated asking for the Zero Protocol to be enacted in the case of Nathan Zradce. Daniel had been asked to sign it and several were shocked when he refused. Several of the officers had signed it, including Jackson Sebring and Martin Phoenix, but in the end, Captain Aaronson had refused to sign off on the order.

"I'll remind everyone that Zradce's body remains in excellent shape and Dr. Schrader has informed me that Zradce's organs have potential value should we need them at some time in the future. As for his taking up of valuable resources, his consumption is minimal. I will revisit this decision in six months after we have established Sagan Base."

The decision was a sound one, since the technology for growing organs would have to wait, possibly years, for the colony to grow and create a hospital facility that could handle the more complicated procedures.

The oceans were a deep blue-green, the clouds were white, and along the meridian of this tidally locked planet, they could see their futures unfolding. Zarmina's World was nearly twice as large as Earth, and the meridian, where they would soon make a home, was unimaginably large. With more than 5,000 kilometers in width, and a north/south length of nearly four times that to choose from, the Landing Committee had focused on a handful of potential sites. They all had water sources, a good mix of prairie and forest, and mountains in the distance that supplied fresh water. There was ample evidence in the low foothills in several locations of the necessary variety of ores and mineral deposits that they would need in the years and decades to come.

The drones they sent out captured dizzying views of massive waterfalls, sharp mountain peaks, endless valleys, even high mountain deserts in the southern region. In the northernmost part of the Meridian was an incredibly tall volcano, cloaked with drifts of snow at its base, with a scattering of green mixed with the black of hardened lava along its flanks. Several immense freshwater lakes held the promise of untold plant and marine life within their depths.

There was so much to do, so much to explore, and the final days aboard Calypso were consumed with in-depth debates over the best site for Sagan Base, the layout of said encampment, and logistics and planning. An enormous, untouched, unexplored world lay within reach as Calypso entered its final deceleration and established orbit around the enormous world.

There was a large inland saltwater sea that had been on the short list of possible destinations. As the ship passed over mountains, oceans, valleys, and forests, the Landing Committee continued with its final deliberations. It was almost time to leave Calypso and finally set foot on Zarmina's World.

Planetfall

"Perhaps, as some wit remarked, the best proof that there is intelligent life in outer space is the fact it hasn't come here. Well, it can't hide forever – one day we will overhear it." – Arthur C. Clarke

Date: 04.24.2104
Zarmina's World – Unexplored Territory

Daniel Medry stood at the edge of the precipice and looked down. It was at least one hundred meters to the nearest outcropping of rocks, and another one hundred after that before solid ground. On his left, just four meters away roared an enormous waterfall. The water was cold, spray flecking the ground and, when the wind shifted, he was immersed in the fine mist. The vials of water samples in his pocket would be studied by Sam when he returned. She was currently testing the responses of the imported Terran plants in the planet's native water supply. So far, the water seemed the same, although it tasted sweeter than he remembered Terran water tasting. Perhaps it was simply a vast difference from the canned, recycled water they had all been drinking for the past five and a half years.

He was tired, they all were. Sleep was a luxury they could ill afford, however. There was an endless number of things to do and a short amount of time to get it done in. Every day since planetfall had been a bustle of activity, every waking moment filled with projects and tasks. Each colonist was bombarded daily with an alien biology, botany, and environment along with a healthy dose of problem-solving. No matter how detailed the plans had been, the unknowns popped up to bite them when they least expected it.

There had been enormous boulders just under the soil that interfered with the installation of posts and fencing. The housing engineers had had their hands full with several freshwater springs that popped up in the middle of a row of houses just three weeks after the occupants had moved in. This had flooded the floors, ruining some belongings. And those were just two of what appeared to be an endless parade of problems challenging them as the colony settled in.

Wes Perdue had taken a day off from watching the artificial wombs grow their first round of cattle to join Daniel in scouting this ridge.

"I need a break, damn it." He had said jumping into the flitter.

"All I do is hover over the damned wombs, charting every fluctuation. I can't stand another minute of it. And new buildings are on hold until they figure out the source of those underground springs."

Daniel laughed, "Well, I'm glad to have you. You gotta see the land from up on that ridge, it's flat out stunning. I've been trying to get Sam out here but she's crazy busy with the greenhouse and the trial rounds of squash they started last week."

The temperatures varied according to geography, but remained the same, no matter the time of day. And day was quite a subjective thing since this world was tidally locked to its sun and experienced synchronous rotation. It was a constant state of twilight, something that had concerned the scientists who worried that Terran plants would not thrive in this alien environment where there were no direct rays of sunlight. The sky varied from an off-white color to a rose red. Right now, it was especially rosy. This was in part due to a volcano to the west which had greeted their arrival to Zarmina's World with a massive eruption soon after planetfall. This had served to vindicate those who had voted for the northeastern option which was slightly cooler, but without any threats of volcanic or seismic activity.

Daniel tapped the built-in communicator on the left breast of his suit, "NARA, submit my diagnostics to Command, please."

NARA responded.

SCANNING TEMPERATURE AND VITALS FOR MEDRY, DANIEL

The data he was collecting was vital to the future of the colony. Knowing how his body was responding to the unique composition of the planetary atmosphere, the water, and local plant life would provide a road map for future generations. One of the requirements the Landing Committee had set forth and approved were regular monitoring of vitals and real-time reports for the database. And NARA was critical to that.

"I'm pretty sure no one needs to know my temperature and vitals," Wes commented, walking up from behind.

In his hands were several bags filled with plant samples. One of them was a rather familiar dark purple berry.

"Take that purple one there and NARA will definitely need your temperature and vitals." Daniel quipped.

"Are you going to tell me what will happen if I eat the purple berries?" Wes asked.

"What and let you miss out on it? Hell no." Daniel grinned at the younger man. "These experiences build character."

Daniel took another gulp of the sweet, ice-cold water from his flask and handed the container to Wes, who sniffed it and also took a swig.

Daniel grimaced; Sam would gripe at him when she found out. He had sampled several things since landfall, including the dark purple berry which had given him the squirts for a full week.

There was only so much that lab tests could tell you, he reasoned, *after that, you have to just jump off the cliff.*

"Damn, that tastes *amazing.*"

"Sure as hell does." Daniel nodded, "I have to wonder if Earth's water tasted like that once. So sweet, I can barely stand to drink the canned stuff now."

Sam and Carrie had taken turns laying into Daniel about being a good example to the kids that were now running about on the surface, along with admonitions that *everyone* was needed.

He had taken his verbal tongue-lashing, dutifully listed the effects of the purple berry and added a request in the colony files to officially name it *Emesis Colonicus.*

Afterwards, he had behaved, for a week or so.

There was a low-growing bush that had a kind of yellow fruit that apparently mimicked the hallucinogenic side effects of psilocybin mushrooms, but with fewer side effects. He had tripped the light fantastic for a full hour and then, just as suddenly as the hallucinations had hit, they were gone. He had elected *not* to tell Sam about that but had logged it in the records as well. Someone would read it eventually and there would be fallout, but he didn't need another scolding right now.

After all, he reasoned, *man learned by trial and error, so why can't I?*

He smiled, Sam would have plenty to say about that line of reasoning, especially now that she was pregnant. Not by him, and not even with her own ova, but through the seed bank on board the ship. It had been a requirement that they had all agreed to. Not just their genetic heritage, but Earth's, was even more important now.

Daniel sighed and thought of his family. They were never far from his thoughts, really. And especially now that he was here, off of the spaceship, exploring this new world. He wondered if Toby was doing well. He would be in his teens now, and there was talk of increasing the turnaround time in communications, thanks to a project that had been underway when Calypso left. Calypso had dropped relays at every warp jump. In another year, after each of the relays connected, it was possible that they could contact the Earth and communicate in transmission packets that had a twelve-month turnaround time. There was even a chance he could find and contact Toby.

Daniel had finally accepted it. His life was here now, as painful as it was to let go.

He had felt such despair in not knowing what had happened to Luke and Janine, such guilt in leaving his son behind. Sam had held him, not making any promises, not uttering banal reassurances. There was no changing the past, anyway. There was only now and the future.

"How's Sam doing? Still getting morning sickness?" Wes asked.

"Nah, she had it right at first, which made the ride down to the surface rather challenging, and she gets all green when riding in the flitter, but the worst of it seems to be over."

"When will you know if it's a boy or girl?"

Daniel grinned, "Already do. It's a boy."

Wes nodded, "I've been seeing Kit." He stopped, scuffed the ground with his shoe, "informal and all that. Just dinner, a couple of walks."

"I heard."

"It's no rush or anything, I mean, her and Deeks, they..."

Daniel slapped Wes on the shoulder, "Wes, it is okay. You're a good guy, Kit's an amazing woman, believe me, I get it."

Wes relaxed visibly. "You were friends and all with Deeks. So was I, I mean, hell, I miss the guy. I just didn't want you to think I was moving in where I shouldn't be."

"We have the chance to make this world a good place, Wes. If that means you and Kit, then good for you. Don't let anyone else tell you how to think, all right?"

"Thanks man."

"*De nada.*"

It was time to head back. He had found, sketched, photographed and taken samples of a score of plants, dirt, and more. His comm link beeped and he answered it while easing his way down a section of slippery rock. He had almost fully recovered from his injuries sustained in the fight with Zradce, but there were still a few aches and pains that slowed him down.

It was Sam.

"What's your ETA?"

Brief, business-like as always. Sam was not the type to waste words.

"I should be back to the flitter in about 30 minutes and then I'm another half hour out. So... maybe one hour?"

They had maintained Earth time despite the vast gulf in orbits. Zarmina's World jetted around its sun in the equivalent of 1/10 of a Terran year, with little or no change in season at the meridian, or change in light, as the meridian remained in perpetual twilight on the orbitally-locked world. This allowed the colonists to create their own time measurements with little repercussions. Keeping Terran time had helped avoid confusion.

"Great," returned Sam's voice, "I'll see you at home then."

Home.

It was a strange thought. The walls of their pre-fab on the residential side of Sagan Base had been printed with the same 3D printer as everyone else's. They had been given a choice of five hundred different layouts to choose from once the streets had been mapped. Eventually the streets would be paved, but that would take getting the enormous machines printed and before that could happen, they would need the metal mined. Until then, they dealt with mud and tried to ignore how much of the green-tinged earth ended up on the floors of their houses.

The wealth of choice in house design had resulted in a hodgepodge of homes representing nearly 2,000 years in construction design throughout the colony. The houses were guaranteed up to 20 years in their current location and were placed on tracts of land with plenty of room for expansion.

Despite this, many of the colonists were already making plans to move out to larger plots of land once the colony had been fully established. The desire for more space was something that most of the colonists could not shake. They were in the process now of dividing the land plats and allocating them via a lottery system. At that time, they could either move their current building or choose to build a new one.

"See that forest to the west?" Daniel pointed to a dark grouping of trees in the distance and thought of the gnarled wood he had seen there.

Wes angled his binoculars towards the dark spot, "Oh yeah, wow, those trees are enormous!"

"They're huge, gotta be two hundred feet high. I'm going to look into building a house out of them."

"A house made out of wood?" Wes sounded incredulous.

"It used to be the material of choice."

"And you see where that got us."

"We can do it sustainably," Daniel insisted.

"Yeah, I guess so. I think I'll stay with the 3D printed homes for now, though."

"Fair enough."

Daniel couldn't help but dream of a small tribe of children, all with Toby's face, filling those future walls.

This planet was home. Daniel and Sam had formally established their partnership, and their pillow talk at night usually centered on how many children they should have.

Daniel and Wes began picking their way along the ridge, slowly making their way back to the flitter.

"There's a meeting tonight," Wes said, nearly tripping on an exposed root.

"Oh yeah?"

"Yeah. Kit has some ideas on how the colony could co-parent the first generation. She's hoping it quiets down the women who think we are planning to use them as brood mares."

Daniel laughed, "As if any of us could. These women, all their high IQs make them even more formidable foes."

Wes snickered and then swore as he tripped on another rough patch. "Well, several of the older women, those who already had children prior to the voyage and aren't planning on having more have stepped forward with an idea for a communal care facility. Any present and future children can attend."

"Yeah, I heard about that from Sam." Daniel nodded, "Sounds good to me."

They finished the journey back to the flitter and Daniel instructed the machine to return to base, leaned back, and rubbed his face. As the wind picked up outside of the flitter, Sagan Base slowly came into view. The buildings were low-slung, only a handful of them more than one level high. The lights in the greenhouses glowed steadily and Wes and Daniel could see the children playing on a small playground, which was dotted with a native grass that looked more like a moss, but was incredibly hardy.

In the distance on the opposite side of town were the houses. Here at the landing strip were the buildings that housed the enormous 3D printers. Inside, the printers worked almost non-stop printing everything from furniture to buildings to dishes for the colonists.

"See you at the meeting," Wes called, jumping out. "Thanks for today!"

Daniel waved back, dropped off his samples and headed across town. He knew Sam was waiting for him, probably working on dinner, hoping to get it done and eaten before the meeting.

In a back room of the newly established Medical Unit of Sagan Base, the machines beeped steadily. The tiny, darkened room was empty except for one bed. It was near shift change, but that didn't matter, the machines kept the man alive and there was little reason for anyone to ever enter the room. No one particularly wanted to, anyway.

Every morning Dr. Schrader would come in, review the reports and check the man's vitals. She did so with no more emotion than if she were handling a side of beef. In truth, that is how she thought of him. There had been little responsiveness after his brain swelling had gone down, and the only reason to keep him alive was the usefulness his organs might provide if there was a need.

His wife Jennifer had visited only once, while he was still in Medical Bay. She had sat next to his side, murmuring to him, before leaving without a word to anyone.

Jennifer Zradce had been remarkably close-mouthed about all of it after she stood up at the memorial, saying, "I have no idea why my husband did this terrible thing. I cannot understand it, but I am truly and deeply sorry for his behavior."

A few blamed her, but most were sympathetic. After all, he had tried to kill her as well in the Cryo sabotage. She was a victim too.

It was evening now, and Carrie was eager to return home to her little prefab, cook dinner and relax. The extra gravity was exhausting, and her schedule was even more so. She had chosen to implant her ova with donor semen from A.R.C. and she was still struggling to acclimate to the pregnancy. Martin Phoenix was definitely making that easier, having visited twice in the past week to bring her lunch. Tonight, she had promised to cook for him, but she was counting on the former first officer and new mayor to follow through on his promise to bring dessert.

The door closed softly behind her. The machines continued to beep, rising up just a notch or two. There were no alarms for the natural return to consciousness, only ones for a steady decline.

Nathaniel Zradce opened his eyes.

Author Note

Thanks for reading *G581: The Departure*. The series continues in *G581: Mars*, followed by *G581: Earth*, *G581: Plague Tales*, and finally will wrap up in *G581: Zarmina's World* and *G581: Plague Tales II*. The last two books are available for pre-order and will be released by January 1, 2026. I hope you will join me for the rest of the adventure. Here is a link to *G581: Mars* - https://books2read.com/g581mars

Please post a review on your favorite audiobook platform, and/or Goodreads. Put simply, reviews serve as social proof that someone has a) read the book and b) thought enough of it (either way) to post a review of it. Your opinion does matter and I would really appreciate it.

You may also be interested in an adjacent series, *War's End*. A series of two novels as well as a short story anthology, these books are about The Collapse that is referred to in *G581: The Departure*.

Follow the links to find these books on your favorite bookselling platform:

War's End: The Storm - https://books2read.com/we1

War's End: A Brave New World - https://books2read.com/we2

War's End: Tales of the Collapse - https://books2read.com/we3

Acknowledgments

No book is written alone, or in a vacuum.

I am endlessly grateful for my friends – they have provided me with everything from laughter, love, feedback, ideas, patience, and their time during the writing of this book and others. In all moments, I am surrounded by their love and support.

For my dear friend Kerrie for her endless support and an amazing abundance of Yapping Mommy Playdates.

I am also thankful for my former teachers at ILS – Kate, Dori, and Rachel – for allowing me to pursue my passion for writing in a unique and unusual manner in the mid-80s. And especially for Rachel, who directed me to her brother, Michael Lagunoff, a virologist and professor at the University of Washington. His knowledge and advice on viruses were invaluable. However, any errors or inconsistencies on viruses and their transmission are entirely my own.

For my amazing husband David, who is the dog to my cheetah. You keep me sane. You are amazingly patient and supportive; I can't imagine loving anyone the way I love you. Thank you too for listening to me read the book out loud – this helped with edits immensely!

For my children – Alex, Angela, and Ethan, each day I spend with you is a joy (even when I'm grouchy).

A huge thanks to Dorri Partain who works at the Northeast News and was kind enough to turn my chaotic thoughts into a small news snippet for the book.

To Nicole Hosier, thank you for your medical knowledge. I needed a lady who knew the lingo and you delivered!

To Kurt Cross, who was taken from us far too soon. I am grateful for the years I knew you – you and Dan are some of the kindest people I have ever known.

And everyone else. You know who you are. Or you should.

About the Author

Christine Shuck is a multi-genre author, chaos gardener, real estate entrepreneur, and mother of four. She lives with her family in Kansas City and when not writing or gardening, can be found shooting pool competitively with her local APA league.

You can read the first chapters of all of her books at: http://christineshuck.com.

Sign up for her monthly newsletter and receive a free ebook and free short stories at: https://mailchi.mp/c05ceb84e66a/subscribe-me

Follow her at:

Twitter: @christineshuck

Facebook: Christine.D.Shuck

Instagram: christinedshuck

X: x.com/ChristineShuck

Don't miss out!

Visit the website below and you can sign up to receive emails whenever Christine D. Shuck publishes a new book. There's no charge and no obligation.

https://books2read.com/r/B-A-BOLF-TZXT

BOOKS 2 READ

Connecting independent readers to independent writers.

Also by Christine D. Shuck

Benton Security Services
Hired Gun
Smoke and Steel
Broken Code
Benton Security Services Omnibus #1 - Books 1-3

Benton Sicherheitsservice
Heiße Gefahr

Chronicles of Liv Rowan
Fate's Highway

Gliese 581g
G581: The Departure
G581: Mars
G581: Earth
G581: Plague Tales
G581: Zarmina's World
G581: Plague Tales II

War's End
War's End: The Storm
War's End: A Brave New World
Tales of the Collapse
War's End Omnibus - Books 1-3

Standalone
The War on Drugs: An Old Wives Tale
Get Organized, Stay Organized
Winter's Child
Short-Term Rental Success

Watch for more at christineshuck.com.